KING'S EXILE

Christine Marion Fraser began her life in the tenements of the Govan district of Glasgow just after the war. At the age of ten she contracted a rare muscular disease, and has been in a wheelchair ever since. She now lives with her husband in Argyllshire.

A keen reader and storyteller, Christine started writing at the age of five, and got the idea for *Rhanna*, her first novel, while on holiday in the Hebrides. She has gone on to write six more volumes: *Rhanna At War*, *Children of Rhanna*, *Return to Rhanna*, *Song of Rhanna*, *Storm Over Rhanna* and *Stranger on Rhanna*. She has also written three volumes of autobiography: *Blue Above the Chimneys*, *Roses Round the Door* and *Green Are My Mountains*. *Noble Beginnings*, the first in an exciting new series set in an Argyllshire powdermill town, has just been published.

King's Exile is the third volume in the popular series which follows the fortunes of the Grant Family and is set in rural Aberdeenshire and in Glasgow.

THE KING'S SERIES

King's Croft
King's Acre
King's Exile
King's Close
King's Farewell

CHRISTINE MARION FRASER

King's Exile

This edition published by Grafton Books, 1999

Grafton Books is an Imprint of
HarperCollins*Publishers*
77–85 Fulham Palace Road,
Hammersmith, London W6 8JB

This paperback edition first published by HarperCollins*Publishers* 1995
1 3 5 7 9 8 6 4 2

Previously published in paperback by Fontana 1989
Reprinted four times

ISBN 0-26-167349-1

Set in Sabon

Printed in Great Britain by
Caledonian International Book Manufacturing Ltd, Glasgow

To Ian McLachlan (the 'Big Yin')
for the unstinting help and friendship
he so willingly gave me
when he was with Collins.
Slainte, Ian

Wood Cottage

Knocke Farm

Clyde Coast

ken. C. Ashfield

Dunmarnock Estate

Glasgow

The Grange

Bracken Ridge Cottage

Fern Cottage

Home Farm

Dunmarnock House

River Threep

ACKNOWLEDGEMENTS

The author would like to thank Ken Hinshalwood,
Local History Dept. Renfrew District Library
and William L. Scott, Local History Librarian,
Argyll & Bute District Council, for the willing help
they gave in the writing of this book.

PART ONE

Winter 1917/18
Dunmarnock House,
Renfrewshire

Chapter One

Evelyn awoke, her pulse pounding, the remnants of her dream following her into her awakening so that she had to press her hand to her mouth to stifle her sobs of fear.

Sinking back against her pillows she lay listening, every fibre of her being on edge, worrying in case the sounds had been heard.

But the house was quiet and still around her, the night breezes hushed over the rooftops; somewhere in the distance a dog barked in a desultory fashion.

It might have been the lands of Rothiedrum out there, with only the wind and the farm dogs to disturb the sleeping parks; but it wasn't Rothiedrum, it was Renfrewshire, a strange place to her as yet and one which might always be so, for she had had neither time nor inclination to explore the vast acres that made up the Dunmarnock Estates.

Her bedclothes lay in a rumple around her for it had been warm in her dream, a damp, cloying warmth, like the mists that had swirled round her that lonely day she had climbed the hills above Rothiedrum towards the two dark, satanic stones that made up what the locals called The Devil's Door . . .

Quickly she pushed the dread vision from her mind. The raw cold of the November night swept over her making her shiver. Drawing the bedclothes up to her chin she lay shaking in a mixture of cold and fright, her stomach churning with a nausea that was always with her these days.

Clenching her teeth to stop them from chattering, she forced herself to lie still while her eyes raked the darkness, gradually adjusting to it so that the lumpy shapes of everyday objects came somberly to her out of the gloom.

The tiny attic room at the top of the Big House had become familiar to her these last few weeks. She had wanted to live with her parents in Wood Cottage which, with its leaded casement windows, tiny towers and parapets, had been built after the fashion of the Big House and was altogether a charming and pleasing abode. But Lady Elizabeth Baird, gazing at Evelyn in a dreamy way, had said in her kind but twittery fashion, 'Evelyn, it would be better if you live in. Mrs McWhirter likes her girls to be ready to start at six sharp and no nonsense about it. I know the cottage is only half a mile away but half a mile in the early hours of a cold winter's morning is enough to make anyone snuggle down at the very idea. You'll be fine at the top of the house with Effie, Peggy, and Violet for company.'

Evelyn had been given no time to protest. Lady Elizabeth had fluttered quickly away, muttering something about 'seeing to Richard'.

And well she might. Behind Colonel Sir Richard Baird, KCB, there lay an honourable and distinguished Army career from which he had emerged still in his prime and ready for anything; all his life he had been blessed with a marvellous business acumen and, in common with his friend and colleague, Evander Forbes of Rothiedrum House, he hadn't been slow to exploit the profits to be made from war; nevertheless, he was hopeless when it came to the small details of everyday life and his wife was forever at his beck and call, be it searching for things he had mislaid or simply making sure he emerged each morning from the bedroom with everything properly tied, buttoned and generally secured.

Lady Elizabeth, on the other hand, appeared to be easy going in a fluttery, faraway fashion, but what she said was law in her own home and Evelyn already knew better than to argue with her.

'It might be for the best, Evie,' Margaret Innes Grant had later told her daughter. 'Six in the morning is an early enough start for anybody and too early from the look o' you. You've been gey peekit this whilie back.'

Evelyn, avoiding her mother's keen eyes, had unconsciously straightened and pulled herself in, all the while praying that Maggie wouldn't notice anything amiss.

'I'll be fine, Mam,' she had reassured. 'It's no' any earlier than the mornings at King's Croft – and anyway it won't be for that long.'

'What do you mean, Evie? No' for that long?'

Maggie had sounded strange and Evelyn hastened to add, 'Ach, don't look like that, Mam. I only meant I won't be working to the Bairds any longer than need be. I'm nineteen now and wi' the war on I feel I could be doing more to help. I had thought to move to Glasgow and do something really useful – like going into munitions – or something like that,' she had finished lamely.

'You'll do nothing o' the sort!' Maggie had returned sharply, 'You'll bide here and be glad to do it. The Bairds have been good to us and we canna let them down when they most need us.'

She had said not another word on the subject but once or twice Evelyn had caught a puzzled frown on her face and, thinking of that in the quiet of her little attic room, she broke out in a sweat. Her hands moved unwillingly over her stomach. It was no longer flat but rose gently above her pelvic bones. It would be a while yet before the betraying contours became evident and before that happened she knew she had to do something about getting right away from here – she had to!

More than three months had passed since she had walked with Davie over the heather braes to the great gap in the crags known as The Devil's Door. There in the cool shadows they had succumbed to the passions that had smouldered in them during those brief, wonderful summer days of his sick leave from the trenches.

Afterwards he had gone out of her life again, leaving her to loneliness and the sick fears that had beset her since discovering she was carrying his child. No one knew except

13

her sister Grace, and Grace would never tell, although more and more lately she had been urging Evelyn to unburden herself to her parents. Restlessly Evelyn moved her head on her pillows. She thought of her old home in Aberdeenshire, a small grey house known as King's Croft sitting amidst the loamy parks and shadowed houghs of Rothiedrum.

There she had grown, had wandered and played and had finally loved Johnny Burns of Birkiebrae. But Johnny had died young and in her sorrow she had found solace in the arms of a Gordon Highlander, David Alexander Grainger. The war had seen to it that their times together were few but oh, how they had filled them with love, with laughter, with passion. Far off these days seemed now: she had lost him as surely as if he had died too — and for all she knew he might have. He hadn't written, she didn't know where he was; he had gone out of her life as easily as he had come into it.

Yet she couldn't forget him, even though she had come near to hating him that autumn day in the Aulton when she had met a girl who was also carrying his child. In her torture of body and soul she had made a lone pilgrimage to The Devil's Door with the intention of ending her own life and that of her unborn child; but the attempt had been unsuccessful and now here she was, unsure of her future, not knowing which way to turn.

Sleep was beyond her. Sitting up, she pulled her shawl about her shoulders and with an unsteady hand put a match to the stump of candle at her bedside. From beneath her pillow she withdrew her diary, a smile touching her lips. She was really too old now to keep a diary but somehow she couldn't bring herself to relinquish the habit of years. As a child she had wanted to be a writer but the hard facts of life as a crofter's daughter had soon chased the fancies out of her head.

Her literary outpourings had gone into her diaries so that now there was quite a pile of them, all of them handbound and kept tied together in a battered tin box hidden under her bed.

14

Bending over the pages she began to write, shivering as the cold seeped through her nightdress.

November, 1917. We've been here at Dunmarnock nearly a month now. The Bairds are fine people and don't seem like gentry at all. Sir Richard prefers just to be called Colonel and would forget his head if it wasn't screwed on. Often he forgets to wear his teeth and her ladyship sends Raggy Annie to fetch the glass from his bedside. Raggy Annie does the rough work of the house and never looks tidy but she's got a big heart and I love her. A lot of the staff went off to do war work and the Bairds have to make do with what they can get. Raggy Annie swears and smokes and just laughs when the rest of the staff talk about her and can't understand why she gets on so well with Sir Richard.

The Bairds have a daughter, and a son who is a major in the army. He is with the 74th Battalion of the H.L.I. and was badly wounded in a gun-pit fire at the end of April. I haven't seen him yet, he spent months in an English War Hospital and from there went to stay with his sister at Craigdrummond, Sir Richard's other residence in Invernesshire. Seemingly she went there specially to look after him as he wouldn't come home to Dunmarnock owing to bad burns he sustained in the fire. Rumour has it that he suffers from hallucinations but that he is getting better . . .

Fiercely she chewed the end of her pencil, a great sadness in her for the Bairds of Dunmarnock whose only son had been so badly injured that he would never fight again — yet, was that so terrible? He was alive, for him the war was over, no more uncertainty for him or for his family. It was the not knowing that was so terrible, never to be sure if someone you loved was alive or dead . . . Her heart went cold within her breast, she had to force herself to go on.

*   *

15

Christine Baird comes home whenever she can. She's very bonny, tall, sophisticated but with a great sense of humour like her father. She's not in the least snobbish though she's a dab hand at organising people like Seal McWhirter. She was down last week when the Lanarkshire and Renfrewshire hunt met at Dunmarnock. The hunt finished early owing to bad weather and a few of Sir Richard's cronies came back here for afternoon tea.

Seal McWhirter, Cook with a capital 'C', nearly went daft altogether when Ferguson brought the order. She was in the middle of making the Christmas cake and in a bad mood because she didn't have enough sultanas or currants. She bawled me out for not fetching enough eggs from the Home Farm and nearly killed a stray cat who was sneaking about looking for crumbs. 'Barbarians, the lot o' them!' she stormed, referring to the hunt crowd and raging at the poor cat who was under the table nursing his sore paws. 'Chasing after God's own creatures then coming back here demanding tea and expecting fancy cakes and all these shortages going about the now!'

She stomped about grumbling and complaining and taking her time about everything till Christine came down to the kitchen and, cool as you like, made the tea herself and ordered Seal to have it sent up at once. The minute her back was turned the old lady nearly exploded and sent both me and the cat scurrying about our business. She's devoted to all the Bairds but hates blood sports and there I agree with the bad-tempered besom but would never dare tell her so.

I think of Rothiedrum all the time. I long to see Coulter's twinkly brown old face and to hear Hinney singing into her whisky.

It will be deep winter in Aberdeenshire and Bennachie will be covered with snow. Mary wrote to tell us it was three feet deep on the turnpike and McDuff the Guff had to trudge up to Cragbogie to deliver Tina O'Neil

16

of a son — her third and still she isn't married. Florrie would smile at that and call the bairns Dolly Mixtures. I wonder what she would have to say about me.

I miss Florrie, sixteen was too young to die. If she and Johnny had lived I might not be here in Renfrewshire a million miles away from everything I love. I was to marry Johnny — yet — he wanted to go to Canada and then of course there's the war, there's always the war. He would have joined up and I might have lost him anyway.

Nellie wrote from Kenneray. Wee Col is well and happy. We all miss him but Father misses him the most, he doesn't say much but I ken fine his heart is hungry for a sight of his bonny son. He'll never grow up to be like other bairns. It might sound selfish but one of the things I liked most about my wee brother was his eternal innocence.

Both Mam and Father like it here well enough but I can tell they miss the old ways and the old speak of Rothiedrum.

I wish I could see Gillie again, dear Gillie, he was as much a part of my life as Johnny and Florrie, even Davie.

Davie. How sweet a sound. But he never loved me as I loved him. I can't bear to think of a future empty of him but I must. His child is strong within me, yesterday for the first time I felt the throb of it deep inside of me —

That throb came again, more a flutter really, barely felt but reminding her of its Presence all the same. That was how she thought of it, a Presence with a capital 'P', a growing entity that she was forced to carry around with her whether she liked it or not ... The pencil dropped from her frozen fingers. She huddled miserably over her knees, her rich red hair falling about a face that had grown thin of late. The childish contours were going yet she looked so young that the Colonel had asked her what she was doing working to him when she ought still to be in school.

Closing her diary, she slipped it back under the pillow and, snuffing the candle, she lay back and shut her eyes. Sleep came unwillingly, creeping through her weary frame like some timid creature of the night, but come it did and for a few blessed hours she was free of the looming black vision of The Devil's Door, within whose portals the seed of Alexander David Grainger had known its turbulent conception.

She awoke, heavy and sick, roused from her slumber by an impatient staccato of bony knuckles on her door. Effie Jordan came in, her face an eerie white blob in the light of the candle she carried.

'Come on, madam, get yourself out your pit.' Her hard voice came out in a rasping whisper. Sitting herself on the end of the bed she gave Evelyn a leering, knowing smile. 'Nae wonder you canna waken. I heard you again last night, crying out like a spook in your sleep. What ails you, Evelyn Grant? Have you some dark and terrible secret that haunts you in your dreams?'

Evelyn struggled to place her thoughts. She had dreamed she was back in King's Croft and for a moment had fully imagined that the hand on the door was Nellie's.

'None o' your business, Effie.' Evelyn spoke sharper than she had intended. No one took Effie's innuendoes seriously though often enough she could rouse even the placid Peggy to angry rebuke. She had needled Evelyn from the start and only by a supreme effort had she held her tongue. She was made of spirited stuff but was well aware of how much her family needed to show themselves in a good light to the Bairds.

Effie was filled with a sense of her own importance and was worse than ever since the parlourmaid had left and Effie had stepped into her shoes. She was a big-boned girl with a nondescript sallow face, a sullen mouth, small,

18

darting eyes and a quick tongue to match. She had two redeeming facets to her nature; one was her staunch loyalty to her employers, the second was her cleanliness. She bristled with it to such a degree that her starched aprons rustled with every step and was such a source of annoyance to the rest of the staff she had soon been nicknamed 'The Rustler'.

Her room being adjacent to Evelyn's, she had taken it upon herself to rouse the girl at 5.30 prompt every morning. She invariably wore the look of a snooper and even at that ungodly hour her eyes would flick rapidly all over the place, even into the corners, as if she fully expected to find someone hiding in them, possibly of the male gender, for she never tired talking about men, especially Major Andrew Richard Baird, over whom she romanticised in such a silly, schoolgirl fashion she had become a source of ridicule, amusement and embarrassment among those below stairs.

'None o' my business, eh?' Her heavy hips crushed Evelyn's feet. "Tis my business when Miss High and Mighty Kitchen Maid wakes me up at all God-forsaken hours. You get a grip o' yourself, madam, or I'll be forced to put in a complaint. Only the other day her ladyship mentioned that I was looking pale. I never said anything for I'm no' the sort who likes to get anyone in trouble but if you don't mind your manners I'll have no choice.'

'Ach, away and look for a man, Effie. Who knows, if you're lucky you might find one lurking under your bed.' Evelyn spoke wearily but added with a flash of spirit, 'And see you dinna waken the rest o' the house when you're getting yourself into your crackling whites, they're enough to frighten away a bogle man, never mind one made o' flesh and blood. Oh, and next time you chap me up I would be obliged if you would bring me in my early cuppy. I canna think straight till I sup at least one cup o' tea.'

Effie had no sense of humour. She glared at the younger girl, snorted, 'Cheeky wee upstart,' and flounced away out of the room, banging the door as loudly as she dared, leaving Evelyn to light her candle and hurry into her clothes – a blue wrap-around dress and a hopsack apron.

She tied the last loosely – the dress was getting a bit tight but didn't show under the apron, and there was always the shapeless peeny she wore for the dirtier kitchen work.

Night still lay beyond the window. Rubbing a circle of condensation from the pane she looked out. The grounds of Dunmarnock stretched, acre after acre, taking in dairy farms, workers' cottages and rolling fields with little woodlands dotted here and there. It was a pretty countryside, soft, undulating, so different from the bleak winter parks of the north-east lowlands . . . yet – how she longed for that harsh landscape – and more – for the couthy crofters and farmfolk who had made up her life.

She missed the speak of them, the dour, droll sense of humour, the laughter and singing that had filled the rooms of King's Croft during the long nights of winter dark.

A sense of terrible desolation seized her. Little had she thought, in those far-off days, that one day she would have to leave it all behind. Life in the farmtouns had never been easy, every day had brought its hardships, but they had been offset by summers of good hairst when the corn was golden on the stalk and everyone had sung on the way home from the fields. She could almost hear the steady clip-clop of the Clydes' hooves, smell the richness of the tumbled hay in the carts.

Everyone had helped each other gather their respective hairsts and afterwards had come the 'meal-and-ale' celebrations held in big, airy barns that had fairly rung with music from melodeons and fiddles and the wild 'hoochs' and 'yoochs' of people enjoying themselves after weeks of hard work in the fields.

The window pane was cold against her brow but she wasn't aware of it; the eyes that gazed out over a strange landscape were unseeing, she was back in Rothiedrum, back among a people that she knew and loved ... A quiver deep in her belly brought her back to reality — yet even that wasn't real somehow. She felt detached, an onlooker, staring at shadows that were insubstantial yet oddly alive. Back, back it all went, into the mists of time, mysterious, forgotten, buried but always just there, beneath the surface of her mind. She seemed to see her mother, her grandmother before that, someone she had never known but with whom now she shared an affinity, for Megsie Cameron had conceived a child out of wedlock — Evelyn's mother, Margaret Innes Grant — whose father had been a man of noble birth. Quite suddenly the baby that was in Evelyn seemed to float before her vision, face-less, featureless ... until Davie's face interposed itself upon that white blob of living flesh ... He wasn't the Davie she had known, he was ill-looking, drained of the vitality she had loved so well ...

She shivered herself out of her strange, dark mood. Hinney had told her she had been born with the second sight and Hinney had known what she was talking about for she too had 'the gift'.

In Evelyn's case it wasn't always the future that she glimpsed; things that were past came to her too.

'I dinna want it, Hinney,' the child Evelyn had protested fearfully.

'Nor me,' Hinney had spoken grimly, 'but I've got it and so have you. It won't aye torment you, just occasionally and often when you're least expecting it.'

'I'll — I'll fight it, Hinney.'

'Oh ay, you will — I did — and in the end I learned to live wi' it.'

But though Evelyn had gradually accepted her sixth sense she had never lost her fear of it and she turned away from the window as if it was a window to her soul and she had had enough of looking into it for the moment.

Going to the dresser she poured water into a pewter basin. The freezing douche took her breath away but she kept on splashing until her face tingled. A memory came to her of her sister Mary throwing cold water over her naked body in the attic bedroom she had shared with Nellie, the eldest Grant girl, and of Nellie's voice, prim and shocked, scolding Mary for being so immodest. 'Ach, it's only a dowp,' had been Mary's mischievous, laughing reply. 'If you took a peek inside your own breeks you would see the exact same thing.'

A giggle escaped Evelyn. Going to the mirror she brushed her waving tumble of waist-length hair before piling it up and securing her cap in place. The face that looked back at her was ghostly pale in the wan candlelight but thinking about her sisters had brought a sprite into her green eyes and very softly she began to hum *Soldier Laddie* under her breath.

On the stairs she met up with Violet Henderson, one of two housemaids left at Dunmarnock. Violet was small, fair and gentle-looking but her meek looks belied a spirited nature and an even more able tongue. A slight speech impediment was an embarrassment to her though Evelyn thought the lisping burr was utterly charming.

'I know that song,' Violet greeted Evelyn. 'A wifie in our close is always singing it in a wee quiet voice like a bird. Her son is away in the war and she sits at the window, watching for him to come back and singing her song. The bairns are scared o' her and call her a witch.'

Behind them, Effie announced her presence with an almighty rustle of starched frills. 'I know that thong,' she mimicked cheekily. 'Mith High and Mighty Kitchie Maid ith always thinging it.'

Brushing past the two younger girls she went on downstairs, sniggering at her own wit.

'Glaikit bitch!' Violet spoke with feeling. 'She was always unbearable but she's worse than ever since she took Cathie's place. I heard her going into your room, Evie. She's had it in for you ever since you came – jealous, o' course. You might just be the kitchen maid but somehow you manage to look like one o' the gentry whereas Effie will

22

aye just be The Rustler, no matter how hard she tries.'

Evelyn laughed. 'Maybe she starches her knickers as well. That would account for her sharp tongue.'

Violet let out an enormous snort. 'Ay, and maybe that's the reason she canna get a lad to look at her. What boy in his right mind would want a girl wi' starch in her knicker frills!'

Chapter Two

Seal McWhirter, Cook with a capital 'C', was shuffling about the kitchen in her slippers, complaining about her 'stiff joints' in between grumbles about the hardships war had brought to her life.

'Girls these days is no' the same,' she was complaining to Ferguson, an ancient butler with a shock of white hair and feet nearly as bad as Mrs McWhirter's. 'I miss Maisie, that I do, she was a whittrock betimes wi' her sulks and glowers behind my back but she could work, oh ay, she could work her fingers to the bone and still come back for more.'

Ferguson – his head 'half up the lum and his hands roasting themselves at the fire' to quote Hugh Kerr, the head gardener – merely grunted. At that hour of the day he always grunted though later, when he had been fortified with several cups of tea, he might argue a bit with Seal about the lamented Maisie's shortcomings, for the only time she had ever hurried was when she had left Dunmarnock for the last time and good riddance was his opinion.

'This new one now,' continued Seal with vigour, 'twice yesterday I had to tell her to do the gravy pan properly and even so there were wee bitties o' dirt clingin' round the erse o' it.'

Ferguson nodded a placid head and let Seal's moans wash over him. Both he and she had been with the Bairds since leaving school, Seal bidding farewell to her crofting home in the Highlands and a mother so steeped in folklore she had rashly named her eldest daughter after a most revered sea creature; Robert Ferguson sailing over from Islay to seek his fortunes on the mainland and finding for himself the Bairds of Dunmarnock whom he'd never had reason to leave, a fact that owed itself to contentment with his lot and the good fortune to have been either too young or too old to fight in any of the wars between 1854 and 1914.

From bootboy to butler, Ferguson had worked his way up and with no further to go he ambled peacefully through his days, occasionally allowing his dignity to slip in good-going arguments with Seal that added all the spice he needed in his life.

By comparison, Seal McWhirter's lot had been tinged with adventure of a domestic sort. From humble kitchen maid to chief cook she hadn't so much worked her way up as wangled it by a series of wily manoeuvres and much diligent application to whatever position she happened to find herself in. Twice married, first to a stable hand, next to a footman, she was once again 'footloose and fancy free' to quote herself, and quite content to stay that way, she had confided in Ferguson, much to his relief; she had been quite a lass in her day and before her marriage to the footman had cast her eye speculatively in Ferguson's direction though nowadays with no more serious intent than to pick his brains as to the best methods for dealing with chapped skin and other domestic ailments.

'Wear gloves,' was Ferguson's oft-repeated advice which Seal always chose to ridicule to his face though bedtime saw her hands smothered in layers of cold cream and encased in a pair of old cotton gloves.

With the passing years she had grown more like her name. She was stout, soft-eyed and barked a lot when she was on her high horse. On her chin she sported a goodly number of hairs the same colour as those on her sleek grey head and when she was being suspicious about anything her nose twitched a good deal. But her bark was worse than her bite and every girl who had ever worked under her started off fearing her and ended up loving her for underneath her bristles and grunts she was as gentle as her name implied and many's the young and frightened girl she had rocked in her arms or cooried to the soft swell of her bosom.

Both she and Ferguson were institutions whose status granted them certain unspoken concessions. Neither Lady Elizabeth nor Colonel Baird would have dreamed of telling Seal to wear shoes in the kitchen instead of slippers or to advise Ferguson to trim his mop of silvery hair and not to sniff into his hanky whilst crossing the hall to answer the door. He had been a grown man and doing these things when the Colonel was still wet about the ears.

Seal had no such reservations. She kept Ferguson in his place all right – he was scolded for sniffing and scratching his head in her kitchens and was reminded to wear his jacket properly when the bell rang for his services – but, all things considered, the pair were the best of friends and always enjoyed this sleepy morning hour before the rest of the household was properly astir and they could discuss favourite topics to their heart's content.

'If you ask me, something is ailing this new lass,' hazarded Seal, settling herself opposite Ferguson with her second cup of tea. 'She looks white and drawn for a girl fresh frae the country and I've a mind she's more on hers than is good for her.'

'Ach, she's young, it will be a lad,' Ferguson nodded sagely. 'At her age it nearly always is. She's a bonny one and no mistake and will no doubt hae a few lads at her beck and call.'

'Ach, havers!' Seal said firmly. 'Young men are gey thin on the ground these days.'

Ferguson nodded and said heavily, 'Ay, you're right, and Evie will likely be pining for one that's far away . . .'

The door opened and Evelyn came in, slightly out of breath from her rush downstairs. 'You're late, Evie,' was Seal's greeting.

A faint smile touched Evelyn's lips. 'No, Mrs McWhirter, I'm on time. It's you who are early – as usual.'

26

She had been longing to assert herself and, as always for Evelyn, the time had to come for her independent personality to make itself known. Every morning the old cook's salutation was the same and while the new kitchie maid's tongue had fairly itched to do battle she had felt too strange and new to dare say one assertive word. But this particular morning was different. Evelyn was on her mettle. Subservience to anyone, whatever their station, had never come easy to her, a trait common to many folk of the north-east soil and particularly so of the Grant family.

Her words fell like pebbles into the sudden silence of the kitchen, broken almost at once by Ferguson's wicked chuckle which was barely quelled by the black look thrown at him by the cook.

'Hmph! You're finding your voice, madam,' snorted Seal, her round face pink with surprise. 'Just see and keep a civil tongue in your head while you're working in *my* kitchens – and while we're on the subject o' work the pans from yesterday will have to be done all over again. I will no' stand for slovenly behaviour frae a fart o' a farmtoun lass, so see you and get your peeny on and be quick about it.'

Evelyn went to work but under her breath she was humming *Mormond Braes*. Something was in her that day, something that had always been a part of her but which lately had been swamped by all the new experiences cramming themselves into her life. Now her natural good spirits were bubbling up, spilling out. For no good reason that she could explain she felt uplifted. It was going to be a special day for her, she could feel it in her bones, sense it in her soul. Sleeves rolled to her elbows, she scrubbed energetically at the pans to the accompaniment of a rather panted version of *The Ploughman's Laddie*.

'I'll say one thing for her,' Seal murmured to Ferguson, 'the lass has spunk.' Ferguson's eyes twinkled. He liked Evelyn, he enjoyed the way her green eyes flashed and the little defiant toss of her head whenever she was on the defensive, and this morning, watching her animated

27

face, hearing her singing, he liked her even more. Nothing would ever keep that lass down for long, by Jove it wouldn't!

'Smeddum,' he drily corrected Mrs McWhirter. 'Where she comes from they call it smeddum.'

Mrs McWhirter put a bowl of eggs on the table. 'Well, whatever it's called she's got it – and I just hope she's no' got too much o' it. A kitchie maid has to know her place and I for one will no' stand for any sort o' cheek in *my* girls!'

'This is for you, Evie, open it when you have a spare minute on your own.'

Jamie handed his daughter a letter, glancing up quickly as if to ascertain that the action hadn't been observed; but everyone was too busy enjoying the morning break to pay much heed to the Grant family. Ferguson was dunking a biscuit in his tea while he pored over small snippets of news he had missed in yesterday's newspaper; Seal McWhirter was massaging her feet by the fire and murmuring something about chilblains; Effie was over at the sink, frantically trying to remove a tea stain from her sparkling white apron; the others were just enjoying their tea while they made desultory conversation.

Maggie picked up the teapot and poured Jamie another cup of tea which he took but didn't immediately drink, his sinewy brown hands carefully setting the delft cup in its saucer as if he was afraid he might spill the contents. He and his wife and daughter sat together at the end of the table, letting the talk of the others wash over them. They still felt out of place sitting in a strange kitchen in someone else's house after a lifetime of living in King's Croft with only themselves and perhaps a fee'd lad sharing the family table.

The Dunmarnock kitchens were large and airy: two pantries, a scullery, a laundry room and small dairy led off from a short passageway. Seal McWhirter grumbled long and loudly about the distances she had to cover in her daily routine, but when the house staff gathered for meals the walls seemed to shrink and absorb any intimacies that might be shared by its occupants. If anything private had to be discussed it had to be done in whispers or else it had to wait; and since Evelyn could only be with her family in Wood Cottage on her afternoons and days off she was often beset with a sense of terrible frustration.

Maggie as housekeeper had her own little office where she could have had her meals if she so wished but that would have meant being separated from her husband and daughter and it was little enough she saw either of them these days. So she took her meals along with everyone else though her natural reserve had already earned her the label of Lady Hoity-Toity. But Maggie was used to such tasteless sarcasm; she had always carried herself with such pride of bearing she had been the subject of much sour comment among the farmwives of Rothiedrum. Her dignity had manifested itself in her children though neither they nor Jamie knew that her natural father was one Lord Lindsay Ogilvie who had 'had his way' with Maggie's mother when she was a maidservant at the royal house of Balmoral.

'She has more airs and graces than Lady Elizabeth herself!' Mrs McWhirter had bellowed into Ferguson's hairy lugs when Maggie had been at Dunmarnock only a few days. 'She'd better watch! Pride like that aye has a fall, it's the natural way o' things.'

'Ay, and pride like that picks itself up, dusts itself off, and starts all over again,' Ferguson proclaimed drily, smiling to himself at the recollection of Cook with a Capital being taken to task over a small matter concerning the hours of the new kitchen maid.

'Just because the lass is her daughter she thinks she can lay down new laws to a body like myself who has been in this house all her days,' Seal had fumed, snorting so heavily she reminded Burton the groom of a sick old horse he had once nursed through an illness. 'Well, I'll no' have it, I'll no'. Lady Hoity-Toity can talk herself blue in the face for all the good it will do her and that's an end to the matter.'

29

'She'd have a job there,' Ferguson sniggered, 'the wife hardly opens her mouth but, by God, when she does she means business and no mistake.'

The very next day Evelyn's hours were adjusted in accordance with Maggie's wishes and from that time on a distinct coolness had existed between Mrs McWhirter and Maggie.

Jamie sighed to himself and wished he was back in the old days and the old ways. This sort of life wasn't for Maggie or Evelyn though he himself had fared well enough in his new job and enjoyed working alongside Hugh Kerr, the head gardener, but it wasn't Rothiedrum, it wasn't King's Croft, and his heart was often sore whenever he thought about the places and the people he had left behind. Yet everyone at Dunmarnock liked Jamie King Grant. Though he had grown quiet since leaving his old home he was still blithe of spirit, though that more often than not owed itself to the furtive sips from a bottle he kept hidden in one of the greenhouses. King Jamie he had been in his travelling and crofting days, a combination of King being his middle name and such title having been bestowed on him when he had been head of his particular band of travelling people. He was of true Romany stock. His father had been a seer of great repute and it was from this source that Evelyn, his seventh child, had inherited her gift of second sight.

He glanced at her and saw that she was clutching her letter so tightly that her knuckles were white. 'It willna bite you, lass,' he smiled, a small sadness in him on noticing how nervous and strained she looked. Of all his daughters she was the one most like him. Happiness had always come easy to her but this last year or two had seen a great change in her and he wondered quietly to himself if she would ever get over the young soldier to whom she had so obviously given her heart.

Evelyn didn't know why her hand had shaken as it did when she had reached out for the letter. Something inside her had gone still and quiet before rushing on in great bounding heartbeats that robbed her of breath and made her sit unmoving in her chair, the letter clasped to the rough material that covered her surging breast.

Maggie looked at her daughter, at the bonny young face framed by glowing hair that seemed always to be touched by bright fingers of sunlight; her eyes fell on Evelyn's hands – they were red and rough from too much steeping in dirty suds and harsh starches – and a knife-like pain twisted in the heart of Margaret Innes Grant. Something ailed this youngest daughter of hers; she felt that she of all people ought to know what it was and right enough, the knowledge of that something was there, tantalising her with its nearness yet always remaining just out of reach, elusive and mysterious.

The room had gone quiet suddenly; dust danced in the sun rays filtering in through the windows; Ferguson's spoon rasped in his cup, reminding Seal he had been helping himself to more than his share of her precious sugar; Hugh Kerr was fiddling with his pipe; Violet was watching Evelyn; Effie's ruffles crackled loudly in the silence which she further broke by saying in her harsh voice, 'More secrets, Evelyn? From morn till night your life seems full o' them. Has your prince written to say he's coming to carry you off on his dashing white charger? If so I hope he comes soon, then we all might get some sleep at night.'

'Ach, hold your tongue, girl!' Hugh said sharply. 'It's no' the lack o' sleep that ails you, it's bad manners, pure and simple.'

'Away you go and read your letter,' Maggie told Evelyn. 'Your time is your own for a good ten minutes yet.'

'Your letter can wait,' Seal spoke in a peremptory tone. 'Her ladyship is having guests to lunch and the tatties have still to be done, no' to mention a hundred and one things you should hae done earlier.'

Maggie got up and walked regally over to the fire, there to pull herself up to her full height and glare down upon Cook with a Capital. The room held its breath. Seal McWhirter was a forbidding force at any time but when she was annoyed she was formidable.

31

But Margaret Innes Grant, the new housekeeper, was promising to be a match for anybody.

'You will have to do something about these feet o' yours, Mrs McWhirter,' Maggie began pleasantly.

'Indeed? And what business is that o' yours?' questioned Seal with an ominous glower. 'Bad feet or no' I do my day's work and have never had any complaints frae anyone.'

'No?' Maggie's tone was still pleasant though a dangerous glint shone in her green eyes. 'Well, there's a first time for everything and that time has come.' The room gasped, everyone eyed everyone else, even Effie was shocked out of her customary air of haughtiness. It looked as though the Grants were about to waken Dunmarnock in no mean manner.

'And what would you be complainin' about?' demanded Seal. 'You that's only been here five minutes and most o' *them* spent wi' your nose up in the air.'

'I'm no' complaining, I'm *telling* you, Mrs McWhirter, ay, and no doubt I'll be saying things that all the poor wee skivvies you ever put through your hands would like to have said themselves. You moan and grumble about your feet yet half the time you sit wi' your nose up the lum, drinking tea while you order Evie to jump this way and the other.'

The old woman's lips curled. 'Oh so, the wee madam has been running to Mother, has she?'

'Indeed she hasn't, Evie is no' that sort o' lass and fine you know it. I've got eyes and ears, I've seen and heard you at it, and forbye all that you grudge her every minute o' the spare time that's due her.'

Evelyn could have died in those minutes and wished the ground would open and swallow her up. Why, oh why, had her mother tackled old Seal in such a manner? Couldn't she have waited to talk to her on her own – if she had to talk to her at all? Didn't her mother realise she was perfectly capable of fighting her own battles? She'd had to do that often enough at Rothiedrum House, both with Lady Marjorie Forbes and Mrs Chalmers, the housekeeper. It wasn't working, it simply wasn't working, she in the kitchen, her mother in a position of authority above stairs. The sooner she left Dunmarnock the better, and for more than just one reason . . .

The eyes of everyone in the room were darting about, from Maggie and Seal to Evelyn and Jamie; Hugh Kerr's rugged brown face wore an embarrassed look; Ferguson was thoroughly enjoying himself; Peggy looked bewildered; Violet seemed ready to erupt into one of her snorting fits of laughter; Effie was wearing that smug look, as if she knew something and was valiantly holding it back till the proper time and place presented itself.

Jamie found Evelyn's hand and squeezed it. 'Away you go and read your letter, Princess. Your mother is holding the fort and doing it right well. Dinna be angry at her.'

He looked pleased, and something else — proud, ay proud of a wife who had taken up the challenge of a new life with vigour and enthusiasm and a determination to see justice done to the family she had loved and cared for all her life.

Evelyn bit her lip. She looked at her mother, at the proud tilt of her head and the strong set of her shoulders. A small stab of unwilling admiration pierced Evelyn's embarrassment. Suddenly, ridiculously, she wanted to stand up and cheer. The notion was strong in her, making her smile at her father, at Violet who was watching Maggie with big blue admiring eyes.

'As for your feet,' Maggie was saying, 'I'll give you a good cure for chilblains — if you're a big enough woman to take it.'

Evelyn held her breath, surely — surely — not that!

Seal pushed out her bosoms, stuck out her hairy chin. 'Say your piece, Mrs Grant, no doubt you are bursting to impress us all wi' your knowledge, though it will just be a lot of old wives' tales that you have brought here frae the north-east. I've heard tell you and your like believe in witchcraft — ay, and maybe practise it as well. Here in the west we are more civilised. My mother aye told me . . .'

'Urine, Mrs McWhirter, good, plain, old-fashioned urine.'

Cook with a Capital gaped. 'Urine, Mrs Grant!'

'Ay, urine, Mrs McWhirter. Gather up a good big basin o' bedroom slops and steep your feet in it. The heat will go out o' your chilblains in no time at all.'

Seal McWhirter looked both aghast and suspicious. 'I've never heard the likes in all my life! Have you any proof o' a thing like that working?'

'Oh, ay, it worked on the sore hooves of our old cow, so I'm sure it will do the same for you.'

The old cook let out a yell of outrage; Jamie clapped his hand to his mouth; Violet snorted into her hanky; Ferguson emitted a great gust of wheezy laughter; a crimson-faced Evelyn rushed outside to stand against a wall and give vent to mirth such as she had never known since the Rothiedrum days.

Chapter Three

When she had recovered from her merriment she walked away from the house, her feet crunching on the gravel, swishing through the grass as she made for a little wood at the foot of the slope. It was a calm, misty day, rich with the scents of wet leaves and wood smoke. She looked back at Dunmarnock, a gracious old house with turrets and tiny, mysterious windows and blood-red ivy covering the north wing.

She thought it suited its name, as it looked more like a castle than a house. She liked to just stand and look at it: it reminded her of Rothiedrum House where she had wandered with Forbes the Younger of Rothiedrum. How sweet the memory of those days, she and Gillie, Johnny and Florrie, sitting in the kitchen of the big house while Martha the cook plied them with doorsteps of bread and jam and buns straight from the oven . . .

Her fingers curled round the letter in her pocket. For some nameless reason she had put off opening it, but now she took it out and stood staring down at it. For long moments she looked at Mary's untidy script with the dots flying off the paper, then, with a touch of impatience, she tore open the envelope.

A single page was folded over a length of dog-eared card but she ignored the card and read the letter first, playing for time. She acknowledged the fact without knowing why.

Dear little sister,
    Postie asked me to forward the enclosed. Old McDuff says it's important so I thought I had better send it right

away. Greg wrote, he is well but very tired. Hinney, Coulter, Carnallachie, and all, send much affection. Wee Donald misses you terribly. Will write more later.

God Bless, Mary.

Carefully Evelyn tucked the note back into its envelope and put it into her apron pocket. Almost unwillingly she looked at the dirty brown postcard reposing in her hand, stared and stared at the address till her eyes grew dry and hot: *Miss Evelyn McKenzie Grant, King's Croft, Rothiedrum, Aberdeenshire.*

Her lips moved, forming the words, before she turned the card over; a squiggle of numbers and foreign words blurred in front of her eyes, then *Prisoner of War* leapt out at her.

'Prisoner of War,' she said the words aloud, as if to convince herself they were real and not a figment of her imagination. At first nothing penetrated; she stood there at the edge of the woods, a crackle of dry leaves under her feet, and rooks calling noisily amongst the tangle of bare branches above.

Slowly, slowly, the message sunk in. Davie was alive. He was alive! And he hadn't forgotten her, he had remembered, and by directing that this postcard be sent to her he was letting her know the reason for his long silence.

Davie, her Davie, was alive – but was he well? The question crept into her mind and hammered at it persistently. She had heard rumours concerning prisoners of war, grim rumours of experimentation and torture . . .

Nausea swept over her. Hastily she sought the support of a stout tree and stood leaning against it, her legs trembling beneath her, one hand held dazedly over her eyes . . .

A muffle of hooves, the crunch of crisp leaves, brought home to her that she was not alone. Her head jerked up, she made a valiant attempt to muster her senses. A big, powerful-looking roan was picking his way through the woods with surprising delicacy; on his broad back sat Colonel Baird who was a keen equestrian and, as well as being an enthusiastic member of the hunt, he rode out most mornings, sometimes to visit the estate farms, more often just for the pleasure of it.

The advent of war had left him with a vastly reduced stable, which inconvenience he had taken philosophically since almost all the stable hands had joined up leaving only Burton, the elderly groom, and two local lads to carry on.

At the sight of the red-haired girl standing so silently under the tree he brought his horse to a halt beside her to frown down at her, his fierce blue eyes sweeping keenly over her.

'Are you all right, child?' he questioned in his precise, military voice. 'You seem – disturbed.'

Evelyn held the tattered postcard to her fast-beating heart and said in a queer, breathless voice, 'Someone I thought dead – is alive.'

The words just tumbled out and she wondered what had made her confide in her employer so readily. It might have been that he was the first human being to find her in her present, confused state, or because he was a man of experience in matters pertaining to war. She didn't know but wished now that she hadn't spoken. He was staring at her without comprehension, thoughtfully stroking his neatly clipped moustache with his thumb. All she wanted was to escape those penetrating blue eyes that looked at her yet seemed not to see her at all. 'Excuse me, Sir Richard, I – I must go.'

She made to move away but he had spotted the dirty piece of card in her hand. With great agility he dismounted and, taking Evelyn by the arm, he marched her over to a fallen tree and made her sit down on it. The roan wandered off a little way, reins trailing, snorts of pleasure puffing out as he snuffled his nose into the mossy ground beneath the trees.

Seating himself beside Evelyn, the Colonel held out his hand. 'May I?' Wordlessly she handed him the postcard. He glared at the jumble of numbers irritably. 'Can't make out a thing –' He began searching his pockets. 'Damned

37

specs, I'm sure I brought them . . .'

'Hanging round your neck, sir,' Evelyn spoke quietly but couldn't keep from smiling.

'Bless me, so they are, can't think why Beth strings them round my ears, I keep forgetting they're not in my pockets – ah, that's better –' He had applied the specs to his nose. 'David Alexander Grainger – lot of jargon – Prisoner of War – hmm – so you thought he was dead, eh, Ellen?'

'Evelyn – Evelyn McKenzie Grant, the new kitchen maid.' She spoke her name with unconscious pride. 'I came wi' my parents to Dunmarnock a month ago, I kent Davie in Rothiedrum and yes – I thought he was dead. My sister forwarded this card, I've just read it.'

She looked Sir Richard straight in the eye, 'Would it be better if he was? I've heard things about these prison camps.'

'Don't believe all you hear,' the Colonel advised sagely, as he handed the card back to Evelyn. 'One hears all sorts of things but I'm sure the Boche are treating our lads well enough. Your Davie will be fine and there's an address here you can send letters to. Write dozens of 'em, even if they don't all get through there's a fair chance he'll get one or two and you'll feel better for unburdening your heart.'

A sudden upsurge of hope manifested itself in an odd way. She began to shake, keeping her fingers clenched tightly on the postcard, as if just by touching it she could extract from it some of the beautiful virile power that she had known and loved in David Grainger.

The Colonel placed a fatherly arm about her slender shoulders, whereupon she immediately planted her face into the fine tweed of his jacket and burst into a flood of weeping. Tension spewed from her, she felt her limbs growing weak and helpless; she was ashamed of her outburst but was quite unable to stem her tears.

'There, there, child,' the Colonel soothed kindly, 'let it all go. Wish men could cry – my son, you know – he'll never be the same again. Beth and I thank God he's at

least alive, so many killed, a bloody war, Evelyn, bloody
and vicious . . . There now, blow your nose and you'll feel
better – dammit! There's one around here somewhere . . .'

He was searching his pockets again and with a watery
giggle Evelyn extracted her own hanky from her sleeve
and blew her nose soundly. 'I'm sorry, Sir Richard, for
behaving like that, I just couldna seem to help myself.'

'Think nothing of it, Evelyn – and enough of that "sir"
business, I prefer Colonel, or . . .' he grinned, 'just plain
old Beardie Bum. That's what they called me at school,
you know. I didn't like it then but now I think it's bloody
funny. Me and Beth have great fun with a little rhyme I
made up – it goes like this:

'Beardie, Beardie Bum, Bum,
'Sitting up the lum, lum.
'Sneeze, yawn, sneeze all day,
'Blow, blow the soot away.
'Oh, ooh, Beardie Bum, up the lum . . .'

He burst into loud and raucous song, slapping his knee in
time to the beat, his eyes sparkling in his fresh, handsome
face. In a flurry of delight Evelyn joined in the ridiculous
chant, her heart taking wing, in her mind, substituting her
own words so that 'Davie's alive, Davie's alive' beat and
pulsed into every cell in her body. She was invigorated,
intoxicated with the euphoria of these timeless moments
in the company of Sir Richard, Beardie Bum Baird of
Dunmarnock House.

But then she sobered, moved away a little, saying,
'Sir Richard – Colonel, I shouldn't, it isna right.'

'What's right?' His face was still aglow, 'I made you
laugh, that's what's right. All this stiff and starch, never
could stand it, that's why I get on so well with Evander
Forbes, we're of the same mind.'

He found his pipe, miraculously coming upon it almost
at once in his top pocket. Lighting it he sat there puffing
peacefully, grinning at Evelyn in a mischievous small-boy
fashion.

She gazed at him. 'Ay, you are like Evander Forbes, but even more like Lady Marjory's uncle, Lord Lindsay Ogilvie. He asked me to call him Oggie – it was a kind of a joke between us.'

'Old Oggie, a marvellous character, no put-on with him, holes in the seat of his breeks, an endearing penchant to be as ordinary as possible amidst elevated circumstances such as his.'

They sat there reminiscing in the woods, the young red-haired girl and the laird of Dunmarnock, till Evelyn suddenly jumped to her feet with a cry of dismay. 'I forgot all about time! Seal McWhirter will be furious. She said that you and Lady Elizabeth had guests coming to lunch. Bugger it, she'll have my guts for garters!'

'Oh, Lord!' The Colonel also jumped to his feet, 'I forgot, dammit! Beth asked me to be home early in order to dicky myself up for the Conways. Bloody nuisance! I detest dressing up – oh, and don't worry about old Seal – I'll see you home, she won't dare come any of her snash with me.'

Calling his horse, he held the reins and bade Evelyn mount. She hesitated. It was only a short walk to the house but the temptation of sitting again on a horse's back was too much. With a breathless acceptance she stepped lightly on the Colonel's cupped hands and settled herself on the saddle.

It was heavenly to be up there, so high and free with the earth moving away effortlessly on either side. Memories came flooding back: the beat of the Clyde's hooves beneath her, the parks of Rothiedrum gliding past; Queenie, Nickum, Swack, and Fyvie, she had ridden them all, with or without a saddle. A surge of sadness took away her happiness. Where were they now, those beloved animals who had given so much to the Grant family?

'You're not new to this, lass?' The Colonel broke into her thoughts and in a rush she told him something of her days of growing up surrounded by horses and dogs at King's Croft.

'Come down to the stables in your spare time,' the Colonel told her. 'Burton won't mind and I'll see you get the chance to keep in your hand.'

'Och no, sir – Colonel – it wouldna be right, the others would talk . . .'

'Damn the others! All this right and proper business is just balderdash. You heed what *I* say and not another word on the subject.'

She was silent. Pregnant, unmarried maidservants did not jump about on horses or take liberties outwith their station. A welter of emotions seized her. All at once everything that was good seemed to be happening to her. Davie was alive – the knowledge of that alone made her heart sing – and on top of that her new life at Dunmarnock had taken on an entirely new dimension. Quite suddenly, the idea of staying on here seemed very desirable – if only things had been different – if only . . .

Burton the groom gaped openly when she clattered into the yard on Major's back, the Colonel leading the way, the family spaniels, who had joined them halfway, bounding along in front, tongues lolling, ears flopping; and his jaw hung even wider when the Colonel courteously helped Evelyn climb down and said he would walk with her back to the house.

'Oh, and by the way, Burton.' The Colonel paused and appeared for quite a few moments to have forgotten what he wanted to say. 'Ah yes –' his brow cleared – 'Evelyn here is an experienced young horsewoman. Let her muck about in the stables whenever she has a mind and if she wants to ride out, give her Darling.'

'Ay, Colonel,' nodded Burton, throwing Evelyn such a bemused glance she had to hide a smile. Come dinner time, the whole of Dunmarnock would know of the incident but – unconsciously she tossed her red head – let them talk! She hadn't done anything so wrong – and anyway she liked the Colonel and had enjoyed the time spent in his distinctly unique company.

Seal McWhirter almost dropped a pan of gravy when

the master of the house appeared with Evelyn in her kitchen to tell her that it was entirely his fault the girl was late.

'I kept her back – blethering about horses,' he delivered succinctly and went away muttering something about finding Beth.

'His fault!' Seal exploded the minute the Colonel was out of earshot.

'Ay, you heard.' Evelyn smiled pleasantly and, turning a deaf ear to Cook's ravings, she set about her neglected duties with a song on her lips and her mind fixed firmly on the precious postcard reposing in her pocket.

'A prisoner o' war!' Maggie's brow furrowed as she looked at her daughter's glowing face. 'So, the lad is alive after all.'

Evelyn, bursting to tell someone her good news, had left Seal napping by the fire and had slipped away to find her mother. They were enclosed in the privacy of Maggie's office, a small room with scuffed leather armchairs, a small mahogany writing desk and windows looking out on the River Threep meandering its way through the meadows at the back of the house.

'Ay, Mam, alive.' Anxiously Evelyn scanned her mother's face which had closed up at mention of David Grainger. 'Say you're glad, I ken fine you never ever really took to him but I – I love him – I've loved him from the start and I – I'm so relieved he's alive I could shout for joy even though I feel like crying at the same time.'

Dizziness swept over her and she sat down suddenly her face bereft of colour.

'Evie, never mind David Grainger for the moment.' Maggie swept him aside as if glad to be rid of the subject. 'I'm more concerned about you. Ever since we left Rothiedrum I've noticed a difference in you – yet strange, ay, strange, I canna lay my finger on it. I kent your sadness at having to leave the croft but it's something more than

42

that – something much more.'

'Ach, havers, Mam,' Evelyn spoke as lightly as she could though her heart was racing so fast in her breast she felt she must faint with it. Wildly she debated with herself if she ought just to tell the truth and get it over with – but no! She couldn't – not yet – she needed time, time to grow more accustomed to the idea of it herself and also to adjust to the discovery of Davie's whereabouts. He might set her free, be allowed to come home, he might even be glad to learn about the baby – they could get married and it would be all right – everything would be all right. She could go to Glasgow and work till the baby came and when Davie came back she would have some place for him and the baby to live . . .

Sitting there in her mother's little sanctum she deluded herself into believing these things; she forgot Davie's passionate desire to roam the world, to be free of domestic fetters; at that moment the road ahead of her was smooth and straight . . .

'I'm fine, Mam, really,' she spoke rapidly, willing herself to stay calm, to speak rationally. 'It's just that everything's so new and I pine for everything I left behind. You won't be pleased at me, I know, but I'm leaving Dunmarnock, whatever you say. Glasgow has plenty o' work for young women and I don't fit in here. I was drudge enough when I worked to Rothiedrum but at least I was above stairs. I'm – I'm just no' cut out to be a servant. There was a time when you hated the idea o' the likes o' that yourself and made such a fuss when I got a place working to the Forbes family.'

'You're right, Evie, you dinna fit in here.' Maggie's voice was suddenly soft. She looked down on her daughter's bowed head and wanted to crush the sweet youth of it to her bosom. Once there had been opportunity enough for such things and with a sigh she put out her hand to stroke tenderly the girl's silken hair. 'I've heard how you and the Colonel met up today and came back here like bosom friends. The whole place is buzzing wi' the gossip

43

o' it, but bugger the lot o' them. You aye did mix well wi' the gentry, it's in your blood, Evie – but that doesna make it right. It might be better if you made your own way, more than any o' my daughters you aye had independence – so you go to Glasgow, you'll take my blessings with you.'

It was what Evelyn had wanted to hear yet the harsh reality of the spoken word weighed down on her like lead. Already she felt bereft of family, of security, of the love that had surrounded her since first she had drawn the sweet air of Aberdeenshire into her lungs.

Chapter Four

That night she went upstairs early, eager to start writing to Davie, in her mind composing the things she would say to him. She still could hardly believe that he was of the world and that he cared enough for her to let her know what was happening to him. But even so, recollections tormented her – the pale haunted face of the girl in the Aulton who had named David Grainger as the father of the child she was carrying; Evelyn's own despair of mind that had guided her footsteps to The Devil's Door with the intention of taking her own life and that of her unborn baby. She was glad now that the attempt had been unsuccessful; despite everything life was still very sweet and the girl could easily have been mistaken – or lying, one of the two – and yet – the thought came unbidden – why should she? Evelyn had been a stranger to her, she'd had no reason to lie – and Davie had certainly behaved childishly that day he had come upon Evelyn and Gillie walking arm in arm together in the Aulton. He had gone off in a huff and it had been quite some time before he had deigned to come looking for her again. He had had plenty of time to console himself elsewhere, he was a man of many passions ... She shivered. She, of all people, knew the truth of that only too well: he was jealous and possessive, he could hate as easily as he could love ...

She took a deep breath, willing her black thoughts to depart back into the deepest recesses of her mind. Davie was alive, that was all that mattered just now, all that would ever matter to her. She loved him whatever he had done, she would always love him ...

Lost in thought, she opened the door of her room and there was Effie, over by the bed, an oil lamp in one hand, Evie's diary in the other, and in a flash she knew the reasons behind the smug, knowing looks the sly whittrock had been throwing her lately – Effie knew! She knew everything! And she had been awaiting her chance to divest herself of her ill-gained knowledge, to point the finger of scorn and blame whenever it suited her to do so. And why? Because she suffered from that most unreasoning emotion, jealousy, plain, black, simple jealousy, and, as Evelyn knew only too well, there was no logic on earth that could easily deal with that primitive state . . .

Outwith the halo of lamp light, the room was darkly shadowed; menace came leaping towards Evelyn to close its fingers round her throat and squeeze the air from her lungs. Effie's face was a waxy blob of shocked surprise; tossing the diary away from her as if she had been scalded, she stepped backwards in an attempt to melt into the waiting shadows.

Rage rose up in Evelyn, it boiled inside her breast, white-hot, bubbling, before it came spewing out like an erupting volcano. She made no sound as she lunged towards the other girl, her body as taut as a bowstring, her hands outspread in the manner of some wild creature about to pounce on its prey. Her shadow cavorted on the wall, large, looming, terrifying.

'Evelyn, I didna mean anything – I never looked, really I didna! You caught me, you caught me in time . . .' Effie's voice was a pleading whimper of fear. They were the only words she managed to get out before the livid fury that was Evelyn McKenzie Grant enveloped her and began to tear at her hair, her face, her clothing.

In a struggling heap they landed on the bed, panting, kicking, scratching. Evelyn was the smaller and younger of the two but Effie was no match against the strength of her inflamed temper. Her limbs went weak and helpless, she tasted hot blood on her lips. Terror was paralysing her; she truly believed in those fearful moments that her end was nigh and, opening her lungs, she gave them full throttle.

Her screams split the night asunder, brought returning sanity to bear on Evelyn who, fighting for breath, sat back on her heels to clutch at her side where a pain, deep and raw, knifed into her.

Doors were opening along the landing, halos of light met and merged and finally illuminated Evelyn's room. Both Ferguson and Seal had puffed up from their respective quarters; Ferguson's hair was standing on end, Seal wore squiggly curlers under her mutch cap, her hands were encased in cotton gloves, her whiskers were fairly bristling with the fright she had received on hearing Effie's lusty cries.

Violet and Peggy had been first to arrive on the scene and stood just inside the door, wide-eyed and frightened looking.

'She *attacked* me!' Effie burst out before anyone could speak, her tongue licking frantically at the blood frothing from her nose. 'Like some heathen wild animal she came at my throat and would have killed me if I hadna screamed.'

Evelyn could say nothing in her defence; her hands were clutching at her side, her face was deathly pale beneath a cloud of hair that had come cascading down from her torn-off cap.

Seal bustled, grabbing hold of Effie and pulling her away from the bed while Ferguson spoke urgently to Evelyn, 'What was it, lass? What made you do it?' Evelyn groaned and fell back just as Raggy Annie arrived on the scene, without flurry or fuss, her rat's-tail hair hanging limpidly about her long, pale, melancholy face, a soggy, skinny cigarette dangling from her thin, nicotine-stained lips. She made the cigarettes herself and kept them in a tin in her apron pocket which was full of little bits of shag all mixed up with tiny balls of oust gleaned from her habit of picking up fluff and hairs from carpets and floors in her travels through the house for, despite her untidy appearance, she was a most methodical worker and kept the place shining.

Annie McMahone came from a line of Irish immigrants who had settled in the Gorbals district of Glasgow. Widowed twice over, she was, at fifty-seven, as hard as nails with a view of life so broad she could take in any situation at a glance and seemed always to know how best to cope. Her niece, Violet, had secured the job for her at Dunmarnock at the start of the war when domestic help was at a low ebb and Raggy Annie herself was down on her luck.

The Bairds had never regretted their decision to take her on. She was reliable and hard-working and though she took a devilish delight in ruffling the feathers of the more correct members of staff she never intruded her presence into the above-stairs household but went quietly about her business. As a result she was a firm favourite with the Bairds as a whole, much to Cook's oft-voiced chagrin.

At her entry, Seal blew disapproval down her twitching nostrils and removed her person from the cleaner's nicotine-tainted path as, without hesitation, she shuffled to the bed in her down-at-heel slippers and took Evelyn to her bony bosom.

'There, there, lassie,' she soothed, pushing the girl's hair from her brow and at the same time expertly flicking a curving oblong of grey ash from her cigarette into the bedside candleholder. 'Lie you back like a good girl, Annie will hae you tucked up in nae time at all and gie you something to ease your pain.'

'Oh, you'll no' do that in a hurry.' Effie had found her voice and was glaring at both Evelyn and Raggy Annie with cold dislike. 'She's a wicked, sinful girl who doesn't deserve any sort o' sympathy and I doubt she'll no' be here for long when the maister and mistress find out she's expecting a bairn out o' wedlock.'

A shocked hush stilled everyone for a moment then Seal spoke, her voice ominously quiet. 'And how do you come to know the like o' that, my girl?'

'It's all in her diary,' Effie sneered, her beady eyes

darting defiantly round the room. 'She's up half the night writing things in it and then she has screaming nightmares that make my flesh crawl to hear . . .'

'So – that was why she went at you.' Violet spoke for the first time, her blue eyes glittering angrily. 'She caught you reading her diary – you bitch – you sly, deceitful bitch! You've had it in for Evie ever since she came and now you go snooping amongst her personal belongings like the sneak you are.'

'Ay, she's jealous o' Evie,' Peggy stated laconically, 'aye has been.'

'And forbye all that –' Raggy Annie had loosened Evelyn's collars – 'the besom's wrong about the lass no' being married. This postcard fell out her pocket, her man is a prisoner o' war – the poor, poor sowel – and see, she wears his ring around her neck . . .' Triumphantly she pointed to the gold band nestling against the white skin of Evelyn's throat. 'A kitchie maid canny very well go about wearing a gold ring while she scrubs pots and pans, can she now? So, what have you to say to that, Miss Know-All?'

'She never said anything about being married,' mumbled Effie, her face flaring to crimson.

'No, she wouldn't, she's the reserved sort,' snorted Seal, glaring at the much subdued parlour maid. 'She's no' the type to go gabbling her head off about men and what she would like to do to them.'

'No, she's already done it.' Effie made a sullen last stand which rattled in her throat as Seal took her and shook her, then bulldozed her out of the room.

'Should we no' get a doctor to the lass?' Ferguson asked anxiously. 'She looks gey pale lying there.'

'You would be pale too if you had fainted,' snapped Raggy Annie. 'There will be no need o' a doctor, I'll see to her. I've had seven pregnancies o' my own, two o' them stillbirths, the rest alive and kicking and terrorising the Gorbals when they were bairns. I've seen three o' my grandchildren into the world so I know fine what I'm talking about. Away you all go ben to your beds, you'll do no good standing here gawping at the girl.'

'Hmph.' Seal mustered her dignity, puffed out her bosom and threw Raggy Annie a look that said all too plainly, 'How dare *you*, a common cleaner, speak to *me* like that?' Nevertheless, she did not tarry but shuffled away to pour her grievances into Ferguson's patient, experienced lugs.

'You stay behind, Violet,' ordered Raggy Annie, 'I'll want you to fetch some cold water and a cloot to bathe the girl's brow.'

'Ay, Auntie,' murmured Violet and went obediently to get the necessary requisites.

Some time later, when Violet had departed and there was only Raggy Annie sitting half-drowsing in a chair beside the bed, Evelyn's eyes fluttered open. In a panic she made to sit up but, immediately alert, the older woman made her lie back, tucking the covers under her chin as she did so.

'Wheesht, wheesht, my bonny one, there's naught to worry about, it was only a stitch you had, the bairn will bide its full term.'

But Evelyn wouldn't be stilled, her hands were out from the bedclothes, scrabbling around in a frenzied searching.

Raggy Annie held up the postcard. 'Here's what you're looking for, Evie, the paper telling you your man's been taken prisoner. Ach my, you must hae made a bonny pair at your wedding, him in his kiltie uniform, you in your best frock. His ring looks a mite big for your wee finger but that can be easily enough sorted and then you can wear it on your days off.'

'Och, but Annie!' Evelyn's eyes were big and dark in the soft light. 'I dinna ken what you're talking about – I'm not married – I could never tell lies like that.'

Raggy Annie gave a hoarse chuckle. 'No, but I could – and the rest o' them will be none the wiser, you can take that from me, hen. I knew fine you weren't wed, you had all the signs o' a lass wi' a heavy burden to bear.'

Evelyn bit her lip. She seemed to hear Davie's voice inside her head, saying half-jokingly, half in earnest, 'Who knows, someday you might need my ring to fool the world.'

He couldn't have known then just how true his carelessly spoken words would be — or had he? It would have been an easy enough matter for him to foresee. He was no fool when it came to playing with women's emotions and by then she had been hopelessly under his spell, ready to give him anything he asked of her . . .

'Ay, Annie, heavy indeed,' she said wearily, 'and in more ways than one. Mam — my mother doesna know, nor do any o' my family except Grace.'

'Ay, you have that to face.' The older woman's voice was unusually soft. 'But you have courage, Evelyn Grant, and will face what's coming wi' a stout heart. I'll get a hold o' your parents first thing tomorrow — before any o' these buggering gossips get to them first.'

'Och, Annie, you're so good.' Evelyn found the woman's rough hand and squeezed it tightly.

'Ach, no, I only hae a long memory.' Raggy Annie's voice was suddenly faraway, 'I was barely eighteen when I got caught wi' my first — ay — and the lad that later wed me wasna the bairn's father, just a good, kind man who gave my firstborn his name. So you see, lass, we're sisters in need, you and me, we hae that in common.'

'Sisters in need.' Evelyn smiled, her fingers relaxed in Annie's hand — she was asleep.

The house was quietly a-bustle. Evelyn could hear faintly the closing of doors; the subdued murmur of voices; the metallic clatter of a kitchen pan followed by a cat's yelping snarl of pain. Seal McWhirter waged a continual war against the farm moggies who found their way into *her* premises. She kept a special supply of ancient saucepans by the back door and Evelyn had a fancy she showed disappointment if she didn't get a chance to use them at least once a day.

This morning would have found her in a rare old temper. Peggy had been dispatched to take Evelyn's place and Peggy had never been known to hurry for anybody – 'No, not even if the King himself was to step over the threshold and demand his tea,' was Seal's grim and oft-repeated remark.

Raggy Annie had brought Evelyn her breakfast on the third-best silver tray, set with dainty cups and jugs, and a yellow chrysanthemum in a tiny vase, thoughtfully provided by Seal herself who, despite her bad mood, was not lacking in sympathy for Evelyn's plight, coupled with twinges of guilt whenever she thought about how she had sent the girl running hither and thither from morn to night with hardly so much as a thank-you or a moment of consideration as to the girl's state of health – for she had often been tired-looking with little dark smudges under her eyes at day's end when sometimes she declined to sup her cocoa with the rest of them but just crept wearily up to her bed.

'Of course, I wasn't to know,' she had excused herself hastily. 'These young girls nowadays will try anything to get out of working.

'Now I know why the girl's mother spoke out for her yesterday,' she confided magnanimously to Ferguson. 'Any mither would worry about a lass in Evie's condition though why it was all kept such a secret is beyond me.'

'Och well, that's plain enough to see. When the Grants left Rothiedrum they must have been gey anxious to make a good impression at Dunmarnock. If the girl's state had come to be known they maybe thought the Bairds wouldna have taken them on.'

Seal was unconvinced. 'Ach, that's rubbish! Surely they should hae known that the Bairds wouldna hae turned them out.'

'These is no' your usual gentry, I'll grant you that, but the Grants weren't to know that,' Ferguson persisted. 'Most o' they big houses are snobs wi' their noses in the air when it comes to servant lassies and their troubles.'

'But surely no' in wartime,' Seal argued, 'they just have to take what they get nowadays and be glad to do it. Look at that Raggy Annie for instance, the woman is as common as dirt wi' a tongue to match yet her ladyship grabbed her as if she was gold. And the wifie is living in, *living in*, Ferguson! All she knows is backcourts and washing at the steamie once a week and there she lies, among the best cottons and flannels and giving me orders, *me*, Ferguson, who knew these things from birth. We might hae been only humble crofters but we had clean sheets and *no* fleas between them! That wifie looks like she's been bitten wi' bed bugs and fleas all her days for the wee marks o' them are all over the skin o' her body — even her face.'

'The pox, Seal, the pox,' Ferguson explained knowledgeably. 'These is pox marks she has on her. Glasgow is full o' pox and fevers and black plagues that maim you for life if they don't kill you first. Mistress McMahone can as much help the wee holes on her face as you can help the dimples in your elbows.'

So they went on, discussing, bickering, Seal almost forgetting the subject that had started it all off but remembering in time to put flowers on Evelyn's tray and a tiny woollen cosy on her boiled egg.

But Evelyn had barely touched anything on the temptingly-set tray, except for the tea, of which she had drunk two cups to moisten her dry throat. Now she sat on the edge of the bed, feet placed neatly together, David's postcard held in hands that were clasped tightly together while she waited for her parents to come upstairs.

Every imagined footfall, every creak on the stairs, set her pulses wildly racing and when finally Maggie and Jamie appeared in her room she felt sick with apprehension. Her father came at once to her side to place his arm around her shoulders and give her a reassuring smile. He smelled of whisky, at just eight-thirty in the morning he smelled of whisky, but his youngest daughter didn't draw away from him. More than anything she was aware of his love for her, reaching out to give her strength and she could have laughed at that if she had felt at all like laughing. Neither of them had much strength to give the other just then but she knew she had his love, all through her life she had had that, and in those moments she hated herself because in a very short time she had to rob him of the trust he had placed in her from the start.

Maggie was more aloof, as if she already knew the things that were about to be revealed and was bracing herself to meet them.

'Well, Evie,' her voice was tight and controlled, 'Mrs McMahone informs us that you have something to tell us.'

'Ay, Mam, I have — only I dinna know how I'm going to be able to say the things I have to say.'

She paused to stare down at her clasped hands, her bowed head shaking so much that an alarmed Jamie took her to him and said firmly, 'Evie, Evie, it's us, your parents, surely you canna be afraid to tell us of the things that are troubling you? When you were a bairn you told me everything.'

'Oh, Father,' she raised her head to look at him, 'I'm not a bairn now. For a long time I've had my secrets from you — and Mam. Last night Effie Jordan sneaked in here and read my diary and she discovered my worst secret of all — I'm having David Grainger's baby! I wanted to go away so that I wouldn't bring shame on my family . . .'

Her voice dropped to a whisper. 'I'm sorry, I'm so very, very sorry —'

Maggie's hand went quickly to the bed rail which she gripped tightly for a few moments before sitting down heavily beside her daughter. 'I think I knew, all along I knew, but, fool that I am, I tried to pretend to myself that you were still as innocent as the babe I birthed and raised and to whom I talked myself blue

in the face about the rights and wrongs o' this world.'
She gave a short, bitter laugh. 'I should have kent better.
David Grainger is no' the sort o' man to content himself
just holding hands – and you –' she eyed her daughter's
ashamed face – 'you were aye too eager for life, to take
what it offered without thinking o' the consequences.'

'What's done is done,' Jamie spoke with a firmness he
didn't feel. 'It willna do a bit o' good harping on things
that are over and past.' He turned his eyes away. 'We all
have our weaknesses – however much we try to hide them
from others.'

'Ay, and well you may talk,' Maggie threw at him.
'You gave her too much freedom! You and she were
aye alike, carefree spirits thirsty for love and romance
– only these days it's no' romance you're after, and the
only spirits in you are those you sup from a bottle – as
for you, madam –' she rounded on her daughter – 'it was
a fine way you arranged to have your wee speak wi' us
– to be waylaid by Annie McMahone and told that our
daughter had something to tell us – ay, and second-hand
news at that! No doubt she and the whole jing-bang o'
them heard it all first!'

'I told you, Mam,' Evelyn was white to the lips, 'Effie
found my diary. She's aye snooping around and for once
I forgot to lock it up. But only Annie kens the truth, the
others think I'm married, they know about the postcard,
they saw this ring that Davie gave me a long time ago.'

Maggie stared at the gold band in her daughter's hand.
'Ay, he kent what he was about wi' you, Evie. He took
you in good and proper.'

The hurt in Evelyn's wide green eyes halted her mother's tongue. Taking the girl to her breast she rocked her
back and forth as she had done in far-off days of innocent
childhood. 'Wheesht now, my lassie, your father's right,
what's done is done, but heed this, you might have fooled
Mrs McWhirter and the others but I will no' allow the
Bairds to be deceived. If nothing else they deserve to ken
the truth and whatever the outcome we'll see it through

together. We're still a family even though we've lived such an unnatural kind o' life since leaving the croft behind.'

She caught Jamie's eye. He was still smarting over her harsh words to him but there was no anger in him, only the defeated look of a man who had been ensnared in the cruel twists and turns of life.

She put out her hand to him. He took it and held it tightly. She was his strength this fine, handsome woman, with her flashing grey-green eyes and her dignified carriage, and more than ever these days he needed the strength of her in his rather uncertain existence.

'Wood Cottage isna so bad, Maggie lass,' he said softly. 'A man's home is his castle wherever it might be and I've known a contentment here I never thought to find after King's Croft — funny it came to be kent by that name — eh?'

'Ay,' nodded Evelyn, 'and now the folk here are calling the cottage Jamie's Castle, as if they had somehow discovered that Father was once king o' the gypsies.'

Jamie winked. 'Now, I wonder who told them that, eh, princess?'

Maggie said nothing. She didn't want to remind either of them that they might not have a cottage for very much longer — whatever its name might be.

When Jamie and Maggie finally took their leave Evelyn felt exhausted after the meeting with her parents and was poorly prepared for a visit from Effie Jordan who, after a peremptory rap at the door, slipped soundlessly into the room.

'A pity you werena aye so careful of a person's privacy!' The words sprang to Evelyn's lips but she never uttered them. Effie was in a pitiable state, her small eyes were smaller still from a recent attack of weeping, brought about by her own state of mind and triggered into action by a severe lecture she had just received from Maggie's able tongue.

Surveying the younger girl through red-rimmed slits,

she sniffed mightily into a stiff cotton square and blurted out, 'Evelyn, och, Evelyn, I hardly slept last night for worrying and wondering about what was going to happen to me. I never meant to look in your diary, honest I didna, it was just you were aye so quiet in your room at night except when you were dreaming and I knew there was something wrong wi' you . . .'

'Last night wasna the first time you looked in my things – was it?' Evelyn said shortly.

'It was almost the first, I only had a wee peek before that and never took much o' it in,' Effie spoke desperately, her fingers working nervously on her apron frills so that the rustling of them got on Evelyn's nerves. 'Say you willna tell on me,' Effie went on, a trembling pleading in her voice. 'My position here at Dunmarnock means a lot to me and the Bairds might no' want me if – if they knew. Oh, Evelyn, I've nowhere else to go, you see. I was brought up in an orphanage and have no family that I know of. The Bairds are like family to me, Dunmarnock is like my home and I – I *need* to be here, Evelyn. Nobody else would want me, no one has ever really taken to me, somehow they didna seem to like me. No' like you, Evelyn, everyone likes you, that was why –'

'You had it in for me,' Evelyn interposed grimly, not allowing herself to be taken in by Effie for one moment – and yet unable to stop feeling a pang of pity for the girl with her unfortunate nature and her nondescript appearance. Just then she looked worse than ever with her red eyes and her nose swollen to a bulbous blob after coming into sharp contact with Evelyn's flying knuckles the night before.

'A jelly nose,' Evelyn murmured, unable to hide a smile.

'What did you say?'

'Your nose, it's swollen. I'm no' going to say I'm sorry because you deserved it – at the time I felt like killing you and might have done if I hadna been stopped.'

'I know,' Effie agreed miserably and with a certain amount of venom. 'You're stronger than you look – I

57

'— I aye admired your dainty wee hands and feet,' she muttered grudgingly.

'They're about the only bits o' me that will be dainty in a few months time.' Evelyn couldn't resist saying that and laughed outright at Effie's look of absolute outrage.

'This is no laughing matter, Evelyn.' The old Effie was returning in no mean manner, her thin lips had curled at the other girl's words but somehow she managed to lift them into an ingratiating grimace that was meant to be a smile. 'You havena said yet if you'll tell on me or no?'

'Of course I won't tell,' Evelyn spoke disdainfully. 'I've more to do than carry tales to my employers — but heed this, Effie, someone else might say something, there was quite a crowd in my room last night, remember.'

'They don't matter,' Effie said scornfully, 'and you can tell that Violet and Peggy to hold their tongues — they'll listen to you — they aye do,' she finished bitterly.

'You make people turn against you,' Evelyn said bluntly, 'and you're wrong about everyone disliking you. Jock Pringle would take you out if you would let him, he's a nice boy and good-looking as well.'

'Jasper Pringle's son?' Effie was horrified. 'But he's only a gamekeeper, always stinking of earth and fish and rabbits. I would never walk out wi' the likes o' *him*.'

'You're a snob, Effie Jordan!' Evelyn gasped. 'You think you're better than anybody else!'

Effie sniffed and straightened her cap. 'I see no harm in trying to better myself — and I will, Evelyn Grant, I will, you mark my words. Major Baird has a great respect and liking for me. He isn't a well man now from all accounts, his hands were so badly burned he wears gloves all the time to hide them. These uppity madams o' his own class will turn their faces away from him but no' me, in time he'll come to know how much I care for him. For when he comes home I'll be there at every turn and he'll notice me all right — I'll make him.'

Evelyn could not help staring as suddenly she realised that Effie Jordan was a girl possessed; her inflated sense of her own importance, her pointed loyalty to the Bairds, her superior attitude to the other servants all told of someone trying very hard to be something she wasn't nor ever would be – but this – this cold, calculating view of her future hopes was something quite different altogether . . . Evelyn shivered, she felt herself to be in the presence of a malevolent spirit . . . Effie was twisted, twisted and sick . . .

She was watching Evelyn, her face mask-like, calculating. And Evelyn knew that she was not sorry for the sly act of last night, she had enjoyed sneaking through Evelyn's personal belongings – it was being found out that had upset her so terribly – and she would say or do anything to ensure that the Bairds never found out about her underhand activities . . . It suddenly struck Evelyn that no word of apology had yet been uttered, only fears concerning Effie's future, Effie's position at Dunmarnock . . .

'Effie, you are sorry for what you did last night, aren't you?'

Effie was arrested on her way to the door; she threw back her head so that she was looking down her grotesque nose at Evelyn. 'Sorry? Of course I am, I came here to say that, didn't I?'

'No, Effie, you never.'

'Och well, I don't have to say, you know fine I am.'

'I want you to say it, Effie.'

A strange light came into the girl's slit-like eyes. 'Ay, you would, you would like us all to bow and scrape to you and be humble all the time, you're a madam, that's what you are. You sneer at me for wanting to better myself when all the time you and yours act like gentry wi' your noses stuck up yonder.' Effie was really getting warmed up, she was panting a little as she went on. 'Lady Hoity-Toity, your mother, canna see where she's going she's that proud o' herself all the time; you have chapped hands and a big belly and eyes that would look better on a cat yet you really think you're something – oh ay, and your father, we mustna forget him, a man wi' earth on his boots and his brains that soggy wi' drink he doesna ken half the time if he's growing weeds or flowers. But, of course, we must give him his proper place now that he's living in his own wee castle as befits someone who was once king o' the gypsies, king o' the tramps more like, crowned in some back alley wi' a wine bottle and a garland o' cabbages and a punch in the face to soothe him to sleep . . .'

All through this tirade Evelyn appeared calm enough but her eyes burned like coals in her livid face and a tiny muscle twitched in her firm, smooth jaw.

'Take every word o' that back, Effie Jordan, or you'll be sorry your mother ever gave you your miserable life. Last night I wanted to kill you for what you did to me and the way I'm feeling now I might just finish the job.'

She had spoken quietly but Effie recognised fury when she saw it. 'Why should I?' she muttered defiantly, licking her lips and eyeing the door furtively.

Evelyn advanced, 'Because I say so, that's why.'

Effie backed away. 'All right, I'm sorry, I'm sorry,' she gasped and with a little yelp of fear she turned and rushed away.

Evelyn watched her go. She had had the satisfaction of extracting those grudging words of apology but it was a small triumph – she now had a deadly enemy in Effie Jordan and the thought made her feel terribly uneasy.

Chapter Five

Lady Elizabeth Baird put her head on one side and said, 'Well, Evelyn, your mother tells me you're going to have a baby and that the father is at present a prisoner of war.'

As she spoke she had her eyes fixed on a large bowl of bronze-coloured chrysanthemums on a table and had such a thoughtful, faraway air about her Evelyn began to wonder whom she was addressing – if indeed she was aware of addressing anyone in particular.

Evelyn had been called into the Bairds' sitting room, a pleasant homely apartment with big, bouncy sofas, and tapestries and paintings adorning the pale green walls; a huge Persian square decorated the polished floor, bowls of flowers stood everywhere; the mellow red of fine old mahogany glowed richly against the walls. Whisky and Golden, the family spaniels, lolled lazily beside a roaring fire, eyeing Evelyn with polite interest but too warmly comfortable to do more than wag their stumpy tails in acknowledgement of her presence.

Colonel Baird was over by the elegantly recessed windows, sitting on a high-backed Regency chair with red padding. He was seemingly engrossed in filling his pipe from a cracked leather tobacco pouch but a tiny flush high on each prominent cheekbone showed that he wasn't as calm as he was making out.

Evelyn, rather taken aback at Lady Elizabeth's direct approach, waited nervously to hear more, her legs a trifle unsteady beneath her so that she wished – oh, how she wished – she could bury herself in the luxurious depths of one of those fluffy big armchairs and never come out.

The silence in the room stretched, her ladyship seemed to have sunk into a kind of trance; the Colonel fiddled with his pipe, coughed, dropped his tobacco pouch, and went down on all fours to look for it. He had forgotten his specs again – they were dangling on the end of a gold chain that had once been attached to a pocket watch – but so busy was he fumbling for both them and the pouch that he failed to locate either of them. The spaniels, thinking he was playing some sort of game, padded over to sniff and snuffle and push their wet noses into his oxters, forcing him to temporarily abandon his search and fuss over them instead.

Despite the seriousness of having been called into the Bairds' presence, Evelyn had to repress a terrible desire to laugh. Beyond the windows she saw her father pushing a wheelbarrow along the path; a brilliant sun had broken through the mists of morning and was spreading golden light over the lawns; Twiggy May, the amply proportioned ragwife, was making her determined way along the field path to the back door where she was sure of a warm welcome and a cup of tea from Seal McWhirter. Cook with a Capital was most partial to having her cup and perhaps her palm read, which Twiggy May would willingly do in exchange for the cast-off clothes she collected from all the big houses in the district.

Jasper Pringle and his son Jock were striding along by the banks of the Threep; arguing as was their wont but every so often a hearty, ringing laugh would break from one or the other of them; Shepherd Tam was out in the fields with his dogs, his crook fairly swinging in time to his long, loose, easy lope that never seemed to falter from the time he set out in the morning from the Home Farm to when he returned for his dinner and a rousing welcome from his five children, all of whom were under school age.

Evelyn sighed. Everyone seemed to be out of doors this bonny day and she was seized with a longing to run out there also, to be as free as she had been in the old days when the only restrictions in her life had been those binding her to home and family. They were fetters she hadn't wanted to shake off, they had allowed her all the freedom she needed, and a vision came to her of the Clydes out there in the winter parks, her father at the plough, gulls gliding on sunbeams that spilled to the earth in rays of misty light. In her mind's eye she saw the waves of rich soil falling away either side of the plough; she could almost smell the tang of loam and dung and the sweet moistness blowing down from the hills . . .

Her reverie came to an abrupt end. Lady Elizabeth had jumped up and was almost frenziedly rushing about the room, punching cushions into shape, re-arranging the flowers, moving pictures on the mantleshelf till a completely new arrangement quickly took shape.

The Colonel sighed, Evelyn stared. Her ladyship was a most disconcerting little woman altogether with her sudden contrasts of mood that one minute gave the impression of a plump robin sitting cosily on its nest, the next fluttering about, restlessly moving from one thing to another and giving half-finished orders that fairly sent the maids scuttling hither and thither and bumping into one another.

She appeared to have forgotten Evelyn completely, her attention being now arrested by the order of books reposing in a corner what-not.

'Has Annie been shifting these?' she muttered. 'Oh dear, she really is *too* thorough. I must have a word with her . . .'

'Beth!' The Colonel's reproving growl came forcibly from the window. 'I can't hang about here all day, you know, and neither can Evelyn.'

'I know, I know.' The words came out in a troubled sigh and the little woman put a small, plump hand to her brow. Across a divide of tables and chairs she looked at Evelyn with worried blue eyes. 'I'm sorry, my dear, it's just – well, to be truthful I hate it when trouble crops up like this, I sometimes think I was never meant to be – och well – enough of that.' She became brisk though the fingers that played with the cameo at her neck were somewhat nervous. 'We'll find another girl for the kitchen, Evelyn, you can't work there now in your – em – condition. Oh, how lovely – a baby – I loved having mine. Your young man will come back safe and sound, I know it, then you can all be happy together.'

'Ay, Lady Elizabeth.' Evelyn felt lightheaded. So that was that! Another girl for the kitchens. She had been dismissed in the most pithy manner she could ever have imagined, but dismissed just the same. She turned away. 'I'll pack my things –' Her voice was low, she kept her head averted. 'I – I hope this doesna mean that my parents have to leave also, they're happy here, you've been so kind to them.'

'Leave?' Lady Elizabeth gave a puzzled frown. 'Oh no, my dear child, I simply couldn't do without them about the place. Your mother is a most efficient and able woman and your father – well – he's a dear, good man – and fancy, king of the gypsies!' She was a plump little robin again, cosy, contented. 'Mrs McWhirter told me – not that she thought it was anything to boast about but then, she has no romance in her soul.'

Evelyn barely heard any of this; on her way to the door she kept her red head high though she wasn't aware of doing so, it was part of her inherent pride. Whenever anything threatened to undermine her dignity up went her head and out jutted her firm little chin.

'Oh, by the way, Evelyn.'

'Ay, Lady Elizabeth?'

'When you're ready I'll get your father to take you home in the jaunting cart, so much easier to hitch up than the trap and such good fun, don't you think? It's small, I know, but adequate for you and your luggage and Mr Grant will see you safely settled in.'

'Home, Lady Elizabeth?'

'Yes, Evelyn, I hope you will consider the cottage your home for the time being. Oh, I know you will want eventually to set up on your own, you and your young man, and the baby too, of course.'

'But –' Evelyn turned, her face crimson with the relief that suddenly swamped her. 'I thought I was being dismissed.'

'Dismissed!' Her ladyship looked blank. 'Whatever gave you that idea? Richard and I decided it would be better for you to be at the cottage with your family. I want you here as long as possible, Evelyn, we thought perhaps you could assist the other girls with their above-stairs duties, they really have too much to do since the others left – but didn't I say all this before?'

'No, Lady Elizabeth, you didn't.' Evelyn's voice was hushed, even though a huge bubble of affection for the Bairds of Dunmarnock was bursting out of the breast of her.

'Oh, I'm sorry, child, I do forget what I haven't said sometimes –' She giggled. 'That doesn't sound right somehow, my Highland blood coming out. Well, Evelyn, that's all settled then. You can stay here at long as you want and never mind the gossips . . .'

'Hear, hear!' The Colonel spoke heartily, 'I believed you were going to take all morning, Beth, and was damned well about to tell you so! Just enough time for a canter over to Knocke Farm, Currie's mare's due to foal anytime and I'm hoping to be there when she does.'

Striding across he took Evelyn's arm and propelled her out of the room. 'Damned glad you're staying, Evelyn,' he said brusquely. 'Too bad about you and Darling, you sit well on a horse – but maybe later – ay, later.'

Evelyn held onto him, glad of his support. Reaction had set in, making her feel slightly giddy. Effie rustled past, her small eyes widening at the sight of Evelyn and the Colonel stepping out arm in arm. Evelyn experienced a rush of gratitude towards the girl, after all if it hadn't been for Effie and her snooping none of this would be happening now and Evelyn might still be moping and worrying about everything. As it was, a great burden had been lifted from her mind and she threw the older girl a radiant smile that few who had felt its warmth could ever resist. But Effie was made of stern stuff. She bristled and glowered and made herself look so positively unpleasant that even the Colonel noticed. Eyes twinkling he put his mouth close to Evelyn's ear and mouthed two words which had the effect of making her go red in the face in a terrible effort to stifle her rising mirth.

Effie rushed on, amidst a positive crackle of starch, her face a study of shocked disapproval. Evelyn wondered what she would have thought if the Colonel, instead of whispering to her, had boomed loudly and succinctly into the depths of the hall, 'Beardie Bum!'

She was in time to partake of a piping-hot 'cuppy' in the kitchen before going upstairs to pack her things. Seal McWhirter, in a bland and mellow mood after hearing from Twiggy May that wedding bells were in the offing for the third time together with a small fortune, insisted that Evelyn's cup should also be read.

Twiggy May, named so in her youth when she had been as thin as a stick, folded her podgy hands over her ponderous stomach and watched as the girl hastily drained her cup.

'Bairns,' Twiggy May eventually pronounced, peering knowingly into the depths of the cup. 'Plenty o' bairns and all wi' different faithers.'

Both Seal and Evelyn gaped at the old woman.

'All within wedlock,' she amended hastily, 'though of course, there's no telling if that makes them legitimate,' she added cryptically and with meaningful emphasis on the word 'legitimate'. 'And men,' she went on, 'lots o' men, one who has aye been in your life and whose heart you own — the other . . .' Her broken fingernails gently probed the leaves and her already grimy face went darker still. 'The other will bring you trouble and strife and through it all you'll love him and care for him right to the end.'

'The end?' Evelyn asked, trying hard to keep the amusement from her expression.

'Ay, he'll no' live long.' Twiggy May sounded triumphant. 'But after him there's more will follow, you'll never be short o' men in your life. I see a much older man who will gie you more bairns and a life o' hell into the bargain but over and above all there's the first man, he'll be popping in and out o' your life like a bubblyjock wi' the skitters, in and out, in and out, a fine man wi' breeding in him and Money wi' a capital "M" – his name begins wi' "G" – it's here – see – next to the ruins o' war and want.'

Evelyn was no longer laughing, she immediately thought of Gillan Forbes of Rothiedrum House who had never hidden his love for her.

'War and want?' she spoke the words unwillingly, rather fearfully.

'Ay, the one you await now is in among the ashes o' war but he'll rise up out o' them – and there will come a day when you and he will know happiness – of a sort . . .'

She peered at Evelyn out of eyes that were black and mysterious and Evelyn knew she would never again take Twiggy May lightly for she saw in those eyes a wise woman who knew more about the fates than anyone would ever give her credit for.

'You're one o' us.' Twiggy May made the statement in a soft voice which had the effect of giving it extra credence.

Evelyn's flesh crept. She knew again the strange and terrible fear of the thing Hinncy had once, long ago, given name to, the second sight, mystic powers which had been endowed in her from ancestors long dead . . .

'Ay, indeed I am.' The words were drawn from her unwillingly, fearfully. During the utterance of them she tried to tell herself that the only reason the old woman was able so accurately to tell her things from the past and the future was because she and Seal had had a real good chin wag about her before her appearance in the kitchen. But it was no use. Twiggy May's eyes were on her, compelling, hypnotising, the eyes of a wise old seer who went through her life in the humble guise of a ragwife making her sparse living from the amused charity of the better-off in society.

Twiggy May put her grimy hand over Evelyn's. 'Go you in peace, my child,' she murmured, 'your life will never be easy but you have the strength — and the power — to live it to the full.'

Seal McWhirter was utterly mystified. 'What are you two gabbling about?' she demanded truculently. 'You seem to be in cahoots wi' one another and are lookin' at each other as if I wasna here, like — like a pair o' witches makin' spells. Evelyn, go you and fill my cup, there's plenty tea left in the pot.'

'I'm sorry, Mrs McWhirter, I have to pack my things, Father will be waiting . . .' Evelyn got up quickly but at the door she turned. 'I'll see you again, May.'

The old woman nodded. 'Indeed you will, child,' she said with conviction, 'our paths will cross many times before yours will take a different course.'

Evelyn didn't stop to question that. Twiggy May was a dramatist, an actor on the stage of life, speaking her lines in a way that drew the best possible reaction from willing audiences in almost every big house in Renfrewshire, but today, just for a little while, she had stopped acting, allowing one young fellow being to glimpse the real person behind the stoor and the grime and the rag bag that was her passport to warmth and companionship and — more than just occasionally — a glimpse of the future.

Grace was delighted when Evelyn recounted to her the interview with the Bairds. 'Oh, Evie, I canna tell you how relieved I am,' she said, hugging her sister to her, 'I've been worried this whilie back, wondering how it would all turn out and now it's all right, it's all right, Evie.'

Grace had grown thinner of late. Evelyn held onto the fragile body of this beloved sister and a pain pierced her moment of happiness. Grace had never gotten over the loss of her surgeon husband who had been killed in a field hospital in France. Theirs had been a brief but wonderful marriage but it was over almost before it had begun. At first Grace wouldn't accept that he was dead and then she had undergone an operation for stomach ulcers from which she hadn't wanted to recover. She had always been the least strong of the Grant girls and for a time everyone had been afraid they would lose her, but gradually she had fought back though she never seemed to regain her strength, however frail it might have been. She was like a madonna, all the life of her seemed to be contained in her huge, dark eyes which burned with a feverish intensity in the pale oval of her face with its frame of shining, chestnut hair. She had found a job at a nearby country house which had been given over to the military for the duration and though she never appeared strong enough for a nursing career she loved her job and wouldn't have been happy doing anything else.

The close proximity of The Grange to Dunmarnock meant that she could be with her family at the cottage and now it was like the old days again, the sisters sharing a room, one with camped ceilings and casement windows that looked out over the rolling countryside of Renfrewshire. Evelyn could have had a room to herself but Grace had requested that she move in with her and that first afternoon they arranged Evelyn's treasured possessions around the room: the little corn dolly made for her by Johnny was fixed above her bed together with Florrie's sampler with its simple words: *Evelyn and Florrie – Best Friends. 1913 and beyond.* On her dresser she placed the beautifully-carved jewel box David had given to her on her seventeenth birthday, taking from it the exquisite pearl drop presented to her by Gillan for Christmas 1914. For a moment she held the cool little drop to her face, remembering Gillie, wondering where he was, how he was, feeling sad to think she might never see him again . . . '*A man whose name begins wi' the letter "G" will always be popping into your life . . .*' Twiggy May's prediction spoke inside her head and tenderly she put the necklet away and shut the lid of David's box, her fingers tracing the carvings on the wood; the thought came to her that two men were represented in these gifts, two men who were very dear to her heart, one to be taken out and remembered now and then, the other always there, tormenting her with his continual presence in her heart. Of the two, Gillie was the most true but it was David she wanted above all else, always it was David . . .

'Where does this go, Evie?' Grace indicated the battered tin box sitting on the bed. In it were Evelyn's diaries – and something else she had all but forgotten.

'It goes under the bed,' Evelyn laughed, 'beside the chanty and the slippers. Look, Grace, did I ever show you this?'

From the depths of the box she withdrew the ugly garnet necklace given to her by Lord Lindsay Ogilvie last time he had come home to Rothiedrum House for a holiday.

'The stones are lovely,' Grace said politely. 'In a different setting they would be beautiful, it must be worth a bit o' money.'

'Ay, it is,' agreed Evelyn. 'Oggie – that's Gillie's great uncle – told me to keep it for a rainy day, till then I like to just look at it occasionally and think o' him. I would never change it; it's not a bonny thing but in some ways it's beautiful – like the old man who gave it to me out o' the kindness o' his heart.'

'You're a romantic, Evie.'

'Ay, so is he. It's strange, Grace, but when I showed it to Mam she laughed and called Oggie a cunning old fox and said that one day she would tell me about him and her – as if she had always known him – yet, as far as I know, she had hardly ever clapped eyes on him.'

'Mam aye had a bit o' mystery about her,' Grace said slowly. 'She started off disliking the Forbes family but in our last year or so at Rothiedrum she and Lady Marjorie became good friends and it was thanks to her we were able to start a new life together in Renfrewshire.'

'Och well, maybe someday we'll know what it was all about.' Evelyn gathered up the necklace and, stuffing it in beside her diaries, she locked the box and shoved it under the bed, taking care to hide the key in the brass knob at the head of her bed.

That night the sisters went upstairs early to sit talking by the window till, exhausted, they grew quiet and just sat gazing out over the dark countryside, picking out landmarks that were growing more familiar with each passing day: the lights of Knocke Farm; the tall chimneys of Bracken Ridge Cottage poking into the sky; the sturdy silhouette of the Home Farm; in the distance the windows of The Grange winking through the trees.

'You would think it would be a sad place,' Grace said softly. 'Men lose eyes and limbs and loved ones but they seem never to lose their courage – at least only in the night when it's just themselves and God alone wi' each other. There's one lad, Gavin Galbraith, he lost both legs at Passchendaele and when he came home he found that he'd lost his girlfriend as well. It was a "Dear John" of the worst kind, she was all he had, yet he jokes and says his knobbly knees never looked good in a kilt anyway.

'I was thinking to bring him home here sometime, when he's able to get outside, that is. The other men get visitors but Gavin gets none and though he tries to make out he doesna care I see his eyes and know his pain.'

'Oh, bring him, Grace,' cried Evelyn, 'he could come for his tea or whenever he likes. Father would collect him in the trap or you and I could push him along in a chair, it isn't far, and it would do him good – to be wi' a family.'

She gazed into the distance. Grace's mention of Gavin made her think of Davie, so far away from home and his own family. She touched his postcard which, since its arrival, she had kept in some safe pocket or fold of clothing. It was more tattered than ever and she only handled it in the quiet, secret hours between gloaming and dawn lest her fingers wear away the writing or tear the disintegrating corners.

She had written to him. It hadn't been easy. Page after page had been discarded as being too eager or too stilted. In the end she said simply:

> Davie, you're alive, and so now am I. I can't begin to tell you how much I've missed you so I won't even try. We've left Rothiedrum, Mam, Father, Grace and me. Mary's still there, Nellie's in Kenneray, Murn in Australia. I'll tell you more next time I write.
>
> Please, oh please, dearest Davie, stay well. I'll send you a parcel filled with food and soap and socks; remember the socks, Davie? Father swore you were keeping the feet of the entire regiment warm with all the socks I sent – he still laughs about it –

She hadn't said much more and hadn't written any of the things she really wanted to say, such as how much she loved him and how empty her days had been since their last meeting. Nor did she mention the baby. Davie was a man to whom freedom mattered a great deal, imprisonment must be torture for him, and she couldn't risk him thinking that he might step out of one prison into another since the idea of domestic fetters might frighten him off altogether . . .

'I'll knit him socks.' She spoke almost to herself, as if trying to convince herself that everything was as it had been when she had had only him to consider. 'Once every week Isa Currie holds a knitting Bee at Knocke Farm and all the womanfolk go to it. Alice Kerr collects sheep's wool from the fences and Grannie Currie spins the yarn. It makes lovely things, soft and warm. Last week Cook with a Capital baked girdle scones to hand round and Lady Elizabeth arrived in time for tea and a good chin wag about knitting patterns. Seal told me I should go along and start knitting things for the baby.'

'Did you tell Davie about it?' Grace asked quietly.

'No, not yet – I think I should wait.'

'For what?' Grace said a trifle grimly. 'You both had a hand in the making o' it and if he has any decency at all he'll surely want to know about his own child.'

'He has enough to cope with just now, he might be ill or injured – or both – he certainly canna be happy stuck in some Godless prison with only his memories to keep him going . . .'

Her voice faltered and Grace got up to pull her gently to her feet. 'Don't, Evie, Davie isna the sort o' man to give in easily. At least he's alive, you have that to hold on to.'

Shame flooded Evelyn's being and she upbraided herself for behaving so miserably to a sister who grieved silently for a big, gentle bear of a man who would never return from the war.

'Och, I'm sorry, Grace,' she smiled. 'Come on, we ought to get to bed, you look tired and we've both to be up early.'

Ten minutes later a small voice disturbed the silence of the room. 'Grace?'

'Ay?'

'Can I coorie in wi' you – just for a whilie?'

There was a short silence. 'Will your belly allow for a good tight coorie?'

'Ay, just about.' Evelyn snorted with laughter and rushed across to snuggle in at her sister's back. She felt safe and good and warm. Grace smelt of rose water and just a tiny hint of surgical spirits.

The room suddenly breathed of King's Croft and of two young girls whispering their childish secrets to one another. From the kitchen below, Maggie's voice filtered, Jamie's laugh rang out.

'Are you remembering, Evie?' Grace's voice came sleepily.

'Ay, I'm remembering.'

For a few blissful minutes Evelyn was lulled into a sense of peace and security – then the child in her womb stirred and in her half-dreaming state she imagined she heard it cry out, as if something had disturbed its tranquil, floating existence.

For a moment, The Devil's Door loomed darkly, then dissipated into the mists of night as Grace made a little murmur of sound that was oddly reassuring.

'I wonder if it will be a boy.' The thought intruded into Evelyn's mind. She sighed and relaxed and drifted into the deepest, most dreamless slumber she had known for many weeks.

Chapter Six

It was snowing; little mounds of it were piling against the window ledges; windblown flurries spattered against the panes to go slithering downwards in ragged patterns. With her fingers Evelyn traced the journey of individual flakes, a smile of pleasure lighting her face. It was so lovely to see the snow, to watch it billowing over the fields and plaster itself against walls and trees. It was her day off and she was free to spend it as she liked; a part of her wanted just to relax and laze about the house but the youthful side of her rebelled against such a waste of her precious free time. She decided on a compromise; she would enjoy a lazy morning, then she would go out and just walk and walk; she might even visit the stables to talk to Darling or go over to Knocke Farm to see the new foal which was all legs and soft hair and a wet little nose that nuzzled her face . . .

A movement below caught her eye; she saw the figure of a man, dark against the snow, striding along the path, looking neither to the right nor the left of him but just staring straight ahead — as if he knew exactly where he was going and was in quite a hurry to get there . . . Then the illusion was shattered; he paused, shook his head as if to clear it, and glanced around him dazedly, giving the impression he was trying to decide where on earth he was placed at that particular point in time.

He was cold, Evelyn could sense it and, as though to verify her thoughts, he began swinging his arms across his body and stamping his feet. On his hands he wore gloves but Evelyn knew they weren't there for the reason of keeping him warm. His movements were clumsy, almost mechanical, it looked as if his reflexes weren't obeying the commands of his mind quickly enough.

Quite abruptly he began to walk on, jerkily, like someone caught up in a meaningless march leading nowhere. Then he fell. It was a heavy fall and he just lay where he was, making no attempt to get up, but cowering down like a frightened dog waiting for a sadistic boot to urge him to his feet.

Without hesitation Evelyn ran downstairs and out of the door. The man watched her coming, his eyes straining through the snow eddies that whirled about him. It was only a shadow that he saw, one that floated in front of him yet never seemed to get any closer; the sounds of war were back inside his head, exploding silently, burst after burst; a wall of fire rose up before him and in that torturous hell the shapes that were men flitted, and screamed their silent, eternal screams. He was outside of it all but he knew he had to get in . . . the shadows were growing black, the stench of charred flesh filled his nostrils . . . someone had to get them out . . . someone . . .

'Barrett! Is that you, Barrett? I'm coming, I'm coming, it is you, isn't it?'

'No, Major Baird, it's me, Evelyn Grant, it's only me.'

He had come home two days ago, urged to do so by Christine, who had arrived back with him. A friend was coming to see him, she had said, one with whom he had shared some of his early boyhood and part of his young manhood. This particular friend had been wounded in the Third Battle of Passchendaele and was coming home after spending some weeks in hospital. So Major Andrew Baird had at last come home to Dunmarnock, a thin but perfectly normal-looking young man – except for his hands which were encased in black leather gloves which he never removed, not even for meals.

He had been brief in his comments about the war, cheerful about everything else – but there was something so terrifying deep in his eyes Evelyn had had shivers the length of her spine the first time she looked into them. He had seemed pleased to be back, had joked with the servants and pacified his mother who had been inclined to fuss, making certain everything was to his liking.

Effie had been overjoyed at his return. She had rustled around him to such a degree that Lady Elizabeth had been moved to admonish her but Effie had paid little heed. She had all but 'kissed his arse' as Hugh Kerr had neatly put it, but she had tossed her head in disgust at such comments and had thrown Evelyn a look that plainly said, 'See, Miss Snooty, the Major likes me to see to him, he trusts me which is more than he'll ever do with you.'

Compassion filled Evelyn's heart at sight of him lying there on the snowy path. He had eyes like his father, deep-set, piercing, dark blue, watching her from beneath very fair brows. His hair was fair and crisp, curling a little over his coat collar. Altogether he was a very attractive man but his lean face was tired and far too pale.

'Let me help you up, Major,' she said quietly but he held back, staring at her as if she wasn't quite real and he expected her to disappear at any moment. 'It's all right,' she spoke in a calm, reassuring voice, 'you're not in France, you're here at Dunmarnock and I'm your friend.'

'I've never seen you before.' He sounded suspicious.

'Ach, of course you have,' she smiled. 'I work at Dunmarnock, you've just forgotten, that's all, there were quite a lot o' faces to take in.'

'Did you tell me your name?'

'Ay, it's Evelyn Grant. Look, get up out o' there before you catch your death or I catch mine. I'm no' wearing a coat and I havena got all day.'

She was deliberately brisk. During her time at Rothiedrum House part of it had been given over to the military and she'd dealt with young men like the Major in her own distinctive way. And it had worked. They had grown to like and trust her and she saw that it was having the same effect on Andrew Baird.

He was grinning at her, a slightly crooked grin that took away his haunted look and changed him into the young man he was.

'You sound a bit of a targe but all right, I give in.'

Grabbing his sodden sleeves she helped him to his feet, dusted him down, held onto him when his feet threatened to slither away from him again.

'Evelyn Grant?' Her name on his lips was a query. His deep voice was cultured, strangely pleasing to the ears. 'You're not from these parts. Do I detect a north-east twang there?'

'Ay, indeed you do.' Without another word she led him into the cottage, sat him at the fire and thrust a mug of hot tea at him. He drank, lay back, looked around, and smiled, a slow, wide smile that smoothed the hollows in his face. 'Wood Cottage. Of all the houses on the estate I liked this one best. I thought it was like a small castle with its leaded windows and tiny turrets. When I was a boy I used to come here to visit Rosie and Geordie Brownlea, then Geordie died and it was just Rosie, Old Rosie, and she was rosy, everything about her was pink and white and smelled of roses and spice. She would give me bread and bramble jam and hot pancakes straight off that very girdle there . . .'

She let him talk, he relaxed, loosened, expanded about his boyhood days roaming the countryside round Dunmarnock. The aura of war slipped from him, making him seem lighter, buoyant, more attractive . . . Then the door opened and Grace came in amidst a flurry of snowflakes and a blast of cold air. The sharp air had turned her nose into a little red cherry, her eyes were sparkling.

'Evie,' she began, 'I've got a couple of hours off and I rushed over to tell you that Gavin is coming tomorrow for his tea. Last night I asked Mam and Father said he would collect him . . .'

She broke off, suddenly noticing the visitor. 'Oh, I'm sorry, I didna see –'

'Grace, this is Major Baird, he was cold and I brought him in for a cuppy.'

Grace extended her hand. 'Pleased to meet you, Major Baird, I'm Grace, Evie's sister.'

He didn't let go of her hand. 'Grace.' He spoke her name slowly, as if savouring the sound of it. Looking at him Evelyn saw a strange expression on his face and she knew at once that Grace had made an instant impression on him. He was staring at her, as if he couldn't bear to tear his eyes away from her till she grew uncomfortable under his scrutiny and, making her excuses, she went into the hall to remove her cape. She stayed out there for as long as she could, composing herself, unwilling to go back and face those penetrating blue eyes but when she eventually returned to the kitchen he was laughing at something Evelyn was saying and on the point of drinking another cup of tea.

Grace took the cup Evelyn handed her. The atmosphere in the room was more relaxed now and it was very peaceful sitting there by the fire, just the three of them, the logs crackling in the grate, General washing his whiskers on the rug before settling down to purring contentment.

Outside the snow whispered, the wind murmured round the house, Andrew began reminiscing again, his voice was very soothing. A sense of intimacy pervaded the room as word-pictures of his past flitted out, slipped away, gradually leaving the boy behind, bringing the man nearer . . . The doors of childhood closed on the boy, he was a man again, one freshly emerged from the carnage of an unholy war that seemed to have no ending. His voice became slower, eventually tailed off altogether and just when it seemed no one knew how to break the silence that suddenly prevailed there came a scratching at the door and when Evelyn went to open it Whisky and Golden rushed into the room, rumps fairly wagging at the welcome they received from the Major.

'They must have got my scent,' he laughed, awkwardly

fondling two pairs of ears with his gloved hands.

'Or else they've run ahead of someone who brought them out to look for you,' Evelyn pointed out. She froze suddenly. Beyond the window she saw the figure of a man emerging from the edge of the woods. He was tall, slim and dark and he was wearing the uniform of the Gordon Highlanders. Her heart missed a beat, her hand went to her mouth. Surely — surely that was Davie out there, his Gordon tartan kilt swinging about his knees, his stride swift and sure as it had been in those halcyon days last summer when he had come hurrying to meet her — but no, this man was taller, slightly broader . . . She gave an involuntary gasp. It couldn't be. He was a figment of her imagination, as impossible a vision as she had imagined Davie to be . . .

Grace came to join her at the window. 'You aren't seeing a ghost,' she smiled, 'I can see him too. Go on, Evie,' she urged, 'away you go and meet him.'

Evelyn went, hardly aware that Grace had thrown a jacket over her shoulders. She walked in a daze, seeing nothing but the figure of the man coming along towards her.

A mist of tears blurred her eyes, his name was already on her lips, one she hadn't thought to utter in his sight ever again. He had seen her, his steps slowed, stopped . . . then: 'Princess, is it really you?'

His voice was a hoarse cry of disbelief. She could bear it no longer, her feet took wing, he became clearer, more real. He watched her coming, like a young deer running. She hadn't bothered to pin up her hair that morning, it tumbled about her shoulders, a startling mane of burnished red against the backcloth of snow. His arms were out, it seemed the most natural thing in the world that she should fly into them, that they should enclose her and that his lips should meet with hers in a long, lingering kiss that seemed never to end and which wiped out the long, uncertain months since last they had met.

'Gillie!' she cried at last, staring at the dark, handsome

face she knew so well, with her finger touching the line of his jaw as if to ascertain that she hadn't just kissed a ghost who might slip away at any moment, 'What on earth are you doing here?'

'I might ask the same of you. I thought I would never see you again, you never wrote, you never even said goodbye.'

Cold reality came flooding back, she remembered the baby, Davie's baby, somehow she hadn't wanted Gillie to know about it, she had been too ashamed, too despairing.

'Och, Gillie,' she breathed. 'Dinna look like that, all black and thundery and sulky. Surely you kent where I was, didn't your mother tell you? Grace is here too, and my parents.'

He explained that his parents were abroad at the moment. 'Mother felt she needed some sunshine so with France being out she and Father girded their loins and went out to see Uncle Lindsay in South Africa. They're all three of them holidaying in the Orange Free State. Mother did write to say you had left Rothiedrum but didn't say where you had gone.'

He further explained that he had been staying with friends in Edinburgh when Christine Baird had paid him a call, had told him about her brother, wondered if he could help.

'I jumped at the chance,' he said rather bitterly. 'I had thought of going to Rothiedrum for a spell but couldn't bear the idea of it without you, so here I am. I only arrived last night, slept late and came out just now to find Andrew.'

'Your mother's a besom,' she said frankly. 'She aye was feart that you and I would run away together and that you would bring me back to Rothiedrum as your wife, all grasping and greedy wi' great sharp talons on me to rake in the family fortunes.'

He laughed at that but immediately became serious. 'Mother's not as bad as she once was, she's mellowing with the years. I suppose she would eventually have told me your whereabouts, probably when I was too old and decayed to care anymore about these wild passions of yours. Oh, Evie, Evie, I've missed you, I want you so badly . . .'

Pulling her into the shelter of the woods he took her to him roughly, his lips merging once more with hers till a groan of longing broke from him and she pulled herself away with a sob, 'Gillie, please don't, oh, please . . .'

At that inopportune moment Willie the Post came whistling along, the cheerful sound dying on his lips at the sight of the young people standing close together at the edge of the woods.

'Good day to you, Evie – sir.' He eyed Gillan curiously then recognition dawned over his ruddy countenance. 'Well, well, if it isna young Gillan, I mind you fine when you and Mister Andrew played here together as laddies.' His gaze travelled over Gillan's uniform. 'So you're wi' the Gordons, eh? A fine regiment, near as good as the H.L.I. I see you're a captain, too, ay, well, good luck, laddie, from all I hear about this war you'll be needin' it.'

He turned his attention to Evelyn, selecting from a bundle of mail a buff-coloured envelope which he waved at her. 'I have a letter here for you, lass, I'll give it to you now, it will save me a wee trek to the house – unless . . .' he cocked his head – 'you're maybe going back there to put the kettle on. Old Seal was in one o' her moods and bundled me out the door before I could blink and in such a bitter day too.'

Something about the postman's confidential manner never failed to irritate Evelyn. He was wont to poke and pry and deliver more gossip than he did Royal Mail and she was in no mood to listen to his prattles. 'I'll take the letter, Willie,' she said shortly. 'Grannie Currie will give you tea till it's coming out your ears if you get along there quick and tell her how you saw me in the woods wi' a young man and no' a bit o' shame on me when you caught me at it.'

Willie the Post stared and stuttered and tightened his

lips. 'Well, well, now, there is no need to take that attitude, lass. We all have our wee secrets and I'm sure I'll no' be lettin' on about yours. After all, it must be gey lonely for you wi' your man away and what more natural at your age than to pass the time o' day wi' a young gentleman friend.'

He winked heavily at Gillan and handed Evelyn her letter, tapping it with a damp thumb. 'It's from your man,' he nodded confidingly. 'All I do these days is deliver letters from soldiers so I know what I'm talkin' about. Effie was after tellin' me he has been taken prisoner and she happened to mention the baby too. You must be mighty pleased that the bairn will have a father after all – both o' them alive and kickin' so to speak, eh, lass?'

He winked again and departed, his whistle thin now on his lips, his nonchalant air proclaiming the triumph of his knowledge of other folk's affairs.

Evelyn's face burned. Effie was wasting no time in setting the cat among the pigeons and Evelyn knew that she hadn't for one moment swallowed Raggy Annie's story about the ring. Pushing Effie to the back of her mind she looked at her letter in a manner that suggested it was only of passing interest when all the time she knew it was from Davie – at last from Davie.

She hardly dared look at Gillan but knew that he was staring at her intently, willing her to meet his eyes, and with a toss of her head she said, 'Ay, I'm pregnant, Davie's the father though he doesn't yet ken anything about it. The ring you see on my finger is only there to fool the world. The Bairds know all about it. The others? Well, they can think what they like, Raggy Annie saw to that. Now you see why I didna write to you, I couldn't, I just couldn't tell you.'

'David Grainger, eh?' He spoke softly but even so his voice vibrated with feeling. 'Always him, from the moment you met. I wish to hell he'd never been born! Or that I'd never been, one of the two, take your pick. I've tried to forget you, to pretend that you just weren't worth all the pain but it's no use. I do love you, Evie, I'll never stop loving you but I'm not a fool. I see now you'll never be mine so – to hell with you! I'm going to find Andrew, the dogs took off so he can't be far away, I'll see you around.'

Turning on his heel he began to walk away, his face like thunder, his shoulders hunched into his jacket.

'Gillie, don't, please don't go.' She caught up with him and held onto his sleeve, 'I canna let you go like this, you and I have aye been such good friends.'

He shook her off. 'Friends!' Scornfully he spat the word at her. 'What kind of friend is it who wants to hold you and love you and lie with you as a man with a wife. I want to touch you and kiss you till in hurts! Is that your idea of how a friend should think and feel?'

He was the same passionate, sensitive Gillie she had always known and – if things had been different – might even have loved. As it was, he owned a part of her heart and always would, wherever their footsteps might eventually lead them.

'Darling Gillie,' she whispered, 'you are very, very dear to me, you've always been special to me and a part o' me will always love and cherish you. I never wanted to hurt you . . .'

'I am hurt!' he all but shouted. 'I hurt so much I bloody well ache with it.' He looked exhausted suddenly and she remembered that he had been ill – *was* ill.

She took his hand, it was warm, Gillie's hands had always been warm. 'I won't let us part like this, I need you, Gillie, I need you very much just now. How long will you be staying at Dunmarnock?'

'Over Christmas anyway. Christmas needs the country, the snow and the holly boughs, the chestnuts and the roaring Yule fires.'

She held her breath, tears caught in her throat. 'Let me share your Christmas, Gillie, we could have such a bonny time together. Grace is bringing a lad for tea tomorrow, he lost both legs at Passchendaele and is recovering at The

Grange. You come too, Mam and Father would love to see you again.'

'Maggie and Jamie,' he nodded. 'All right, I'll come. There was a time I thought your mother was a bit of a bogle but she's a marvellous woman once you get to know her. That's settled then, princess, I'll see you tomorrow evening.'

She laughed and tucked her arm in his. 'You'll see me tomorrow morning, all prim and staid in my starches and much too humble and lowly to pass the time o' day wi' a fine gentleman like yourself.'

They laughed at that, he brushed the snow from her hair and made to walk away. 'I really came out to look for Andrew Baird, Chris thought it would be better if I went, she thinks he's beginning to feel that she's always on his heels, watching him. I don't suppose you've seen him.'

'Ay, I have, he's at present ensconced in that cottage, *our* cottage, drinking tea and talking to Grace.'

'I'd better fetch him then.'

'No, leave him, I saw his eyes when Grace came in, let them be for a whilie, the dogs are there too. You and I, young Rothiedrum, will walk and talk together, and maybe even pelt one another wi' snowballs the way we did when we were bairns playing together in the winter parks of King's Croft.'

Grace remained at the window, watching her sister running to meet Gillan, something in her rebelling against joining the man at the fire with his compelling eyes that had looked at her too intently.

'Grace, come over here,' he beckoned to her and she went slowly towards him to sit down on a little raffia stool by the fender. He kept his eyes on her, his attention caught by her hands folded peacefully in her lap. Slender hands, he noticed, the long thin fingers so delicate he felt that the least pressure would break them; then he saw the shining band of gold reposing there and a small part of him went cold.

She felt him watching her and glanced towards him enquiringly. He laughed, a slightly embarrassed laugh and said, 'Forgive me, I've taken to looking at people's hands, a part of the human anatomy I never used to give much attention to till this . . .' He indicated his own hands, enclosed in their black leather. She said nothing. In time he might bring himself to talk about it but she knew better than to ask questions.

'You're married then, Grace.' It was more a statement than a question and he hadn't really wanted to say it but he had to know more about her. The light from the fire was on her hair, polishing the chestnut waves that so sweetly framed her bonny young face. She was an exquisite creature, so delicately formed, so calm and gentle, yet so finely strung he could sense strange, deep passions in her that few would ever reach. She was not conventionally beautiful but there was something about her that went far deeper that mere perfection of face, he had been aware of it from the first moment their hands had touched. He couldn't explain that to himself. Forty per cent of normal feeling had been burned from his hands yet he could have sworn that some strong magnetic charge had passed from her into him.

She raised her head, he held his breath. Those eyes! Great black pools that glowed with life, that burned with the hurt of it.

'I was married, Major Baird, his name was Gordon Chisholm. We met in an Aberdeen hospital, he was a surgeon, I was a nurse. We were only married a few brief months before he was killed in a field hospital in France. It was the only time in my life I ever really lived – I loved him so. My family think I've accepted his death but I never will. I still feel he's alive, somehow, somewhere he's alive, he was too strong to die.'

He touched her hair, expecting her to move away from the cold, unnatural feel of lifeless leather which revolted even himself, but she didn't flinch.

'Gordon Chisholm was a lucky man, Grace – I can

call you that, can't I? And please, call me Andrew, I'm like my father, I hate to be formal.'

A smile touched her mouth. 'Ay, I've heard about Colonel Baird, Evie thinks the world o' him — and talking of her, she's a long time coming back, she kent Gillan Forbes in Rothiedrum and they aye had so much to say to one another.'

'He's a grand chap and the reason I came back here. I'm glad I did now, otherwise I might never have taken the plunge and would never have met you. I'd better get back —' He stood up, towering over her, his hair had dried to a crisp fairness, his blue eyes were smiling at her though she noticed in them that same fathomless expression that had struck Evelyn so forcibly.

She stood up also. 'I'd like to walk back wi' you, Andra, see you get home safe.'

'I'm not going to refuse an offer like that even though I'm fine now and all the better for hearing you say my name like that.'

She coloured a little. 'It's the north-east dialect, I'll never be able to change it.'

'Don't try, it's charming, I love it. Come on, Whisky, Golden, home.'

The dogs were unwilling to abandon the cosy hearth but, once outside, they pranced along, their noses snuffling, stumpy tails wagging, bundles of red-gold fur that matched the bracken poking through the snow all along the path. A cock pheasant flew up from the undergrowth, a blur of colourful plumage. The dogs jumped, made to give chase till Andrew called them to heel.

The snow was thinning; blackbirds were 'chukking' in the woods; a tiny wren perched itself briefly on a nearby bush; a robin followed them along the path, flitting from branch to branch, its distinctive 'tic-tic-tic' scolding them all along the way. The sky to the west was lightening, a pink blush shone through the snow flurries; a cockerel crowed from the Home Farm, the boisterous notes carrying clearly over the fields.

'Andra' Richard Baird breathed deeply; he forgot the war; forgot for a while the face of Barrett that wasn't a face but a charred and blackened blob that had reminded Andrew of the crackling skin of roast potatoes thrown into the white heat of Hallowe'en bonfires.

Grace was muffled into the warm folds of her winter cloak; little wisps of chestnut hair had escaped the hood and were curling over her high, smooth brow; one bare hand held the garment tight to her throat – he thought that her fingers looked cold and all at once he wanted to cover them with his, to crush the rest of her slender beauty to him and never let go . . .

'Grace.' His voice was low.

'Ay, Andra?'

'Let me hold your hand. Mine aren't completely dead, you know, I can still feel quite a lot and hold onto things.'

Obediently and without hesitation she gave her hand to him. She was used to young soldiers holding onto her hand, it gave them something real and warm to cling to when war wounds had smashed their bodies and very often their private lives as well.

Andrew Baird was no exception. He was walking a thin rope that might snap tomorrow, or next year – or never – depending on how resilient he was. He had come home with shadows in his life; he was haunted by the ghosts of comrades maimed and killed in front of his eyes and he couldn't forget. Some did, others couldn't; he was one whose mind wouldn't let go and if he didn't destroy his shadows they would, in the end, take and smother him . . .

A fuzzy sun was throwing yellow splotches over the virginal landscape, giving an illusion of warmth to the scene. It was a clean world, clean and bright. Once, long ago so it seemed now to the young man, he had been invigorated by days like this, every breath had cleansed his body, cleared his mind.

'Grace, you're a nurse,' his voice was hurried, as if he was trying to rid himself quickly of things he ought not to voice – not to a woman – not to her . . . 'Can you tell me – will I ever feel – clean again?'

'Och, Andra, Andra,' she chided gently, 'you mustna think like that but I ken fine what you mean. You've come home to a house and people you've kent all your life but it and they are like strangers. You've touched death and watched hell on earth and suddenly you're here where everything seems the same but more fragile, more clean than ever you remembered. It's all right to feel like that, Andra, it will pass, everything passes – in time.'

He faced her, his blue eyes filled with a strange, intense light. 'Barrett Bradbury, pals together since boyhood. We joined up together, made it all through the war till last April. He was trapped in a dug-out when enemy fire ignited a box of Very lights. Shells were exploding, cordite charges burning, dug-outs and gun-pit were enveloped in flames. We tried to get Barrett and the others out but were beaten back. Later on I saw him, he wasn't a man, he wasn't anything, I cried, like a baby I cried – grown men shouldn't cry . . .'

His eyes were burning into hers, desperate, hopeless; she put her hand on his arm. 'A safety valve, Andra, women use them all the time, it's foolish, not brave, to deny them.'

'You understand, Grace, you, so lovely and pure and soft. How can you understand?'

Her eyes were luminous with unshed tears. 'I've been there, Andra, I worked in France while Gordon was there. We got the boys coming down the line from the forward casualty stations –' She paused, hideous memories engulfing her, the sickening stench of gas gangrene; the tortured cries of the injured; the uncanny silence of the dying; the hopeless, empty faces of young boys whose early heroism had died somewhere back there in graveyards of mud that had embalmed so many bloody corpses the numbers wouldn't be known for years to come . . .

Andrew saw the horror written on her face; his own personal tragedies seemed suddenly flimsy compared to those she had suffered. 'Don't, Grace,' he whispered, 'I'm sorry I brought it all back – yet you're tougher than you look. I could never have imagined you among any of that – you're such a wee thing.'

'Havers,' she said lightly. 'You only think that because you're so big.' She glanced at her watch. 'Oh, look at the time, I must get back! Listen –' impulsively she laid her hand on his arm – 'why don't you come to tea at the cottage tomorrow night? Gavin might be glad of your support, he tries to hide it but I ken fine he feels embarrassed about his legs.'

Gladness rushed through him 'Tomorrow night, Grace, I'll look forward to it.'

He stood there, watching her walk away from him; there were no shadows, only one young, lovely girl who was living and whole and very, very real.

David's letter was short, filled with more constraint than words. Evelyn hadn't had a chance to read it till after tea but the knowledge of it had lain at the forefront of her mind, she felt like a child anticipating some delicious treat, hardly able to wait for the minute, the moment and now . . . one sheet of grubby paper, the pencilled writing running off the page, odd, shaky writing, so unlike David's clear, sure hand.

Lucky to be sending this. Christmas, the time of Good-will among men, even Jerry. God bless Jerry, they do a good job. I remember the summers at Rothiedrum, it's difficult to see it all clearly but the little things stand out. The smell of warm grass, the grey granite of Aberdeen, the colour of the heather, your eyes, and your hair. You're not there anymore, I can't place you now. Light a candle for me on Christmas Eve, who knows, Someone up There might see it. Keep warm, keep well.

Yours as always, Davie.

She read and re-read it, trying to read between the lines, to imagine the things he had really wanted to say, to try and make sense of those that he had said. 'God bless Jerry, they do a good job.' A good job of what? Of starving their prisoners? Of torturing them?

And what had he meant when he said, 'You're not there anymore, I can't place you now'? Did he mean she wasn't where he had last seen her? In Rothiedrum? Or was he trying to convey that she wasn't much in his thoughts now? That he was unable to find a place for her in his heart?

She tormented herself, went over and over the letter till her eyes blurred and she could make no sense of either word or meaning. Kissing the laboured writing she placed the page neatly into her diary, smoothed out the creases, ran her fingers over it again and again telling herself as she did so that Davie had touched the precious paper that she was touching now. But it was no use. Nothing but a terrible foreboding came to her. He wasn't the Davie she had known, she sensed his despair, his lethargy . . .

Grace came into the room, her steps light. 'I've asked Andra Baird to come for his tea tomorrow, he and Gavin will be company for each other. Mam said it would be all right.'

Evelyn stared. 'And I've asked Gillie —' She got off her bed, hastily tucking away her diary as if it contained some dark secret instead of one badly written letter from the man she loved. 'I'd better go down and tell Mam, it will be quite a party.'

Grace laughed. 'Och, let's make it a party, Evie, it's a long time since any o' us enjoyed ourselves.' She took Evelyn's hand and held it tight. 'You're no' smiling, Evie, is Davie all right?'

'He — didna say very much.'

'He will, Evie, give him time, men like Davie and Andra and Gavin need time.'

Evelyn said nothing. She went to the door, Grace went with her. 'Let's go down and raid the larder. We'll make

91

some scones and maybe a cake, if I'm minding right, Gillie aye had a weakness for home baking.'

'Gillie.' Evelyn breathed the name softly and went with Grace to the warm kitchen to bake scones for three young men who were sore in need of enjoyment in their lives to help them forget the shadows.

Chapter Seven

Gavin Galbraith arrived at Wood Cottage in style, driven there by Gillan in the Colonel's Rolls which, because of petrol restrictions, was only used when he went into town for the occasional Board meeting.

On hearing about Gavin the Colonel was more than pleased to instruct that the big, comfortable automobile be used for the occasion and so the Rolls slid to a halt outside the cottage, quite literally so for it was a freezing night of moon and stars with ice diamonds glittering on the frosty roads and on the moon-bathed tracts of snowy countryside.

Amidst flurries of laughter, instructions, and a few muffled curses, a crunch of wheels on crackling ice, Gavin made his entry into the welcoming warmth of the cottage with Grace at the helm, for he had insisted that she be with him at The Grange to tide him over the awkward first minutes of meeting with Gillan and Andrew.

'They're posh these friends o' yours, Grace,' he had told her with a bravado he was far from feeling; every time he looked at the rug that covered the lower half of his body he broke out in a sweat and wanted only to remain in the familiar security of the place that had been his home for the past few weeks.

But there were no awkward first minutes. Both Gillan and Andrew were keyed up themselves and seemed neither to see nor care about his legs — or rather the lack of them. To each of them it was nothing out of the way to see limbless men and between them they bundled him into the Rolls and secured his wheelchair into the boot in a haphazard fashion.

Andrew was silent and preoccupied in his thoughts. It had been a long time since he had allowed himself to mix with anyone on a social level and his young face was tight with tension till Grace squeezed his arm and whispered, 'Mam and Father willna eat you, Andra, they'll enjoy having you just for yourself, so dinna try to be acting as if you werena there.'

His mouth relaxed, he burst out laughing. 'You have a lovely, quaint way of expressing yourself, Grace, I love it.'

'Have I?' Grace had looked at him doubtfully, thinking perhaps he was laughing at her. One look at his eyes quelled her doubts but not a strange catch at her throat. Something was happening that she didn't want and a frown creased the smoothness of her brow as she settled herself into the back seat beside Gavin.

Gillan hunched himself over the wheel, concentrating on manoeuvring the vehicle over the snow-bound road. In the course of that day he had caught glimpses of Evelyn, as she had said, all prim and proper in her white cap and apron. She had behaved towards him as she would to any of the Dunmarnock house guests, but before setting off for home she had run into him in the hall and had whispered, 'Tonight, Gillie.' His heart quickened at the thought of seeing again the natural, spontaneous girl he knew and he cursed himself for feeling this way about someone who so obviously belonged to another.

Arriving at the cottage, silence dispersed, nerves dissipated in the bustle of getting Gavin and his chair out of the Rolls.

'Watch my bloody legs!' he mouthed at one point whereupon a rather breathless Gillan replied sarcastically, 'Don't worry, we'll chuck them out in the snow for collection at a later date, they'll keep.'

Gavin loved it. It broke the ice between them for all time; Andrew forgot his hands; Grace her apprehension. They fell over one another laughing and trooped into the house in high spirits to be met by Christine Baird in the hall. Earlier in the day she had partaken of tea with Maggie in her little office and had casually mentioned how glad she was that Andrew had been persuaded to 'come out of hiding' as she put it. In an uncharacteristic fit of impetuosity Maggie had issued her with an invitation to come and complete the party and had been rather taken aback at the readiness with which Christine had accepted.

She was fair with dark blue eyes that were quieter than her brother's, her smooth skin was golden brown with a warm flush on her cheeks that gave the impression of some perpetual inner glow that wouldn't be quenched. She had an air of great vitality about her, her smile came readily to her generous mouth, one sensed her strength of character and the kind of determination that would brook no nonsense from anybody.

Introductions were made, everyone spoke at once. Maggie, who had seldom dealt with any meal more elaborate than a harvest dinner, peered into the oven for the umpteenth time, her face flushed with a mixture of heat and anxiety. She had never been one for entertaining, the crofting life called for plain fare, hard work, and little time for life's frivolities. She had only bargained for one young man from The Grange; now, somehow or other, there was a whole army of young folk to feed and entertain. But Jamie was holding the field in the latter score. He was laughing and joking, his black eyes sparkled, his thin face was animated and altogether he looked more alive than he had done for months.

Maggie had made him wear his Sunday-best suit. He had hummed and hawed but had finally capitulated but with the proviso that if it got too hot he would loosen his collar and 'to hell wi' toffs'.

Maggie had also warned him not to drink too much and now she could only pray that he would respect her wishes. For too long now he couldn't get through a day without a good drink warming his belly and when Maggie told him, 'You'll kill yourself wi' the evil stuff, Jamie. It will corrode your liver, ay, and maybe your mind as well,' he just turned a deaf ear and crept guiltily away from her naggings and warnings.

These days she seldom nagged, having finally realised that it did more harm than good. Sometimes she hated him for what he was doing to himself and to his family but more often she felt a deep sadness for, no matter what, she still loved him and would to the end of their days together.

From his place on the hearthrug, General, the big ginger tom who had, some weeks before, defected from the Big House in favour of the Grants' more homely cottage, yawned, stretched, panned his large, green calculating orbs over the assembly, then with mincing deliberation he arose and jumped straight on to Gavin's knee, there to purr, rub, and mew his pleasure.

'The buggering wee moggy!' Gavin yelled. 'I canna stand the damt things. When I was a wean in my pram one nearly smothered me to death, another tried to scratch out my eyes, and one peed against my leg in front o' the drill sergeant at training camp. He thought I'd smuggled the brute in on purpose!'

Gavin was from the Gorbals district of Glasgow, his dialect was richer than black treacle and so thick you could cut it with a knife. He had black curly hair, brown eyes and a nose that had taken too many bashings at the Glasgow boxing clubs. He had made good money at the booths and had hoped one day to be a champion but then the war came and his dreams were no more. He had shoulders on him like an ox and hands so strong everyone had winced in their introductory grip. He was straight, frank, outspoken and believed in 'calling a spade a shovel'. His wit was ready and abrasive, his sense of humour bawdy but there was another side to Gavin Galbraith, one that was mainly apparent when in the company of the fair sex: he respected and considered them, the tongue, that could be so coarse, became gentler when he addressed himself to them; and he had manners on him, had Gavin, the kind of manners instilled in him from the cradle by the mean

96

thongs of a leather strop and, when that wasn't to hand, by the near equal sting of his father's heavy hand.

His three older sisters had died in their infancy, his mother of the Bubonic Plague when he was just two years old, and his father had seen him into his teen years before 'flu had carried him off, and so Gavin was virtually alone in the world except for aunts, cousins and uncles for whom he cared little and who cared less for him.

Christine Baird was fascinated by him. He called her Chris and passed her the salt and told her outright he couldn't understand her posh accents but that she had a nice voice just the same. 'Sort o' plummy,' he grinned, 'I feel I could put you into a jar and scoop you up wi' a muckle great spoon.'

'And I could say the same about you,' she retaliated readily, 'only in your case it would be a tin and a knife and a big hunk of bread just asking for black treacle squiggles running all over it.'

He laughed. 'Ach, I'm sure you have better things to do wi' your time – or have you?' he said pointedly. 'The hunt came over by The Grange yesterday, Cuddles – she's the Matron – rushed to the window to watch. She said that "Miss Christine of Dunmarnock" would likely be out there wi' them. Were you? Do you really enjoy chasing a poor wee fox over the countryside only to watch it being torn to pieces by the hounds?'

She reddened slightly and Andrew laughed. 'Chris doesn't see it like that, do you, Chris?'

'I enjoy riding, I love the chase, it isn't like the way you describe it, Mr Runny Black Treacle.'

He grinned again but persisted. 'Och, c'mon, Chris, or should I call you Plummy? You don't seem set in the same mould as the usual run o' the mill idle rich. What are you doing to help out in the war, for instance? Should you no' be driving an ambulance or wearing a Red Cross uniform, or something like that?'

'No, I shouldn't,' she replied, bristling a little. 'As you say, I'm not your usual run of the mill, I hate uniforms and I hate anyone bossing me about. To put it simply I'm a non-conformist, I do my own thing and I do it my way. Myself and my friends visit and try to help injured soldiers. Sometimes we take them to recuperate at Craigdrummond — that's my father's other place in Invernesshire. Occasionally we go to his shooting lodge at Ross Dhu but mostly it's Craigdrummond. Father keeps a small staff there and a section of the house open for the soldiers. They have a wonderful time. We go fishing and walking and we do a lot of talking, talking helps. By the time they're ready to go back to the front they feel like men again and have stopped talking about death and dying.' Her blue eyes looked directly at him, 'If you behave yourself and want to come, I'd like to take you there when you're fit enough.'

'Och, I don't know,' he hedged, trying to appear only mildly interested. 'The country and me might no' go too well together. I'm more used to backcourts and busy streets.'

'Think about it,' she advised with a little half smile and let the subject be for the moment.

The soup course over, Maggie brought a sizzling roast pork to the table. It sat in a savoury lake of bubbling gravy and when Jamie plunged the knife through the crackling skin a spurt of juice descended on Gillan's trousers, and likewise on Andrew's jacket. Grace rushed to fetch a 'cloot' and both young men grinned at her as she anxiously dabbed at their clothing.

'I understood I was being invited to *tea*,' commented Andrew. 'If this feast goes by that humble title in this house then I'll have to instruct our new housekeeper to alter the Dunmarnock menus.'

Maggie smiled self-consciously. 'It started out being just a simple meal but when these daughters o' mine told me they were inviting so many o' their gentry friends I couldna very well serve up mince and doughballs.'

'I love mince and doughballs,' Gillan told her. 'As for gentry friends, I hope you haven't shoved me into the same category as this lot, Maggie, not after the Rothiedrum meal and ale celebrations and all those cuppies supped at King's Croft fireside.'

'That doesna alter the fact that you are who you are,' interposed Evelyn. It was an argument that she and Gillan had often indulged in and he reddened now in chagrin as he had done in the old days. 'Mam's right,' she continued, cutting her meat with great concentration and avoiding his eyes, 'we did put on an extra effort because the folk from the Big House were coming. You are who you are in this life no matter how you might try to pretend differently. Class exists in Scotland though it's no' nearly as important or as snobbish as it is in England but that doesna alter the fact that some o' *your* posh friends might look down their noses if you were to tell them you had dined here wi' us.'

'Now, now, bairns, dinna get carried away,' Jamie said warningly, but it was too late, a good argument about the class system was already well underway and by the time dessert arrived everyone had held forth an opinion, even Maggie whose own feelings had always been strong on the subject, and Gavin whose colourful expressions concerning 'toffs' had the table laughing whether they agreed with him or not.

Maggie had excelled herself in the cooking of the main meal but the simple dish which she now put down brought forth the most delighted comments of all.

'Atholl Brose!' cried Gillan, grabbing his spoon. 'I only ever tasted it once before at a Ne'erday dinner in Edinburgh.'

Gavin, who had, at the start of the meal, wondered which item of cutlery to use first, dispensed with formalities and used the first thing that came to hand, a serving spoon bearing traces of mashed potato. 'To hell wi' class,' he spoke the words like a battle cry, 'this is the food o' the Gods and if I eat enough o' it who knows, I might grow a new pair o' legs.'

'You might grow several,' Christine laughed, 'and chomp round the countryside looking like a giant caterpillar.' She tasted her dessert. 'Mrs Grant, this is delicious. How is it done and why has Seal McWhirter never made it for us?'

'She maybe thinks it's too common a dish to set before the queen,' sniggered Gavin.

'Ach, tis only oatmeal, honey and whisky topped wi' thick cream and set to chill in the outside larder,' explained Maggie, flushing a little.

'There's a fine wee story attached to it.' Jamie, avoiding Maggie's eyes, loosened his collar. 'Away back in the dark days, when folk didna ken any better, only water was used in the making o' the Brose, but in 1475, a bit before I was born, the Earl o' Atholl beat his deadly enemy, the Earl o' Ross, by replacing well water wi' whisky into Atholl Brose the drink. The Earl o' Ross just gulluped it down and fell into a drunken stupor, and the other Earl won though I forget now what it was that the mannie needed to win so badly.'

'Well, if earls can eat and drink it surely old Seal can make it for us.' Andrew looked at Grace who had been rather silent during the meal and had avoided his eyes at every turn, 'What do you think of all this class nonsense, Grace? You haven't said very much.'

'Oh, I agree wi' Evie, we're all alike in the eyes o' God but no' in the eyes o' each other, if like doesna stick to like the tongues start wagging and nobody is very happy.'

'I don't agree!' Gillan half-shouted, not at Grace but at the whole subject under discussion. 'In my case I would have married Evelyn Grant and bugger the gossips but she wouldn't have me! So it cuts both ways, a crofter's daughter can be just as snobbish and pig-headed as any of your so-called gentry and I should know what I'm damned well talking about!'

It was out in the open. At last. The table fell silent. Evelyn stared at Gillan's excited dark face and, seeing there the flush of shame spreading over it, something that was already in her for this young son of Rothiedrum, took firmer root that oddly controversial night of December 1917.

'In your case, Gillan,' Maggie spoke softly, almost to herself, as if she was remembering again the poverty and struggles of Megsie Cameron, her mother, who had once, long ago, been taken in by the sweet words of love spoken to her by Lord Lindsay Ogilvie, who had later married and whose children had all died in infancy. If he hadn't paid so much court to class he would have known his only living daughter, would have watched his grandchildren growing up. Later, when it was too late, he had wanted to provide for Evelyn whom he had met and had loved . . . He was a fine-looking man . . . Maggie recalled that day at King's Croft when he had appeared at her gate, awkward, regretful, offering all kinds of things in compensation. She had shown him the door . . . Sometimes she wished she hadn't, he was her father after all but that didn't make any of it right . . . Strange to think that young Gillan was her cousin . . . Evelyn was watching her, sometimes she wondered if the girl knew more than she let on but she couldn't – one day she would tell her about her grandfather, Lord Lindsay Ogilvie, one day . . .

'In your case, Gillan,' she repeated, 'you would have wed Evelyn but you are the exception to the rule and it is high time we all stopped blethering about such nonsense. Evie, go you ben the house and see to the fire; Grace, clear the table; go you out, Jamie, and fetch in the coal and dinna be all night about it and see you dinna leave a trail o' wet footmarks all over my clean floor.'

Her homely words lightened the air, chairs scraped, dishes clattered. Christine insisted on helping Grace and when that was done everyone trooped through to the kitchen to help wash the dishes so that there was a line of guests from sink to sideboard, washing, drying, putting away, smilingly ignoring Maggie's protests that the visitors' place was in the parlour where 'a good fire was going to waste up the lum'.

'Nonsense, Mrs Grant,' said Christine firmly. 'I for one am quite used to kitchens. You know yourself that I go down to ours and sort out Seal *and* I have been known to soil my fair hands making tea and even baking the odd cake.'

'Very odd,' smirked her brother, dodging a swipe from the dish cloth.

Maggie gave in with good grace and when everyone voted that they would rather pass the remainder of the evening in the homely and much warmer kitchen she just sighed and went to 'smoor' the fire in the parlour, her inherent thrift never allowing that good coal should go to waste.

Jamie sank into his chair, allowed himself to relax. Taking a wax spill from its holder he held it to the fire then applied it to his pipe. Leaning back, he puffed contentedly, the bowl of the stubby Stonehaven pipe held lightly in his cupped palm.

'Evie, go you ben the parlour and fetch me my fiddle,' he directed. 'We'll have a wee ceilidh here by the fire – oh, and while you're about it, bring the whisky through as well.'

'Ay, Father,' nodded Evelyn and went off to get the things, her heart singing in her breast. It had been a long time since Jamie had looked at his fiddle, let alone shown any inclination to play it, and lovingly she lifted the instrument from its red velvet case and bore it through to the fire.

Maggie grabbed the whisky bottle and dispensed the drinks. It had been a good evening so far and she was determined that it should remain so for when her man had partaken too freely of the Uisge Beatha he was inclined to get maudlin and sometimes she was afraid that he might say something he shouldn't, like mention his term of imprisonment in Craiginches prison where he had been incarcerated for eighteen long, weary months for half-killing a man who had attempted to ravish Evelyn in a house in the Aulton. When Maggie's cousin, Lady Marjorie, had secured a place for the Grants at Dunmarnock, she had thought it better not to mention that unsavoury part of Jamie's past to the Bairds, and there were occasions when Maggie broke out in a sweat for fear it ever became known.

But James was only for singing and playing that night by the fire with a bitter east wind soughing round the house and ice spicules whispering against the window panes.

Everyone joined in the singing for they were tunes of Auld Scotia that Jamie extracted so hauntingly from the fine old fiddle that had once raised its sweet voice round the smoking fires of gypsy camps in long ago days of boyhood. The music that he played told of the hills and the glens, the oceans and the rivers of the Scottish Highlands, then the tone changed; peesies and skylarks birled into the room, borne on the wings of song; the Clydes came in too, so real you could almost hear the swishing of their silken fetlocks; and then the plough, gliding through the furrows, leaving in its wake a rich concoction of dung and earth and wriggling worms that brought the gulls descending to the soil in great drifts that were like snowflakes swirling down; the bothy ballads came next, haunting, evocative, telling the stories of an old land and an old speak that came to life there in a cottage kitchen with the fire's warmth all around and the faces of young and old, wistful for a land that some of them had never known, but who felt the poignancy of those who had loved and left their homeland behind. Purple moors; lonely houghs; vast skies; acres of parkland smothering under quilts of bitter-green corn, emerald grasses; yellow tattie shaws.

Grace and Maggie stared into the fire with eyes that were too bright, Evelyn looked at Gillan and saw on his dark face an echo of her own longing for places and days and laughter long gone. She put out her hand to him, he took it and held it tight, and she was afraid for a moment because she wanted to take him into her arms and hold him to her heart. He looked vulnerable, somehow lost, and the thought came unbidden that there would come a day in both their lives when they would go their own ways and she would never see him again.

The idea of that was so sad that she shivered a little in the room's warmth and was glad when the atmosphere lightened. Christine Baird had brought out her comb, round it she folded a piece of tissue paper into which she blew, giggling as her first efforts at playing a tune tickled her lips. But perseverance extracted a gay little melody, followed quickly by another. Not to be outdone, Gavin found his comb and joined his efforts with hers. There followed quite a scramble to find combs and suitably thin pieces of tissue till before long a good-going 'Comb Orchestra' was underway. Even Maggie allowed herself to relax and blew as good as the rest of them till, slightly out of breath, she got up to fill the teapot.

General, who for most of the evening had ensconced himself on Gavin's knee, stretched luxuriously, treated himself to a good scratch, yawned mightily, and was highly indignant when tea came and he was deposited on the rug without ceremony.

'Do you still hate cats?' asked Christine curiously.

'Only if they don't like me,' he grinned and threw General a morsel of cake.

'I haven't heard you singing.' Andrew addressed himself pointedly to Grace, his blue eyes glinting with some annoyance since she had spent most of the evening avoiding him at every turn. 'I've heard your father and Evelyn, music seems to run in your family – yet your voice is noticeable by its absence.'

'Ach, it's been so long now I've forgotten how, you'll be no less the richer for not hearing me, I assure you o' that.'

She was very lovely that night with a pale green ribbon holding back her chestnut tresses and a soft green blouse emphasising her fragility, all the life of her seemed to be contained in her huge burning dark eyes fringed with lashes so thick the shadow of them was fanned out on the delicate curve of her cheekbones. Andrew could hardly take his eyes off her. Since their meeting yesterday he had thought of little else but her. So consumed was he with his thoughts that he had forgotten the shadows that had plagued him for so long; now there was a new kind of torment and he ached to hold her dainty hand next to his cheek in the hope that some of the gentle, sweet life of her would flow like music into his soul.

'Och, Grace, sing *Rowan Tree*.' Jamie tapped out his pipe, his voice was coaxing, gently persuasive. 'There's no' another lass in all the land who could sing that song like you.'

A red stain of embarrassment flooded the girl's otherwise pale cheeks. 'No, I canna,' she faltered, 'I've forgotten the words.'

The lie confused her, she shrank into herself. How could she say that? That song, that poignant, lovely melody was imprinted in her heart for all time. She had sung it to Gordon the last time she had ever seen him. Three days only they had had together. He had been exhausted, worn out from too many nights battling to save lives that slipped away beneath his hands, leaving bloodied shells that had once taken the form of men.

She had held him, letting him sleep whenever he needed to, had comforted him with her love, soothed him with her singing.

'You have the body of a tiny wee wren and the voice of a skylark,' he had laughed, and then he would join in her song, his deep, strong voice blending with hers . . .

'Rowan Tree, oh Rowan Tree . . .' She could hear herself singing it, heard the dark timbre of his voice coming in . . . 'That's aye so dear tae me-e.'

It filled the room, cancelled out all other sound . . . With a start she glanced up. Maggie and Jamie were singing, watching her, with their eyes encouraging her to take up the melody; her voice soared forth, her small, sweet soprano mingling with that of her mother's, with her father's musical tones. She was singing it for Gordon – only for him 'entwined am I wi' many ties o' hame and family.' She didn't want any of it to be for Andrew Baird of Dunmarnock, but how could she help some small part

105

of her rushing out to embrace that thin, young man with the haunted blue eyes that watched her in such breathless, reverent silence?

'Is it all right to cry in this house?' Christine asked when the song was finished, throwing back her head as if to suppress the tears that glimmered on her lashes. 'You sing like an angel, Grace Grant, if I had a voice half as good I'd be up there on the world's stage, trilling my lungs out.'

'I need all my breath just for living,' Grace returned with a shy smile and a positive refusal to sing one more song.

Gavin took up the cudgels. With a dead pan expression he told them a story of a young man called Gavin Galbraith who went to be a missionary in the Gorbals, and ended up being converted into heathenism by the natives. It was ad lib all the way, flowing out of him, rich, earthy, colourful and so funny told in his broad dialect he soon had everyone laughing and General complaining in raucous mews about all the din plaguing his lugs.

'I can honestly say it's the best night I've ever had,' said Christine at the door when finally they took their leave.

'Ach, away wi' you,' said Maggie. 'Surely you're forgetting the hunt balls and the parties you have had in your life.'

'Mrs Grant — Maggie — this is *real*,' Christine said warmly. She lowered her voice. 'Andrew would never, never have come out of his shell if he hadn't had this night with you and your family; as for me, I'll never forget the music and the singing and . . .' She giggled and gave Gavin's chair a push. 'Gavin Galbraith, the heathen missionary who found his vocation in a Glasgow pub.'

Gillan hung back to the last when he took Maggie's hand in his and squeezed it tightly. 'It's been like old times, Maggie, I honestly believed I would never again know the hospitality that once I had at King's Croft.'

106

She looked at the dark-haired, dark-eyed young Rothie-drum and a wave of real affection sprang up in the breast of her for this youthful cousin of hers. Strange to think there had been a time when she had avoided him and had truly imagined that the likes of King's Croft would be too humble a place for the likes of him to visit. To her in those days he had been young Forbes, she had been Mrs Grant to him. Now he called her Maggie and held her hand and she knew a terrible longing for things that might have been . . .

'Gillan –' she pulled him back inside and closed the door – 'has Evie told you . . .?'

'Ay, Maggie, I know all about it.'

'This might sound shameless, Gillan – but I wish to God it had been yours.'

'No more than I, Maggie,' he said softly. 'If I had my way I would marry Evelyn tomorrow and to hell with what Mother would have said.'

'Ay, she was aye a powerful force to reckon with – yet, thinking o' the way she is now, kinder, more likeable than she ever was, I think in the end she would have tholed it wi' good grace.'

'It wasn't to be, Maggie.'

'Who knows, Gillan, who knows? Life has a funny wee way o' turning us upside down just when we think there's no way out the midden. Maybe some day . . .'

'Some day, Maggie,' he said softly, bending down and kissing her cheek just as Jamie came back from saying his farewells.

Chapter Eight

Gillan joined the others to find them having a good-going argument about who was to go home with whom. Andrew wanted to drive both Grace and Gavin back to The Grange then bring Grace home. He was quite adamant about it, desperately so, proclaiming vehemently that he could drive quite well despite his hands and this no one disputed as he had taken the wheel once or twice since his return from the front.

Grace was equally adamant that they should all go back to The Grange with Gavin since she would need more than one pair of hands to get Gavin and his chair out of the Rolls.

'Och, c'mon, Grace, you know fine that Cuddles will be there to help,' said Gavin in all innocence. 'She could throw the lot o' us over her shoulders and carry us up to bed if the need arose. Thon wifie might have been born a woman but somewhere along the way she turned into an elephant.'

'Oh! For Heaven's sake!' Christine spoke with exasperation. '*I'll* run Gavin back and you lot can get along to your beds or to one another's beds, whichever you fancy! I'm freezing standing around here arguing, so scatter, the lot of you.'

'Whatever you say, Plummy,' grinned a delighted Gavin, patting the driver's seat invitingly. She got in, ignoring her brother's look of outrage though she knew he would have something to say later on about her indelicate tongue.

The vehicle spun away in a flurry of slushy ice leaving behind an oddly tense silence.

'You two girls had better get along in,' Gillan said at last. He took Evelyn's hand. It was icy cold; his were, as always, warm, strong. 'Goodnight, princess, I've loved every minute.'

She took matters into her own hands. 'I'll get our coats, Grace,' she threw over her retreating shoulder. 'We'll walk the boys home, turn the tables for a change.'

Grace stood immobile, frozen to the spot, not daring to protest for fear of sounding ungracious.

Evelyn was back in minutes, wrapped up warmly, avoiding her sister's accusing black eyes as she gave her her coat and helped hap the garment round her.

They walked in awkward silence, their breath frosting out in uneven puffs, ice crackling under their feet, keeping all together on the glittering path leading through rimy woods, frost-bound fields. Somewhere in the ice-happed woodlands a barn owl hooted; above their heads winter-black branches creaked under their weight of snow.

Leaving the trees behind they came into a brighter world, all around them the virgin countryside lay sleeping under the stars, pinpricks of light shone from farmhouse windows, the moon rode out from imprisoning snowclouds, looking haughty and aloof away up yonder in the realms of time and space.

Evelyn and Gillan found themselves lagging behind the other two; Grace seemed in a terrible hurry to get on though she kept looking back as if to ascertain that she wasn't being left alone with Andrew Baird.

Gillan halted and, taking Evelyn to him, he kissed her gently. His lips, like his hands, were warm. 'No fights tonight, I promise,' he whispered. 'I won't even torment you about the baby or David Grainger. Last night I decided that while I'm here you and I are going to enjoy every minute of the time I have left. We'll all enjoy it, you me, Grace, Andrew, Gavin and Chris. Do you think I'm being very stoic and sensible?'

'Oh, Gillie,' she smiled shakily, 'I do love you, I think I always have, not in the way I love Davie, a different thing

109

altogether. For you I feel something very special. I'm being selfish, I know, but I want always to feel that you're there, that I'll ken where to reach you and talk to you. You're far too good for the likes o' me, and I dinna mean the class thing, someday you will meet a lass who will love you as you deserve to be loved.'

'Ay, maybe.' He moved restlessly. 'Don't let's talk about it any more, I'm tired to death of the subject.'

Grace felt very strange walking beside Andrew, just the two of them together. If she had not been so aware of his feelings for her, things might have been different; as it was she wanted to break away from him, to run and run to a place where he would never reach her . . .

'Grace.' He stopped walking and pulled her to him with a suddenness that took her completely by surprise. 'I want to kiss you, I've wanted to ever since I first set eyes on that lovely mouth of yours –'

His mouth came down on hers. It was a sweet, gentle kiss, undemanding and faintly pleasurable, but then it went deeper, his tongue touched hers, his hands brushed her breasts, he pressed himself into her. She could feel the hardness of him at the pit of her belly and, quite unbidden, a small flame flickered in some deep, private part of her body. Guilt seared her soul, combining with a feeling of such loathing for herself she pushed him roughly away.

'Andra! I canna have that!' she half-sobbed. 'And I tell you this, I will no' bide by your side a minute longer if you are going to carry on like that.'

'Grace, I'm sorry, I couldn't seem to help myself.' He spread his hands in appeal, a look of misery on his intense young face. 'I promise it won't happen again, not if you don't want it to . . .'

A shout of laughter came from behind them. Gillan and Evelyn had started a snowball fight. Grace saw it as the excuse she needed to break the tension between her and Andrew.

She ran to join the others with Andrew following slowly at her back though minutes later he was just as caught up in the fun as everyone else. Lumps of snow flew through the air, bringing forth peals of laughter and shocked gasps as some of them found their mark and went slithering over warm skin to melt in icy rivulets into places where they were least welcome.

Christine, coming back with the Rolls, found a scene of abandoned jollity and, jumping out, she joined in the fun till they were all hot and panting, with roses in their cheeks and bright beacons for noses.

'Let's sneak into the kitchen and make some cocoa,' she suggested and without more ado they let themselves into the Big House to creep down dark passageways.

'We could make it in Ferguson's pantry,' suggested Evelyn in a whisper, but Christine was having none of that.

'It's warmer in the kitchen, don't worry, old Seal will be in bed, we'll have the place to ourselves.'

But there she was wrong. A faint glow of light illuminated the big, warm room and there by the fire sat Cook with a Capital, steeping her feet in a basin from which steam arose in clouds.

'Something smells bad,' choked Gillan. 'It's either her feet or the stuff she's soaking them in.'

His last guess was the right one. The old cook almost had a heart attack when the five young people materialised before her vision, Christine to murmur some half-hearted apology before going to find the milk, the others to busy themselves doing nothing because the look on the old woman's face was so comically shocked, each and every one of them had perforce to turn their eyes from it lest merriment got the better of good manners.

Nothing was said, no explanations made. Cook appeared to have lost the use of her normally expressive tongue, she just sat there at the fire, her feet in the basin, gaping at the subdued bustle in her kitchen as one in a state of shock.

Evelyn did not need to look closely to realise that her mother's advice on a chilblain cure had been followed by the old lady to the letter. The basin was filled to the rim with a clear yellow fluid from which an obnoxious acrid odour arose in such strength it filled every corner of the kitchen premises and caused the new arrivals to cough discreetly into hastily sought hankies.

'Cocoa, Mrs McWhirter?' Christine's question was made with the utmost politeness though a gleam in her eyes and a tightening of the lips showed all too plainly the effort she was making not to laugh outright.

Cook emitted an oddly strangulated sound which the young lady of the house chose to interpret as acquiescence. A steaming cup was set before Mistress McWhirter, everyone else took theirs to the further corners of the room to sit and sip in utmost silence, not daring to look at one another as each of them knew only too well that one smiling glance would force them to abandon manners they were finding hard enough to maintain.

It came suddenly to Evelyn that the old woman had made no complaint about chilblains for the last few weeks so it was obvious that the cure was working. She hugged herself with glee and determined to transmit the news to her mother at the first opportunity but at that moment Seal found her tongue and in a queer, quavery, voice said in near-pleading tones, 'You'll no' be lettin' on aboot this tae another living soul? I would never live it down for the rest o' my days and would be the laughing stock o' the place. I truly thought I had the room to myself –' Her voice became stronger, more like the Seal everyone knew. 'It never even entered my head that *my* kitchens would see intruders at this time o' night. It is little enough privacy I get to myself and it was far too cold in my own room to see to a wee part o' my toilet that is very personal to me . . .'

At that moment she lifted her feet from the basin to set them into another of clear warm water reposing beside the first. The sight of the dripping wet appendages did nothing to stop the mirth so valiantly suppressed in five young breasts. As one they erupted, exploded, boiled over. Snorts, grunts, shouts of laughter filled the room. They clutched, held, embraced one another in their total, unrestrained throes of rude and utterly enjoyable hilarity.

One after the other they fled the kitchen, leaving Seal to muster what dignity was left to her in the suddenly empty room.

'Now I have seen everything,' Christine wiped her streaming eyes and leaned against the wall for support.

'And *smelt* everything,' added Andrew with feeling.

'Shh! What was that?' Grace held up her hand. A faint rustling sound came to them from the depths of the dark passageway. They were all quiet suddenly as they stood there in the flesh-crawling darkness, listening to the sounds which were becoming louder with each passing second.

They were almost glad to see Effie hoving into view, though the candle that she carried, and the rustling noises that she emitted, imbued her with such ghostly qualities it was an easy enough matter to believe that she might not be real after all.

But real she was, as large as life as her harsh voice soon proved. 'There you are, Major Baird.' She spoke in a way that suggested total surprise at seeing him there in the dark passageway in the dead of night, and she addressed herself only to him, as if his four companions did not exist. 'I knew fine you would be cold and tired when you came home so I took the liberty o' putting hot bags in your bed and another in your night things.'

Andrew's face had lost its carefree look. From the minute he had come home, the parlourmaid had been there at every turn, fussing, clucking over him like a mother hen with an injured chick; she had anticipated his every move so that he'd hardly had to lift a finger; he recognised in her a soul who craved attention and affection and in his heart he was sorry for her though she made his flesh creep. If, for any reason, she came in contact with his person, a happening

113

that was all too frequent and unnecessary in his view, he found himself hating her with a violence that sprung from some dark inner font of his mind that had been warped by his war experiences. She cloyed, she clung, she disgusted him. She had pointedly never mentioned his hands and in her presence they loomed larger than life. She was adept at making him remember everything he was trying so hard to forget yet she could not have been kinder, more caring.

He cringed at her mention of his night wear. Somehow or other she always managed to inflect a tone of intimacy into her words even though she might only be speaking about his toothbrush, his sheets, whatever.

'Thank you, Effie,' he said sharply, 'but there really is no need . . .'

'Och, of course there's a need,' she broke in, smoothly and placatingly. 'You need looking after and I'm going to see that you get all the care you deserve. If you were my brother —' here she looked pointedly at Christine — 'I would make right certain no' to keep you out till these ungodly hours and in this bitter weather too. You look frozen and done in and I'm going to bide right here by your side and see you get into bed safe and sound.'

With a belligerent glare in Evelyn's direction she made to take his arm but he shook her off and was never so relieved when Gillan took matters to hand by saying calmly, 'Come on, old son, you and I will go up together and if you need tucking in you can damned well do it yourself because I'm dropping with fatigue.'

Both men went quickly away leaving Effie staring after them. 'Och, the soul,' she said blandly, swallowing her chagrin against Gillan, 'he's bound to have these wee tantrums after all he's been through.' Her eyes slid slyly to Christine. 'You and me must look after the young maister, Miss Christine, for, besides his parents, we're the only two who really know how to nurse him back to his full health and strength, is that no' right now?'

So saying, she rustled away, her candle casting a ghostly

glow on the walls, and throwing brooding shadows over her face.

Grace, Christine and Evelyn looked at one another but said nothing – they didn't need to, the disquiet of one was reflected in the eyes of the other, like mirrors absorbing shadows that were yet to come but not knowing who they would fall upon.

In bed that night Grace's voice came clear and vibrant: 'Evie, about Andra, dinna do this to me or to him. I ken you mean well but it will only bring more pain into his life. I'll never love anyone but Gordon, I dinna need any other man but him, so dinna you go throwing Andra at me again.'

'But, Grace,' Evelyn's voice was gentle, 'Gordon is dead, you must start to live your life again.'

'He isna dead, Evie.' Grace sounded unusually passionate. 'He'll come back to me, one day he'll come back.'

Evelyn held up her candle to look at her sister's face and saw that she really believed what she had just said. The realisation hit Evelyn like a douche of ice water. Grace, her beautiful, darling sister, would waste her young life waiting and watching for her man to return from the ashes of war. Yet Evelyn understood, she had felt the same about Davie long before the arrival of that fateful postcard telling her he was still of the world.

Chapter Nine

The days that followed were days that none of them would ever forget. Whenever possible they collected Gavin from The Grange and together they roamed the winter countryside, three young men, three young women, pushing Gavin's chair over the hoary earth, walking, talking, laughing, Grace feeling safe because she and Andrew went in a crowd, Evelyn feeling guilty in the knowing that for the first time in months she was really and truly happy and managing to achieve that state without David by her side.

She almost forgot that she was carrying his child: she was no longer sick in the mornings, she felt fit and young again, and strangely carefree. They gathered great bundles of holly and mistletoe and got Hugh Kerr to cut down a little tree to decorate the cottage. 'A castle must have a tree!' laughed Gillan and so they piled into Maggie's parlour to hang holly and mistletoe on pictures and walls and to garland the tree with the home-made decorations that had once graced King's Croft.

In the evenings they gathered round the fire to make hot buttered toast and to roast chestnuts and later Jamie would play his fiddle accompanied by the 'Comb Orchestra'.

When Seal was in the mood she held little tea parties in her kitchens, inviting along Twiggy May to read cups and palms and even suffering the presence of Raggy Annie who, with the able support of Gavin whom, to her delight, she had known in the Gorbals, told stories about her girlhood in the tenements that even had Cook with a Capital wiping her eyes with enjoyment, though she threw in the odd 'tut, tut' of disapproval just to show that she was not accustomed to such earthiness of tongue.

Grannie Currie, a snowy-haired old lady of eighty who lived with her son and his wife at Knocke Farm, was also a firm favourite at these gatherings. Her speciality was ghost stories and her quavery old voice was adept at bringing spooks and hobgoblins clanking along the corridors of the Big House: bogles came chapping at the doors; witches screeched at the windows while mournfully sad grey ladies sobbed their ghostly way in and out of the empty rooms in Dunmarnock's east wing which Grannie Currie knew fine was haunted, for hadn't she seen a headless old woman wandering there when she had worked to Dunmarnock as a young girl?

Ferguson snorted his scepticism and muttered something about her being the old woman, 'Brainless wi' the drink'; Violet uttered little yelps of terror and begged for more; Effie threw everyone dark looks which made Christine liken her to one of Grannie's bogles; Peggy gaped into space as if expecting to see a grey lady at any moment; the rest plied Grannie with tots of warmed sherry which flushed her cheeks and fired her imagination still more so that by the end of the evening Violet was afraid to go upstairs and Seal made bold to escort her though with frequent glances of fearful expectation thrown over her shoulder.

Gillan and Andrew resurrected the old family sleigh from the stables, complete with seats and sleighbells. With Jamie's help they spent two days making it road-worthy, hitched it to Darling, and off they all went, jaunting through the snowy acres of the estate, rugs round their knees, singing, giggling, drinking flasks of hot broth provided by Maggie. They gathered kindling and wood wherever they went so that as Christmas drew near the wood shed at the side of the cottage was stacked high with Yule logs.

The sharp air brought colour to Grace's pale cheeks,

a sparkle to Andrew's eyes; Gillan lost his tired look; Gavin positively glowed with returning health; Christine was busy and happy; Evelyn's nightly entry into her diary was just a repetition of the last: I never want tomorrow to come, it could never be as happy as today.

But tomorrow came, and the next, bringing Christmas ever closer, bringing Mary from Rothiedrum, all rosy smiles and burdened with messages from old friends and neighbours, bringing Wee Donald with her, and fast on their heels Willie the Post, bearing letters from Murn in far-off Australia together with presents, cards and a letter from Nellie in Kenneray.

Murn, the second eldest of the Grant girls, wrote glowingly of her new life in that far-flung continent to which she had fled after her cherished hopes and dreams of marriage to Kenneth Mor, Nellie's big, red-bearded Highlander, had perished when wedding bells had tolled for them.

She had secured a good teaching post in Sydney, the weather was warm, she was well and quite happy, she occasionally pined for the Scottish lands she had left behind but more for the family she had loved in the oddly detached way that only Murn was able to love.

'Will we ever see our lass again?' Jamie asked Maggie, and Maggie merely shook her head and said, 'Who ever kent wi' our Murn? She'll come home if it pleases her and no' before and only when she's able to boast a good bittie about all her achievements and her ambitions yet to be fulfilled.'

Nellie's letter was entirely different from that of her sister to whom she had never been close and whom she had never understood. In her strong, bold script she penned all her news, she spoke of Croft Donald, of the family, of Wee Col and his progress, of the oceans and beaches so beloved by Kenneth's first wife Jeannie who had died tragically young.

Enclosed in her letter was a card from Wee Col, laboriously decorated with robins of his own creation. *To Mam and Dadda, Evie, and Grace, love from Col,* was all it said but it was enough to make the recipients look at one another with tears neither of sadness or gladness shining in their eyes.

To Evelyn, Nellie had written a short, personal note:

Dear little sister, Mam wrote to tell me of your condition . . .

At this point Evelyn could picture the tightening of Nellie's lips for though she had lost a lot of her primness her opinions and views of life still adhered to the good old-fashioned moral standards of her upbringing.

Far be it for me to lecture you on the rights and wrongs of what you have done, enough it is that you have thrown away the best years of your life for a moment's foolishness, but you must realise that already so I am not going to say another word till I see you and have my wee speak with you face to face, for I am hoping that you will come and visit us at Croft Donald before very long. I think of you all with great affection and love. I remember so clearly the nights at King's Croft when all of us sisters used to coorie in bed together and whisper our wee secrets to one another. They were hard days but the goodness and love of them lives with me still and always will to the end of my days. Kenneth sends his fondest love and Wee Col a big cuddle. Cal and Isla Nell are well and happy. I think of them as my own bairns and hope Jeannie would approve of the way I am rearing them. I miss you, you wee whittrock, of us all you were the most carefree and impulsive. Give my love to my bonny Grace,

Nellie.

Grace smiled when Evelyn showed her the letter. 'Our big sister has changed, Evie, there was a time when she would have been shocked to the core at you, marriage to Kenneth has made her bonny and loving and she's no' feart any more to show it. One thing is certain, she's true is our Nellie, true and strong and good. In my mind I aye likened her to the Scottish hills, hard and dour wi' a sullen face but a good place to hide and a rock to lean on when the road gets shaky underfoot.'

Evelyn liked that description of Nellie, she went immediately to write it in her diary and while she was at it she wrote a letter to Davie telling him all the news but omitting to mention Gillan and all the happy times they had shared in the past week or so. She had good reason for doing so. David had told her quite plainly that he couldn't bear the idea of other men in her life and she had learned that it was wiser and safer to have her secrets from him.

For the hundredth time she read the letter he had sent and she thought of him in that far-off cheerless prison, lonely, ill – he *must* be ill to have written in such a stilted, detached fashion – bereft of home and family. She hoped he would get the parcel she had sent. Isa Currie's Knitting Bees were wont to produce more gossip and giggling than anything else but it was only once a week after all and in between times Evelyn had knitted and knitted till her eyes and fingers were sore and she felt she never wanted to see another sock or Balaclava helmet again.

With a sigh, she rose and went to the window. Mary was out there with Wee Donald, building a huge snowman in the garden, their frost-stung faces bright with gaiety. She wanted to laugh with them, to be happy while she could, for something told her that the days and months ahead of her would hold more sorrow than happiness.

Christmas came and Christmas went, wonderful days of family and presents and trips into the countryside with Gillan and the others; companionable nights of roaring Yule fires and spontaneous ceilidhs; tables piled high with clootie dumpling and jellies, roast chicken and cold ham, scones and hot pancakes straight off the girdle.

Hogmanay saw a differently-laid table: shortbread and black bun; rich fruit cake and fingers of sponge cake; bottles of whisky and sherry and port that winked in the firelight and made you think that rubies, amethysts and ambers were captured in the bottles. For weeks Maggie had been saving sugar and flour so that she could indulge in a huge baking spree, and now the results sat temptingly on the kitchen table, ready for the first-foots to admire and drool over and finally guzzle.

Just before the bells Evelyn rushed up to her room to light David's candle as she had done every night since Christmas Eve. 'Keep him safe, Lord,' she whispered, gazing beyond the small tongue of flame to the dark lands beyond her window; then she went back downstairs in time to join everyone as they toasted in the New Year. Poignancy seized her, it always did at this time, but this year more than ever. A whole procession of memories flitted through her mind, the Hogmanay nights at King's Croft, the skirl of the pipes, the plaintive notes of the fiddle, the melodeons, the singing, the streams of merrymakers that came and went all through the wee sma' hours. Silently she saluted neighbours and friends, well-known, well-loved, gone from her life now but never forgotten.

She thought of David, of the child within her; she wished Nellie was here, Murn too for all her self-centred ways . . .

'Happy New Year, princess.' Her father kissed her on the cheek, squeezed her tightly, his black eyes conveying so many emotions that would never be uttered. Everyone was kissing everybody else, Andrew was making full play with the mistletoe, catching Grace, claiming her mouth, his fair head blotting out her dark one. When finally he released her her face was flaming red but there was no anger in her, it was New Year, it was all right to kiss men who weren't Gordon, ay, the mistletoe, the goodwill, the sherry, that made it all right.

'Princess.' Gillan was there in front of Evelyn, his

brown eyes watching her quizzically, his well-shaped mouth quirking into an odd little smile in his dark, attractive face. Funny, he called her princess like her father did, long before he had heard the endearment used . . . It was a dear and special thing to her and seemed completely natural coming from the two men whose love for her never faltered through thick and thin. A thought struck her: all the men who had ever meant anything to her were of the same colouring – Gillan, Father, David, three dark men . . . But how could she say that? Johnny, darling Johnny, so fair, the exception, the first of her loves. Johnny, Florrie, they came to her as real and clear as they had been in life, their voices were in her head, their laughter was locked in her heart . . . She shivered and was ready to meet Gillan's kiss with a mouth that was tremulous and warm . . . She was ready to press her breasts against him and to rejoice in the knowing that their heartbeats were merging, mingling and beating, such a fiery, sensual beating, reaching and reaching, into her pulsebeats, her throat, her belly, down, down . . .

'Gillie!' She wrenched herself away from him, he held onto her hands, gazed deep into her eyes . . . He knew!

'I – I shouldn't drink sherry.' Her voice was faltering, unsteady . . .

'Ben the parlour!' Jamie's shout saved them both. Everyone made haste to the table. It was splashed with light from the hundred tiny candles Jamie had lit on the Christmas tree, the air was savoury with the combined smells of a mountain of mashed potatoes and a vast steak and kidney pie brought piping hot from the oven. The knife fell, pastry, golden, light and flaky, disintegrated, gravy ran in rivulets over the edges of the ashet. Everyone ate, everyone drank. A traditional Ne'erday supper, designed to soak up the whisky soon to be drunk.

The first-foots arrived, Big John Currie, dark, rugged, carrying a lucky lump of coal, shouting, 'Lang may your lum reek.'

In at his back toddled Grannie Currie, helped along

by Isa, John's wife. The visitors came, the visitors went, Hugh Kerr played his pipes, Jamie his fiddle, Burns was sung, quoted, recited, Gillan excelling himself at the latter. Burns was his favourite poet; he kept a treasured collection of his works at home but more precious than any of them was a volume given to him by Evelyn some years before with her inscription on the flyleaf.

'Ae fond kiss and then we sever —' he looked at her as he sang these words, she turned away to hide her tears — 'never met and never parted, we would ne'er be broken-hearted . . .'

The tomorrow that Evelyn had dreaded came early in the New Year when the hunt met at The Grange and the men who were fit enough collected in the grounds to watch the colourful gathering. All that morning the woodlands and the coverts echoed with 'tally-ho'; with the baying of the hounds; the rallying blow of the horn. Looking from a window Evelyn neither saw nor heard anything of such rude excitement; instead she heard the tinkle of sleighbells, the crackle of runners on frozen snow; the snapping of twigs in the woodland; the laughter, the singing; she saw five young faces, rosy and sweet, smiling for a while in the exuberance of youth, the pain, the shadows forgotten.

She knew none of it would ever happen again, the brief moment of joy was over. It had been the happiest Christmas she had ever known. She hadn't expected it to be, but she had taken it all while she could for all along she knew it wouldn't last, that dark tomorrow had to come and it was here — she sensed Gillan's presence before she saw him and she turned to meet him with the sad face of her buried inside and the bright, brave face she kept for such moments shining its light to the world.

He held out his hand: wordlessly she took it and they climbed together to one of the empty rooms at the top of the Big House.

'You dinna have to say anything, Gillie, I ken fine

enough what you have come about.'

He looked fit and strong and handsome, ready once more to go back to a war that had broken so many hearts the tears might never end.

'I want you to come back, Gillie – I want – so much for you to – live.'

He said nothing; instead he took from his pocket a thin gold band and placed it on her finger. She opened her lips to protest but he placed his fingers over them.

'Shush, shush, my darling, I ask only one thing of you. Keep this and remember me. You might never be my wife but my heart will always be yours. This ring will bind us together, in memories that are yours and mine alone for all the years to come. Look on it as a marriage of our hearts if you like. Take very good care of yourself, princess, I want always to think of you as the beautiful, eager, happy girl I knew. You were never quite mine but I like to think you might have been if the fates hadn't decreed otherwise.'

'Will I never see you again?' She spoke huskily, her throat tight with the tears she fought to keep back but which wouldn't be stemmed.

He couldn't speak. They both knew they were only prolonging their pain by questions that had no answer.

Briefly he took her into his arms, brushed her tears with his lips, then he was gone from her, never looking back, never once slowing.

She stood there for a long time, empty and alone. Far, far in the distance the huntsman sounded his horn, the hounds bayed. The sounds were like death knells that reverberated in her head and echoed down, down, into the depths of her soul.

PART TWO

Spring 1918

Chapter Ten

Spring seemed slow in coming that year but when it did it came with a rush, as if the earth was suddenly glad to shrug off the fetters of winter that had bound it for so long. Snow melted from the low hills of Renfrewshire; burns shed dripping fangs of ice and tumbled down into the Clyde Valley to meet and converge with fast-flowing rivers that hurried their turgid way into the waiting waters of the River Clyde.

Jasper Pringle, gamekeeper and earthstopper to the hunt, made his last nocturnal round of the season and next morning hunters and hounds skirled their noisy, colourful path through the blossoming countryside, starting off at Hartfield Moss then towards Threepgrass and Bardrain, up the hill to Gleniffer, through by Game Wood and Cuffhill where the fox got to ground in a drain. Hounds screamed for blood but none was forthcoming that day.

'And a good thing too,' declared Seal with vigour. 'Foxhunting might be the best way – so *they* say – to keep the poor craturs down in a humane manner, but *I* say myself that the laws o' nature have their own role to play without interference frae a pack o' bloodthirsty hounds.'

'Ay, well, Big John Currie would have somethin' to say aboot that,' sniffed Willie the Post who privately enjoyed the colour of the hunt but didn't dare tell that to Seal. 'He lost a wheen o' chickens to foxes over the winter and is only too pleased to see hunters wi' hounds fleein' over the countryside.'

'Ach, drink up your tea, Willie,' scolded Seal grimly.

'You're like an old woman the way you prattle on.'

Wiping his hand across his moustache, he hurriedly rose, knowing how easy it was to get on the wrong side of Cook with a Capital. 'See and give Evie her letter now, she's been like a hen on a hot girdle this whilie back and I've a notion this might just be frae her man. It's a similar sort o' writing that was on the last one but no' as shaky and the envelope is cleaner. A Glasgow postmark too. Maybe he's come back in time to marry her before she drops the bairn . . .'

Seal turned an ominously thunderous face. 'What was that you said, Willie Nairn?'

'Och, come on now, Seal, there is no need to pretend to me that you don't know the girl made all that up aboot bein' marrit. Effie was there that night and she . . .'

'*That* weasel! I might hae known she would be spreadin' her mischief about. I was there too that night, I'll have you know that, my man, thanks to Effie and her snooping. I saw the wedding ring wi' my own een and there's an end to the matter. Go you along now and get on wi' your work, you spend far too much time sniffing your nose into other folk's affairs.'

Willie escaped gladly, leaving Seal to turn Evelyn's letter over in her hands. Despite her staunch outburst she too had often wondered about the girl but och! she was a good lass, bright and kindly, always with a song on her lips and a cheerful willingness to do anybody a good turn; and if her past might just be a shade on the dark side, well, that was her business, she would pay for her sins and would need all the goodwill she could get to see her through the next few difficult months.

Evelyn put her letter in her pocket and walked away down to the quiet banks of the River Threep where primroses were peeping shy faces and a blackbird trilled from some hidden branch.

This time she wasted no time in opening the letter.

It was succinct, to the point. He was home! He had been repatriated much sooner than he had expected and could she come and visit him at the above address? He had simply signed himself: *D. Grainger.*

She jumped up as if she had been stung. Home! He hadn't given her any warning. She had heard from him only once more since his first communication. He had had little to say and now this! Home! Repatriated!

This time she didn't keep the news to herself. She went fleeing back indoors where everyone was drinking tea in the kitchen.

'Davie's home!' She half-shouted the words. 'He's been repatriated and wants me to visit him at his parents' address.'

'Funny way to treat your wife,' Effie said sourly. 'Why did he no' tell you to meet him at the station instead o' sneakin' home to be wi' his parents?'

It was exactly what Evelyn had wondered herself and the first flush of her joy faded a little.

'Ach, he'll be ill,' Ferguson hazarded stoutly. 'The lad maybe didna want a lot o' palaver to start him off.'

'And him wi' a pregnant wife?' persisted Effie, glancing slyly at Evelyn.

But she wasn't listening. 'Ill?' she whispered, staring at Ferguson's placid old face.

'Ay, he's been repatriated, Jerry wouldna let him go if they could make any more use o' him.'

Violet was peeping at the letter over Evelyn's shoulder. 'That's *my* address,' she said in some astonishment. 'Grainger, I should have known but I never connected – Och! remember I told you, Evie, Winnie Grainger, sitting at the window singing that song you aye sing, watching for her son to come home from the war.'

'Ay, ay, I do mind you saying that, Violet,' Evelyn spoke automatically, her mind racing with the implications of the old butler's words.

'Evie –' Violet took her arm and propelled her into a corner – 'let me come wi' you when you go to see Davie.

I could show you the way. I'm due a day off and Auntie was coming wi' me to visit her sister – that's my mother.'

'Three o' us would never be able to get off together, there wouldna be anybody left to see to things here.'

Raggy Annie solved the problem. 'You get along to see that lad o' yours, lassie,' she told Evelyn later that day. 'I can take my day off another time, there are no braw young soldiers in my life – more's the pity,' she chuckled, flicking her cigarette ash into a nearby flower pot with expert aim.

'Annie, you're so good. Oh! I canna believe this is happening! Mam went all queer and dour when I told her but Father gave me his blessing.'

'You havena telt the lad aboot the bairn, have you, Evie?'

'No, not yet, I thought it better to wait and explain . . .'

'If he hadna come home in time – would you have telt him at all? Or would you have landed him wi' a ready-made bairn as a homecoming present?'

'Och, Annie, I dinna ken, I canna really think straight just now. The question is solved now anyway and I – I hope he'll be pleased.'

'Gie him a breathing spell tae get used tae the idea, hen,' advised the older woman wisely. 'From what you've told me aboot him he's no' the domestic sort – so don't expect too much all at one time.'

Evelyn dressed carefully, a state that was difficult to achieve as she was all fingers and thumbs and so nervous she forgot to put on her petticoats and had to start all over again. She could no longer wear corsets. Seven and a half months into her pregnancy she was heavy and ungainly and was only able to hide her condition under loose-fitting garments which had the effect of making her look childishly young, almost like a besmocked schoolgirl who had no idea how to get the most from her figure.

When finally she was ready she gazed anxiously into the mirror; her hair was fine, rich and thick around her head;

but her colour was too hectic, her eyes too anxious which always had the effect of making them seem greener than ever. With a click of impatience she applied a powder puff to her nose and cheeks, ran her hands over her moss green frock, tugging, straightening, patting the white collar into place. She wondered if she should tie a sash loosely round her waist. What waist? She sighed. She already looked like a sack of potatoes, without emphasising it any further.

She stood back, examined herself critically. The glass told no lies. Once – oh, such a long time ago – she had been perhaps a bit too proud of her appearance but that was before the Presence began to make itself known. As if it could read her thoughts it gave her an extra hard kick in the groin. It was strong! Dear God! Did it really have to punch and kick her like that? Perhaps it was as impatient to be free of her as she was of it.

She had never liked the feel of it inside of her. It gave her the creeps, especially in the middle of the night when she had just turned over. Then it started, kick-kicking, pushing sleep further away, almost as if it wanted all her attention *now* – before it was even born. She occasionally felt repulsed by it and it was then she prayed, 'Dear God, let me like it more, especially afterwards, I want to love it, it's Davie's child after all.'

Perhaps her present attitude towards the child owed itself to the fact that it disturbed her most when she was dreaming about The Devil's Door. That particular nightmare never seemed to diminish in strength and it might be that her fears transmitted themselves to her unborn child. She didn't know, she didn't particularly want to know . . .

Grace came into the room. 'Evie, you look bonny,' she cried warmly. 'Davie will love you –'

'Ach, Grace, I don't, and he won't! But it's kind o' you to say so.'

'Evie, look at yourself.' Grace made her face the mirror. 'Those eyes, that glorious hair, your skin, like golden peaches without flaw.'

Evelyn giggled. 'Tis a pity I canna leave my body behind and just let my head float along, you've made it so big wi' your fancy talk it might just do that, but what would Davie have to say when my head glides up to him, kisses him on the lips, gives him a wink, drinks a cup o'tea and splashes it all over his feet!'

'Ach, Evie, you're still as daft as ever you were, nothing will ever change you.'

Evelyn studied her sister's face. 'Maybe, but something *has* changed you. You look so different from the lass you were when we came here, sort of glowing and floating.' She giggled. 'Maybe you and me should haunt people, me wi' my floating head, you wi' yours in the clouds . . .'

They fell against one another in a fit of merriment. 'Seriously –' Evelyn wiped her eyes – 'Is it Andra Baird?'

'Andra Baird!' Grace was genuinely surprised. 'Och no, it isna Andra, though I like him a lot and enjoy seeing him when I have the time. No, it's just me. I feel better than I ever did and because o' that I'm happier in myself. I think it all started before Christmas. They were such good times, Evie, I'll never forget them. I felt alive, whole, ready to face the world again.'

'Ay, it was a wonderful time,' Evelyn spoke wistfully, picturing it all, seeing Gillan's face in her mind, 'I felt like you, free, happy. I'm so glad you felt that way too, you're young, Grace, you have to forget, to start to live again.'

'Oh, but Evie –' Grace turned a serene face – 'I'll never forget, in fact I'm only now starting to remember all the good times I shared wi' Gordon. It was all dark before, my mind was full o' darkness and death. I was beginning to think it would aye be like that but now I ken better. Gordon will come back to me and when he does he'll find a fit young woman, ready and able to take up life where we left off.'

Again Evelyn saw that same gentle conviction on her sister's face and she knew it was useless to argue. Instead she said, 'Andra loves you, Grace.'

'I ken that.' Grace shuddered suddenly, a strange, haunted expression coming into her eyes. 'That's the reason I havena encouraged him . . .' She swung round to face Evelyn, fear stark on her face. 'You dinna think I have, do you, Evie? I couldna bear it if he thought I had — it would be like Martin Gregory all over again. In many ways Andra puts me in mind o' him, he's so intense, so serious and — and — there are the other things, the times he seems to forget I'm there and talks to someone called Barrett! I shoudna tell you this but I ken you willna say. Barrett was his friend, he died in a fire, Andra burned his hands trying to save him!'

Evelyn put her arms round her sister and held her tightly. No one, least of all Grace, would ever forget Martin Gregory who had taught at the little school in Rothiedrum. His wife had died in childbirth and in his loneliness he had turned to Grace for comfort. She had been but a lass of sixteen when first it had started, he a man old enough to be her father. For many years Grace had given him her affection and devotion and in the end that had been her undoing. He had mistaken her kindness for love and when she refused to marry him he had hung himself from the rafters of his fuel shed. Later it was discovered that he had been suffering from a brain tumour that had warped his whole personality but Grace had always blamed herself for what had happened. Soon after the affair she had married Gordon and had never mentioned Martin Gregory again and the thing about Andrew might not have seemed so ominous if that had been all there was to it. But a few weeks ago a letter had come from Martin's lawyers. In the event of his mother's death he had willed everything to Grace. The letter was to tell her that Mrs Gregory had died and Grace was now the sole beneficiary of the will.

The incident had opened up old hurts, stimulated half-forgotten terrors. She hadn't touched a penny of the money but had directed that it should go to a benevolent fund for handicapped soldiers.

When that was done she wore the look of one who had shaken off some dreadful burden but Evelyn now saw that she still remembered, still worried and fretted about that dreadful, unhappy episode in her past.

'Andra isna like Martin,' Evelyn said gently. 'He's young and he'll do something wi' his life. Chris said something about him taking over the running of one o' his father's factories. He'll get better, Grace.'

'Ay, he'll get better.' Grace lifted her head and smiled, an odd little smile that didn't reach her eyes. 'Go you away now and meet Violet, she'll be waiting.'

Evelyn gave a gasp and rushed away as fast as she was able. Violet was waiting impatiently at the stables with Burton who had been persuaded to take the girls to the station in the pony cart.

'Come on, Evie,' he greeted her, 'we'll miss the damt train if we're no' careful and Auld Dobie is a mite too long in the tooth to hurry himself for anybody.'

But Auld Dobie must have been feeling spring in the air that day for he cantered to the station in double-quick time, allowing the girls a few spare minutes to catch their train and settle themselves comfortably with their bags and parcels carefully deposited in the overhead racks.

The journey to Glasgow wasn't long enough for Evelyn. She found herself wishing it would last forever as, now that the moment of meeting David was almost here, she felt sick with apprehension and hung on to Violet's arm as that young lady guided her confidently onto an electric tramcar.

'Upstairs,' she directed, leading the way with great agility up the twisting steps and plonking herself down on a seat at the front.

It was Evelyn's first experience of a tramcar and she giggled a little as the vehicle rattled and swayed along streets that abounded with horse-drawn traffic of every description.

'Fares please.' The conductress staggered up to them, very businesslike and severe, dressed in a hip-length belted jacket, a long checked skirt, and wearing on her head what looked to Evelyn like a tin helmet with a badge on the front.

Swaying back and forth to the vehicle's rhythm, big, sensibly-shod feet splayed out as an aid to balance, she rung her little ticket machine and raked in her leather bag for change.

'I wanted to be a tram conductress,' Violet confided in her friend the minute the woman was out of earshot. 'Glasgow was the first town to take on women tram conducters and it was said they made so much money they were out buying themselves fur coats and fancy furniture. But Mammy wouldna let me, she's a bit o' a snob is my mother, as different from Aunt Annie as chalk from cheese though they might be twins to look at them. Anyway, Mammy wouldna let me leave Dunmarnock, she said I would learn some genteel manners there and I'm glad really for I like the country fine and the Bairds put up our wages when it looked as if they might lose all their staff to the public services and the munitions factories. Forbye that,' she settled herself more comfortably, 'I would never have met Jock Pringle. We've been walking out steady since Effie stood him up a few months back. What he saw in *her* I'll never know but that doesn't matter now.'

Violet chatted on, every so often breaking off to indicate to Evelyn the change in women's fashions since February when the vote had been conferred on women over the age of thirty. Skirts had become shorter, hair was neatly bobbed.

'I would get mine done but Jock likes girls wi' long hair,' prattled Violet. Evelyn wasn't listening, she was watching the bustle of life that was Glasgow: the townies, the wanderers, men in straw hats carrying walking canes; women in fringed shawls carrying huge shopping bags and quite often babies too. As well as the foot traffic there were horses and carts; men riding single horses; motor cars and tramcars whizzing by.

As they left the city centre behind the scene changed, tenement buildings rose up on either side, dusty and black from the putrid smoke spewing from household fires, mingling with the nauseous gases that belched from the tall columns of industrial chimneys. Ragged children played marbles in the gutters; monumental women leaned massive elbows on window sills and watched the world go by; skinny small girls in dirty print frocks played skipping ropes to the chant of rhymes that had known their beginning in some distant time.

'Ach, don't look so worried,' Violet laughed at sight of Evelyn's face. 'This is the stinking side o' Glasgow. Govan's much nicer, it's more like a village and it was here long before this smelly city. We get off here then we walk for a bit.'

Alighting from the tram they traversed so many streets Evelyn knew she would have lost the way without Violet's able guidance.

'We're nearly home,' Violet spoke at last. 'Dive into this close here and we'll give ourselves a bit o' a toosh-up.'

So saying, she pulled Evelyn into a nearby close, got out her mirror and comb, and began to preen herself.

'Violet, will you come in wi' me? Just for a wee whilie?' Evelyn spoke anxiously.

'What? I thought you were dying to see Davie!'

'Och, you ken fine I am – but – it's his parents. I've never met them – I – oh, please, Violet! If it had just been me I wouldna have minded so much but – there's this . . .'

With her eyes she indicated her stomach and her companion laughed. 'Och, all right then, but only for a wee minute, mind. Mammy will be looking out for me. It's no' that often I get to see my folks and they like to hear all the gossip o' the Big House.'

They went on, Evelyn wondering when they were coming to the village Violet had spoken of. She could deal better with a village. It might not be as rural as the small clachan of Lums O'Reekie but anything was better than Glasgow with its fumes and dusty streets.

'We're in Govan,' Violet pronounced cheerily. 'I told you it was better, didn't I?'

At first glance it appeared to country-bred Evelyn much the same as Glasgow. Women pushing squeaking prams along the pavements; children bawled in rickety go-chairs parked at close mouths; little girls played peever in the streets. But there was no congestion of traffic; the buildings looked cleaner, the streets wider, the trees in a nearby park swayed gently in the April breezes.

'This is our street.' There was a hint of pride in Violet's voice. 'Here's our close.'

Evelyn was never to forget her first glimpse of 198, Camloan Road. It wasn't much different from the other closes in the street but, seated at a downstairs window, was a woman with a calm, sad face and dark eyes that looked outwards and saw nothing. Her expression was vacant, her long, fragile fingers played idly with a narrow piece of dirty blue ribbon that was attached to the end of a straggly rope of hair that had once been fair but which was now a faded yellow-white. She was singing *Soldier Laddie* in a voice that was high and tuneless yet held an oddly sweet nuance.

Evelyn felt tears pricking her lids. So this was Davie's mother, singing, watching and waiting for a man-child who would never return from the wastes of war. Poor, poor, lost soul!

'That's Mrs Grainger,' whispered Violet. 'Witchie Winnie, the bairns call her. She used to be a lovely singer; when she and my mother were girls they used to sing at concerts in the Town Hall and Mrs Grainger had everybody saying she would go on the stage one day. Now look at her, poor wifie. She *must* be daft. Her lad's come home yet still she looks for him and sings her wee song, aye the same one, over and over again. Even my da says she's no' the full shillin' but she's harmless and wouldna hurt a fly.'

'It isna Davie she waits for,' murmured Evelyn. 'She

looks for Danny, he was only sixteen when he got killed at Le Cateau. Davie said his mother's hair turned white after that. I – I never gave her a second thought at the time. She was just Davie's mother – now . . .'

'Oh, you mean Daredevil Dan, that's what we called him. The wee bugger used to pull my plaits in the playground. He was a wild one but clever, he would tell the teacher how to do sums. He was the apple o' his mother's eye. David used to get jealous and take it out on Dan who was too wee to fight back but aye got the better o' his brother wi' the big, fancy words he used. It's all coming back now, wi' me being away from home so much I miss a lot o' what goes on. Right, come on then, Evie, only ten minutes – mind that.'

Chapter Eleven

As it happened they were met at the Graingers' door
by Violet's mother who was, as Violet had said, so like
Raggy Annie the two might have been twins. But Mrs
Henderson had none of Annie's easy-going, likeable ways.
She was prim and precise and was only saved from prudity
by a humorous tongue which acknowledged Evelyn with
off-handed warmth followed by an oblique reference to
her girth which she slyly chose to put down as 'too much
o' that stodgy gentry food'.

'Douglas Grainger asked me to set the table in case
he wouldna get hame on time. He's taking the afternoon
off and should be here soon,' explained Mrs Henderson
as she led the way through a tiny, dingy lobby and into
the kitchen. It was the only apartment, a single-end as
it was known in Glasgow. On one side of the door was
a four-by-six recessed bed, under it was stuffed another
bed on wheels together with trunks and numerous other
domestic items; two worn armchairs reposed either side
of the massive black-leaded kitchen range which domi-
nated the room. There was a dresser, a coal bunker, a
shelf running the length of one wall on which reposed a
motley collection of crockery and pans. The sink was in
a small enclosure covered over by a flowery curtain; over
by the window sat Mrs Grainger, still singing her song,
oblivious to whoever came and went from her home . . .
and in one of the armchairs sat Davie, only Evelyn had to
look twice before she recognised anything in the unmoving
figure that reminded her faintly of the young man she had
known. This boy was like a stranger, his harrowed dark

139

eyes were sunk into the skull-like mask of his face, his skin was yellow and unhealthy-looking, stretched tightly over the frail bones of nose and jaw, yet sagging loosely beneath his chin in little crêped furrows. His pitifully thin body did not fill the clothes that encased him. His shoulders were hunched like those of an old man, his bony hands lay on his lap, the crooked palms upturned.

'Davie,' she whispered, hardly able to get the name to come out of her dry throat, 'Davie, it's me, Evie, I've come as you asked.'

There was no response, he went on breathing in the same shallow manner as before, and she ran to him to kneel beside him and take his pitifully thin hands in hers. Swallowing back her tears so that her throat became sore and tight with the effort, she said gently, 'Davie, you dinna need to say anything, everything's going to be all right. I'm here now, I'm here.'

She might not have spoken, there was no sign from him to show that he knew she was there.

Mrs Henderson coughed. 'I'll get away back upstairs, lass. If you need me for anything it's the first door on the right, two up. You come along, Violet, and stop gawping like a loony.'

'I'll stay for five minutes, Mammy,' stuttered the loyal Violet, looking as if she would like to turn and flee the scene.

'Five minutes then,' Mrs Henderson said, and let herself out.

Left alone, Violet rushed to put her arms round her friend. 'Sit down, Evie,' she directed. 'You look – awful.'

But Evelyn pushed her away. 'No, Violet, I'm fine, it's just I didna expect ... Oh look, put the kettle on and we'll make some tea, we must do – something.'

But Mrs Henderson had not only made tea, she had set a big pan of broth to heat on the range and left a pile of somewhat thick sandwiches on the scrubbed kitchen table over which she had thoughtfully draped one of her own tablecloths.

The heat in the room was oppressive, Evelyn saw beads of sweat standing on David's brow and, filling a bowl of cold water, she went to kneel by him and bathe his face till it was cool and fresh to the touch.

A child was playing ball in the close, marking time with a rhyme that dirled steadily into the room: 'One, two, three a-leerie, four, five, six a-leerie, seven, eight, nine a-leerie, ten a-leerie post-man.'

The *thud, thud* of the ball on the wall beat into Evelyn's head. 'Violet,' she began, but Violet already had her head outside the door and soon sent the offender packing with a few well-chosen words.

The door had no sooner shut than it opened once more to admit a tall, harassed looking man dressed in working jacket, trousers and stained cloth cap. His face was prematurely lined, his head of jet black hair was threaded through with wiry strands of grey. He looked tired and terribly defeated but Evelyn didn't need to look twice to know that this was David's father, his eyes were of the same velvety brown, somewhere in his rugged face there lurked the ghost of the handsome man he had once been and still was in a powerfully magnetic way.

Before he even spoke Evelyn liked him at once and was ready to take his big, rough hands in hers when he held them out to her and said, 'You're Evelyn. Forgive me, lass, for no' being here to meet you, it's a fair trek from the shipyard but I see Jenny Henderson has been and seen to the table.'

'I'll get along up.' Violet went to the door. 'I'll meet you in the close at five, Evie, and don't be late like you were this morning. It's a good long journey back to Dunmarnock.'

Left alone, Evelyn and Douglas Grainger looked at one another, 'You've seen our lad, Evelyn.' His voice was soft, tinged with bitterness. 'I didna believe any o' the newspaper stories till I keeked at my son through the grimy window o' a train and went on past thinking he was some other poor bastard's lad. Bloody Jerry have half-killed him! He's probably starved himself trying no'

141

to eat filth full o' disease and chemicals. 'Tis little wonder he's nearly as crazy as that poor bitch who sits there at the window, singing her madness to a world which neither sees nor cares if either she or her boy is alive or dead!'

'The letter?' She spoke haltingly. 'He didna write it, did he?'

'No, lass, no, you can thank or blame me for that, whichever you like. Before this happened he spoke a lot about you. I found your new address in his pocket book and lured you here in the hope that a sight o' you might stir some recollection in that sick mind o' his.'

'Och, please dinna speak like that. You never lured me, I wanted to come, it's what I've waited for! There's so much I want to tell him!'

'Ay.' Douglas Grainger eyed her ungainly little figure. 'I can see that, you've waited well, lass, and I'm thinking you'll have to wait a whole lot longer before he can take in the fact that he's fathered your bairn. It is his, isn't it?'

'Ay, it's his.' Evelyn spoke wearily and at once Douglas Grainger was filled with compunction for his lack of manners.

Indicating the table, he bade her sit down but she shook her head. 'No, Douglas Grainger, you and me have things to do, people to see to.'

His sudden smile recalled to his face some of the vitality which had been trodden into the ashes of his life. 'Ay, lass, we have that. We'll sup later and we'll talk. I have good neighbours, grand friends, relatives I like and some I can do without, but none o' them have what you and me have in common, love for that boy who sits there in his lonely prison and knows not how to break free. Only love can help him do it and I can see you have a powerful lot o' that in your heart.'

He lifted the pan of broth from the fire, ladled some into two bowls, before going to the window to fetch his wife to the table.

Evelyn took David's arm, led him to the table. Obediently he sat, allowed her to feed him and wipe his mouth and break his bread into manageable pieces.

The room was silent. Outside, the children chanted their rhymes, cawed their skipping ropes, chased their peevers; inside, a man and a young girl sat, spooning broth into two mouths, the one of the son uncaring and feeble, that of the mother eager and slavering yet as easily diverted as a small child. Winifred Grainger grabbed at the big patient hand that held her spoon; toyed with the saltcellar; sang snatches of song; bubbled her lips into her broth. Douglas Grainger caught Evelyn's eye. 'Who would have thought, lass, eh?'

'Ay, who would have thought?'

'Where will you have the bairn?'

'I havena really decided, maybe at my sister Nellie's place in the north-west.'

'My grandchild, I canna right believe it's real.'

'It's real enough — and big enough. It fights wi' itself inside o' me — only a boy could kick like that.'

Winifred Grainger keeked up suddenly from her plate, her eyes strangely interrogative.

'Have you seen my boy? Is he coming home? Does he know I'm waiting for him?'

It was as if she had seen and heard Evelyn for the first time. The girl hesitated, unsure how to answer, then she said boldly and clearly, 'Ay, Mrs Grainger, he kens you're waiting. One day he'll come home, if you wait long enough he'll come home.'

Douglas Grainger frowned a warning at her but she was unrepentant. 'It's what she needs to hear, the sort o' thing she wants someone to tell her. She'll still wait and hope, it's the only thing left to her, but she might no' be as anxious as she was. You should try it, it might do some good.'

'You seem to know a lot about it for a lass o' your tender years.'

'Ach, no' really, I only know that she maybe feels more

143

shut out than she needs to be. She wants to hear Danny's name but everyone is too afraid to say it.'

'Danny.' Winifred Grainger spoke the name softly and looked at Evelyn with an odd light in her eyes. 'I'll wait for Danny, he knows I'm here, he knows I'm here, eh, lass?'

'Ay, he kens all about you,' Evelyn nodded. She looked at Douglas Grainger, 'Did it make any difference to her when Davie came home? Doesn't she know he's here?'

'He might as well no' exist, Evelyn. When she heard about Danny her mind just seemed to snap, she grew more and more into herself till now I have to feed her and tend her as if she was a bairn. She won't get better.'

'But Davie will?' She tried to keep her voice calm but everything hinged on that brief question.

'Ay, the doctors say it will take time – but he'll get better.'

Evelyn never forgot the terrible sad strangeness of that afternoon. When it finally came to an end one part of her longed to escape the claustrophobic prison of the cramped room, the other half wanted to stay by David's side and care for him as he so badly needed her care and love. She also longed to relieve Douglas Grainger of his dreadful burdens. It must have been bad enough looking after a woman who had once given him the intimate companionship of a wife and who was now no more than a bairn living out her fantasies in a half-world of dreaming and watching. But now he had David to contend with as well and, taking his hands warmly in hers, she said quietly, 'I'll come back, as often as I can, I've left some things, scones baked by my mother and a few bit things I made myself.'

'You're a good lass, Evelyn,' he told her gruffly, 'I'm right glad my son found your like, there's no' many would look at what you looked at today and want to come back for more.'

'I love Davie,' she said simply.

He seemed to have heard, for when she went over to him he reached out to pull her in close and buried his head into the pit of her belly. She stood stock still, afraid that one move from her might frighten him back into his previous semi-comatose condition. But he remained where he was, burying himself deeper and deeper into her till she imagined that he must surely feel the heart of his own child beating there inside her womb.

'Davie, dearest Davie,' she whispered huskily, reaching down to stroke his hair. It was harsh and dry, no longer the soft warm brown head that she had kissed and caressed in the days of blithe loving when the carefree beauty of their youth had allowed neither thought nor heed to things that were ugly and dead.

At the feel of her touch upon him his shoulders trembled; great dry, painful sobs broke from him and he cried into the still, quiet oasis of her flesh. 'I should have died! I never wanted you to see me like this! I never wanted . . .'

She took his head to her breast and allowed him to weep till, spent, he lay back to look at her, his empty burning eyes once more receding inwards as if gazing at phantoms flitting in and out of his mind.

Douglas Grainger's hand on her shoulder pulled her back to reality. 'It's worked, lass,' he told her with such gratitude she felt it wouldn't be wrong to take him and hold him and soothe away the hurt of him, so patiently and silently endured. 'It's the first response I've seen in him since he returned home.'

'Ay, it's worked, Douglas Grainger.' She wanted to laugh, to share her small, triumphant joy with him, and that must have been there in his own mind too for he took her to the huge, manly wall of his chest and squeezed her so hard she gasped and laughed and finally broke away panting to say, 'Faith! Look at the time, Violet will be out there champing at the bit! Goodbye, Douglas Grainger, my thanks to you for writing that letter. You'll never ken how much I've longed to see Davie and though none o' us would have wished it to be like this, he's alive, we have that to be thankful for.'

It was dark when they got back to Dunmarnock, a soft darkness that still retained some of the gloaming above the low hills to the west. Violet went rushing away indoors to get herself 'tooshed-up' for seeing Jock Pringle while Evelyn told Burton she would walk home as it was such a fine evening.

She had barely taken two steps away from the Big House when a familiar rustling sound made her stop in her tracks, the hairs crawling on the back of her neck. She waited, her heart strange and swift in the breast of her, and when Effie finally stepped out of the shadows she knew that the parlourmaid had deliberately prolonged her appearance.

'Oh, it's yourself, Evelyn Grant.' Effie had the audacity to sound surprised. 'Just back from Glasgow, I see. How was your man? Pleased to see you, I hope.' Her tone of voice suggested otherwise and Evelyn shrank away from the cold, hard note of it.

'Ay, I'm back, Effie,' she returned stiffly, 'your powers of observation astound me though I shouldna really be surprised. Anyone who goes creeping about the way you do is bound to see and hear things that normal folks might likely miss.'

Effie did not rise to the bait, so eager was she to say the things that had fermented in her mind ever since the two younger girls had driven way with Burton in the pony cart.

'You're no' exactly bubbling over wi' joy, are you, Evelyn? And after all that time o' waiting to see your man. My, my, you and he didna fight, I hope, and the pair o' you wi' such a happy event just round the corner. It's a good way to get a man, eh, Evie? And whether he's pleased about it or no' he'll take you to the altar in the end. It's the way o' things, especially when mothers and fathers

146

are involved and no' wanting a bastard to be born into the family. I've heard tell there's many a pregnant bride has gone to the altar just to keep a good name from getting tarnished.'

Evelyn's face burned and her fingers itched to slap that slit-eyed pale moon of a thing leering at her out of the darkness. She made to walk on before her temper got the better of her, but Effie's hand shot out to hold her back.

'Wait you, Evelyn,' she implored playfully, trying to inject pleasantness into her voice, 'I'm no' for spreading it about that you and that common wee keelie, Raggy Annie, cooked up your wee fables about husbands and wedding rings in order to show you in a good light. She's the sort to understand that kind o' thing, I havena a doubt she opened her own legs to a man before the meat was even half-cooked for she's the type to start breeding while one foot is still in the cradle.'

Evelyn could hardly believe the evidence of her own ears. She had never heard such coarseness of tongue, not even from the hard-drinking men of the farmtouns, and with a shiver of disgust she realised that Effie's prim and correct ways had all along hidden a nature that might have sprung from the gutters of the meanest alley.

She began to walk swiftly away, an odd frightening sensation curling in her belly. She saw now that Effie hadn't waylaid her merely for the sake of tormenting her. She was leading up to something and Evelyn did not wish to wait and find out what it was. The little wooded knoll ahead of her was a pleasant place to look at in the kindly light of day, but now it seemed full of menace, the black twisted trunks of ancient oaks spread grasping gnarled fingers; gnomes and hobgoblins and all manner of fabulous creatures escaped from the bounds of her imagination and seemed to come leaping out of the shadows towards her. A shiver of terror crept on her flesh and went trembling into her very marrow so that she jumped when Effie's voice came at her back, again with that forced jocosity polishing its edge.

'Evelyn, Evelyn, dinna run from me like a tinker from death, I'm no' trying to scare you, I just wanted you to know that I'm grateful to you and would like to thank you.'

'Thank me, Effie?'

'Ay, for showing me the way. I wasna right sure before but now I know what I'm going to do. Sinning will no' come easy to a well-brought-up lass like myself, but I see now you have to chase after what you want in the world in order to get it. It took a tink's daughter to show me the way and for that I salute you — oh, and Evelyn, I'd like us to be friends from now on, it is no use bickering and fighting wi' someone as helpful as you have been to me.'

'Friends?' Evelyn's voice was flat and dull. In normal circumstances, anyone who had called her father a tinker would have had their hair pulled out by now but Effie's conversation was anything but normal. Evelyn could feel the evil of the girl all around her, black, ruthless, terrifying. She wanted only to take heel and run but instinct warned her that to show fear to the older girl would only invite further ridicule, both now and in the future.

'Ay, friends.' Effie spoke evenly but with a peculiar heavy vibrancy in her tones. 'Oh, and that goes for your sister as well. I know fine she's been trying her hardest to get her clooks into Major Baird, but I dinna mind any o' that now. It's me he'll want, ay, and in the end, it's me who will get him.'

At that moment a wonderfully normal sound infiltrated the gloom. Jock Pringle came whistling along the path, kicking up the leaves as he approached.

'Evening, ladies,' he greeted cheerily.

'It's you, Jock.' The words quavered weakly out of Evelyn's throat. 'Violet said she was seeing you tonight.'

'Ay, I'd better get along or she'll accuse me o' being late. Violet might be easy-going in some ways but lateness she canna abide.' He paused and glanced at Effie. 'My, my, Effie, here you are, just you and Evie, all cosy together in the dark and here was me believing you went to bed to read your Bible at set of sun. At least, that's what you led me to think when you refused to spend your nights wi' me.'

'Rabbit-man!' she muttered under her breath and went hurrying away back to the house.

Jock Pringle stood looking after her. 'You wouldna think it to look at her, but underneath these starches walks a Venus. Her face might no' be up to much but her body makes up for it.'

'Oh, and how do you come to ken that, Jock Pringle?'

'Because I saw it, that's how I know.'

'You *saw* it?'

'Ay, the one and only time she came out wi' me. We ended up in the chaumer above the stable and one thing led to another. Just when I thought she would slap my face she gave a weird sort o' groan and began tearing off her clothes. I tell you this much, Evie, I'm no' the sort of bloke to slap chance in the face but I was taken aback at the sight o' Miss Prim and Proper lying there in the straw wriggling about like a worm. If it had been any other lass I would hae leapt at the chance but this was Effie, you understand, Effie wi' the orphanage upbringing and that stiff wi' correctness I often had the notion she would snap wi' its weight.'

'I ken fine what you mean, Jock,' nodded Evelyn when he paused to take breath, his eyes wide in his face, as if he was seeing in his mind's eye the vision of Effie attempting to seduce him in the cobwebby twilight of the chaumer.

'She was full and ripe and ready for a man,' he went on musingly, 'but something in me held back from her, a kind o' half-fear o' this wild lookin' cratur lickin' her lips and holding out her arms to me wi' fingers that beckoned and clawed at the air. I know you willna tell on me, Evie, but I upped and ran out that place feeling a' the witches o' hell were at my back, and I didna stop running till I reached the safety o' my ain house. Effie hated me after that, she wouldna look the road I was on and called me a' the dirt o' the day behind my back. She'll never tell o' it and knows pride will hold my ain tongue – and it has – until the night. When I came by just now I got the feeling she was harassing you so I telt you about her just to let you see she's a dangerous woman under a' that starch and to be careful o' her. You'll no' let on will you, Evie?' he repeated, anxious now that the fire of his tongue had burned itself out.

'No, Jock, I willna let on and I'll be careful – you can be sure o' that.'

Andrew Baird was wakened by the most exquisite sensation of pleasure pulsing in his loins; heavy with the effect of last night's sleeping sedative he was confused but had no time to try and collect his thoughts; fast on that first erotic feeling came others; an awareness of cold and heat; of someone there in his room, doing things to him that were quite outwith the normal concept of decent human behaviour.

His heart bounded into his throat, he became fully and intensely awake. Impressions piled in on him. His blankets had been pushed aside, he lay in a state of semi-nakedness, the morning flowed over him in chilly waves – except on the lower half of his body where soft, burning flesh met with his own.

Struggling to sit up, he saw in the pre-light of dawn the shape of a woman crouched over him, her full, firm breasts pressed down on his throbbing hardness, drawing from him wave after wave of sensual excitement. She was moving herself back and forth, back and forth in an oddly primitive motion that was both fascinating and frightening . . .

Recognition leapt in on him. 'Effie!' He spoke her name in a gasping protest and tried to struggle free of her. But it was too late. She was on him, on top of him, her hands pinning him down, her knees imprisoning his thighs in a painfully powerful grip. But he was beyond feeling pain, beyond feeling anything but her warm moistness pushing down hard on him, her flowing buttocks pounding back against his knees, pounding, pounding till he no longer wanted to break free but only wished for a release from that ecstasy that was very nearly a pain.

'Relax, Major.' She spoke for the first time, the words jerking out of her in small breathless gasps. 'This is what you need. I told you I would look after you, I told you . . .'

Her tongue was washing over her lips, her back was arched, animal-like moans broke from her throat – he stiffened – relaxed – gave himself up to his unbearable agony, but even at the height of his rapture some separate part of him knew loathing for himself and repugnance for her so black and bitter he could feel the taste of it in his mouth.

When at last she was done with him he was drenched in perspiration and he was aware of a nausea rising in his belly.

She lay beside him, struggling to regain her breath, her mouth hot and damp against his ear. 'There now,' she rasped, 'I knew I did the right thing coming to your room. I'm no' the starched miss everybody takes me for, eh – Major? That frozen bitch you think you love could never give you what I've just given.'

'If you mean Grace you had better watch what you say . . .' He paused. Grace! How could he face her after this? How could he look at that beautiful sweet face knowing what he had done, who he had done it with?

'Never mind her now, Major, it's me you'll want and want again.' She was regaining her control in no uncertain manner. 'And if you have it in your mind to try and make me lose my position here you had better think again. I would haunt you, Major, no' as a ghost haunts but in the flesh, there at every turn, and forbye there's your parents to think about. I wouldna like to do anything to harm them for they've aye been good to me but if need be I

151

wouldna think twice about it. I want you, Andrew Baird, and I mean to have you, by fair means or foul, it makes no difference to me.'

He stared at her, at the twist of her mouth, the gleam in her narrow eyes, and he knew she was perfectly capable of carrying out her threats without compunction. 'Get out,' he threw at her, 'get out of my room and never dare appear to me in this manner again!'

A sardonic smile flitted across her sallow face. Wrapping herself in her dressing gown she padded from his room like some soft-footed cat, closing the door soundlessly behind her.

He lay unmoving on the bed, his face bathed in sweat, his eyes staring unseeingly ahead. Dawn was on the horizon, light filtered in through the drapes, softening the shadows that minutes before had crouched in secret corners, as if waiting to pounce on him and carry him back to that dark world of faceless men and fires that seared the peace from his soul.

He didn't sleep again. Morning brought Effie back into his room, the Effie everyone knew, wooden-faced, dour, setting his tray on the bedside table, drawing back his curtains.

She was efficient and starched to the last apron frill, clean and white and fresh-smelling. He stared at her and at once saw the difference in her now that she was standing close by. Beneath the unsmiling exterior she was excited, smug as a cat who has stolen the cream. He could sense the tremendous effort she was exerting not to crow over him. It was as if she had won some personal triumph known only to herself.

'You'll be feeling better this morning, Major?' She leaned over him to plump his pillows, deliberately allowed her breasts to brush his shoulder. She stood back, a slight flush staining her sallow skin, her narrowed eyes reminding him of a vixen he had once watched pouncing on its prey. 'Ay, and you look better too – Andrew.' She used his Christian name like a trophy, somehow managing to imbue a husky note into her hard voice.

When she had gone he left his food untouched and drank only his tea. He felt soiled and degraded, his hips were tender where she had gripped them with her knees.

Rising from his bed he went to the window. The sky held all the promise of a glorious spring day. From this elevated position he could see the snow-capped peak of Ben Lomand and the distant hills of Argyll, soft and blue against a honey-tinted sky; the parklands of the estate swept green and umber on every side, grazed by sheep and cows, broken by greening woodlands and little white houses whose chimneys puffed hazy-blue woodsmoke.

He took a deep breath. Life was full of promise and sweetness. At last he was emerging from the shadows that had darkened his days for so long. Very soon now he was going to manage one of his father's business projects but only till he had saved enough capital to buy himself a good stable. His ambition was to breed horses. As a boy he had haunted the Dunmarnock stables and loved riding but had never gone out with the hunt. He hated it, all that noise, the unholy howling of hounds – the poor bloody fox, running its heart out only to be torn to bits in the end . . .

A light tap on his door and Christine came in, dressed for riding. She looked fresh and bonny and so normal he wanted to reach out and touch her fair face with his hands – quite presentable-looking hands now that the operation scars were fading . . . Then he remembered and his hands fell back to his sides.

Surely she must see the stain of self-loathing that suddenly sprung to his pale face. He drew back from her, knowing that he would never feel clean in her sight again.

'Father and I are going out in fifteen minutes,' she greeted him, 'and I wondered – as it's such a beautiful morning – if you would like to come with us. The fresh air would do you good. You used to love your early morning ride.'

'Thanks, Chris, but I think I'll stay around here for a bit, I have some papers I want to go through.'

She took a step forward. 'Andy, are you all right? You look a bit — odd — and you haven't touched your breakfast.'

'I'm fine, Chris, really, I've just gotten used to lazing around in the mornings but all that will change soon. You go along and enjoy yourself.'

She went to the door. 'I'll see you later then. You know we promised Gavin and Grace that we'd drive them into Renfrew?'

'Yes, I know, I haven't forgotten. Go along now, I want to get dressed.'

The door closed on her; unseeingly he stared at it. Later that week she was leaving Dunmarnock for the north, taking with her four young men from The Grange, one of them Gavin Galbraith to whom she had given every encouragement in his fight back to strength. His new artificial limbs had been fitted, she had gone to The Grange every other day to coax, berate, bully him into using them so that now he was getting along with only one stick. She was good at helping young men like Gavin, young men like himself. Ever since the start of the war she had thrown herself wholeheartedly into the task of rehabilitating the war wounded, she and her friends succeeding so well they had become much in demand, both here and in the Highlands. Her fiancé, Guthrie Wilson Kerr, youngest son of the Marquis and Marchioness of Inverbrora, was with the Second Battalion of the Black Watch.

She had seen little of him in the last few years but wasn't the sort of girl to sit back and wait for life to come to her. Rather she went at it full tilt and with an enthusiasm that brooked no nonsense from anyone.

His throat tightened. He would miss her, God how he would miss her! She had been a dear and faithful companion to him since that hellish time a year ago now. Panic seized him. How could he cope without her? Sometimes she got on his nerves with her determined attitude to whatever she tackled but he had needed the strength of her in his life ... Mentally he shook himself. What kind of a man was he? Depending on a woman to prop him up, using her shoulder to lean on and cry on whenever he needed it? It was high time he was independent ...

Down below, Christine came from the house with the Colonel close at her back. Both of them looked up and waved. He returned a sort of half-salute and drew back, as if to hide himself in the folds of the curtains, anything to escape that keen, searching gaze of his father's whose long-sight was so devastatingly accurate. He wanted to rush down and go with them, to talk and laugh and quicken to the feel of his horse beneath him. Yesterday morning he could have done that with an easy mind — now ...

The memory of Effie came to him, her face was a blur in his mind — but her body! Who would have thought such a starched miss could possess a body like that? A small, unwilling thrill of excitement trembled through him. Her voice floated into his mind, saying things he hadn't thought he had absorbed ... *'It's me you'll want and want again.'*

'No!' he shouted aloud to the empty room and, sinking down onto the bed, he put his face in his hands and wept.

PART THREE

Summer 1918

Chapter Twelve

Croft Donald was a lively place, full of bustle and life from the first crack of dawn to the evenings of cosy peat fires and Nellie singing untunefully but happily as she went about, seeing the children off to bed, or out there in the dairy shed, turning the butter churn, making pats of cheese.

She had written to Evelyn, insisting that she come to Kenneray to have her baby, and so Evelyn had travelled to the Western Highlands, accompanied by Grace who was long overdue some leave from The Grange and had wanted to spend it with her sisters. They had received a rousing welcome, children and animals had swarmed around them, though Wee Col, who had gone to live with Nellie after her marriage to Kenneth Cameron Mor, was shy at first of his sisters and just stood regarding them out of big, blue, wondering eyes, his thumb jammed into his mouth, the fingers of his other hand curling themselves into the ruff of Mirk, a three-year-old Border Collie who had, from the beginning, attached himself to the little boy as if sensing that he wasn't the same as other children. For Col, the only son of Jamie and Maggie Grant, had been born mentally retarded and was only now, at the age of nine, learning to read and write under the patient guidance of Kenneth's mother who had been an infant school teacher before her marriage.

Of all the people in his life he adored Nellie best and when she had left King's Croft for Kenneray he had pined so much for his big sister she had eventually taken him to live at Croft Donald where he had thrived and learned and was altogether so happy neither Maggie nor Jamie had the heart to take him back, even if their present situation had made it possible.

Calum Alasdair Cameron, better known as Cal, was the same age as Maggie's son and had, from the start, loved and protected his small friend. Cal was a sturdy, handsome boy with eyes and hair almost the same colour as Col's, though there the resemblance ended. Cal had the wonderful strong physique of his father, the same thundering hearty laugh, while his friend was small and underdeveloped with an introverted nature and a dreamy, sometimes vacant expression in his eyes. His speech was limited and stilted, he had only ever managed to stutter out the names of those nearest and dearest to him, to pronounce with difficulty the everyday objects of his surroundings. Most people were too impatient to try and decipher his laboured tongue, even members of his own family had often found it hard going, but both Nellie and Cal had always somehow managed to make sense of his ramblings and were able to carry out his simple requests.

But he had grown bigger and bonnier since moving to Croft Donald. Grace and Evelyn saw the change at once and were about to rush forward and embrace him when Nellie said softly, 'Bide a minute, give the wee mannie time to gather his wits. See if he remembers you before you smother him wi' your love and kisses.'

With scant patience the sisters held back while little Isla Nell giggled as if at some wonderful joke and Cal fidgeted and longed to show the visitors the dainty little butter pats Nellie had allowed him to make in their honour. Another minute ticked by, fraught with anxiety on both sides, and then Col began to chuckle, a chuckle that grew in volume till it became a deep, fat, belly-shaking laugh, the like of which had been peculiar to him from infancy and which was so infectious no one who had ever heard it could resist joining in. The uninhibited peals filled the kitchen, pouring from the happy, blithe heart of him without restraint.

Throwing back his red-gold head as if to give his

lungs more room, he giggled, and laughed and wiped his streaming eyes then he held out his arms and shouted, 'Gwace! Evie!', which fairly sent them rushing over to hug him and lift him and birl him round and round till he was dizzy and dazed but still laughing and saying their names over and over.

And then Kenneth Cameron Mor came striding in, bringing with him the scent of the fields and no wonder Nellie scolded before he was halfway through the door: bits of hay and grass adhered to his Cameron tartan kilt, earth and dung flew off his boots and scattered themselves all over the clean stone floor which Nellie had scrubbed and scrubbed in honour of the visitors.

'It will clean, Nell, lass,' he cried, propping his crook against the door and rushing forward to scoop her into his arms and place a resounding kiss on her indignantly parted lips which brought the colour rising to her high cheekbones, though sweet was that kiss and fine she liked it but not in front of all the delighted eyes taking it in.

Kenneth Mor was a fine figure of a man, towering more than six feet high with eyes that were the cool blue of a Highland loch, though when he was angry a wildness came into them that made them the dark stormy grey of an Atlantic in fury. His face was strong but finely honed and proud was he of his high-bridged nose with the wee bit twist to it as befitted his surname which was 'Camshron' in Gaelic and meant 'crooked nose'.

His kilt, which he always wore, swirled about great hairy knees while the sark of him lay open at the throat revealing a magnificent expanse of chest matted with hairs of red-gold that met up with his ebullient silken beard.

Without further ado he clasped the two younger Grant girls to his heart in a breath-robbing bear hug, the big, booming laugh of him thundering out of his huge lungs as he swung them round and round the kitchen, never once allowing their feet to touch the floor, the laughter of them bubbling out and never stopping when finally he set them down to stagger a bit in regaining their balance.

'You're bonnier than ever, Grace,' he bellowed. 'As for you, Evie lass, you've filled out a bittie since last I clapped eyes on you.'

She looked at him quickly, wondering wildly if he didn't yet know ... But surely Nellie must have told him ...

Seeing her face, he winked and grinned and she knew he was only trying to put her at ease, and so he did, not just her but everyone else. They were smiling at his wit, including Iain and Irene, his parents, who had come in at his back and were standing around looking a wee bit shy till that moment when tension broke and the children ran to swarm over their father, even Col who now thought of him as such, all of them in a ferment of delight when he scooped them into his arms and jigged with them around the room.

And that was the sisters' welcome to Croft Donald, a wonderful day for everyone, a day filled with lark song and sunshine that sparkled on the distant ocean and sent the lambs so daft with the pleasure of it they skipped and called and jumped over their staid, recumbent mothers in frisky gangs.

Croft Donald was the sort of house that could comfortably accommodate a fair number of people. Leading off from the large, airy kitchen was a scullery and a larder. A short, dim hallway led to a back bedroom and a parlour with views to the beach and the sea. Upstairs were four more bedrooms and into one of these piled Grace and Evelyn, giggling with the rapture of the moment, throwing themselves down on the enormous, double, feather bed to snuggle their heads into their folded arms and from that relaxed position to look beyond the window to the shimmering blue of the Atlantic Ocean.

'Ach, it's so good to see Nellie again,' sighed Grace. 'I didna ken just how much I had missed her till I glimpsed her waiting with the cart at the station.'

'Ay, and did you ever dream such cart tracks existed as the ones leading to Kenneray? Bumps and stones and

162

breaking bones but our Nellie no' even noticing and gabbling away nineteen to the dozen wi' the words rattling in her throat.'

'She's so different now, Evie, blithe and bonny wi' her fair skin glowing and the eyes of her so big and bright for love o' Kenneth and the bairns.'

'Ay, she's changed a lot, Grace, but there's still plenty o' the old Nellie there and aye will be. I ken fine she means to have a good talk wi' me and that I dinna mind just as long as it doesn't turn into a lecture.'

She had guessed right. That night, everyone went early to bed but Nellie hung back to the last and grabbed a hold of Evelyn as she was about to make good her escape. But she needn't have worried; there were no barbs in Nellie's tongue as they sat cosy by the fire, peat sparks crackling in the lum, the clock, the dogs, the cats, ticking, snoring, dreaming, according to their nature. The wind from the sea rattled the sashes, the skylarks were still trilling high above the machair, somewhere in the distance a curlew bubbled its golden song into the sigh of the ocean's breath.

Evelyn held out a bag of 'black strippit balls' and they both sat for a while, saying little, sucking peacefully at their sweeties, till Nellie smiled at her little sister and said mischievously, 'Faith! These are as hard as the rocks out there by the reefs! If it's your intention to hold my tongue by feeding me your minty boulders, you can think again, you sly wee whittrock.' Her face softened. Evelyn looked so young sitting there, the firelight glinting in her hair, the small lithe fingers of her playing nervously with the cameo at her throat, her body thrown awkwardly back on the chair to better accommodate the huge swelling of her belly.

'Ach, Evie,' Nellie sighed and shook her head, 'what have you done wi' your life? You that was aye so quick and clever wi' your books and your writings? I had thought to see you making something o' yourself. Now here you are, carrying the bairn o' some young soldier who only ever cared about what he could get from you.'

'Dinna you speak like that, Nellie!' Evelyn cried, anger springing swift in her breast. 'I love Davie and he loves me! He'll get better and he'll want his bairn as much as he'll want me!'

'Och, dinna fash, quine, I'm only sad to see you wasting your youth on things that could well have waited a whilie, but Mother was right about you, she aye said your heart ruled your head and now look where it's got you.'

'Dinna rub it in, Nellie, I hate myself enough for what I've done to me and mine but it's too late now to turn back the clock.'

'Ay, quine, what's done is done, there's no going back now and I'm no' going to lecture you on the rights and wrongs. Three years ago I might have had plenty to say but now I would be a hypocrite if I started preaching to you about the lusts o' the flesh for I was no saint when I married Kenneth. 'Tis the babby you have to think about now. Would to God our positions were reversed but fate is no' a fair provider so I'll just have to bide my time a whilie longer.'

Evelyn was forcibly struck by the irony of the situation. Here was she, unmarried, only nineteen, as yet unreconciled to David or his child, and here was Nellie who pined for a baby of her own but hadn't yet conceived. More than two and a half years had passed since her marriage and still Nellie waited, saying little but fretting inside herself to give Kenneth a bairn of their own flesh and blood.

She took a deep breath and stared at her sister, her eyes wide and frightened as she blurted out, 'Oh, Nellie! I've never told anyone this but I'm telling you though you might no' understand what I have to say. I dinna want this thing that lives and breathes inside o' me! I never wanted it and I'm feared because I think there must be something wrong wi' me.'

'When it comes you'll want it,' Nellie assured softly.

164

'You feel as you do because you had to thole the worry o' it on your own but once it's here that will all change.'

After that the talk turned to other things and then Nellie asked, 'What about our Grace? She seems better than she was last time I saw her but it's difficult sometimes to ken what lies behind those great eyes o' hers.'

Evelyn told her about Andrew Baird. 'He's besotted by Grace, his eyes just fasten on to her as if there was no one but her in the world. I thought to encourage their friendship but Grace got mad at me and told me to mind my own business. It's strange, Nellie, but she talks about Gordon as if he was still alive and says she believes he'll come back to her one day.'

'Oh, my darling sister!' Nellie's eyes were moist with love for the one amongst them who had incurred in her the least wrath in girlhood days. They all adored Grace but Nellie and Evelyn adored her the most. 'She'll never get over Gordon. He was such a fine big chiel wi' a heart o' gold. If I could have chosen a man for Grace I would have chosen him. I can understand how she feels but she'll never go forward if she keeps on looking back at the past. It's no' healthy and she'll never find happiness and she of all people is the one who needed happiness in her life. She's never been strong, Evie, yet she gives everything o' herself and asks little in return.'

It was well past midnight when Nellie finally smoored the fire and saw Evelyn to her room by the light of an oil lamp. Grace was fast asleep when Evelyn crept quietly in. Despite her long day she wasn't in the least bit tired and for a long time she stood at the window, staring out at the scattered white houses of Kenneray lying peacefully under a night awash with stars. She felt oddly at peace with herself after her talk with Nellie, then the child lurched and struggled inside her womb and suddenly her peaceful mood was gone. Something strange and sad curled into her senses and she knew a terrible fear now that her time was almost here. It wasn't just the physical pain she was afraid of though God knew that was terror enough to face. But that kind of pain would pass and would soon be forgotten. The dread that seized her was for the changes about to take place in her life, for now and for all time. Never again would she be an entity unto herself and the thought of that alone accelerated her heartbeat.

She remembered the night Wee Col had been born, her mother's cries of pain, the long hours of loneliness lying in bed, waiting and wondering and finally creeping downstairs to the kitchen to share her apprehensions with Grace. She had been ten years old then and knew little of the facts of life beyond what she had witnessed in stable and byre. Later she had asked Florrie, who had come right out with the truth and had laughed when Evelyn refused to believe that her mother and father behaved in the same way as the beasts in the field. Her attitude to her father changed after that. No longer was he merely the smiling, dark-eyed being who coal-carried her up to bed and kissed her goodnight. He had become less a fun-loving playmate, more of a man-creature with secrets he kept hidden from the world except those he shared with her mother in the still, quiet hours of the night.

Now all that was done with, the mystery had been gently explored, finally exploited, and now there was only herself and the stranger within, one that wouldn't remain so for very much longer. Soon, soon, it would show itself and the final mystery would be over, the flesh of her flesh would be revealed and no more would she think of it as some dark, faceless creature that had warped her visions of herself and Davie lying snug together in the cool, black cavern of The Devil's Door.

She shuddered. If only David was here. She had gone to see him several times since that first shocked visit but though he was responding little by little it would be a long time before he came to the full awakening of his being.

Exhausted suddenly, she went wearily to bed. It had

been a long time since she had made any sort of entry into her diary. Now she wrote briefly:

May 28th 1918. I'm at Croft Donald in Kenneray. The night is dark and quiet, Grace sleeps peacefully in the next bed. Davie's child will come soon, and I'm afraid to sleep, the violent stirrings are with me all the time now and I fancy I'll wake up and find it there, so eagerly it struggles to get out. I don't want to shut my eyes in case it decides to surprise me so I'll stay awake as long as I can . . .

She was asleep almost before the last word was written. In her dreams she seemed to hear the silent cries of her child, weeping, weeping, in the warm, dark shell of her womb, as if it sensed the harshness of that other world it must soon enter.

The June days were long and golden and it seemed there was no night in the fragrant world that was Kenneray. The larks sang all day and every day and well into the small hours of morning as well; the machair bloomed with a myriad of wild flowers so that if viewed from afar it appeared as plains of gold that reached down to shimmering white beaches lapped by petticoats of surf billowing out from the azure blue of the western ocean; from the wooded hill corries the notes of the cuckoo echoed and rebounded till it seemed the rock faces vied with one another to see which could produce the loudest song of summer.

Kenneth Mor and his father took advantage of the good spell of weather and were up each morning at the crack of dawn for an hour or two in the fields before coming home to a breakfast of porridge and new-laid eggs and thick, crusty bread spread with crowdie cheese and home-made butter. With the enthusiasm of crofting men well-pleased with promising crops, they ate and talked with rude enjoyment and never seemed to notice that the womenfolk were quieter than usual with nothing much to add to that which was already said. The day they had all awaited had come and gone with nothing to show for it but nerves growing tauter by the hour and a strangely silent Evelyn who smiled and spoke automatically without any enthusiasm at all.

More than a week over her time, she was heavy and bloated and arose from her bed each morning to gaze hopefully at the horizon for a sign of cool cloud, but every dawn was cloudless, every gloaming a blaze of crimson that spilled into the sea till it looked like a vast lake of molten blood. The treeless machair offered little or no shade and so she spent a great deal of her time in the house, finding solace there from the beating sun but none at all from Nellie whose anxiety had made her revert to the Nellie of old. Round the house she flounced, sweeping, scrubbing, baking, cooking, taking her temper out on the cats whom she sent packing from her kitchen with broom, mop, anything that came to hand.

In spite of her discomfort Evelyn smiled a little and often felt herself to be back in King's Croft with Nellie fleering about the place, going daft altogether if one single footprint, be it animal or human, dared to mar her clean floors.

Grace was her usual serene self, taking the children for walks when they came home from school, wandering off into the gloaming with Irene Cameron who was only too glad to escape her daughter-in-law's flashing eyes and quick tongue.

'I've never seen the lass like this,' she confided to Grace. 'Anyone would think it was she who was expecting a bairn.'

'Would that it was the case,' sighed Grace. 'But she's anxious about Evie and maybe minding the times when our Mam gave birth to one bairn after another and her a bit quine having to see to the house and maybe assisting at the deliveries forbye.'

'Ay, life hasna been easy for Nellie,' said Irene thoughtfully. 'She often seems older than her years and can even put me in my place wi' her sharp tongue.'

'Oh, she's a lot better now,' laughed Grace. 'At King's Croft she ruled the roost and could easily send Father away wi' his tail between his legs wi' just a few choice words. Only Mam could ever stand up to her and I wish she was here now to give Nellie a piece o' her mind but, och! she's my sister and I love her and can thole the way she is now, knowing it willna be for long.'

But even Grace lost her temper when Nellie barked at her for allowing one of the dogs to coorie into bed with her one night.

'Ach, Grace! I thought wi' you being a nurse you would have had more sense!' Nellie ranted. 'Peg is aye rolling in the dung and seems aye to have fleas and I'll no' stand for such a thing in *my* clean beds!'

'Och, Nellie!' Grace retorted, her black eyes flashing. 'In the state o' mind you're in the now there's nothing that pleases you and if you go on as you're doing I'm leaving Kenneray and good riddance too.'

She banged away downstairs, Nellie muttering and scolding at her back, but when they stepped into the kitchen all enmity between them was instantly forgotten.

Evelyn was stretched out on the inglenook, her face twisted in pain and neither of her two sisters needed to look twice to tell them she had gone into the first stages of labour.

Kenneth Mor was instantly dispatched to fetch the doctor who resided seven miles along the coast, but the doctor was out on a case and there was nothing else for it but to leave a message and come all the way back, stopping off on the way at the Clachan of Kenneray to oust old Jenny Ryan from her rickety garden seat where she was wont to spend a greater part of her day, gossiping to neighbours while she soaked up the sunshine, not to mention sips of rum, and smoking her clay pipe which was kept well-filled by the good folk of Kenneray to whom she administered her natural medicines along with oddly primitive little rituals that sounded good and harmed only those who objected to such 'heathenisms'.

There was one like Jenny Ryan in every Highland village, one in every street or close, nurse, midwife, faith healer, their knowledge gathered from vague sources, from mothers who had passed it on, or simply from the vast experience of age and wisdom along life's way.

Jenny Wren, as she was known in the locality, hailed Kenneth Mor with delight and sprachled willingly into the cart beside him. She had known him when he was a lad in short trousers and was apt to treat him as if he was still wet behind the ears.

'Your sister-in-law you say? Havin' her first bairn? Well, get along, laddie, and dinna sit blethering. We might be in time for one o' your Nellie's dinners for it can be gey long wi' a first and I never work well wi' an empty belly.'

She got her dinner, her tea as well, and when, by supper-time there was no sign of the baby arriving, and she heard the rattling of dishes, she came spryly downstairs to sit herself by the fire and partake with great relish of a small feast of oatcakes and cheese followed by slices of dumpling and several scones.

'There's nothing wrong wi' your stomach, Jenny Wren,' commented Nellie acidly, pouring at the old woman's request, her third cup of tea which she instantly laced with rum.

'Indeed no, lass,' nodded Jenny Wren placidly. 'All my kin had appetites as big as horses' and none the worse for it except maybe occasionally when out would come the castor oil or maybe a medicine o' my ain mither's recipe that was better than anything else in all the land.'

'Och, never mind all that now,' Nellie said irritably.

'Surely the doctor should be here by this time – unless he's lying drunk in a byre somewhere,' she added scornfully.

'Ach, dinna exaggerate, Mistress Cameron,' returned the old lady placidly. 'Joe McDonald can take a dram wi' the best, I know that better than anybody, but he's never the worse o' it and will likely be held up at the McTavish croft. Jessie was warned no' to have another after her seventh but she lets that man o' hers do what he likes wi' her and will likely be having a bad time o' it. But you have no need to fear, I'm here and I'm all you need, so stop cacklin' like a broody hen and take a sup o' tea while you can.'

The menfolk said nothing and ate very little, all their former lightheartedness having departed in the drama of the moment.

Upstairs, Grace was administering to her younger sister, so cool and efficient it was difficult to believe she was the same tranquil young woman everyone knew.

'I canna bear it, Grace,' cried Evelyn, her eyes dazed with pain, her racked body awash with perspiration. 'Will it come soon? Will it?'

'Wheesht, wheesht,' soothed Grace, her lovely eyes filled with compassion for Evelyn's plight but the nurse in her not giving anything away. 'Try and relax, Evie, and just you do as I tell you.'

Nellie came in to stand rather helplessly watching Grace bathing the patient's brow. For once she was lost for words and was relieved when Col's voice floated from the landing, requesting a drink of water which she went to fetch with the utmost alacrity.

Grace smiled faintly. 'She would give anything to be in your place, Evie.'

The remark brought an answering smile to Evelyn's hot face, 'Ay, Grace, anything, that was why she flew out the room just now, Wee Col just might die altogether if he doesna get that drink o' water.'

She had no breath left for further foolishness, her body felt as if it was being torn apart, every shred of her strength, every part of her mind, was concentrated on her agonising struggle to rid her being of its excruciating pain – except one small part that pined for Davie – and oddly enough for Gillan's sensitive dark face conveying to her the depth of his caring.

The child burst from her body, an enormous boy, weighing all of twelve and a half pounds, the lungs of him filling with air before anyone had time to even realise he had been born at all, so swift was his gushing entry into the world. Grace and Jenny Wren between them delivered him from his mother, with Nellie a stunned onlooker, quite unable to move one finger in those first dramatic moments. Only the sight of Evelyn's sweating strained young face galvanised her into action and her limbs took flight, carrying her over to the bed to cradle the girl's head to her bosom while she uttered soothing words of reassurance.

It was just going on midnight of 9 June 1918. A moment or two later the grandfather clock in the hall chimed out the hour as if proclaiming to the world that Evelyn McKenzie Grant had been delivered of a son.

Grace and Jenny Wren were jubilant, the latter chuckling triumphantly, one gnarled old hand going to her pocket to withdraw a hip flask from which she swigged a generous amount of rum, before proceeding to assist in the washing and cleaning of both Evelyn and the bairn, till one was happed in a fresh white cotton nightgown and the other in hippens and a long 'goonie' which Nellie had fashioned herself as soon as she had heard the child was to be born at Croft Donald.

'Is the bairn here?' Iain Cameron's voice floated from below.

'Ay, he's here,' Nellie called from the landing. 'Big, bonny and in perfect health.'

'And how is the wee mother?' came Kenneth's anxious

enquiry.

'Och, she is just fine — and will be all the better for a good strong cuppy,' Nellie added meaningfully.

'I'll fetch it,' Irene's voice came readily, as if she was glad of something to do after a night spent in the decidedly gloomy company of both Kenneth and his father.

A few minutes later a hauntingly familiar sound came floating in through sashes that had been thrown wide to catch any wisp of air that hot summer's night. The notes swelled and throbbed and grew in volume till Evelyn felt a shiver of wonder in her marrow at the realisation that it was Kenneth Mor who was out there, striding up and down playing the pipes, playing them as he had played them once before on a still, frosty night, away up yonder in the parks of Knobblieknowe, heralding to all and sundry that a daughter had been born to him and his bonny Jeannie, a daughter who was little Isla Nell lying snug now in her cot just two doors along the landing.

'That man!' Nellie tried to sound stern but the sweetness of her love for the big, red-bearded Highlander spilled out of her oddly beautiful amber-green eyes. 'Just listen to him, he'll have the whole o' Kenneray falling out their beds and sprachling down here thinking Croft Donald is ceilidhing.'

To the window she hastened with Grace, the pair of them to lean on the sill and watch the tall, proud silhouette that was Kenneth Mor, marching up and down on the fragrant machair, his pipes ringing, ringing, far and away over the beaches and the ocean — and — who knew on that scented hot June night with lark song still in the sky and curlews calling sweet from the shore? — perhaps carrying way and beyond to far-flung islands sailing blue and serene in the rose-tinted horizon.

Evelyn, lying there on her pillows, spent but replete with the fullness of peace that filled her now empty belly, every emotion raw and alive, allowed the tears to spill from her eyes and down over her cheeks to soak her hair and her goonie. She loved them all, everyone there, they who had sat with her through the night watch and those of her kin who were scattered and gone but remained in her heart wherever she went – yet, strange, she had no notion yet to look at the bairn for whom the pipes chimed and echoed out there in the evening hush.

Exhausted after such a long and agonising labour, she barely had strength to lift her head to look at him – but she made the effort – this was Davie's son after all, a living proof of those stolen hours so carelessly shared.

With more curiosity than wonder, and glad that everyone was too occupied elsewhere to mind what she was doing, she pulled back the shawl to stare at the being who had lived within her for nine long, weary months. He was so big, not like a new-born baby at all, no more like Davie than the man in the moon. With an odd sense of detachment she looked at the chubby knuckles punching the air, at the round, red, bulging face, the hairless head. He reminded her of a small, fat Buddha and the only response he stirred in her was a curious feeling of wistful compassion, together with a dislike of her own self for not readily accepting him as her son. He was a stranger she didn't know and had no great desire to know and she was glad when he spat bubbles down his chin and twisted his face away from her as if to let her know he didn't much care for her either.

She was relieved when a commotion on the stairs took her attention away from the new little soul who shared her bed. The doctor came into the room, piped through by Kenneth Mor who only stopped playing when he himself was over the threshold, two long strides taking him to the bed to fold Evelyn into his arms and plant a bounteous kiss on her warm cheek. So enthralled was he with her and the baby he forgot to lay aside his pipes so that they were sandwiched between him and the girl. They were still filled with air and gave off such a droning mournful wail she laughed even though it hurt, and playfully tugged the red beard just inches from her face.

'God, lass!' Doctor McDonald was staring at the baby. 'You must have been gorging yourself to produce such a big lad as that! He couldna be described as a puny wee fart, that's a certainty.'

'Ay, and her such a wee quine,' supplemented Nellie, pointedly ignoring the doctor's rude tongue. 'But faith! He's a bonny, bonny bairn and just as well he was strong enough to see his own self into the world and lucky he had Grace and Jenny to meet him when he came.'

'Ach, Nellie! You're an awful lass for peckin' round the edges without coming straight out wi' what you really mean,' cried the doctor, his red face gleaming for he liked nothing better than teasing the young Mistress Cameron. 'If you must know the truth why no' just ask, but seein' you enjoy a wee game I'll have you know I was lying drunk at the roadside for nigh on fourteen hours and dreamt I was over at Mistress McTavish's fighting to save her and a skinny pickle o' bones that looked more like a drowned rat than a bairn.'

'Ach, stop your blethers, Joe McDonald,' skirled Jenny Wren who was viewing the world through a rum-induced haze. 'Tell us straight, did you save Jessie and the wee one?'

'Ay, indeed I did, but no thanks to Jim who nearly went spare at the thought o' losin' his poor wife and himself to blame for the state she was in. It was that eldest wee lass o' his who ran back and forward, fetchin' and carryin' and greetin' her eyes out all the time but able enough to assist me at the birth and even to get me a good dinner before she would let me out the house to come over here.'

'Come down and have a sup o' tea when you're finished here,' muttered a shame-faced Nellie, hurrying from the room.

Kenneth Mor winked. 'Ay, man, I'll make sure it's *strong* tea you get. We must wet the bairn's head and Jenny Wren looks as if she's discovered the right way o' doing that.'

*   *

175

A good while later, when the doctor had taken himself off downstairs and it was only Grace left sitting at the end of the bed, Evelyn sighed and turned her face on the pillow, her purple-smudged lids so heavy with weariness she couldn't keep them open a moment longer.

'Evie,' Grace whispered the name, unwilling to disturb her sister's repose but a need in her to ask an imperative question. 'What will you call your son?'

The answer came slowly, but with such definition it had obviously been thought of some time ago. 'Alexander – Alexander David Grainger.'

'Ay, that's a bonny name,' breathed Grace, 'and fitting for such a proud, strong boy.' Then, hesitantly: 'You do like him, don't you, Evie?'

A long moment of silence, a grudging reply. 'I dinna ken him yet, Grace, and I'm too tired now to think about it.'

'Ay, you sleep, Evie, you've had a long, terrible day but you bore your pain well, I'm right proud o' my girl.'

Evelyn softened, relaxed, tears glinted on her lashes, she put out her hand to her sister. 'Oh, Grace, I'm a selfish besom and I'm nothing to be proud of. It was you, I never could have tholed it if it hadna been for you.'

'I couldna have managed without Nellie and Jenny Wren . . .'

'No, Grace, it was you I needed, you who came to Kenneray for a holiday and who ended up nursing me.'

'Ach, I enjoyed every minute, it's a long while since I've delivered a bairn, it made such a change, to see a young life coming into the world instead of watching one slipping out o' it. But wheesht now, dawn will be here soon, I hear the birds starting already.'

She turned down the oil lamp. Dawn was here, a faint golden flush on the edge of the world, silhouetting cows and sheep and fence posts and far-off islands dreaming on the breast of the ocean.

'Grace.'

'Ay, Evie?'

'Take the bairn and put him in his cradle, the bed is too hot for him.'

Grace lifted the sleeping bundle and tiptoed over to place him in the beechwood cot that had once cradled the bairn who was now Kenneth Mor.

The child stirred and whimpered a little, so recently severed from the womb, too soon separated from the security of his mother's breast.

Grace placed her lips against his smooth plump cheek. 'Bide quiet, my wee man,' she murmured. She made no objection but was glad when Nellie came in and stole the baby away to her own bed and her own breast that yearned so much for children that were not of other women's making.

Chapter Thirteen

Evelyn had to remain in bed for several days after the birth of her son, an enforced confinement and one which made her irritable and morose and filled with longing to be out there in the sunshine. The fragrance of summer floated in through the open windows together with shouts of laughter and banter. Everyone was carefree and happy, only she seemed to have lost her freedom, and she chafed restlessly in the confining comfort of the big feather bed. It was too hot, too soft, it had lost all its previous charming qualities and she only wanted to shake herself loose of its shackles.

Jenny Wren sprachled along to see her and to murmur quaint little rhymes over both her and her son and to wrap a shiny new penny in clean cotton and fix it over his navel because she was of the opinion that it was protruding. Into his fat little fist she pushed a shiny new sixpence 'for luck', treated them both to a few more incantations, then left the room in a cloud of pipe smoke.

Nellie rushed in with a newspaper to fan away the toxic cloud and told Evelyn that Doctor McDonald said she could get up.

'Really, Nellie?' cried Evelyn gleefully.

'Ay, but only to sit at your bed and maybe walk up and down a wee bit. And no sulks from you, madam! It's all for your own good though anyone would think we were your jailers the way you carry on.'

A few days later she was ready to go home. Grace, her

leave being up, had already left and now that the time had come Evelyn wasn't looking forward to the journey with only a newborn baby for company.

The day before her departure Nellie pulled her into her own bedroom, made her sit in a cane chair by the window, and paced up and down the floor for a few minutes before coming to the point.

Abruptly she halted and spoke urgently and swiftly, her fair skin flushed. 'Evie, let me keep the wee one for a while. It would give you a chance to get on your feet and allow you and David some time on your own. The responsibility o' a bairn might be too much for him the now. From what you tell me he's no' yet ready to face up to anything far less a ready-made son.'

'Och, Nellie, I canna let you do that!' The falseness of the protestation mocked her with its hollow beat. 'And anyway, why would you do this for me?'

A wistful smile flitted across Nellie's strong face. 'Because you're my sister and also because you're a troubled soul just now. I do it for the bairn because I love him more than you love him at this moment in time, and I do it for myself because I want him more than you and canna seem to have any o' my own.'

'Oh, Nellie, you'll just have to be patient a whilie longer – there's plenty o' time.'

'Is there, quine? I'm thirty-one years old and so far I've done nothing but collect other folk's bairns.'

'Ach, you've done more than that and fine you know it!' cried Evelyn passionately. 'You're a mother to Cal and Isla Nell, you've given them so much of your love, Jeannie would be proud o' you. And look at what you've done for Wee Col, you're a wonderful mother, to them, and will be to your own when you have them.'

'Ay, maybe you're right, but stop your blethers, I want to show you something.'

She opened the bottom drawer of the dresser to reveal a pile of baby clothes, all beautifully knitted, crocheted, sewn. 'I've been saving these for a long time now, Evie,'

179

she said softly, 'and I'll go on making them as long as there's hope for me, but it seems such a waste just to have them lying there. I want you to have some for wee Alex, or at least let me dress him in them till you come back for him.'

It was obvious that she had made up her mind about the baby. Evelyn opened her mouth to make a further token protest but the look on her sister's face stayed her tongue. It was shining, her beautiful eyes begged the other girl to say yes.

The next day Evelyn left Kenneray – alone.

Maggie was furious when Evelyn returned from the north-west minus her son. 'You selfish wee bitch!' she fumed. 'Did it never occur to you that your father and me might like to see our grandchild? And what on earth were you thinking of? Leaving the wee mite wi' Nellie? Do you no' think she has more than enough bairns to look after without taking yours as well!'

'Nellie wanted him!' returned Evie with equal asperity, the depression that had beset her since leaving Kenneray, coupled with terrible pangs of guilt, making her throw respect for her parents to the winds. 'It was she who suggested it but I dinna see why you should think it so odd to place a bairn in her keeping. You did it willingly enough when you let her take Wee Col for you never could abide the wee man about your skirts.'

It was a hurtful barb, all the more so since it was partly true for, in the beginning, Maggie hadn't wanted her flawed son, though as the years passed she had come to love him and had been heartbroken at having to part with him . . .

'Oh, I'm sorry, Mam!' cried Evelyn, shocked at her own cruelty. But it was too late. Maggie, her green eyes blazing, slapped the girl's face. She recoiled, holding her hand to the crimson skin, then, turning about, she fled away upstairs, banging her door viciously behind her.

180

'Maggie, Maggie,' sighed Jaimie, filling his pipe with a slightly shaky hand. 'You and she aye could set the heather on fire wi' these awful tempers you share. Can you no' see the lass is tired out and needing this while to herself to sort herself out?'

'No, I canna see!' Maggie threw at him. 'And 'tis high time you were firmer wi' the girl. You were aye too soft for her own good and now look what she's come to. She lay wi' a man and had his son and thinks it's all and fine to turn the responsibility o' him over to some other body. Well, I'll no' have it, Jamie! She'll just go right back to Kenneray and fetch the baby home here and by Dyod! I'll see she rears him properly or she'll have me to answer to!'

Maggie was not the only one that Evelyn came up against. Everyone at Dunmarnock had something to say about it. Twiggy May stared at her in a most peculiar fashion and said cryptically, 'Dinna blame the wee one for the manner and place o' his conception, Evie.'

'And what would you ken about it?' demanded the girl. But a glance into the other's eyes forbade further comment. Need she ask? she thought bitterly. Her life was an open book to this wise old woman and she was the first to turn away from her penetrating stare.

Lady Elizabeth was the next to air her opinion, 'Dear me, Evelyn,' she fluttered, punching cushions with such vigour one lost some of its stuffing, 'your mother tells me you have left the baby with your sister. And here was me looking forward to having him about the place. I made Burton bring down our old pram from the attic. As good as new with hardly a scratch and I had thought that the little one could sit outside in the sun, all safe and cosy while you got on with your work and plenty pairs of eyes to watch over him.'

Both Seal and Ferguson were shocked to the core at what Seal called her 'hardness of heart'. Even Violet looked at her askance and with a sigh Peggy sadly put away the little jacket she had knitted for the baby's homecoming.

But Effie was loudest of all in her condemnation. 'But surely, Evelyn, you wanted to show the boy off to your husband,' she said slyly, a coarseness in her voice that made Evelyn think for the umpteenth time there was more to the Rustler than quite met the eye. 'After all, a sight o' his very own son might be just the thing he needs to bring him out himself. It takes two to tangle and he'll no' be pleased at you for denying him his rights as a father.'

'Oh, Grace,' cried Evelyn in desperation. 'What am I to do? Everyone hates the sight o' me, even my own mother, and Father has hardly spoken one word to me since I came home.'

'Ach, he doesna ken what to do or how best to handle the situation. Mam warned him no' to be soft wi' you and the only way Father kens how to be strict is to keep a hold o' his tongue. If you really want my advice I would tell you to leave the baby wi' Nellie meantime and bring Davie here.'

Evelyn stared, hardly able to believe her ears. 'Bring Davie here?'

'Ay, you heard, bring him here.' Grace's smile was soft and secretive. 'I saw how you reacted to wee Alex, you kept calling him a stranger and in many ways so is his father. What do you and he really know about one another? In three and a half years you've only met a few times and I feel you'll never want to know your son till you get to ken his father better.'

Evelyn could say nothing for a few moments. With her fingers jammed in her mouth she just gaped at her sister out of eyes that were too bright.

'Oh, Grace,' she breathed at last, 'do you really think I could do that? It would solve so many problems. Davie will never get well in the tenements, he needs the country, fresh air. I could see him all the time, no' just for a snatched hour or two — I could really look after him . . .' Her face fell. 'Mam would never allow it — she never liked Davie, she couldna thole the thought o' him under the same roof as herself.'

Grace shook her bright head, her smile widening, her eyes growing darker, deeper. 'Och, use your imagination, Evie, no' the same roof, Fern Cottage has been empty since we came. I'm sure the Bairds would like to see it fired and aired. I could move in wi' you — just till you and Davie are truly wed,' she added hastily. 'Neither Mam nor Father would approve any other way. Later on you can fetch the baby home, meantime we could pay the rent between us.'

'Grace, oh, Grace, you darling, wonderful sister! I never thought you could be so — devious!' Evelyn bubbled, so stunned with sudden joy she became the girl she had been before care darkened her life.

'There's a lot you dinna ken about me . . .' Grace began but got no further. She was seized, birled round the room in a mad dance of abandonment that left them both breathless and flopping onto the bed where they giggled like a couple of schoolgirls.

'I wonder what Mam will say.' Some of Evelyn's euphoria left her.

'You leave Mam to me.' Grace sounded unusually determined. 'You're a big girl now, Evie, it's time you led your own life.'

'You want your — er — hm — husband to come and live in Fern Cottage, Evelyn? Well, yes, it seems a very good idea.' Lady Elizabeth was so taken aback by the request she forgot to flutter but just stood with her head on one side, twittering instead, 'Yes, well, if you'll just come with me we'll see what Richard thinks about it.'

'A thundering good idea,' approved the Colonel, glancing round vaguely as if certain he had forgotten something but not quite sure what. 'We should have thought of it before, eh, Beth?' he appealed to his wife as if the idea had been of their making. 'Do the cottage good to be lived in and give your – er – young man a chance to get on his feet. Your mother will know where the key is – damned reliable housekeeper. You go along and get the place sorted out, hasn't been lived in since old Gus Ferrets retired. Mind you, the lad will have to get one of the village girls in to help with his meals and everything, he'll need a lot of looking after at first.'

'Oh, but Colonel,' Evelyn spoke hastily, 'I'm going to move in with him, he would never manage otherwise.'

'Eh? What?' He peered at her over the top of his specs which he had just found hanging by one leg from the chain of his pocket watch. 'Well, now, this puts a different light on the affair. I'm aware that everyone thinks that you're married, Evelyn, but Beth and me know different, eh? Don't want to pry and all that but your young man – what did you say his name was?'

'David.'

'Ah, yes, David, well, don't know quite how to put this but – oh – dammit! Will he be fit enough to face up to his responsibilities? You and he alone together in the cottage, we must get you to the altar first – principle and all that.'

At this his wife hastened to explain that Grace would be living there too and Grace was not the sort of girl to suggest such a thing without first making certain it was all seemly and above board.

The Colonel's brow cleared. 'Grace. Ah, lovely girl, definitely not the sort to . . .' His brow furrowed once more. 'No, sorry, Evelyn, can't have it, two girls and a young man, unmarried, all living together, wouldn't be right, must marry your David first, Evelyn.'

Her heart sank; the possibility of marriage to David was the last thing on her horizon. Even if he had been well enough to discuss it there was no knowing if he would ever consent to it.

'Cheer up, Evelyn,' The Colonel was looking very downcast, it was obvious he disliked disappointing the young maidservant of whom he had grown very fond. 'When you get back your – er – seat you might ride Darling for me. Andrew seems to have lost interest and Christine is away gallavanting again – took a notion to whisk some young man off to London to show him the sights as she said – the one who went with her up to Craigdrummond . . .'

'Gavin Galbraith,' supplied his wife.

'Ah, that's the one. I say, Beth, you don't think she's forgotten young Wilson-Kerr, do you? The Marquess rang me up the other day asking if she would come up to visit him and the Marchioness at Inverbrora and I had to . . .'

Evelyn slipped quietly from the room. When the Colonel and his wife got talking about family matters they very often forgot anyone else who might be in the room and she had no wish to eavesdrop on their conversation – though, not unnaturally, she did wonder about Christine Baird and Gavin Galbraith.

Christine arrived home with Gavin and was the means of solving quite a few problems. At first she was annoyed when she heard about the plans for Fern Cottage as she had wanted it for Gavin for whom it was to have been a surprise.

She was anxious, she explained, to assist in his rehabilitation and, as he had been a ship's cabinet maker before the war, she had planned for him to stay at the cottage where he could perhaps restore some pieces of antique furniture that had been set aside for the attention of just such an expert.

'I don't want him leaving here till he's quite ready,' she told Evelyn and Grace, her blue eyes shining with enthusiasm. 'He needs a quiet place where he can gradually adjust to his disability, feel that he's independent, and at the same time start earning his keep. He's got plenty of courage and ought to be quite well able to look after himself. That was why I thought . . .'

'Och, Chris, there's no need for you to justify yourself to us,' chided Grace gently. 'You're the daughter o' Dunmarnock and can have anything you want of it, I'm sure. But why can't Gavin and Davie share the cottage? Your father willna hear o' me and Evie living there alone wi' Davie but I'm certain he won't object to the two men making use o' it.'

Her eyes were shining. Gavin had been one of her special patients and she could see that he had become a bit more than that to Christine. 'The house is all on the one level so stairs will no' be a problem and when one or another of us isn't popping in, Gavin can keep an eye on Davie.'

'Grace, you're a genius!' enthused Christine who rushed off at once to get her parents' permission before going to break the news to Gavin.

'Aw, you're too good to me, Plummy,' he told her, his eyes shining. 'I thought you might have wanted rid o' me by now. An ancient aunt has turned up from Bridgeton. She's offered to take me in and give me a good Christian home as she puts it.'

'You're staying here,' she said firmly, 'I'm not the sort to shirk my duties so just you start getting your things together – you're moving to Dunmarnock.'

'So, I'm just another duty to you,' he teased, the sweat breaking on him with the effort of standing too long in the one spot. 'I suppose you do this sort o' thing for all the lads who come under your wing?'

'Nonsense!' she returned briskly. 'There wouldn't be room for them all!' Her face softened, she took his hand and squeezed it. 'You're different, Runny Black Treacle, I've never met anyone with quite so much cheek.'

She was about to rush off, her face pinker than usual, but she paused to throw over her shoulder, 'Don't forget to tell Cuddles you'll need your wheelchair, those wooden pins of yours are all very well but we'll be walking a lot at Dunmarnock – and I want to do the pushing.'

*   *

Gavin, with the help of Jamie, and Hugh Kerr, went to the Big House to personally convey his gratitude to Lady Elizabeth and the Colonel who both fully approved of the new plans for Fern Cottage. In the hall he bumped full tilt into a hurrying Effie. With a hastily suppressed oath she bent to rub her shin where his wheels had knocked it and he received the full brunt of her belligerent scowl.

He had seen her before of course, at Seal's tea parties last winter, but she had remained in the background and the room had been suitably dim so that Granny Currie's ghost stories could have their full effect, but today the hall was flooded in sunshine and the parlourmaid's face was caught fully in the light.

'Here, do I know you from somewhere?' he asked, his brow creased in an effort of remembering.

Without answering, Effie hastened away, her starches positively crackling, and the incident was forgotten, except by Effie whose thunderously dark face was twisted with rage.

Her heart was beating swiftly with apprehension. She leaned against the door of Ferguson's pantry, her knuckles clenching and unclenching at her sides. Why did *he* have to turn up? she fumed inwardly. It had been bad enough when that filthy little rat bag, Annie McMahone, had come to work at Dunmarnock, but even though they worked in the same house their paths had seldom crossed and, anyway, the cleaner went about in such a perpetual haze of smoke she only ever seemed to see what was immediately in front of her nose. She had given no indication of suspicion but Gavin Galbraith was different. He had sharp eyes on him, she would do well to keep out of his way, not that they had ever known each other well in the old days but still, it was better to be safe than sorry. Fancy seeing him again after all this time. It brought all the past rushing back, the filth, the shame, the degredation. He had been just another face in the teeming flotsam of her life but she could tell he was all there and could cause trouble for her if he ever found out more than was good for them both – and she couldn't afford to take any risks – not now – when everything was going her way and she had Major Baird eating out of her hand.

Douglas Grainger had willingly accepted Evelyn's proposal to take his son away to Dunmarnock.

'The best thing that could happen to him,' he told her when she arrived with Jamie at 198 Camloan Road.

He and Jamie got on well from the start. They sat at the table, eating, drinking, talking about everything, while Evelyn fumed with impatience and only supped a little of the delicious broth Douglas had made himself.

His face fell when his eyes went to her plate and she hastened to say, 'Och, Douglas, it's lovely, but I'm sorry, I'm just no' hungry, I'm . . .'

'I know fine, you want to be on your way and get Davie settled. I told him you were coming for him and he went to pack his things.'

'Really?'

'Ay, really, he loves it when you come, Evie, and just shrinks into himself when you go away.'

Over by the window, Winnie Grainger was singing, her sweet little voice trilling like a bird though a few moments later it was drowned out by a raucous chorus of children's voices in the street outside, chanting: 'Witchie, Witchie Winnie, dirties her clean pinnie . . .'

'No,' whimpered Winnie Grainger, in the tremulous tone of a child, 'I'm waiting for Danny to come home. Have you seen him? Have any o' you seen him?'

'Danny's deid! Danny's deid! Jerry! Jerry! Jerry! Conked him on the heid!'

The cruel chants grew in volume. With a snort of anger but with the resignation of one who has often performed such a task, Douglas got up and hurled out some well-chosen words which soon sent the offenders packing and left his wife to go on, undisturbed, with her monotonous little drone.

'She'll miss her lad,' Jamie commented, a small wonder in him at the patience with which the other man had fed his wife, had later taken her out to the lavatory in the close, had washed her face and hands and finally settled her at her place by the window.

'No, Jamie,' sighed Douglas, 'her memory only serves her for one lad and that was her youngest. After that there was no one –' he spread his hands, well-shaped hands with good long fingers though the flesh was hacked and calloused from years of battering rivets into big ships at Fairfields of Govan – 'not even me. I've become someone who is at the edge of her life but never intruding into it. In her own way she's happy, all I can do is see she's comfortable and fed.'

Evelyn grasped hold of the emery-hard hands, her eyes wide and sad for this gentle big man who had asked for little in his life and had ended up getting almost nothing, 'You'll come and visit Davie,' she urged, 'he'll feel strange at first – homesick.'

'Homesick? For this?' He glanced round the cramped, dingy room. 'No, lass, he'll no' miss this, it's been his jail for too long, out o' one and into another. But I'll come and see him if I can. Bessie Fullerton next door is a good soul, she'll see to Winnie if I ask her.'

They left soon after, Davie still too thin, but a new awareness in his eyes as Evelyn led him to the door.

At the last minute Douglas threw his arm round his son and hugged him briefly before turning away, the throat of him tight and sore with words left unsaid, tears left unshed.

Evelyn's heart went out to him, she wanted to rush back, to comfort him in his lonely grief but Jamie threw her a warning look and pulled her away, out of the close, away from 198 Camloan Road where Winnie Grainger sat at her window singing her endless, meaningless song to unlistening ears.

Chapter Fourteen

Fern Cottage was reached by a little rustic bridge which spanned a purling burn that wound its way through golden meadows towards Primrose Wood. A tangle of roses and honeysuckle grew round the doors and windows which were painted a bright red and gave the house the appearance of a happy little gnome of a place with smoke puffing and drifting from the red chimneys.

The hearths blazed warmly, the polished floors sparkled, vases of foxgloves and delphiniums sat in the deep window ledges and on top of the round, mahogany table in the parlour; Evelyn had thrown multicoloured crocheted bedspreads over the beds and over the back of the faded chintz couch.

From the kitchen wafted the mouth-watering aroma of roast chicken, prepared and cooked by Maggie herself who, at the last minute, had relinquished the last of her objections to Davie's coming and who had, rather shamefacedly, set out to do all she could to make him feel welcome.

'Well, Davie?' Evelyn, holding tight to his hand, waited with bated breath while she prayed for some reaction, anything to tell her that he knew, that he understood.

He faced her. A strange, shining mist wavered in his beautiful brown eyes.

'Evie,' he whispered. Tentatively he put his face close to hers. His lips were warm, warm and soft, and very gentle.

A great bubble burst in her heart, spilling happiness into every fibre. Davie was hers again – and he had come home.

The arrangement with Gavin and Davie was a huge success. Every spare minute she could get, Evelyn rushed over to Fern Cottage and every time she found Davie more alive, more responsive to everything around him. He lost his frail, old-man look, the bloom of youth came back to his face, the shine to his hair and his eyes.

He and Gavin got on well together, they shared much in common. Davie too had been learning the carpentry trade before the war and between them they lovingly restored prized bits of furniture over which the Colonel and his wife enthused prolifically and for which they paid generously.

It was the therapy they both needed to restore their sense of usefulness and make them take an interest in themselves and the world again.

Gavin proved to be a great, if messy, cook. Bawling out a song at the top of his voice he would sit at the kitchen table, sloshing eggs, flour, and other ingredients into a vast yellow bowl, and from that carelessly-mixed concoction somehow producing an appetising dish.

Pigs' trotters and spare ribs, dripping with nuggety-red juice, served up with roast potatoes and cabbage, topped their list of favourite meals, and that was what the Grant family were served when they were included in an invitation to partake of dinner at the cottage, in return, Gavin said, for all the meals he had had at Wood Cottage.

Andrew and Christine were there too and while they waited at the table for their meal, Gavin was at the stove, stirring gravy, presiding over pots and pans, leaving David to play host, which he did, impeccably and politely but laughing at Gavin's antics in the kitchen.

Evelyn was very proud of him that day and when his velvety brown orbs met her green ones it was like that time over three years ago in Bert's Tea Shoppe in Cobbly Wynd, when they had looked at each other over a pile of hot, buttery pancakes and he had been kind and sympathetic about young Johnny Burns who had died too soon.

They all sat at the table, gentry folk and working class, stripping flesh from their spare ribs, sucking flesh from their pigs' trotters, juicy red gravy dribbling down their chins, enjoying the meal without manners or restraint for that was the only way to eat such mouth-watering fare.

'Fingers were made before forks,' stated Jamie, plunging his fingers into his plate with gusto, for once not having to be 'heedful o' his manners', as everyone else was doing the same thing. Soon all that was left were heaps of picked bones lying on the plates, likened by Christine to 'dinosaurs' graveyards'.

When Maggie rose to help with the dishes David pushed her back into her seat, gently but firmly. 'No, Mrs Grant, you're a visitor, remember? Visitors don't help wi' the dishes in this house.'

It was still 'Mrs Grant', Evelyn noticed, formal and polite, while Jamie was just that, and she sighed to herself and wondered if he and her mother would ever grow to like and trust one another.

But otherwise the day was a huge success, and when the Colonel and Lazy Elizabeth were invited to avail themselves of a 'thank-you' meal, they were served up the same as the others, and so well did they relish it they went home to seek out Maggie forthwith and ask her to see that pigs' trotters be included in the Dunmarnock menus. When Cook with a Capital heard that, her eyes nearly bulged out her head and she went off muttering to herself, something about not knowing what gentry people, who, in her opinion, were mixing too much with common folk for their own good, were coming to.

It was a happy time for the young people. The days were long and hot, filled with the perfume of dog roses and wild honeysuckle and the heady fragrance of meadowsweet.

The rolling countryside of Renfrewshire was richly green and inviting and they met as often as they could, Gavin and Christine, Evelyn and David, Grace and Andrew, to walk in the cool woods, picnic by shady banks, Christine pushing Gavin's chair, all of them laughing and singing and young together. They boarded a paddle steamer and sailed down the Clyde to Dunoon and Bute; they fished in the rivers, picked wild flowers, never tiring of mists and soft rains, summer breezes and hot sunshine, and grew brown and glowing.

Evelyn wished for that summer to last forever, her hand in Davie's, his eyes regarding her in that secretive, intimate way that set her pulses racing.

War was still raging through Europe but they didn't want to think about that, especially the three young men whose lives had been affected by it one way or another.

But Evelyn never quite forgot Gillan and the fact that he still fought in that life-extinguishing hell-hole across the sea. She was apt to remember with nostalgia that last lovely time they had shared, when side by side they had roamed the winter countryside; to recall also, with great sadness, his unforgettable farewell when he had given her the fragile gold band that now reposed beside her other treasures in the tin box under her bed but which she often brought out to look at and occasionally to slip onto her finger, especially in the uncertain days of Davie's illness and before the birth of her son.

Nellie kept her well-posted about the baby's progress. He had been a discontented infant in the early days and the first weeks had been sleepless and difficult. But he was settling down now, growing bonnier with each passing day.

Every time a letter came from Nellie, guilt tore Evelyn apart. She knew how wrong and selfish she was being, that it was she and not her sister who should be rearing the boy, but these were the only times she really gave him a thought, when she was forcibly reminded of him like that, and, though she wrote back, telling Nellie how grateful she was, that she would come to collect him as soon as she could, she never could bring herself to say that she missed him — and — God forgive her — she didn't! Not really. Only those letters recalled her to the fact that she had ever borne a child – them and the tiny, livid stretchmarks which marred the skin of her belly and which she hated as she would the evidence of some disfiguring disease.

The time was coming for her to tell Davie about the child; if she didn't someone else would. None of those closest to her had breathed a word but very soon his horizons would broaden and he was bound to hear the news from someone. Willie the Post would have given it away long ago but he was on his annual holiday and the temporary postman was tight-lipped and dour and a newcomer to these parts anyway.

Oh ay, she would speak to Davie soon but not now, not when he was only gradually starting to accept life again and all the wonderful things it had to offer.

Only Andrew remained pale and withdrawn all through that summer and only seemed to come alive when he was with Grace with whom he was more besotted than ever. But he made no attempt to touch her now and while she was glad enough about that she often wondered if he was really getting better or if part of him was still living in the past. She was struck by the haunted expression that seemed to have permanently settled on his quiet young face, but when he saw her watching him he made a great attempt to cheer up and join in the banter of the others. He felt lost and terribly alone, there was no way he could unburden himself, no one he could turn to in his humiliation and bitter self-loathing.

Effie's hold on him was becoming more and more vicious. She clung to him tenaciously, sapping the little strength he had gained in his struggle out of the darkness, and as he became weaker she became stronger, till he now fully believed that she was perfectly capable of bringing some dreadful retribution to bear on his family if he so much as breathed one word about her to his parents. The day for family discussions was coming soon enough, she told him, and when it did he wouldn't dare denounce her but rather tell them how much she had come to mean to him and see how it went from there.

Meantime she came to his room every other night, whipping him into frenzies of desire that were barely satisfied until her next visit and the next. She had become a drug to him, one that he longed to be free of but was powerless to resist.

Outside the bedroom her attitude towards him was exemplary in the extreme but when she spoke to him the oil of intimacy smoothed her throat and there was an inflection in her tone that said, 'tonight, Andrew'.

Gradually he lost interest in everything, even the horses he had once loved. Half-heartedly he applied himself to managing his father's munitions factory and when the Colonel had pulled him up sharply, telling him to get his head out of the clouds and bloody well start working for a living, he had retaliated disgracefully, bawling that he had never been damned well interested anyway and had only consented to it to keep everybody quiet and off his back.

With the passing days he became more depressed and miserable, the only highlights in his life being those times spent in the company of Christine and the others, and of course his darling Grace, whom he longed to touch but never would again, not until the taint that was Effie was somehow, miraculously, cleansed from his system.

Ironically, the nights that Effie didn't come were the worst, for then the dead face of Barrett came to him instead and the awful, living reality that was Effie was infinitely better than anything that other dread world had to offer.

On a sultry, thundery day in late July, Davie learned about Alexander David Grainger but he didn't hear it from Evelyn. She came over to the cottage that evening to find Gavin out with Christine and David sitting alone by the dead embers of the kitchen fire, his brows as dark as the gathering clouds, his fingers reaching nervously for a cigarette when he heard her light footsteps in the passageway.

'Davie,' she began but got no further, the look on his face swiftly stilling a tongue that had been ready with some lighthearted greeting. 'Davie,' she repeated, staying over by the door, her quick senses warning her that it would be foolish to approach him in his present mood. 'What is it? Is there something ailing you?'

'Ay, you could say that,' he interrupted rudely, 'something you could call mistrust and disgust for a girl whose bonny honest eyes hide a heart as black as the sky out there.'

'Davie —' she took a few steps forward — 'I dinna ken what you're talking about . . .'

'Better no' come too near!' he warned sharply, his fists curling into tight balls. 'I want to see you properly when you tell me it isn't true you've birthed a bairn, one that is supposed to be mine wi' my name branded on him — oh — and seeing as I'm supposed to be your husband, how would it be if you and me went through to bed right now to enjoy our marital rights?'

She had gone deathly pale at his words. 'Who told you all this?' She could barely squeeze out the question, so swift ran her heart.

He tossed his half-finished cigarette into the grate. 'Some rat-faced maid I happened to meet when I took a walk away from this prison of a place.' He gave a short, humourless laugh. 'No wonder you kept me tucked up all nice and cosy within these walls, afraid of what I might hear if I escaped into the big, bad world! Was that your idea? Miss Bright-Eyed Innocent!'

'Effie!' She ground out the name from bloodless lips. 'Effie Jordan. I aye kent she would make trouble for me one way or another and by Dyod! I was right!'

'Does it matter who the hell she is!' he shouted, half on his feet, his eyes wild and staring. 'You had no right to spread these lies about — as for the bairn — how do I know he's mine?'

'I did have a right!' she shouted back, unable to control the bitter surge of hurt and rage that rose up in her breast. 'You left me to face the world, carrying your child, just as you left another poor fool to do likewise! What was I to do? I have a family whom I love and respect, I . . .'

'What was that you said?' He was fully on his feet now, coming towards her, menace in every measured step.

'Anna Millar,' she half-sobbed. 'I met her in Cobbly Wynd last October. How strange we should meet there like that, in the place where it all started between you and me. I kent I was pregnant by you and was near out o' my mind wi' worry. I wanted to see again the place where I first fell in love wi' a selfish bugger o' a man wi' the petty values and jealousies o' a child. And there she was, I had seen her once, talking to you at the station, and I went to speak to her. But she was sick and ill and near fainting there in the street so I took her into Bert's Tea Shoppe. She told me about herself, how she had been taken in by a sweet-talking soldier. She told me his name – the name o' the father o' her child . . .'

He struck her face then, his hand crashing down, the jolt of the blow knocking her head to one side so that her hair fell rich and thick about her shoulders. She tasted blood, her head spun, but she went on talking, as if nothing had happened, in a calm, controlled, conversational tone that was utterly frightening in its normality.

'I never told her a thing about myself, or about you, I just listened and felt sick and then I left her and walked to the harbour in a sort o' daze. I stared into the water – oily – I remember that, nothing else. A few days later I climbed the Deacon Hill, up, up. It was misty and strange. I thought I heard you calling but it was only the ghosts o' the hill or maybe Auld Nick himself, who knows. Whatever it was, something unknown and awful drew me on to The Devil's Door and there I tried to kill myself.' She went on, still in the same conversational tone while he stared at her, fascinated, afraid, bewildered. 'I didna see any sort of future for myself nor for the baby, unborn, and still innocent o' the world. I jumped over the edge and later on old Carnallachie found me lying in a soggy bog that saved two lives that day. He spoke about my legs as if they were pigs' trotters and asked me no' to mention his sack o' poached fish to the Gamie. He put me in his cart and he and that daft cuddy o' his took me home. I was in bed for quite a long time. Auld McDuff came to see me and farted in my face and brought me flowers. Only Grace guessed what I had tried to do and I told her that never again would I attempt to kill myself for a man to whom I had been nothing more than a passing fancy.

'Even so, I was in despair thinking you were dead but I had good friends. The Bairds were kindness itself, so was my dear Annie McMahone who tried to save my face by pretending to everyone that you and I were married after Effie Jordan sneaked into my room and read my diary. By then I kent you were a prisoner but when you came home you hardly even recognised me, let alone noticed that I was carrying a child. I went to Kenneray and gave birth to a boy in Croft Donald. I'll never forget how good Nellie and Kenneth were to me. When she offered to keep the baby till you were well enough to accept the fact that you were a father, I jumped at the chance, also at Grace's suggestion that I should bring you here till you were well enough to face up to the truth. If it hadna been for my family and my friends God knows how I would have survived – you either for that matter.'

The monologue came to an abrupt end. He was gazing at her, as if seeing her for the first time, then wordlessly he gathered her into his arms and they both cried, silently and without restraint.

'Forgive me, oh, forgive me, my darling little girl,' he murmured brokenly, his mouth going again and again to the livid weals his fingers had raised on her face. 'I owe everything to you and never thought I could hurt you like this. It was that bitch o' a maid, the way she spoke, wi' a sneer in her voice, harping on about you and that public schoolboy, how you had the time o' your lives together when he was home last Christmas.'

She stiffened. 'If you mean Gillie, say it. He's a Gordon Highlander now, the same as yourself, a courageous one at that. He's won medals for gallantry . . .'

He was angry again, shaking her, telling her to stop talking about other men.

'You brought up Gillie's name,' she retaliated with spirit. 'You've aye hated the idea o' him, right from the start! Well, you can just go and bugger yourself, David Grainger! Gillie's a very special friend to me and aye will be no matter how much you rant and rave about him. God! Why did I want you back, I wonder? All you're good for is picking holes in my life and throwing jealous tantrums — as if — as if you owned me. Well, you don't, no man does. As soon as you're well enough you can leave here, your father loves you and needs you though God knows why. I've done my part, more, I've lied and cheated for you and in the process I've pulled myself and my family into the gutter! Well, no more! Here . . .' She began frantically to tear at the buttons at her throat, the tears of rage and torment pouring down her face. 'Take back your buggering ring! It's served its purpose, I dinna care anymore if the whole world kens I bore an illegitimate bairn for I wouldna have you now in a gift!'

Her rage, her flashing green eyes, her untamed quality of spirit, stirred passions in him he had imagined he would never feel again. His mind spun with a dozen mixed emotions but of one thing he was certain. No one had ever excited him or made him feel more alive than this red-haired beauty with her taut, young breasts and her vibrant, eager hunger for life.

'You bloody little wildcat!' he said admiringly and throwing back his head he roared with laughter and went staggering back into a chair, pulling her with him. 'Bright Eyes! Darling little Bright Eyes! You kept my ring, that gold signet ring I gave you when first we met.'

'Ay, I needed it to fool the world — remember?' she

hurled at him, struggling to break free of his ever tightening arms. 'Raggy Annie told everybody that you and I were wed and got the ring fixed so that it would fit. Only my family and the Bairds ken the real truth. I wore it all through my pregnancy but when I kent you were coming here I put it back round my neck for fear you might start asking questions before you were ready for the answers. We've all been protecting you but that's done wi' now. You're well enough to face the world but you can do it without me, so just you let go o' me this minute or I'll – I'll bite your nose clean off your face and no lass will ever want to look at you again!'

'Hush, oh hush, Evie.' The velvet was back in his voice, the eyes that gazed into hers were deep dark pools filled with tenderness. 'Of course you're going to stay in my world, you have to because we share the same one. From the first moment we met in Cobbly Wynd you were mine and we both knew it. I'll never let you go again.'

He gathered her in close and held her to his heart. She melted against him, cooried herself into him like a tired little mouse that has at last found a safe nest. She said nothing, she was too exhausted, too filled with the wonder of the moment to want to break the spell that had fallen over her like a gossamer mantle. But there was something she had to know, something she had always wanted to know and wonderful though his caressing words were he hadn't yet uttered the one thing that was the most important of all.

'Davie, do you – love me?'

He held her off a little way, pushing the rich strands of hair from her tear-stained face, kissing the tip of his finger and placing it over her lips. 'You know I do.' A tiny frown creased his brow, 'You surely don't need to ask.'

'I want to hear you saying it.'

He laughed softly, 'All right, I love you, and to prove it I'm going to marry you just as soon as possible. Does that make you any happier?'

'No' because o' the bairn? It mustna be for that – it

has to be for us. I would aye be feart you would hate me for trapping you into a marriage you didna want.'

'Oh, come on, Evie.' He moved restlessly, a slight impatience in him. 'Of course it's for us —' he gave a strange little laugh — 'I can't have you any other way — can I?'

'No, never again. They were good days these days we had together but they're over. I was a child then, I'm a woman now, wi' responsibilities I never wanted so soon but got through my own foolishness.'

'Then, it's the altar for us, Evelyn Grant?'

'Ay, Davie Grainger — if first you tell me you willna mind losing your freedom.'

His frown deepened, he sighed. 'Of course I'll mind, I think every man does, just a wee bit. But stop your blethers, I want to hold you like this for ever. I never thought the day would come, Evie, I've been so far away, so alone.'

She gave herself up to the warmth of his mouth, the dear, sweet nearness of his body — but something niggled at the back of her mind — the something that was Anna Millar who had carried his child, a child who would be just a bit older than her own. He had been angry at hearing the girl's name, too angry. He had given himself away so that now she knew Anna had spoken the truth. But she didn't say anything, not then, enough it was she had this hour, this moment, his promise of marriage lying snug and reassuring in her breast.

The days went by quickly after that, the bonny, blithe days of summer, slipping away, shortening. Haar lay over the morning rivers and in the field culverts, birds grew quiet in the trees as they rested and moulted after the hectic months of chick rearing; the corn grew golden on the stalk; burnished hayfields rippled lazily in caressing breezes; the air was heady with the tang of ripening fruits and sweet with the scents of harebells and lilac scabious

201

blossoming in the meadows. On the hill, the lambs and calves fattened, and only kicked their frisky heels in the cool of gloaming; the heather was, as yet, no more than a purple-pink haze blanketing the moors.

The frantic days of earth-turning and seed-sowing were over, harvest was still to come but until then a lazy tranquillity settled over the countryside. Evelyn held her breath, as if savouring the quiet before the bustle, holding to her heart the precious hours and days of this, her last summer of freedom. For she had come to think of it like that and wondered at herself for wanting to hold on to freedom, to that very thing she had once believed to have been so close to Davie's heart.

The marks on her face faded but those that were left in her heart didn't and never would. She still loved Davie but it was a different love from the blind, worshipping passion of a young girl, her vision of him was clearer, more realistic and only the impatient, restless part of her galloped on to that day set for mid-September; the rest of her, the romantic, heedless, carefree part, wanted to cling forever to dreams and heartaches and strange, lonely tears that wept for the Evelyn who had been and would never be again.

Soon she would belong to another, she would no longer be Evelyn McKenzie Grant as she had been for twenty years, and she went through her days, dreamily, lost in pensive thought, letting Maggie, Jamie, and Grace do all the talking, even allowing Cook with a Capital to scold her without retaliation and Effie to make her sly remarks about Davie and the baby.

She stood perfectly still and obedient for Raggy Annie who had been a seamstress among other things in her day and, having offered to make the wedding frock, came furtively to Wood Cottage for 'secret fittings' as she called them, her mouth full of little rows of pins, the famous ash dripping from the end of her cigarette onto Maggie's clean floors.

'Move yourself, quine!' Maggie ordered sharply.

'Take this upstairs to her ladyship and be quick about it,' barked Seal with asperity.

'Surely you and your man will be going soon to collect the bairn,' hinted Effie.

'Och, Evie, you've left the coal scuttle upstairs again!' wailed Violet.

So it went on, the chatter, the orders, the plans, the Colonel frowning beneath his brows at coal dust on the carpet, her ladyship punching cushions and telling Evelyn in a breathless voice that it was all very well but never quite getting to the point.

Nothing or no one seemed able to rouse Evelyn from her trance-like state – nothing that is until she met Effie's mother one hot sultry day when she was making her way back indoors after the morning tea break.

'Excuse me, miss, could ye tell me where I might find Effie Barr?'

Evelyn jumped with fright when the voice came at her elbow, a coarse, grating voice with a querulous ring to it. Spinning round, she found herself staring at a scraggy undernourished-looking woman with stringy grey hair straggling out from a stained black hat and dirty, pox-pitted skin that had an unhealthy yellow tinge to it. Her mouth was very close to the girl's face and belched stale whisky fumes all over it.

'Effie you say? The parlourmaid? But her surname is Jordan.'

The woman's thin mouth twisted. 'Oh, she's that now, is she? Ay well, it'll be a lie like the rest o' her. If her first name's Effie and she's got a tongue like a razor that will be her right enough. Where is she? I want to speak to her in private.'

'She'll be in the house as usual,' Evelyn replied, taken aback at the woman's peremptory tone and the hard voice with a pronounced glottal stop in almost every word. 'But I dinna ken where you can speak in private unless in the wee summerhouse over yonder.'

'Oh – I dinna ken – in the wee summerhouse over

203

yonder,' mimicked the woman with huge enjoyment. Evelyn recognised that mocking voice, the ignorant sense of humour – but surely – it couldn't be . . .

'Never mind the summerhouse,' the woman said firmly. 'I'll wait in the house – it'll be cool in there and I didna come a' this way to stand in the sun like a camel.'

So saying, she marched up to the front entrance with peculiar mincing little steps and her finger was already on the bell by the time Evelyn caught up with her.

'Dinna ring that!' ordered Evelyn in a fluster. 'Ferguson willna be pleased at having to struggle into his jacket only to come out here and find you.'

'Jist whit dae ye mean by that?' growled the woman ominously but, without further ado, the girl grabbed her arm, recoiled afresh at the stale stench of whisky, pushed open the door and marched her inside, taking her to her mother's office which she was relieved to find was empty.

'Wait here,' she said, firmly and coolly, 'I'll fetch Effie. Who will I say . . .?'

'Her mither – jist that – her mither.' She emitted a snort of harsh laughter, quickly suppressed, as if she was enjoying some huge, secret joke.

Evelyn closed the door behind her and stopped to lean against it for a moment. 'But Effie hasna got a mother,' she said to herself before going to seek out the parlourmaid whom she encountered at the foot of the stairs.

Evelyn delivered the message, the older girl frowned. 'In Lady Hoity-Toity's office, you say? But who . . .?'

'She says she's your mother!' Evelyn returned sharply, annoyed at Effie's attitude. Her words had a profound effect. The girl drew back, her face white to the lips, her eyes raking Evelyn's face as if perhaps hoping to see a glimmer of a smile that would tell her the words had been spoken in jest.

'Oh, my God!' she mouthed and then she rushed off, Evelyn at her back, curious to find out more about the strange visitor even though it went against her principles to listen in to a private conversation.

But she needn't have worried on that score as it was obvious by the raised voices coming from behind the violently slammed door that neither of the two women were in sufficient control of themselves to keep their exchanges on a low key.

Effie's voice was high-pitched, verging on hysteria, 'I told you never to come here! What is it you want?'

The other woman's was equally high-pitched with the addition of a whining edge to it. 'A fine way to speak to yer auld ma and me near oot ma heid wi' worry aboot the rent. That auld swine o' a factor . . .'

Evelyn moved out of earshot, a bit red about the ears at having heard so much. But Effie didn't have her visitor for long. The door opened and Mrs Barr, if that was her name, catapulted out, as if she had been helped on her way by a none too gentle hand.

But she didn't seem unduly worried or annoyed. She came towards Evelyn, stuffing some notes down the greasy neck of her blouse, a smirk of pure triumph on her thin mouth.

'She's a snooty messin but I knew she would cough up. Feart I'd get her the boot and a red face forbye. She's aye sent me a pound or two but has missed out this last month or so. Maybe she didna think I'd hae the brass neck to come out here and see her personally but she didna reckon wi' her auld ma, eh, hen?'

She brought down one darkly-smudged lid in what was meant to be a wink and Evelyn made to walk away. A vice-like grip on her arm stayed her. 'Dinna rush away, hen, keen to tell yer pals ye met Effie's auld mither, eh? Ay well, I'll make it worth yer while,' she lowered her voice to what was meant to be a confiding whisper but only succeeded in producing a rasping drone that anybody could have heard. 'Ye wouldna think it to look at the hoor now but once she roamed the streets and took a man tae her bed for a few bob at a time. It was only a means tae an end though, she aye had ambition to better herself, did our Effie. She was mean wi' her money, saved a' she could get

205

her hands on, honestly or otherwise. She learned to speak and act properly, got a position wi' a posh family in the west end and moved up frae there. Ye'd better watch oot –' she began to move towards the door, a fact for which Evelyn was heartily thankful as from the corner of her eye she saw Ferguson shuffling up from the kitchen – 'before ye know where you are she'll be runnin' this place and everyone in it. She aye had it in her to be somebody and she'll no' care how many eyes she claws oot on the way.'

The big oak door closed on her just as Ferguson came up. 'Who was that, Evelyn?' he enquired testily, for the door and all who entered herein was his sacred domain and he disliked anyone coming or going without his knowing it.

'Oh, just some old wifie selling pegs,' Evelyn fibbed quickly without really knowing why.

Ferguson peered at her suspiciously. 'Is that so? Why did she no' come to the back entrance?'

'She couldna find it and as I was in the hall anyway I just opened the door to save you the bother.'

'I never heard the bell.' Ferguson was still suspicious.

'Ach, she just chapped. I saw her shadow on the glass and went to see who it was without thinking.'

'Ay, well, the door is my job, Evelyn. I will no' have all and sundry coming to this house – selling things at the front door – folk have no respect for their betters these days.'

Peeved, he went away, shaking his silvery head and muttering under his breath. A moment or so later the door of Maggie's office opened and Effie came out. She had obviously taken time to compose herself and to allow the old butler to be safely out of the way. Darting quick, nervous glances to the right and the left of her she rushed over to Evelyn and spoke hastily and imperatively, 'Evelyn, promise me you'll no' mention this to another living soul! Promise, Evelyn! I know I've said some pretty nasty things to you and you would have every right to go spreading it about the place. I would if it was me – but –' she eyed the younger girl uneasily, looking her straight in the face which in itself was unusual as normally when she addressed anyone her eyes darted shiftily about — 'I somehow feel you're no' like that — I heard you the now wi' Ferguson and — and I thank you for saying — what you did.'

She was in a pitiful state of anxiety, her face was ashen, a tiny nerve pulsed below one eye.

'I'll no' lie for you again, Effie,' was all Evelyn said before moving away, leaving the parlourmaid standing alone and utterly wretched-looking.

In the days and weeks that followed Evelyn was to wonder many times about the strange incident, especially as the parlourmaid now looked at her with a new respect and ceased to cast her sly innuendoes regarding Evelyn's marital status. She knew it was only a temporary truce, Effie was Effie, and would always find something to pick at; nevertheless it was a welcome interlude and she even found it in her heart to forgive the girl the trouble she had caused and quite often to feel sorry for her.

She had obviously had a hard upbringing and anyone might be excused for turning out the way she had with Mrs Barr for a mother. Little wonder she had rejected her background and had set out to better herself. She had determinedly worked her way up the ladder of the social order of servants till now she had reached the top of the scale. She couldn't do better than that — or could she?

Evelyn remembered how she had fawned over Major Baird and her determination to get him to notice her at all costs. Odd — she seldom spoke like that anymore.

Evelyn frowned at these thoughts. Seldom? Not at all. There was something different about her attitude to Andrew Baird, she was deferential, perfectly polite, utterly and entirely confident in her approach to him.

No longer was she like a giggling schoolgirl eyeing him from afar and the more sure she became of herself the more Andrew was sinking back into his old, unhappy self.

Evelyn wondered about that, she wondered very much, and when Mrs Barr's parting words came back to her – 'before ye know it she'll be running this place and everyone in it' – she wondered even more and might have tried to find out something from Andrew himself had not her days been so busy and full.

PART FOUR

Autumn 1918

Chapter Fifteen

The early days of autumn came quiet and golden to the countryside. Every morning the farmers would scan the dawn skies with anxious eyes, a prayer in their hearts that the weather would hold good for the harvest ahead, then they would take a turn to the fields to look at their corn growing fat on the stalk while the old folk, feeling the morning chill in their bones, would walk with measured tread to their woollen kists to rake out warm vests and flannel knickers in order to air them in the warm September sunshine.

On a mild, sweet-smelling mellow day, when the reapers were being brought from their sheds in shining, oil-slicked readiness for the work ahead, Evelyn and David were quietly married in the scrubbed and polished parlour of Wood Cottage. The Colonel and Lady Elizabeth had wished the ceremony to be held in Dunmarnock's big airy sitting room, but circumstances had decreed otherwise, though they were present that day, along with their son and daughter, rubbing shoulders with Raggy Annie, Violet, Gavin, Douglas Grainger, and Evelyn's own family of course, including Mary who arrived from the north-east, fresh-faced and full of vigour, bringing with her scores of warm wishes from the good folk of Rothiedrum.

Hinney had sent a fragrant herb pillow so that all Evelyn's dreams would be happy ones. Coulter and Carnallachie, for once burying their differences, had clubbed together to buy a canteen of cutlery. Best silver plate it was, with a note tucked into the red velvet lining in Coulter's spidery, old-fashioned script: 'Carnallachie put half but I put a bob more for the nice velvet covers –' she could just imagine him, chortling and chuckling at having got that one over the other old rogue, and managing to secrete it into the box without his knowledge – 'but it was worth it for you, my lassie. King's Croft is no' the same without the Grants. There's another chiel there now, dour as the rainstorms over Bennachie's pow and that mean with his sillar he crawled about in the stoor for two days looking for a farthing he dropped from his pooch. God bless you, lassie, the good fairies will watch over you for you deserve the best. Coulter.'

Numerous other gifts, both humble and grand, accompanied Mary on the journey to Renfrewshire, and she breezed in, rosy-cheeked and burdened down, a breath of Rothiedrum air, declaring herself to be 'fair wabbit and longing for her bed', but throwing herself first on her family, parcels, baggage and all.

Evelyn had been thrilled beyond belief to receive the gifts, but more, to know of the love and thought that lay behind them, and she cried and exclaimed over them all before pinning Mary down for the rest of the evening to beg for news of those beloved people she missed so much.

She was further delighted and utterly surprised to receive through the post a fat parcel from Lady Marjorie Forbes, no other, containing an exquisitely embroidered tablecloth of Irish linen together with a little card bearing flowing, congratulatory words.

'Fancy that,' Maggie said, the handsome, strong face of her taking on a pensive look for she had come to know and like her rich cousin extremely well in her last year at Rothiedrum, so much so there had been times recently when she had stood back from whatever she was doing to recall with nostalgia those meetings and to wish rather wistfully that she hadn't wasted so many years resenting the Forbes family.

'That isna all!' Evelyn was plunging excitedly into the wrappings, lifting out a small package which, when opened, proved to contain a dainty little gold fob watch that could be worn pinned, or hung on the accompanying gold chain. 'It's from Oggie!' she cried, staring at his little card, the tears springing swift to her eyes for she had loved the fine old gentleman who had taken her to his heart as if she was one of the family.

'Lord Lindsay Ogilvie,' breathed Maggie, her own eyes misty for the father she had never known and whom she had rejected so harshly when he had come humbly and warily to King's Croft to try and make amends for his years of silence.

'Ay, the grand old gentleman himself,' murmured Jamie, watching Maggie who had always behaved so strangely whenever that particular name was mentioned. 'What has he to say for himself, princess?'

'Time was golden when spent with you, my dear, dear child.' Evelyn read the firm, bold hand, dashing away her tears with an impatient gesture though unable to keep the tremor from her voice. 'May the years ahead of you be filled with richness and sweetness as you deserve, but may I humbly ask that you never forget the hours you spent with one old man who has never forgotten you. Too short they were and over too soon but dear are those treasured moments and will be for all time. Yours affectionately, Oggie.'

'Oh, I loved that dear old man!' cried Evelyn, her eyes filling afresh. 'I wish I had kent him longer – oh – I wish I could see him again! I wish I could see them all – Evander and Lady Marjorie, Oggie and Gillie!'

'Ay, the old rascal aye did have a way wi' words,' said Maggie softly, her fingers caressing the little watch as if she could extract something of her father from it, no matter how small the measure.

Into the parcel Lady Marjorie had enclosed a letter, marked simply, '*Evelyn Grant, private and personal*', and this Evelyn bore off to the privacy of her bedroom, knowing full well who it was from as she knew the writing as well as her own. Letters from France, bearing the exact same script, were hidden safely in her tin box, neatly tied with a braid of dried heather for she had been unwilling to part with them when she had parted with so much else on leaving King's Croft.

Dearest Princess,

I knew the day was coming when I must finally relinquish any hopes I ever entertained for you. I kept trying to make myself believe it would never really come and so I played ostrich in order to keep myself going. Please don't take that the wrong way, I'm truly glad that romantic heart of yours has at last found its happiness — even though it's with the wrong bloody man and should have been me.

There I go again, saying things I know I shouldn't but I'm not going to take back any of it. I'm still the same hot-headed Gillan and always will be, deep down. The grapevine has been busy. Mother tells me you have a son. That's something else I can't really take in. My skinny, lovely little princess, a mother. So near are the days of the Kelpie Pool and the Rothiedrum hairsts, so near is the memory of a red-haired imp shouting her cheek at me from the back of a homeward bound Clyde. I can't really believe that she and me are all grown up and Johnny and Florrie are no longer with us.

But I have to believe, don't I, Evie? We'll go our separate ways now, gone forever is the wonderful sweet innocence of childhood, so near, so far.

Last Christmas was the best of my life. You and me and the others out there in the woods and the snow, Maggie and her Atholl Brose, Jamie and his fiddle. I love you all, all the Grants that ever were born.

I'll be glad when this endless war ends. I ache for everything I left behind, then remember I won't be coming back to you and the ache goes away, leaving me dead inside.

I might go out to Africa and be with Uncle Lindsay for a bit; if anyone can make me forget he can, just as long as he doesn't start talking about you again. After that I suppose I'll go back to studying law (remember? fusty old wigs and dusty old books?). I might meet and marry a fusty old maid and have countless little fusties running about wearing holes in my fusty old house.

Be happy, princess, spare a thought for me now and then. You can't say I didn't try, eh?

I'll hold you forever in my dreams, keep you for always in my heart. Goodbye and God bless you, my dear, dear girl.

Ever yours, Gillie.

When she had finished reading she threw herself down on her bed and cried as if she would never stop; then she got up, washed her face and put the letter away in her battered tin box, beside all the other treasures she could never bear to part with.

And now, here she was, solemn and silent, her heart strange and sore in her breast, Davie by her side, the red rosebud in his buttonhole like a blob of blood against the dark cloth of his suit; the minister's voice leading up to the words that would make her the wife of a man she had loved for so long, even though sometimes he was a stranger she didn't know at all.

Raggy Annie had done her right proud. With hands that were rough and chapped from years of hard work she had fashioned a dress fit for a princess. Pale green silk it was, delicate and fine, lying neat and sweet upon her small boned body, her glorious red hair piled up and braided through with white Marguerite daisies and bits of green satin and a little veil draped over her eyes though never dulling the brilliance of their emerald green sparkle.

It had felt strange but good coming into the room on her father's arm and he so smart in his best dark suit, the eyes of him black and glowing with a moistness in them though the tears never showing, for he was a man and men didn't cry on occasions like these even though he was giving his beloved youngest daughter to a man he didn't right know yet but would, for he was James King Grant after all, and few men had turned away from the husky magic of his gypsy tongue and the open friendship in his honest brown eyes.

And there was Maggie, white-haired to be sure, but the bloom of youth still there in her fine noble face with its fresh pink skin and bold eyes looking out straight and sharp and the tall, proud figure of her stiff and erect with that little lift of her chin that had earned her the label of Lady Hoity-Toity, among other things, from folk who liked her well enough but were too envious and respectful of her ever really to love her.

Beside her, Grace, beautiful Grace, her slender body happed in white silk and the great burning dark eyes of her casting their haunting light upon the sister in whom she had always confided and trusted all through their childhood and on into young womanhood.

The contrast that was Mary was similar to seeing a wildflower beside a delicate lily. Her vibrant face so bonny and glowing with roses rampant in her cheeks and her glossy black hair imprisoned in the depths of a cheeky big hat with a wide brim that shadowed her face but couldn't dim the laughter tumbling out of her eyes . . .

The minister started the ceremony and then David was speaking, that beautiful, sensual mouth of his saying things she had never thought to hear. She had waited a long time for this moment; now it was here but strange, she felt no joy, only a tight ball of nerves growing and growing at the pit of her stomach . . .

'. . . take this man to be your lawful wedded husband?'

She started, looked round, colour flooding her face. Everyone was waiting, wondering why she didn't answer straightaway. Davie's eyes were on her, dark, compelling, questioning. And no wonder, this was the greatest moment of her life and she had been so keyed up she had barely taken in what the minister was saying.

She panicked, glanced over her shoulder, caught her

father's eyes, bright, as anxious as her own but reassuring, always they had looked at her with that special warm glow.

'I do.' Her voice came out, loud, clear, only a very slight tremor at the back of her throat that no one knew of but herself.

Four years of heartache, sorrow, laughter, rose up before her like a shining mist that trembled with echoes from far-off in the years of golden girlhood, and the pain that was Davie ached her heart sore for the hurt he could give her one minute and the joy the next. But that was Davie, her Davie, she wouldn't know him if he was any other way now and the mists of her past life dissipated and cleared so that her vision of the day was raw and sweet and throbbing with the life that was all around her, life that was her husband, kissing her firm on the lips, life that was her father and mother and sisters, wrapping her in their arms and making her laugh and cry with her love and joy of them, life that was the Colonel and his wife, and Raggy Annie, Christine, Andrew, Gavin, Douglas Grainger, crowding round, kissing and shaking hands as if she was more to any of them than she felt she deserved to be.

And then, the real, near, exquisite life that was Davie, hers to hold and love when all the chatter was done with and it was just he and she, travelling north on a journey that never seemed quite real, on pony carts, and trains that never seemed to get there but did in the end, and there was Kenneth Mor, more real than anybody could be, the sinews rippling in great brown hands that grabbed their cases and threw them into the cart that went bumping and rattling over ruts and potholes on the wild, isolated road to Kenneray on the north-west coast of Scotland.

And at last there was Croft Donald, sturdy and douce against the night behind the hills, the scent of the gloaming dripping round and about it, a huge harvest moon riding its fat-bellied trail in the heavens above it, a soft glimmer

217

of light winking and shining from windows that were like friendly warm eyes gazing out into the purple-shaded night.

Nellie came rushing out to meet them, her long peeny flying in the breeze, her hair soft and flyaway round her face for she'd barely time to get her breath after seeing the children to bed and attending to all the last-minute chores before the black dot that was the cart was sighted on the moonlit road. Her last task had been to confine the cockerel in a peat creel so that he couldn't mix with the hens on the following day which was Sunday, and after that there hadn't been any time left for personal preening. But she had put on a clean peenie and that made it all right. Nellie always maintained that royalty could pass her by and she would feel just as good as any of them as long as she was wearing a fresh white apron.

It was all a blur of breathless greetings and sheepdogs lifting their legs at the cart wheels, all to the accompaniment of pig grunts, cow moos, horse snorts, and clucking hens, in the background.

'Come away in, you must be fair wearied after the journey.' Nellie was patting her hair into place as she spoke, calming down to her normal practical self, while Kenneth led his little Highland garron away to unhitch her and sort her for the night. He and his father had two horses to work their sixty-five acres, though a lot of that was rough hill ground used mainly for sheep grazing.

One of the horses was Bess, a big, placid Clydesdale mare, who never needed to be coaxed from the field to be dressed for a day of hard work: the other was the Highland garron who was worth her weight in gold for she was a hardy little beast, able to graze and survive on the meanest pasture, and was used for a variety of work.

Kenneth Mor was a great man for giving his animals long-winded Gaelic names though the one he had bestowed on the garron was short enough but with a rather rude connotation. It was Allt Buidhe (pronounced Boo-ee) and meant 'yellow stream' and right enough, the beast made an awful stoor when she lifted her tail to relieve herself.

'When yon cratur pishes it's as near as dam't to a burn in spate!' Kenneth would roar at the top of his voice and pretend not to notice the reproving look thrown at him by Nellie.

But for all that he was real fond of the hard-working little animal, and when he had unhitched her he spent a good few minutes talking into her flicking lugs before putting her into the field beside Bess, and taking his time about it for he was a restless creature at harvest time and liked to linger out there in the scented pastures on a fine night such as this.

Evelyn had always loved the old-fashioned farmhouse fireplace at Croft Donald with the big stone jambs on either side of the black-leaded ribs and a welter of earthenware pots and jars decorating the mantelpiece, but Nellie loved it less for it was difficult to keep clean, though an easy enough job to get the sand for scouring the steel bits to a satiny shine.

Even so, she and Irene between them kept it sparkling, and it was a fair joy to feel the heat of it after the bumpy journey in the cold night air and to smell the savoury aroma wafting from the broth pot that was hanging on the swee above the flames.

Irene was presiding over this and no sooner were introductions done with but Evelyn and David were sitting at the table, supping bowls of steaming ham soup while Nellie flapped scones and curled oatcakes on the girdle that had now replaced the huge black broth pot on the fire chains.

They all sat round the fire to eat the piping hot delicacies, swimming with melted butter they were, or thick with tangy cheese, while on the stone hearth sat an enormous pot of raspberry jam for folk to help themselves when they felt like it. The room was quiet and free of bairns and Evelyn hardly dared ask about her son, not that night with herself the new bride of David Grainger and him having had so little time to get used to the idea of that without coping with the idea of a baby as well.

But neither Kenneth Mor nor Iain Cameron had any reservations about that. They laughed and talked about 'the boy and his lungs' and said he had fair wakened up Kenneray with his bawlings and screamings and Irene said he had half-scared the life out of the cats who skulked away with pinned back ears whenever he got going with his tantrums.

'Ach well, it saves Nell the job o' skiting them out the door wi' her broom,' Kenneth hazarded but with a wary glance at his wife who had been, as he called it, 'pricklier than a bed o' nettles this whilie', though he had been gentle with her when she barked at him, knowing that she was dreading the day of having to part with the baby.

'But he's no' so bad now,' nodded Iain, lathering jam onto a scone at such a lavish rate it ran over his fingers and needed a few good licks from his tongue to mop up the spillage. 'He's settled down this past while and taking time off from greetin' to have a wee keek at the world around him.'

'You'll see him for yourself the morn,' was all Nellie said, her fair head down bent, and Evelyn knew fine what was on her mind but pushed such thoughts from her head. It was the first night of her honeymoon, after all, and she was glad when the talk turned to the wedding and was eager to join with Davie in describing the events of the day which lay behind her now but which she knew she would never forget, simple and swift as it had been.

It was no surprise to her when a ceilidh started up, for that was the way of it in the lonely lands above the seas and among the hills, when the Scotland of the mists and suns was immortalised in song and story beside warm, safe hearths of croft and cottage.

It was Kenneth, that great red Highlander, who raised his voice in a song that spoke of the wild hills and the dreaming glens, and while he was singing Iain went ben the parlour to fetch glasses and whisky to set down on the kitchen table, just cleared of its supper debris by Nellie who had then crept quiet from the room to check the bairns asleep upstairs in their beds.

'Whist,' she warned, coming back to the kitchen to a husband whose sark had been torn open at the neck better to allow his big lungs to take their fill of air too hot now for comfort but cooling nicely in the fresh sea air flowing in through the hastily opened sash. 'You'll wake the bairns wi' all your scraichin'.'

But it was too late, the bairns were awakened anyway, up there in their beds, lying quiet and snug, listening with pure pleasure to the magnificent voice of Kenneth Mor, and not minding to have been wakened from sleep that was no novelty at all compared with that of singing and storytelling.

Only the baby slept on, used as he was to a bustle of a house that woke at dawn and maybe before if he was in a mood to decree that it should. He had 'grat right well that day' to quote Iain and was glad enough now to rest his plump limbs in his cosy little cradle.

So down below, Kenneth had his way, and after him Irene sang *The Road to Dundee* with its 'cauld winter howling o'er moor and o'er mountain' and it was good that, to sing about the wreck of winter when outside Croft Donald the rose-flushed Atlantic whispered under the moon and little white crofthouses dreamed under the stars, except for a stirring in Tigh na Beinne under the hill where stout Bella Armstrong turned in her bed and murmured something about Croft Donald ceilidhing whereupon Big Ben Armstrong, her man, said quick as a flash, 'Wheest, woman, and put your bum next to mine, it's Sunday soon but time for a cuddle afore it comes.'

Half an hour later a slightly flushed Nellie, her sleeves rolled to her elbows as was her habit except on the Sabbath, the chapped red hands of her lying peaceful and innocent in her lap, sang a Highland fairy lullaby, the poignant tale of a baby stolen away from its mother by the fairies and never found again no matter how far and long she looked for it.

Nellie was no great singer but there was something so wistful in her voice it was utterly spellbinding. The words of the song rode soft and sad on the whisper of Iain's fiddle, plaintive, plaintive in the hush of the room, and everyone wondered where the brisk, fleering Nellie had gone, for it wasn't she who sat in the ingle but another Nellie, whose eyes were open but watching other things, remembered at night and in the gloaming and in lone secret moments when raw, unspoken yearnings tore at the breast for things only half-glimpsed in the shadowed pattern of life.

Evelyn's heart swelled with compassion for her sister, but then she looked at Davie and he looked at her, and they smiled quietly to one another in shared understanding of that night and that time, and in their youth and their ignorance they knew that they would never be like Nellie looking dark and wanting at the back of yesterday and into the veiled face of tomorrow.

Let that bring what it would, and Kenneth thought so too, for though he looked strange and sad at Nellie's song he suddenly rose up and asked them all to charge their glasses in a toast to the bride.

Nellie got up too, flustered and embarrassed, and joined with the rest in crying 'the bride', looking at her sister with those beautiful amber-green eyes of hers and hugging her close which wasn't like Nellie at all as she had never believed in 'palaver o' that sort'.

'Good luck and God bless you, my babby,' she said huskily, and then she looked at Davie in an oddly intense way, not sure of him yet, not even knowing if she would ever get to like him.

She was like Maggie that way, from the beginning she had mistrusted him and hadn't approved of the manner in which he had conducted himself when first he had come to King's Croft, enough charm in him to melt an iceberg and an eye for the women that wasn't right decent, though even she had to admit it wasn't all his doing since even sensible beings like Irene fell swiftly and readily under his spell.

'You take care o' this girl, David Grainger,' she said softly but with great emphasis. 'She's been through a lot for you and many's the time I thought she would pine away altogether when she was waiting and wondering if you were ever coming back to her.'

'Och, c'mon now Nellie,' he chided, his eyes holding hers teasingly, 'surely you know the reasons for that. Prisoners o' war canna escape every five minutes just to go running home to their sweethearts, can they now?'

'I meant before that!' she replied sharply. 'You have it in you to be selfish, David Grainger, so just you mind what you're about wi' her.'

Her bluntness took him aback. Just for a moment a cold glimmer of dislike sprang like a wild beast out of his eyes, then the moment passed and he was smiling again, his hand on her shoulder, the warm pressure of it urging her to better humour so that she gave a little laughing shrug and told both him and Evelyn that she was just tired and needing her bed. But after that night she and he knew that something existed between them that would never lose its sharp edge, no matter how well they might become acquainted in the years that lay ahead.

'Oh, look at the time!' she glared accusingly at the clock. 'It's Sunday morning and all those glasses still to be washed! I canna abide a Sabbath wi' dirty dishes in it.'

'Relax, lassie,' urged Irene, 'we'll do them between us when we get up. Who's to know if we wash a few wee things on a Sunday?'

Nellie rolled down her sleeves and buttoned the cuffs. 'The Lord will and so will the half o' Kenneray. That Bella Armstrong has long lugs on her and an even longer tongue over which she has no control at all. I thought Kirsty Keith o' Dippiedoon was the world's worst futret until I came here and got to ken Bella. Her hearing's that sharp she can even tell the kind o' paper you use in your wee housie, just by hearing the rustle o' it as she passes by. And if she can hear that she will surely hear the clink o' glasses in the sink, and go to kirk all prim and proper while she gossips about the sinners within Croft Donald.'

Nellie said all this simply because she felt like asserting herself on the matter of the dishes and not because she had ever been one to adhere to the day of rest so strictly observed in God-fearing households all over Scotland.

She had already shocked Kenneray to the core by not only missing kirk services but by sewing and darning on the Sabbath, and – dreadful sin! – by reading secular newspapers and being actually brazen enough not to care who saw her reading them. The only reason she followed the rule of confining the cockerel was because the 'damt cratur' got on her nerves and shutting him away gave her the only kind of rest she ever needed or wanted on the Sabbath as it simply wasn't in her nature to twiddle idle thumbs, no matter the day of the week.

Even so, she respected the routine of Irene and Iain in their own home, and off she went now, helter-skelter, winding the clocks, bringing in the peats, clearing the table of dirty dishes before setting it down again for the Sunday morning repast of cold porridge cut into slices from the porridge drawer.

She exclaimed loudly when she noted that the water pails were empty and both Kenneth and Iain were despatched forthwith, till a row of brimming buckets sat neatly on top of the sink slats, ready for the morning. David offered to help tidy up the kitchen but was knocked aside in the rush as Nellie fleered round with a broom, sweeping away the stoor and the supper crumbs the cats had missed.

'No, no, no,' she told him emphatically, 'just see you smoor the fire before you come up to bed, and mind make sure you put the guard over it, and dinna leave your shoes or anything else on the hearth for fear o' hot cinders . . .'

'Bed!' ordered Kenneth laughingly, putting a firm arm round his wife's waist and steering her to the door. 'You two bide up as long as you feel like doing,' he threw over his shoulder. 'We're supposed to have a long lie come the morn though I myself have yet to experience it.'

After that, quite suddenly so it seemed after all the activity, Evelyn and David found themselves alone, blinking as sleepily as two cats into the last curls of flame in the grate, the room quiet and dark around them, for Nellie had turned the lamp down low as befitted that 'ungodly hour o' the morning'.

David's face was ghostly in the fitful firelight, his head was that of a boy, yet the soft dark of it bowed to the grate as if the weight of it was too much for his tired shoulders. His hands were together, the knuckles loosely clenched, and though Evelyn was weary herself a great swelling of love rose in her breast and she went to sit by him and lay her head on his lap.

He uncoiled one finger and caressed the bright gleam of her hair, slowly, without hurry, time stretching long and golden into the hours and days ahead.

'Nellie's a bitch!'

The words fell like harsh pebbles into the pool of silence that flowed all around them and the ripples they made circled for a while before ebbing away.

'Ach, you'll get used to her,' Evelyn said carelessly. 'People do once they get to ken her better. She's aye been frank and outspoken but you'll never find anybody more honest and you'll aye ken where you stand wi' her.'

'I already do,' he said quietly, 'I think I always did.'

He said no more on the subject, instead he took her hand and they padded to the door, but at the last minute Evelyn remembered the fire and together they smoored it with the contents of the dross bucket before creeping hand in hand up the dark staircase, pausing at every creaking step to stifle their mirth and listen with bated breath to the heartbeat of the sleeping house.

They climbed on, thinking they were never reaching the top but coming to it abruptly, and then to the door of the room Evelyn had shared with Grace on that last memorable occasion.

The girning creak of the hinges shattered the deep silence of the upper floor. Behind a hidden door somebody coughed, from another a child squeaked like a kitten. With tightly held breath and beating hearts they listened, then as one they dived into their room to fall back against the door, smothering relieved laughter, one into the neck of the other, and the kisses came wild then, all traces of weariness gone from lips that sought and fought and kindled passions that had smouldered inside of them all through the day with its ceremonies and travels and music.

When at last they drew apart they saw the white of the bridal bed looming at them out of the surrounding blackness, and the strangeness of that tugged at Evelyn's heart for she had first lain in that same bed with Grace as her companion and there too she had stretched and cried and curled in the cruel torment of childbirth.

David went to the window to pull back the curtains, letting the sea-spangled morning creep cold into the room, and after that there was no time for reflection of any sort. He had done that to see her when he unpinned her hair and let it fall rich and thick about her shoulders.

There was no time to feel shy or hesitant, not now, with the heat of his lips searing her shoulders, and hardly able to wait to kiss her breasts, when at last she rid herself of her clothing and happed herself around him, shivering in the chill of the room, but soon warm and safe in the circle of his waiting arms. They said nothing, there was nothing to say, it had all been said before, and the floating warmth of the big feather bed was ready to enfold them round in its downy caress and to mould itself to the stirring passion of their eager limbs. The sweetness of his kisses lingered for a while on her neck and shoulders and went on and on, down and down, to breasts and belly and secret places afire with wanting and waiting, and all the time he whispered and murmured deep in his throat, sounds that weren't words but strange sighing nuances that her ear couldn't understand but her heart could.

Gently and expertly he took her with him to the heights of desire so that all she wanted was assuagement for the fire that curled and pulsed into every fibre of her being. It didn't seem possible that a small, separate part of her mind should detach itself from such pleasurable sensations and when it did she hardly heard or recognised the weak inner voice that floated into her absorbed consciousness.

'Davie,' it whispered unwillingly, 'be careful, I dinna want another bairn, not yet, not yet . . .'

But it was only a fleeting thought, unvoiced, unheard. Even if she had said the words aloud he wouldn't have heard. He was lost, lost, gentle no longer but forceful, demanding, his body hard against her softness, thrusting itself into her, pushing and twisting and filling every throbbing, aching cell, his breath harsh and swift in his throat, her own echoing his, sighing and breathing as together they strived towards that final release from their fiery agony. Even when it came and she and he were drenched in waves of ecstasy, the fire seemed to leap higher, burn and burn, till the flames of it licked her heart and her breasts before finally receding in a slow dying of heat that left her weak and helpless in his slackening embrace.

And then the heaviness came, creeping over them, curling into them and through them, so that they felt they would never again move from the billowing cloud that was their feather mattress happing them round in its comforting warmth. Nothing mattered then. The world outside the night-tinted window belonged to other beings who slept and dreamed and never knew of their world with its soft breathings and sighings and sleepy murmurings.

Even when a baby's cries shattered the stillness they hardly heard nor cared. It was soon quieted anyway and it mattered not who had stilled the lusty throat. The night was full of shadows that wandered the dark hours and if one of them could rise from its sleepings to lull the other shadows then so be it.

None of them could penetrate the still and peace that lay like a soft blanket over the bridal bed. The Devil's Door and all it meant belonged to another time and another place, and the young girl who had lain too long in its blackness slept the sleep of one who had crept clear and free of nameless phantoms who had once stalked her night world. She was married to David. She was safe.

Chapter Sixteen

Reality came with the dawn, honey-rose outside the window, painting the hills purple, smudging the inky sea with blobs of gold.

The cockerel in his peat creel opened his cramped throat only to emit a sad travesty of sound that died quickly away leaving the Sabbath morning to blink sleepy eyes into the rising sun and to yawn and stretch into the feathers for a few blessed minutes of quiet before the day really got going.

To Evelyn, warm and snug beside David, her head close to his on the pillow, her limbs lazy and incredibly relaxed, it was a beautiful reality. Except for the traces of colour on the western ocean night still lay over the land, serene and barely awakened, the muted murmurings of shorebirds and the sighing of the sea only adding to its tranquillity.

For long, blissful minutes she lay quietly, gazing towards the window, watching gulls drifting on air thermals; seeing the orderly pattern made by a formation of wild ducks against the breast of a fluffy pink cloud; seeing the sky gradually lightening and brightening till the new day was imbued with life and love. She knew it was love. It was there all around her, in the atmosphere, in the softly-lit corners of the room, a room she had come to know well since her first acquaintance of it a year ago when she had come to Croft Donald with Grace for a holiday away from all the sad upheavals of King's Croft.

This room had known her despair of that time. In it she had whispered her fears for David's safety, her uncertainties about her future, her growing certainty that she was carrying the child of a man whom she had thought never to see again.

It all seemed very far away now and she wasn't sorry to push that part of her life to the back of her mind and think instead of things nearer to hand, the birth of her son for instance, somehow unreal, but real enough now that she was back in this room lying beside the man who had given her such sorrow and pain – and finally his love.

Memories of last night came crowding in on her and she stirred and gazed into his sleeping face, so young, so close to her own. The sensual mouth was soft, relaxed, thick dark lashes made tiny fans of shadow on his high cheek bones, a tendril of earth-brown hair strayed over his brow. Gently she kissed it, then his mouth, only a feather touch, she wanted to wake him, yet didn't, for at the same time she was aware of movement in the room below. Nellie was up. She was sure it was Nellie and if Nellie was up and doing at this hour of Kenneray's day of rest then it had to be for a good reason and that reason would likely be Alexander David Grainger, though it might just be Nellie herself who never could lie idle in bed, no matter the day of the week.

But Evelyn knew the activity owed itself to her son. She heard him, mewing and whimpering his greeting to the morning, and quite unbidden a great rush of excitement thrilled her being. Quite suddenly she couldn't wait to see him and hold him in her arms.

She had given him birth and then she had left him, had half-forgotten him by conveniently burying him at the back of her mind and she hadn't missed him at all, so anxious had she been to get back to the silent lost man who was his father.

But David wasn't lost anymore, he had come back from his silent world, back to life, back to her and his son, and Nellie was down below, tending a child who wasn't hers but who might have been for all the love and devotion she had heaped on him since he had been shorn from his mother's arms.

But all that was done with now. Months of suppressed longings came rushing out of her heart, making her leap from the bed that only last night she had imagined she never wanted to leave again.

Marriage and motherhood, one had come before the other, tearing her apart, still tearing her apart for she was as new to the one as she was to the other, and she hurried into her clothes, shivering in the chill bite of morning, hastily splashing her face from the ewer, tugging a brush through her hair, kissing David's sleeping face once more before rushing downstairs and into the kitchen and Nellie sitting by the newly-stoked fire, her untended hair falling soft about her pale, morning face, the baby on her lap, happed cosily in a clean hippen and fluffy white jacket.

His little toes were held pink and squirming to the heat of the fire, his rosebud of a mouth was clamped firm and eager round the teat of a bottle, the gurgles, grunts, and suckings of him falling rude and uncaring into the peat-crackling peace of the morning kitchen with its cats and its snorings and its deeply-recessed windows looking one to the hills, the other to the sea.

'You're up, I see,' was Nellie's somewhat brusque greeting, not lifting her head, her entire being concentrating on the comfort and well-being of the child on her lap. 'Well, see and make yourself useful, the fire is ready to take a few more peats – and dinna be skiting dirt all over my clean grate – oh, and while you're about it take a cloot to the table and make sure you rinse it out afterwards and . . .'

'Right, Nellie,' responded Evelyn, scampering to do as she was bid before her sister could think of anything else as, once she got going, there was simply no stopping her.

When she came back to stand by the little wicker rocking chair that Nellie claimed as her own, the baby had drunk his fill and appeared stupefied in his brimming appeasement, the plump pink cheeks of him sunk deep in his bib, a puzzled frown between eyes that thoughtfully contemplated the fire and seemed to unfocus themselves in the process, while his mouth bubbled froth and his head lolled on his fat-layered neck.

'Here, take him.' Abruptly Nellie thrust the boy at his mother. 'He'll be needing to break wind.'

Evelyn grabbed quickly at her sturdy son, immediately alarmed when he grew red in the face and twisted his features into spasms of pain. 'I – I dinna ken how,' she stuttered, holding the infant at arm's length and staring at his mouth which was opening itself wide in preparation of a good hearty bawl.

'Och, let me,' Nellie snatched him back and walked up and down the floor, the baby held against her shoulder while she rubbed his back with a firm hand, all the while hushing him and crooning soothing nonsense into his lugs.

When at last he opened his throat to emit a series of loud belches it was difficult to tell who looked the most surprised, Evelyn or her son, for the expressions on either face was comical to behold and made even Nellie smile when she handed the child once more to his mother.

'There, you'll ken what to do next time,' Nellie said briefly. 'And dinna be too long gawping at him for he'll be filling his hippen again and will need changing before he goes back down.'

Alexander David Grainger had grown into a bonny boy, bouncing being the proper adjective to apply where he was concerned for he was just that, the limbs of him well-formed and strong and perfectly capable of kicking his displeasure as Evelyn found when he braced his feet against her stomach and pushed with all his might. No longer did his head resemble a gull's egg as Kenneth Mor had laughingly described it soon after his birth, it now boasted a fine sprouting of hair, new and soft, honey-gold with a faint tinge of red to it; his eyes were the most unusual Evelyn had ever seen in a child of his age, one grey-green, the other hazel brown, orbs that both fascinated and disconcerted, not only for their colour, but for an oddly appraising look in them that would still have seemed out of place in a much older child.

For several long moments they regarded this stranger who held him and watched him with a stare as unblinking as his own, then the wondering expression left him, he glowered at his mother, long and hard, his features twisting, his lower lip pouting. Silent tears drowned the colour of his eyes and he turned his head away, blindly seeking the familiar mother figure he had known since birth. His little body was trembling, his strong legs once more bracing themselves against Evelyn's stomach in an effort to push her away.

'Ach, would you look at the petted lip on him.' Nellie's words were light enough but her voice vibrated with pride in the knowledge that the baby should at once turn to her in his need for comfort. 'He was aye good at turning it on but I'm thinking the poor wee man has excelled himself this time.'

The enchantment Evelyn had felt on seeing her son was rapidly departing, leaving cold reality in its place. This was no doll to play with or cast aside according to her whim. This was a child, living and real, one who was of her flesh but who turned away from her in fear and trembling, wanting only Nellie to hold and love him and care for him.

The enormity of the thing she had done made her feel cold and afraid, her extra sense warning her that the deed would have far-reaching effects and never, never, would this, her first-born child, accept her as his first and only mother. But then she shrugged such dark thoughts away, this was only a baby, innocent and ignorant of the world, his needs and wants were only for his own comfort and she could change a hippen as good as Nellie any day, she had done it often enough for Col when he was a baby and she could do it again — by God and she could!

Her head went up, out jutted her chin, she suppressed the instinct to hand the boy back to Nellie and was glad that she did so for David came bursting into the room, so eager and thrusting she knew that he, like herself, had been seized with an irrepressible desire to see his son.

His hair was rumpled, his collars unfastened about his throat, his braces were hanging loose, and she could have laughed at that and at the prim expression that flitted over Nellie's strong face, but the time wasn't right for that and so she smiled instead, a smile that she kept hidden, for David was at her shoulder, gazing down at the baby, *their* baby, the child they had conceived together in pain and in passion.

'He's big.' Pride was in David's voice, Evelyn felt the throbbing of it surging into her ears, singing into her heart. 'But he'll do, ay, he'll do right enough.'

He took the child from her and carried him over to the window as if better to examine him, his hold firm and sure, no hesitancy in him when the child squirmed and mewed and would have cried but for the sudden command that bade him be still.

'It's your father holding you, do you hear that, lad, your father,' he said imperatively, then he threw over his shoulder, 'I might have denied him except for that eye, that definitely is mine, the resemblance is undeniable.'

Evelyn laughed at that, giggling her mirth into her hands, against his shoulder when he came back to the fire with a son who stared entranced at him, as if some sort of spell had befallen him over there by the window.

David looked at Nellie. 'You've done right well by him, Nellie quine, he's trig and bonny and so well-cared for he might be your own.'

He couldn't have riled her more if he had tried, for nothing nettled her as much as people who aped the north-east accent, no matter how well-meant, but worse, in her highly emotional state she read more into his words than he could have dreamed, imagining them to allude to her childless state, and after treating him to a contemptuous glare she jerked a napkin from the wooden clothes horse and threw it at him so that it landed fair and square in his face.

'It's time you looked to your own,' she told him coldly, 'the bairn needs changing. Let us see if your actions are as smart as your words.'

Their eyes met, hostile, challenging. He said not a word but sat down in the ingle to lie the baby on his knee. Without fumble, fuss or hurry he bared the plump buttocks, washed them from the bowl on the hearth set there for that purpose, dried and powdered them and finally happed them neat and firm in a clean napkin.

'Ay, you're able, David Grainger, I'll grant you that,' was all she said and had time to say for the house was up and a-bustle, the children clattering downstairs, Kenneth and Iain pausing only for a mouthful of tea before going out on the morning round of the croft, Irene getting ready the breakfast, sparse though it was that Sabbath morning.

When the men returned they all sat round the table to bow their heads while Iain said grace, his succinct thanks to the Lord heard clearly by everyone since baby Alex lay quiet in his cradle, placed there by David himself with a hush and an order to go 'sleepy-bye'.

'The wee one is deafening wi' his silence this morning,' commented Iain, digging into his fried porridge slices with relish as he had an appetite like a horse and never seemed to mind what he ate as long as it was filling.

David applied himself to his breakfast as if he tackled slices of fried porridge every other day of the week, and indeed, it had been common enough fare in his own home when he was a boy and glad to wolf down anything that came his way.

'All the boy needs is a firm hand,' he said without looking up, not daring to meet Nellie's eye but determined to say his piece just the same. 'He's been spoiled, anyone wi' half an eye can see that.'

There was a short, uncomfortable silence, broken by Kenneth Mor glancing quickly at Nellie's flaring face. 'No bairn gets spoiled in this house, only loved and cared for, which is all any bairn needs to see it through life.'

'Discipline, don't forget that,' David went on, ignoring

Evelyn's warning look, 'I had it myself from my own father and it never did me any harm.'

'I agree wi' you there,' nodded Irene. 'I needed to exercise plenty o' it when I was teaching infants but they were old enough to appreciate it when they came to me.'

'It should start from the cradle,' persisted David and sparked off a good-going discussion in which everyone joined without rancour, except Nellie who applied herself to her food with purpose and was first up from the table and away to feed the hens, Col and Isla Nell at her heels.

'Heed what you're saying in front o' her, lad,' warned Kenneth Mor when the door banged shut, rattling the dishes in the dresser. 'She's a good woman and does a grand job wi' the bairns.'

'I know,' David sounded and looked rueful. 'But she takes far too much to heart and I just don't seem able to say the right things to her without her jumping down my throat. When I said the baby was spoilt I didna just mean by her. You've all done your share o' that and I'm the first to admit it's natural wi' the youngest o' a household. My mother did it wi' my young brother and now she's off her head altogether because he's dead and I might as well no' exist. If it hadn't been for my father I might have gone off my head too, just to keep her company, but thank God he was there, a man I've respected all my life even though I felt the sting o' his hand often enough when I was a bairn.'

For the first time, Evelyn saw that this favouritism of his mother's had affected him far more than she or anyone else realised and later, when everyone else was upstairs getting ready for kirk, she said tentatively, 'Davie, you'll no' spend our honeymoon arguing wi' Nellie about the baby, will you?'

'Ach, no, of course I won't, she's the one who wants to argue but I promise I'll try to hold my tongue and behave like an angel – though I can't promise she'll no' hear the bedsprings creaking at night.'

'Faith! That would be terrible! It's funny, I'm married now and so too is Nellie yet I'd hate to give away any o' the things you and me get up to even though I ken fine she gets up to them too. It's just that she's Nellie and aye will be, no matter how old and grey she and me might become.'

'In other words – she'll aye be Nellie-ish,' he grinned, more relaxed and carefree than she had ever seen him.

'You were great wi' wee Alex,' she enthused. 'I saw you wi' fresh eyes this morning and realised there's so much about you I dinna yet ken. You handled him even better than Nellie herself. Where did you learn all that?'

'From boyhood. I practically brought Danny up, bathed him, changed him, blew his nose for him. I loved him and I hated him. Mother was never strong, she left the dirty side o' him to me and kept all the nice clean and shining bits for herself. He both resented it and loved it and in the end he couldn't wait to break away from it. You know the rest. Dad was the strong one, we all leaned on him I suppose, Mother in her weakness, Danny in his despair, me in my loneliness.'

'Davie, oh Davie,' she whispered, 'I never kent any o' that. It just goes to show how little I know of you.'

He kissed the tip of her nose. 'It goes to show how little we know of each other so I warn you now, you'll get no peace from me till I find out every last wee thing about you, both physically and mentally.'

In those moments she felt closer to understanding him than ever before. The road ahead seemed straight and clear and she looked forward to getting to know him even better in all the years of their life together.

The days sped by quickly, filled with the scents, the sounds, the sights of harvest. From first light till dusk, in bad weather and in good, they were all out there helping in the fields, the crofters taking it in turn to help one another, the children running home from school to join in the fun, for fun it was to them as they ran and laughed down the bouts behind the binder, the older ones stooking almost

237

as swiftly as the adults, corn and more corn, the cropped yellow stalks of the straw, all of it making a pattern on the land that yielded the bounty it had been nurturing since seed time.

Nothing, except maybe the Sabbath, was allowed to hinder the harvest once it got going. Babies were happed in shawls and cried and gurgled through each day in the shelter of the stooked corn; food and drink was brought to the fields in great baskets into which everyone dipped and shared and sat together looking over the bronzed landscape as they talked about this and that but mostly about the weather and the harvest and rarely about the things that bothered them in the normal course of their days.

And somehow the womenfolk found the time to go bramble picking and spent their evenings making jams and jellies and enormous fruit pies that were wrapped in white linen cloths to keep them fresh for next day's harvest fare. Croft Donald's kitchen was steeped in homely smells of baking and cooking with the sharp tang of the dripping bramble juice adding its spice to everything else.

When the work of harvest began to ease off a little Nellie and Irene were inclined to spend more time at home and then the cooking really got going in earnest, delicious mouth-watering roasts and chicken, hams, croudie cheese, homemade chutney, fruit dumplings, spicy cakes, black pudding, and huge haggis whose swelling breasts rattled the lid on the pan hanging on its swee.

Evelyn and David worked and ate as heartily as everybody else and when they weren't doing that they were walking on the hills or by the whispering beat of the ocean. They watched sunsets and dawns, treasured the cool peace of gloamings, wandered in soft rains and brisk breezes and grew brown and glowing and healthy.

David enjoyed controversy and it became a habit for discussion to start up during meals and every night before bed. He and Nellie appeared to have abandoned their rancour. They worked and talked amiably together and one day she said gruffly, 'You're no' so bad wi' the knowing, David Grainger.'

To which he replied, 'I'm as easy to get to know as you are yourself, Nellie Cameron,' and they both laughed rather dourly in silent acknowledgement that one was as good a match for the other.

Evelyn held onto each moment, each hour, each day, wished the impossible wish that her honeymoon in Kenneray would last forever, but the day of departure had to come and with it came a chill rain, blotting out the hills, darkening the sea.

Nellie spent an entire evening packing the baby's things, not coming down to sit with the others at the fire that last evening, and Evelyn could well picture her sister up there in her lonely room, folding the tiny garments, holding them to her face, the big, strong heart of her overflowing with love and sadness for the little boy she had grown to cherish and understand as only Nellie could.

'Don't cwy, Nella.'

Wee Col, missing her downstairs, had come anxiously seeking she who made his life the happy, secure thing it was, and she had taken him to her breast to hide her face in his golden red hair and say brokenly, 'Oh, my wee man, thank God I still have you, you'll aye need Nella and I'll aye be here to see you through your wee life.'

Kenneth Mor held her tight that night in bed and she cooried herself into his comforting hardness like a lost child whose tears had all been shed except for those that ached in her breast. He had no words for her, he had said them all before too many times, but she didn't need his voice to tell her what she already knew, it was there in the big beating heart of him, in the great, strong arms that always made her feel protected and womanly and very, very wanted.

And the morning came, bringing the rain, and the quietness of the land shorn of its crops and empty of the people who had trod its fertile acres these last few happy weeks.

Nellie dressed the baby for the last time, finally happing him warm and snug in the fine wool shaw she had fashioned with her own hands and kept hidden in a drawer filled with tiny garments she had knitted and crocheted with love and hope for the tomorrow that never came.

'Nellie, Nellie.' Evelyn impulsively put her arms round her sister and held her close, ignoring the gruff protests that she knew her action would bring for, though marriage had changed her in many ways, it couldn't change some things, she was still Nellie after all, a young woman who never could abide 'all thon palaver and fuss' since, in her opinion, it was only gentry folk who were weak enough to indulge their feelings in public displays of emotion.

'You're so good, Nellie,' Evelyn said huskily, 'I can never thank you enough for looking after the baby to let me get on my feet and if it was just me I would leave him here wi' you and let you bring him up as your own.'

Nellie pushed her away, her face flushed with the pain of the moment but a spark of downright amazement showing in eyes that often looked cat-like when she was getting ready to be angry.

'What are you saying, quine?' she demanded sharply. 'How can you say it? He's your own flesh and blood yet you could turn your back on him — so lightly.'

'Ach, dinna look like that.' Impatiently Evelyn dashed away her tears. 'I gave him birth but he was yours from the minute I walked away from Croft Donald without him. *That's* when I turned my back on him and I'll never get over the hurt o' it till my dying day — not my hurt but yours — and his. I have this strange feeling that he senses what I did to him. He never lies quiet in my arms and never looks happy till he's out o' them again. Davie can lift him and talk to him at any time and he'll smile and gurgle — but no' wi' me, never wi' me.'

'Ach, stop havering, quine!' Nellie was so astonished she momentarily forgot both her anguish and anger. 'The bairn is no' even four months old, it's daft and wicked to talk like that about an innocent baby. You're as bad a witch as that auld speywife, Hinney, you two were aye in cahoots wi' one another and I'm thinking she's put too much o' her nonsense into your head than is good for you.'

'Hinney was never a witch!' Evelyn cried defensively. 'Only bairns ever called her that, myself included when I was too young to ken better. She and I just kent things that other people were too blind to see. Surely you saw that for yourself, you lived wi' me long enough.'

'I lived wi' a whittrock who grew up and bedded herself too quickly,' flared Nellie who had rarely believed in anything she couldn't touch or see for herself. 'And if you're supposed to ken so much about the future why did you no' stop David Grainger from doing what he did to you and nothing in front o' you but bleakness and worry?'

'I didna want to — some things are meant!' Evelyn shouted back and was glad that David appeared at that moment for Nellie looked angry enough to strike out and was perfectly capable of doing so as Evelyn knew to her cost. Many's the time she had felt the sting of her sister's wrath on her face and knew that, in those amber-green cat's eyes, she was still very much a child who had to be punished if the need arose.

'Fighting? Today of all days?' David said warily. Nevertheless, he went up to Nellie and without ado wrapped his arms around her to embrace her briefly. 'I know we don't always see eye to eye but I'm grateful to you for everything you've done for my son and for this time at Croft Donald. I've loved every minute.'

He thrust a fat parcel at her which contained a dress of softest green wool that he and Evelyn had bought in Renfrew for this occasion, then the room was filled with people, all saying their farewells, allowing Nellie the time she needed to compose herself and to even feel ashamed for attacking her youngest sister with such venom.

'I'm sorry, Evie, I'm sorry,' she whispered at the door.

'Come back and see us, you and David and the bairn, more than anything I look forward to that.'

The hustle and bustle with the luggage put paid to further conversation and in minutes, so it seemed, Kenneth Mor was at the door with the cart and Allt Buidhe, so eager to be off she lifted her tail with excitement and enthusiastically added her generous contribution to the drizzle of the morning.

In a flurry of laughter that successfully disguised the sorrow of parting, the young folk boarded the cart and were soon rumbling away down the rutted road out of Kenneray, leaving Croft Donald behind, waving, waving, till Irene's hanky and Nellie's face at the window were no longer discernible and the sturdy white crofthouse was swallowed up in the mist that swirled in from the sea and down from the corries of the wild, north-western hills.

Chapter Seventeen

Fern Cottage was bright with new paper and paint. The young couple hardly recognised it when they arrived back from the north-west bearing a fretful baby and a longing only for bed.

'Father! You did all this for *us*?' Evelyn cried, throwing her arms round him when he rose up to greet them, tiredness deep in his eyes for he had worked every minute of his spare time getting the little house fresh and cheery for his daughter's return.

'Ach no, I did it for the fairies,' he smiled, 'and of course for my grandson.' He cocked his head at the child, now lying serene and good in David's arms and never a girn to spoil that serenity when Jamie took him and 'hushie-bawed' him round the room with pride soft and kind on his seamed, weather-beaten face.

'Oh, it's lovely to be back,' Evelyn commented, gazing round the cosy kitchen with appreciative eyes before throwing herself into a chair to take off her shoes and hold her feet to a blazing fire that leapt and pranced up the lum. 'How is everybody? Is Gavin settling in all right with you and Mam? And how are the Bairds and all the folk at the Big House?'

'Where will I put these?' Burton asked, coming in laden from the trap that Lady Elizabeth had directed be at the station to meet the young Graingers. In the confusion of the next half hour, Evelyn's questions went unanswered. Maggie and Grace arrived after Burton's departure, followed closely by Gavin who had moved in with the Grants when it had been decided that the newly-weds should have

Fern Cottage. A small downstairs room in Wood Cottage had been converted into a bedroom for Gavin and he was quite happy there, settling into the routine of the household as if he had been there all his life. More and more now he was walking with the aid of his artificial limbs, the wheelchair only being used when really necessary, though there were times when he pushed himself too hard, times like now when he had insisted on walking the half mile to Fern Cottage and couldn't disguise the pain that contorted his perspiring face.

'Och Gavin, sit down,' Grace instructed, pushing him firmly into a seat when he protested that he was fine. 'You try too hard,' she scolded. 'Determination is all very well but there is such a thing as pig-headedness.'

'Ay, Nurse,' he grinned but lay back, very glad to take the weight off stumps that sometimes erupted into raw sores and forced him to rest till they were healed. 'You know, you're worse than Plummy any day,' he continued, 'she gies me hell if I dare to waggle as much as a wee toe and will insist on pushing me in that damt chair till I break out in bum sores.'

'Ach, you love it,' Grace laughed lightly to which he reddened and said nothing. He and Christine Baird had seen a lot of one another that summer. 'Too much,' was the verdict of some, 'that young man o' hers will come back to her after the war and she'll just cast off that cratur like an old coat.'

But they would have been wrong there. Christine had grown more than fond of the disabled young Glasgow lad and in her honest way had told him so.

'Havers, lass,' he had answered with a nonchalant shrug, 'you and me are from different sides o' the fence and besides, what would a fine girl like you want wi' a crock like me? I'm just a novelty, that's all, you'll soon get tired o' me and anyway, I'll be leaving here soon. I'm a townie at heart and a good Christian home is waiting for me in Bridgeton together wi' an old-fashioned aunt who canna wait to convert me to her clean-living ways.'

'We'll see,' was all she said and they had left it at that.

When everyone had stopped talking at once, and they were all gathered round the fire drinking tea, news and gossip soon flowed and Evelyn was saddened to learn that Andrew had slipped back into his world of shadows and was at present residing at The Grange under the care of a specialist in brain disease and psychoanalytic science.

'I thought he was getting better,' said Evelyn, fowning. 'He seemed on the road to recovery – and yet . . .'

'Ay – and yet.' Grace spoke the words softly but with a world of meaning in her tone. 'I've watched him this whilie back, growing quieter, back into himself again. I ken fine something or someone lies at the back o' it but he'll no' say anything. He just sits in a chair all day, staring ahead, seeing nothing.'

'It's as if he's feart to face the world,' Maggie said grimly. 'He's no' a strong lad – no like this sturdy wee cratur who's been kicking me black and blue for the last ten minutes.' Her face softened, she lifted the baby to her face to kiss his smooth cheek which made him grin his toothless grin and pull at her hair with his dimpled fingers.

'It's Chris I'm sorry for.' Gavin banged his cup viciously into its saucer and stared broodingly into the fire. 'She nursed him through hell when he came back wrecked from the war and now it must all seem for nothing.'

'He'll get over it,' Grace spoke as if to herself, and, looking at her lovely face with its white skin and perfectly-shaped brows, Evelyn wondered if her sister had discovered a feeling in herself for Andrew that went deeper than she was prepared to admit, though her next words seemed to rule this out: 'For his parents' sake he has to get over it. The Colonel is so upset he hasna been near the stables for ages and Lady Elizabeth has practically lived at The Grange since it happened.'

Evelyn looked at David, he at her, and she knew what he was thinking, Croft Donald and Kenneray already seemed far behind them. The ocean, the hills, the talk, the

245

laughter, the drama of that small haven on the north-western seaboard, belonged to another world, their world was now here, at Dunmarnock with baby Alex snug in the cradle Nellie had insisted be transported all the way to Renfrewshire, no matter how difficult it may be to get it there.

'He's been used to sleeping in it,' Nellie had told Evelyn at the last minute, 'and might fret if he has to lie in a strange cot. If I ever need it I'll get it back, you can be assured o' that, but I couldna sleep easy myself if I thought my wee man was missing his ain familiar bed.'

And so it had left Croft Donald, going first in the pony cart, on two trains, then in the trap, with Burton mumbling under his breath about its weight, its rockers finally coming to rest in a secluded corner of the kitchen. And that's where little Alexander spent his first night at Fern Cottage, the visitors long gone, the two cats who had come with the house, adding their quiet breathings to his as they slept warm on the hearth though Evelyn, mindful of Nellie's instructions, was careful to fix the cat net over the cradle hood even though she, her sisters and little brother, had slept in a kitchen full of cats and dogs and never so much as a hairnet to protect them from the 'damt craturs' as Nellie was wont to refer to them.

'It's been a long day.' David's lips were warm against her face as he held her close in the strange bed up there in the little attic room with its tiny window peeping out shyly from the eves. 'Kenneray seems so long ago.'

'I know.' A great poignancy seized her. 'Yet it was only this morning we left it.'

'Nellie's face at the window.'

'Irene's hanky fluttering in the breeze.'

'Ken's kilt lifting in the stoor and steam as the train pulled out o' the station.'

'You remember everything,' she said wonderingly, coorying in close to him.

'Ay, even your face, sad and wanting, as we left Croft Donald behind.'

246

'Leaving the sea.'

'And the hills.'

'And the yellow stooks standing in the last-cut fields.'

'Ay, and wee Jenny Wren standing at her cottage door, puffing her pipe and waving wi' a corner o' her peenie.'

'And the feather bed, dinna forget that, warm and safe, so safe . . .' Her voice broke.

'Oh, I'll never forget that,' he pulled her in closer, his arms tightening, becoming more urgent.

'Nellie will be alone tonight,' she sounded bleak, sad for the sister who collected other folks' bairns.

'She's got Kenneth Mor, she'll never be alone or lonely as long as she's got him.'

'I meant for –'

'I know what you mean but there's time and enough for her yet – and Alex is ours after all.'

'You love him, don't you?'

'He is ours,' he repeated, 'mine – he's got that one brown eye, hasn't he? He must be mine.'

'Oh ay, he's yours all right, brown eye or no. I hope he'll sleep through the night. Nellie did all that for me, the lifting, the laying, the night watches.'

'You're his mother, you'll do it and get used to it.' He sounded annoyed for a moment then he relented. 'Poor wee girl, you're no' ready for him yet, nor for any bairn, you were aye such a bairn yourself, all big eyes and trembling lips.'

'Ach, that was years ago, I'm twenty now, that's getting on.'

'God – only twenty,' he breathed, 'so much has happened to us both you might well be ninety, me a hundred.'

'Do you feel a hundred?' Her voice was teasing, light with laughter.

He considered, 'Mmm, maybe not, maybe just ninety-nine . . .' His laughter mingled with hers. 'So just you be quiet, Grannie, and I'll show you what a ninety-nine year old man can still get up to.'

'Ay, Granda,' she giggled. Moments later there was no

laughter, only the night and a silence filled with sounds that weren't words but might have been for all the love and warmth they carried on their passionate breath.

All except their nearest and dearest believed they had gone to the north-west to give David the holiday he needed and to collect the baby of course, and their married life settled into a happy routine at Dunmarnock. Every day Gavin came over to the cottage to continue working with David on the restoration of small pieces of prized furniture that came from the big houses round about. This had started off modestly but as word spread there seemed no end to the supply of work so that eventually Jamie helped David turn a small back room into a workshop. There the two young men employed themselves busily and willingly while Evelyn carried on working to the Big House, occasionally leaving the baby with the two men, more often taking him with her to lie in his pram in the kitchen or outside if the weather was fine, never short of hands to rock him or hold him, croon to him and talk to him and, in Seal's case to sing to him, lullabies and sea shanties that had him gurgling one minute, sleeping the next, for Cook with a Capital was blessed with a sweet voice that had even Ferguson nodding off by the fire if the time and circumstance was right.

Everyone, it seemed, doted on the beautiful baby boy, even Effie, that paragon of routine, finding time in her day to pause at his pram and murmur words of nonsense that were strange coming from her thin, precise lips.

The Colonel found more reason than normal to pass by the kitchen door or pop through it for a word with 'the boy' while his wife positively revelled in the fact that 'Dunmarnock had a baby again' and would temporarily forget her worries over her own son in the joy of paying attention to Evelyn's.

Amidst all the attention and affection he thrived and blossomed. He gurgled more often than he girned and soon found he could twist anyone round his fat little finger if he showed so much as the glimmering of a tear. Only with his mother did he remain aloof and unloving. She told herself she was imagining it, how could so young a child possibly differentiate between her and the others? But he could and he did, till it got to the point where she stopped even trying to win him over but left him there outside on the lawn or inside with his adoring retinue to heed his whims and wants. She fed him and changed him, bathed him and dressed him and often didn't need to do any of these as Maggie or Seal, Violet, Peggy, or Raggy Annie displayed distinct tendencies to get there first.

Raggy Annie was his especial favourite. He just needed to glimpse her melancholy little face to go wild altogether, blowing bubbles, throwing his limbs about, going red in the face till in a flurry of cigarette ash and giggles he was up in her arms, grabbing at her lanky hair, intoxicating himself with whiffs of her nicotine-laden breath, while she pranced and danced him round the room till he chuckled himself into exhausted silence and she collapsed with him into a chair, fag ash, shag fragments and all.

The Grange was a charming old Scottish country house with wide lawns leading up to red brick terraces, and roses and flame-red ivy growing round the windows and over the walls. The curving drive was lined with great horsechestnut trees whose red and yellow leaves were drifting down like huge, sad hands to the ground beneath, sometimes twirling in a little spiral dance according to the whim of the October breezes.

It was a peaceful place to be when body, mind and soul needed rest, and Andrew Baird felt he never wanted to leave its tranquil seclusion for the rest of his life. His room was at the back of the house, facing on to the rolling fields with the River Threep gliding and tumbling by under the trees. Bowls of roses and freesia stood on his windowsills, brought from the gardens of Dunmarnock every other day so that they were always fresh and fragrant and filling his nostrils with reminders of summer. The bustle of hospital life went past in soft footfalls outside his door but he wanted none of that, as long as they went on past his room and left him alone he was as happy as he would ever be. But safe as the room was it couldn't shut out the night and the dreams and then the dread visions came to him to haunt him and taunt him and turn his little haven into a prison from which there was no escape. But as long as Effie didn't come it was all right. He could handle the shadows and the ghosts, in some odd way he had grown used to them though he had never ceased to feel saddened by the white faces of young men he had known and loved and who had departed too soon to nameless graves beyond the night hills. Sometimes he could lie in his bed watching their grey wraith-figures gliding past his vision, marching, marching, in a silent procession that never seemed to end, going on and on into curtains of mist and fire that swallowed them up yet still they came on past, never looking at him, intent only on their soundless, endless march into hell.

He wasn't part of it so he could be quite impassive about it all till the exhaustion came and with it the heavy sinking into sleep that somehow afforded little rest.

But as long as Effie didn't come he could stand anything. Even the very thought of her could fill his peaceful room with shadows of evil and then he would shout, 'No! Don't let her in!' and a nurse would come running to soothe him even though he insisted that he hadn't made a sound, that the voice had come from somewhere outside of himself and had nothing to do with him.

But gradually, gradually, the ghosts and the voices receded back, back into the twilight hills and when that happened he knew that the dawn was coming again, as it had before when his darling Chris had been by his side and had shared his darkness. She had made the dawn come, till the light of it spread over the deep valleys of his mind and he had been dazzled by its beauty. And now it was happening again, the shadows were fleeing before that wondrous shining brightness and now there were people that had substance, people that he loved, his mother and father, looking at him, smiling their love on him, and Chris, her blue eyes matching the October sky outside his window – and Grace. Oh, lovely Grace, a figure of serenity in her nurse's uniform, flitting somewhat wraith-like into his room but smelling of life and hope, not like those other wraiths whose eyes were dead and empty and smelled of death and destruction.

Every dawn endowed her with more human qualities, with a voice that spoke kindly and softly, with burning dark eyes that met his and smiled at him as if he was someone who was worth smiling at instead of a wreck who had perforce to hide his dark secrets from the world even though the dawn had set him free of the shadows.

'Your son is almost ready to talk,' Major McFadyen, a fatherly-looking man with close-cropped grey hair, a pink face, and sharp eyes behind thick glasses, leaned back in his padded green leather chair and looked keenly at the Colonel and his wife. 'Whether he will or not depends on how anxious he is to rid himself of his burdens. He has been through a very bad time and he isn't yet out of the woods. He still has the odd hallucination when he talks to someone called Barrett and occasionally he cowers down in his chair and begs us not to let "her" in, whoever she may be. But he's been well enough to go for a walk in the grounds and talked this morning of his horse, Darling.'

'Will he ever really get well again, Doctor?' Lady Elizabeth asked the question hesitantly, as if she was afraid of the answer.

The doctor looked at her over the top of his specs and spoke kindly. 'My dear Lady Elizabeth, your son didn't receive his medical discharge from the army because he was considered to be – em – unbalanced. The doctor who recommended that – let me see –' he rustled some papers – 'ah yes, Major Black. He examined the lad in December of

251

last year and recommended the discharge on the grounds that he was too finely tuned, so to speak, to risk further military duties. But you must already know that. The point I'm trying to make is this. Some people have great mental resistance and can always come bouncing back, no matter how many shocks they have faced. Your son is of a very delicate and sensitive nature and couldn't withstand the strain of his war experiences. But he's young, he ought to get over this setback and there's a great struggle going on inside of him. Something or someone lies at the root of it and he needs to get it out of his system. Time, of course, is the great healer but I'm certain we could speed things up if we could get him to talk things over with someone he trusts.'

'Oh, come on, man,' the Colonel spoke gruffly, his fingers stroking his neat moustache impatiently, 'we're his family, surely he can trust us of all people.'

The doctor looked at him thoughtfully. 'Hmm, I wonder. In my experience family can often be too close for comfort — loyalty and all that, fear of letting the side down by admitting to something it's thought they might not like to hear. Very often a close friend makes the best confident.'

'All his close friends are fighting in this damned war or have been exterminated by it,' growled the Colonel. He thought deeply for a moment while Lady Elizabeth gazed at him hopefully and wrung her hands together nervously.

'Young Gillan Forbes might be due some leave,' said the Colonel at last. 'He and Andrew were great boyhood chums and did a lot of deep talking when Gillan was home on leave last Christmas. I'll get in touch with his people and see if they've heard anything from their son though I doubt the boy will want to come all this way when he's maybe sore in need of a rest himself.'

When they were leaving, Major McFadyen drew the Colonel back and murmured in his ear, 'Talking of friends, your wife looks as if she could be doing with a good one to take her mind off all this and perhaps help with the running of things for a while. She's been driving herself too hard these past weeks and it wouldn't do to have her going down just when there's a glimpse of hope at the end of the tunnel.'

Startled, the Colonel glanced along the corridor to where his wife stood quietly leaning against the wall as if for support, her face pale and strained-looking. 'I see what you mean,' he nodded. 'Been so wrapped up – *you* know, however, leave it with me, I'll see what I can do.'

Some days later, Lady Marjorie Forbes, with her husband Evander in tow, came sweeping upon Dunmarnock like a ship in full sail, dark eyes snapping with vigorous determination, bringing with her a middle-aged lady's maid who went by the name of Sarah and gave the impression of being very superior and stand-offish. Sarah had flat feet, small, pale, tired eyes, big hands and frizzy ginger-grey hair that sat on top of her head like an abandoned bird's nest. She suffered from a delicate stomach and this fact she made known almost before she was over Dunmarnock's doorstep. At the first opportunity she sent, via Peggy, a list of fads down to the kitchens for Seal's attention.

With the exception of Evander, who was an easy-going sort and the type that tried never to interfere in the running of houses that weren't his own, the new arrivals threw the ordered routine of the house into complete disarray with their caprices and orders.

'Oh, Richard, have we done the right thing?' Lady Elizabeth enquired of her husband while below stairs Cook with a Capital sweated, groaned, and complained and had never been so busy since before the war. The kitchen premises fairly rang with her barked commands and instructions till Molly, the new kitchenmaid, jumping hither and thither, this way and that, dropped a pan of potatoes and went home in tears, vowing she would never return and if she did it would be with feet nearly as bad as

Seal's and 'serve the old besom right if she had to hobble instead of run to her every bidding.'

Both Evelyn and Violet were relegated to the kitchen to help out, leaving Peggy and Effie to carry out all the above-stairs duties and a few more besides. This didn't suit Effie in the least, though that wasn't surprising as nothing had pleased her since Major Baird's departure to hospital. Shedding a good deal of her customary cool along with a few tears of pure rage, she rustled swiftly through the house, her nostrils white and pinched, making life difficult for Peggy who at one point lost all *her* unruffled calm and hid herself in Ferguson's pantry in a flood of weeping. She remained impervious to Seal who coaxed and pleaded till she was hoarse, and also to Ferguson who appeared to have been struck with some sort of brain storm and banged on the door till his knuckles were raw, while shouting blue murder at the top of his voice.

But Peggy only emerged when Lady Elizabeth herself appeared, to kneel on the floor and apply her eye to the keyhole and from that vantage point to talk to the girl in her kindly fashion till a shamefaced and red-eyed Peggy abruptly opened the door and just in the nick of time caught her ladyship in her arms as she fell through the aperture.

'Dyod! That woman! She could cause chaos on the moon if she had a mind!' expostulated Maggie when the menu was altered for the third time in two days.

But she didn't mean it. She was positively delighted to see her cousin again and was further enraptured when Lady Marjorie presented herself at Wood Cottage on Maggie's half-day off.

It was like old times, the pair of them sitting by the fire, drinking tea and exchanging news, hardly pausing for breath, only moving to refill a cup or fetch more scones from the larder.

Lady Marjorie had never been so exhilarated or so relaxed. She spoke openly about Lord Lindsay Ogilvie, her uncle and Maggie's father, describing her trip to South

Africa to visit him, about the journey which had been 'just too tedious for words'.

Maggie watched her cousin's animated face, noting the elegant eyebrows, the exquisitely manicured hands, never still for a moment in keeping with her tongue. She was beautifully and expensively dressed but she had grown plumper in the last year and somehow that lent her a homely air that met with Maggie's full approval.

'He wanted to talk about you – and Evelyn.' Her ladyship looked Maggie straight in the eye. 'He grew quite sentimental over the pair of you and sighed a good deal over the wiles of fate. Oh, Margaret, what a pity you and he didn't make amends when you had the chance. He can't get over how you turned him away yet he admits you had every right to do what you did – though too bad you did it so brutally.'

For once in her life Maggie was the first to drop her eyes and her voice was low when she spoke. 'Ach, dinna rub it in, there's hardly a day passes but I think o' that time and – and I wish I had handled it differently. But what else can you expect from a crofter's wife? I didna have the benefit o' your genteel upbringing and aye believed in speaking my mind.'

'*Now* who's rubbing it in?' Lady Marjorie glanced down at her pinky crooked daintily below the handle of her cup, and hastily she straightened it. Really, the other woman must think her just *too* affected for words. It didn't matter as a rule but somehow here – in this homely little house – some of her mannerisms must stick out like sore fingers . . . At this she smiled a little and, leaning forward, she placed her hand over Maggie's to say earnestly, 'Seriously, Margaret, we all of us really ought to let bygones be bygones. You have denied your origins for far too long and in the process have deceived your own family into believing you despised the Forbes family just because we are gentry and not because you are actually one of us. Oh, look like that if you like, all snooty and distant, but I will say my piece whether you like it or not. Surely it would do no harm to let them know who you really are. Evelyn, I know, adores Uncle Lindsay and would be so happy to learn he is actually her grandfather. It wouldn't matter now that . . .'

'Now that the Grants are safely out o' Rothiedrum and can no longer blacken the good Forbes name.' Maggie enjoyed the satisfaction of seeing her cousin squirm, then she relented, her voice soft as she continued, 'No, Marjorie, it would do no good to rake it all up. Best to bury the past and everyone in it, it's healthier for all concerned.'

'But you can't bury it!' came the passionate objection. 'Oh, well, you can, I suppose, but you can't bury the people who are still very much alive and kicking and who would love to acknowledge you as family. Uncle Lindsay was so wistful and sad. He's an old man now and his dearest wish is that you and Jamie and Evelyn – her family too of course – should go out to South Africa to be with him and live your lives in comfort and style. It would be a new life for you, Margaret, you were never cut out to be a – a drudge.'

'Changed days.' Maggie smiled a trifle sarcastically. 'There was a time when you believed that was all any o' the Grants were good for. Ach, dinna look like that, all black-eyed and soft like a cow wi' the colic. I'm glad we're friends now and can look at one another without fear and dislike. No matter what may happen in the future I'll aye think o' you wi' fondness and respect but the fates put us in different camps and that's all there is to say on the subject – except . . .' Her brilliant green eyes grew misty. 'One day I'll tell Evelyn and the others about their grandfather – and about you and Gillan.'

Lady Marjorie sighed. 'I suppose that's better than nothing – as for Gillan – I never thought to hear myself say this – but I wish now that he and Evelyn had gotten together after all. He loves her, you know, deeply and honestly, and he's never been happy since the Rothiedrum days when he and she were so young and carefree together. Foolish woman that I am, I used only to bother my head about what other people might think, not like Evander who earned everyone's respect and liking by just being himself. Now —' She spread her elegant hands — 'my son's happiness comes first and I wish, oh, how I wish . . .'

'I ken fine what you wish, I wished it too . . .' She echoed her cousin's sighs. 'But life is never so simple. She lost her head to David Grainger and the Lord knows if she'll ever come to her senses.'

'You don't like him, do you?' Lady Marjorie spoke bluntly and with accuracy.

'I dinna trust him,' Maggie replied with equal frankness. 'Oh, he could charm the breeks off his grannie but . . .'

She was interrupted by her cousin who had fallen back in her seat and was giving vent to peal upon peal of helpless laughter, the tears running down her cheeks.

'Margaret, Margaret,' she gasped, removing a tiny lace square from her sleeve with which to mop up her eyes. 'You're a tonic. I've never laughed so much since that old rogue Coulter told me a story about Carnallachie's extreme caution with his "sillar", as Coulter put it.'

'I heard that one,' Maggie volunteered and proceeded to repeat the tale in her rich north-east 'twang'. 'It seemed that Carnallachie was so mean he used to sew his money into his pooches to keep it safe until the day he gave a bundle o' his old breeks to the ragwife. She was a mile along the turnpike before he remembered about his sillar and off he went in hot pursuit o' the poor, bewildered wife. But she was no' for giving him back his rags and there in the road they had a tug o war wi' them till they ripped themselves to pieces and all his precious money scattered into the mud o' a ditch. Though he raked and searched till his fingers were bleeding he only ever recovered half and most o' that in farthings.'

After that they both lapsed into mirthful reminiscence and when Jamie came home he found them still talking and laughing by the fire.

'Jamie, how nice to see you.' Graciously Lady Marjorie got up and took his hand, genuine warmth in her voice for he had always treated her with respect and liking.

They spoke for a while of this and that and then Jamie said, 'How is young Gillan faring these days? No chance o' him getting home on leave, eh? I heard some talk that the Bairds had hoped he might get over here to visit their lad.'

'No hope of that, I'm afraid.' Lady Marjorie sounded wistful. 'He's in Italy, you know, trying to drive back the Austrians, and though there's talk of victory one does wonder when it will come, if ever, especially with the munitions labouring all out for an offensive to be launched next year. Evander is happy enough about that, of course, though being the astute man he is he has quietly been setting his sights elsewhere, just in case. One man's loss and all that, he has always been a great believer in that little adage and can be quite ruthless in setting about his business. Still –' she brightened – 'I'm not complaining, I know which side my bread is buttered and if my son comes home from war in one piece it's as well for him to come home to a thriving inheritance rather than a crumble of poor investments brought about by lack of foresight.'

'You never used to talk about serious things like that, Marjorie,' commented Maggie in some wonderment.

'I know, isn't it awful, the war has changed even me, I'm afraid, and of course everyone and everything else with it. Take that dreadful flat-footed Sarah for instance. Before the war I wouldn't have been seen dead with a poor creature like that but now one has to make do with servants of all sorts and . . .'

'Marjorie,' Maggie said warningly.

They all looked at one another and laughed and the word 'servant' wasn't used again that afternoon. Her ladyship might be flippant about many things and with many people but Margaret Grant wasn't one of them and never would be.

258

Chapter Eighteen

The advent of the Rothiedrums proved beneficial to everyone, with the exception of the staff who felt anything but
benefited by the visit. Evander successfully took the Colonel's mind off himself by talking over business matters with
him and in the end persuading him to transfer some of his
interests to fields other than those relating to war.

'Got to look ahead, old man,' he advised firmly. 'If
victory does come soon we both could find ourselves
with dead babies on our hands, so if you'll listen to me
I have one or two little projects in mind that could well
safeguard us for the future.'

He also persuaded his friend to get back into the
saddle so that most mornings they were to be seen riding
out, accompanied by Christine and occasionally by Lady
Marjorie, though no one relished that very much as she had
never had a good seat and was much happier organising
people and things.

Lady Elizabeth found that she was very much taken
out of herself by her vivacious guest who whirled her from
one thing to the next, never allowing her to mope on her
own for long. Together they visited Andrew, had friends
in to tea, walked and talked and reminisced through every
day.

Lady Elizabeth was very glad to place the running of the
household temporarily into the capable hands of Maggie
and Lady Marjorie, both of whom had never stood any
nonsense from anyone and didn't stand any now. Fretful
servants, domestic crises, persistent tradesmen, were all
firmly dealt with.

Seal, in a state of shock after Lady Marjorie had dared to invade *her* kitchens in order to pacify Molly who had returned but was threatening to leave again, shuffled dourly about her business in such ear-splitting silence Ferguson thought she must be ill, but so thankfully did he welcome the peace he inwardly blessed 'Lady Bossy-Boots and all who sailed in her'. The phrase floating to mind after one glass of cooking sherry too many had played tricks with his mind.

Effie, bullied into a state of near total submission by that same personage, stopped grumbling as she had been ordered but took instead to pulling faces behind the lady's back, only to be caught out one day and sent severely about her duties, during the course of which she wished dire happenings on her tormentor and only succeeded in making herself sick while Lady Marjorie sailed blithely on her way, oblivious to the parlourmaid's scowling white face.

'You really shouldn't interfere too much, Marjorie,' warned Evander. 'Too many bosses spoil the works and that girl Effie looks as if she would like to kill you.'

'Nonsense, Evander,' was the brisk reply, 'Elizabeth has always been far too soft where the staff is concerned. The result is they think they can just do what they like and get away with it. She's always hated having to give orders, I can't think why, she's the daughter of an earl who simply ruled the roost in his own home – or should I say castle. He berated his staff unmercifully and one would think that his daughter might have learnt something from him.'

'She did,' Evander spoke shortly, 'she learned to despise bullies and grew up with the intention of treating her own staff with fairness when she had a place of her own to run.'

'Well, it hasn't worked, that old witch of a cook simply lazes her time away by the fire and the old butler is just as bad – as for Effie, there's something very unpleasant about that girl and I mean to make sure she toes the line – at least while I'm here and able to keep my eye on her.'

* *

The very next day Lady Marjorie was seized with dreadful stomach pains and the doctor had to be called.

'Gastritis,' he diagnosed. 'You must have eaten something that's disagreed with you.'

'Nonsense!' her ladyship told him robustly. 'I've never had any bother with my inner man.'

'Well, you've got it now,' said the doctor who was old and wheezy and bothered with *his* stomach. Directing her to take only liquids for the next twenty-four hours and to stay in bed till he saw her next day, he went off to report to Lady Elizabeth who fluttered and wondered what her friend could have eaten to cause such an upset, till Maggie appeared on the scene and soothed away her worries with a cup of hot tea and a few kind words.

Despite her protests, Lady Marjorie was glad to obey someone else's orders for a change, and she lay in bed, very pale and wan, too ill even to enjoy harping at Sarah, while down below a snigger of relief went up and Seal settled herself by the fire with her feet on a stool and told Molly to fetch her a 'good strong cuppy'.

'Ay, Mrs McWhirter,' Molly acquiesced obediently, 'I'll tell Violet to fetch it.'

'Violet nothing, my girl. The kitchen work is yours, Violet belongs upstairs.'

'No' the day, Mrs McWhirter,' Molly said smugly, her lively eyes snapping with triumph. 'Lady Marjorie has sent for me to sit by her and read wee bits out o' *Kidnapped* –' I got it at school, so I did, and when her ladyship heard that she said it was onc o' her favourites too and now she's ill and wanting me up there.' The dimples in her pretty, mischievous face deepened. 'She's taken a real bonny liking to me, so she has, and told me to report to her if you pushed me around too much – so I'll tell Violet to bring your tea and then I'll go and tell Lady Marjorie that you're getting on wi' your work – just as if she was up and about and keeping her eye on you.'

At that Seal fairly flew out of her chair, yelling 'damt cheek!' and forgetting her sore feet in her anxiety to get at

Molly who let out a screech and disappeared with alacrity out of the door, leaving Cook with a Capital to collapse back into her chair, there to bemoan 'girls these days' to herself since Ferguson wasn't available to listen to her grumbles.

Lady Marjorie spent three full days in bed, days in which she refused all food and couldn't be bothered with anything or anyone. So pale, quiet, and listless was she everyone began to be quite concerned about her and Sarah, who had oft wished a respite from her mistress's lively tongue, actually began to miss the throb of it against her eardrums and said she could hear her own heart beating in the dead silence of the sick room.

'Of course, I respect her wish for complete rest and go about my duties on tip toe,' she imparted haughtily to Peggy when she appeared in her room with her tea tray. 'You must do the same, of course, if you have reason to visit her room – oh, and inform the parlourmaid not to knock too loudly on either her door *or* mine when she brings the morning tea, the girl has hands like a farm labourer.'

'*Tip-toes*!' exploded Ferguson when Peggy relayed the latest news from upstairs. 'Yon wifie has no tips on her toes, she walks like a splay-footed elephant wi' clogs on.'

Seal, forgetting the disruption that the coming of the Forbes had wrought in her easy existence, prepared dainty trays for the sickroom and was most crestfallen and worried when they came back untouched.

'Ach, poor sowel! Poor sowel!' she sympathised, shaking her head so vigorously her mutch cap slid over one ear. 'She had such a healthy appetite when she came and she was generous wi' her compliments about my cooking – whatever else her faults.'

'Ay, she ate like a horse,' supplemented Ferguson bluntly. 'Every dish scraped that clean I was feart she might lift the pattern out the china. It's strange her being taken ill like that and the doctor saying it was something she had eaten. We all had the same food as herself and none o' *us* any the worse o' it.'

On the second day, Lady Marjorie permitted a weak concoction of beef tea to pass her lips and Molly's presence was requested upstairs for a resumption of *Kidnapped*.

'I don't know what the mistress is thinking about, I'm sure,' Sarah confided to Peggy through tight lips. 'That girl's place is very firmly in the kitchen. She has no manners whatsoever for a sick room and furthermore she has leanings towards adenoids. All my previous ladies told me what a nice soothing voice I had been blessed with and often used to nod off when I read to them. As for *Kidnapped* –' her lips tightened even more – 'that's all and fine in its place which I always believed was on a schoolroom shelf. The *classics* were the thing for my other ladies, though mind, I'm not saying I have anything against Stevenson myself, but give me the Brontës any day – such sensitivity, such style.'

'A *soothing* voice, was that what she said, Peggy?' snorted Seal. 'Monotonous as mud, that's what *I* say. And *Kidnapped* not a classic! The woman's ignorant as well as impertinent. Robert Louis Stevenson could beat any o' the Brontës any day – and what's more he was a Scot! Away you go upstairs this minute, Molly,' she directed magnanimously. 'Lady Bossy-Boots might be the limit at times, but she knows a good book when she sees one, I'll give her that.'

Molly fairly revelled in being singled out to attend upstairs and was careful to be very quiet and respectful in the suitably draped half-light of the sickroom, even though the presence of Sarah, sitting nearby looking very industrious with a basket of darning on her knee, was somewhat offputting.

'Molly, be a dear and peel me an orange,' Lady Marjorie requested when Molly had rustled through less than two pages of *Kidnapped*.

'Yes, m'lady.' Molly went to fetch an orange from the bowl by the window, obediently and unquestioningly.

Sarah's head jerked up. 'An *orange*, Lady Marjorie?' she questioned, in a tone that might have been used if her mistress had asked that the pin might be removed from a hand grenade. 'But surely – in your condition – it will make you sick, *such* an acid fruit.'

'An orange, Molly,' said Lady Marjorie when the girl hesitated by the bed with a large orange in her hand. 'And don't bother fetching a knife to cut it, I prefer my oranges half-peeled in order that I can hold it and bite into it so that the juice dribbles down my chin.'

'Ay, m'lady,' complied a rather bewildered Molly, preparing to dig her fingernails into the tough, pocked orange skin. In seconds a pungent aroma filled the sickroom and Sarah, looking slightly green, rose hurriedly and rushed from the room, whereupon Lady Marjorie leaned back on her pillows and permitted herself a most healthy chuckle.

'She hates oranges,' she confided, a wicked twinkle lighting her eyes. 'The very smell of them makes her physically sick and I don't think she'll be back to bother us for quite some time to come. Take the beastly thing through to the dressing room and eat it yourself like a good girl, the very sight of it is making *me* feel squeamish and I have no desire to go through all that again. It was worth it though, just to see poor Sarah's face. I do enjoy tormenting her which is very naughty but then, I was never renowned for being a Miss Goody-Two-Shoes. Now, be quick with that orange, Molly, I'm simply dying to hear more about old Balfour and the House of Shaws, he was such a rogue but he had character and I always preferred him to those simpering heroines my governess used to insist I read. Whenever her back was turned it was *Kidnapped* or *Treasure Island*, by the light of a candle in the dead of night, and how I enjoyed having my flesh creep by all the deliciously wicked adventures Stevenson penned so brilliantly.'

'Oh yes, m'lady,' beamed a delighted Molly and rushed

264

to consume the orange in order that she might get back quickly to Lady Marjorie and *Kidnapped*.

At intervals on that same day, her ladyship requested the company of Evander, Lady Elizabeth, Maggie and Evelyn, in that order, the last two being deliberately saved to the end as a child might savour a much anticipated treat. Once they were ensconced within the portals of the sickroom several small peals of laughter were heard to drift out and Peggy rushed downstairs to report that her ladyship was 'on the mend'.

When Effie brought tea the following morning she was greeted with the sight of Lady Marjorie sitting up against her pillows ready to greet the new day. 'How are you feeling today, m'lady?' Effie intoned as she drew back the curtains.

'Much, much better, Effie,' came the prompt reply and she went on to further inform the parlourmaid that she was 'as hungry as a horse' and wished for a substantial breakfast to be sent up.

'Very well, m'lady, I'll go down and tell Cook right away.'

Effie withdrew and Sarah entered, dressed in a long robe of a serviceable material, her ginger bird's nest separated into thin little sausage segments that were tied up in rag curlers.

'Definitely a Gorgon,' Lady Marjorie muttered, settling herself back on her pillows.

Sarah swallowed, her Adam's apple sliding rapidly up and down within its parchment-like covering. She saw at once that her mistress was almost fully recovered and while she was glad to see health for health's sake she had hoped for one more day of respite from that caustic wit that was so often directed at her appearance.

'I beg your pardon, m'lady, what did you say?' she enquired, fearful of the answer but feeling that some sort of response was expected of her.

'I said, it's definitely a lovely morning.' Lady Marjorie beamed innocently, 'For me, that is.'

'Oh, yes, yes, m'lady, and I'm *so* glad to see you are back to your old bright self.'

Slight emphasis was placed on the word 'old' and Lady Marjorie's smiles turned into a glower. A constant battle of wits raged between the two but without actually saying so both women revelled in the verbal exchanges and were always on their mettle with one another.

'I'll go and get dressed.' Sarah made to withdraw. 'I only came through to see how you were.'

'Oh for heaven's sake, Sarah! This is no time to stand on ceremony. You look all one to me, dressed or otherwise. Fetch me some hot water and a towel and I shall want you to do my hair – oh, and bring me my blue silk peignoir. I feel like a rag and simply must get back to my normal, attractive self. Evander will be through to see me shortly and always enjoys seeing me in blue silk – this gastric thing has been simply too tiresome for words but thank heaven it's over with.'

Propped against her white, lace-edged pillows, her dark hair attractively arranged so that it fell in gleaming coils over the luxuriant material of the peignoir, Lady Marjorie clasped her hands demurely over her stomach and waited for Evander to come through. But Effie came first, bearing a tray set with silver accoutre, dainty slivers of toast, scrambled eggs, butter, marmalade, and homemade bramble jelly.

'Oh, how lovely.' Lady Marjorie clasped her hands together and gazed joyfully at the contents of the tray Effie was setting upon the bedside table. 'Cook may be many things but first and foremost she is a cook of the highest order. The eggs look perfect, not too soft, not too overdone either, everything piping hot – give her my compliments, will you, Effie, dear?'

'Ay, m'lady.'

Something about the tone of the girl's voice made the other woman look up and what she saw in the narrowed eyes made her draw in her breath. There was something strange in the way Effie was looking at her – no, not looking, watching, waiting, like a cat playing with a mouse that isn't quite yet killed – a stab of alarm pierced Lady Marjorie's breast. There was something odd here, something terribly odd about this girl. Some awful, primitive beast lurked in her slit-like eyes – and – would it be too melodramatic for words to apply the word 'sinister' to the girl's entire attitude and bearing?

She sat back on her pillows, forgetting her breakfast, feeling strangely breathless, the oddest sensation of fear stifling her lungs. She felt as if her heart was being squeezed, contracted by clutching fingers, and that she was being suffocated little by little . . .

The door opened, Evander came in.

'Evander, thank God,' she croaked, 'the window, open the window – can't breathe . . .'

Her husband hastened to do as he was bid. Cool, fresh air flooded the room. Two strides took him to the bed, there to whip the tray away and order his wife to put her head between her knees and breathe deeply. This she did, gulping in air till some colour came back to her face. She sank back against him, pale and dreadfully shaken.

'What happened?' he demanded, his strong, dark face a shade whiter than usual.

'I thought I was hungry,' she gasped, 'but the sight of food – made me feel queasy again.'

'Is that all?' Anxiety lent his voice a rough edge.

'That's all, darling.' She made an attempt to sound reassuring but shivered instead. 'Tell – the – the maid to take the tray away.'

He turned to Effie who had stood passively at the foot of the bed all through the little drama, her hands folded meekly in front of her. 'You heard her ladyship, take the food back to the kitchen.' He didn't like the sallow-faced parlourmaid in the least, she had always given him the creeps the way she rustled about yet could come up behind one with such stealth she could make you just about jump out your skin when her harsh voice spoke suddenly in your ear.

'Evander, go after her, tell her not to give it to the cats.' Lady Marjorie clutched her husband's arm beseechingly as the door closed on Effie. She adored cats, not big, fluffy, high-bred exotic creatures as might have been expected, but farm moggies and timid little tabbies who looked at you with their intelligent big eyes and kept themselves more aloof and more dignified than any aristocratic cat ever could.

'Cats! Cats! What do you mean? Cats?' Evander was looking at her as if she had taken leave of her senses.

'Oh, nothing,' she shrugged, unwilling to make an issue out of something that was probably only her imagination after all. 'I'm sorry for all the fuss, really, and I'm feeling so much better I'm getting up out of this bed this minute –'

'Up! But . . .'

'Evander, if I stay in this room one more day I shall go mad. I'm getting up and that's final. I'm starving again but I'll eat with everyone else in the dining room. I've had enough of sick rooms and invalid trays to last me for many a long day.'

Later that morning she slipped down to the kitchen to put her hand on Seal's arm and say warmly, 'I'm so sorry about this morning, Mrs McWhirter, everything was splendid but I'm afraid I was being too greedy too soon. I've so enjoyed your cooking since I got here but as Martha, my own cook, tells me often enough, my eyes are bigger than my stomach.'

Seal went pink with surprise and pleasure. She blossomed, she blushed, and readily forgave and forgot her ladyship's shortcomings.

'Och, that's all right, m'lady,' she began, a small wonder in her for Martha who could address her mistress with such homely ease – if not to say familiarity. Didn't *anyone* have any respect for their betters, these days? 'It's the way o' things when a body has been ill, I've done it myself often enough, especially when I had the colic and would maybe think to myself how I'd like a wee taste o' this or that and being sick all over again at the sight o' food. It was worse when I was young. "Mother," I would say, "I'm feeling better and would like a taste o' buttered tatties" or maybe I would fancy a big plate o' beef broth and Mother would say . . .'

Lady Marjorie cut into this fond discourse with practised ease. 'Ah, beef broth, you make my mouth water but . . .' she laughed, 'we mustn't forget Martha, must we? Oh, and by the way, I know I've already imposed on your good nature a great deal and you've been so sweet lending me Molly when it took my whim to have her. She's so pretty and young but patient for all that and with such a clear reading voice. I do so like her cheerful manner and wonder, if it wouldn't be too much to ask, if she could bring me my morning tea in future. Not her job, I know, but you've already been so understanding . . .'

'Ach, of course, m'lady.' Seal was quite carried away with this charming new side of her ladyship. 'To tell the truth, I myself would rather see Molly than Effie first thing in the morning so don't you worry about a thing and just concentrate on getting yourself properly on your feets. I'm making one o' my special beef and kidney casseroles for dinner since you and − er − Miss Sarah seem so fond of them.'

'Good, good.' Lady Marjorie beamed. 'But you mustn't worry too much about Sarah, you know, Martha never does, she tears up all her faddy little scribbles on likes and dislikes and pops them on the fire.'

'Really?' Seal was gratified and delighted to learn of this and warmed hugely to the unknown Martha. So immersed was she with the novelty of the whole thing she stooped to stroke one of the cats who was warily waiting either to be sent packing with one of the spare pots or to be offered some leftovers, depending on Cook's mood.

'Oh, what a handsome cat.' Lady Marjorie fondled

the animal's ears. 'He didn't happen to eat some of my breakfast, did he?'

'No, he didn't,' Seal frowned, 'that Effie threw it in the fire before I could stop her. A shameful waste, I was reared in a thrifty household and canna abide seeing anything getting thrown away. If the cats don't get the leavings I save them for Grannie Currie's chickens. She often stops by for a blether and a cuppy and goes away wi' a parcel o' good scraps for her hens – they lay bonny eggs too – double yolks, every one. I often have one for my breakfast, hens are like that, they just give back what they get.'

'Indeed they do,' said Lady Marjorie and went off, frowning.

'Christine dear, what is your opinion of the parlourmaid?'

Christine looked at Lady Marjorie in some surprise. 'You mean Effie? Oh, I don't know, I haven't really thought about it very much. I suppose I have never really had much opportunity to come in contact with her. Sometimes she gives me a look – and funny – I get goose pimples on my skin and I've thought once or twice there's something that is slightly peculiar about her.'

Lady Marjorie began pacing up and down the morning room carpet, giving every appearance of being agitated. 'Christine, my dear, I'm going to come straight to the point. I have thought and thought about it and I really think it would be better for everybody if the girl was to leave Dunmarnock at once, right away, in fact, the sooner the better for everyone. I get the shivers every time I look at her, she's – she's eerie that one. In all my days of servants of every sort I've never come upon one quite like her before. I didn't want to worry your parents about it, not just now, so I thought I had better speak to you first, and then, depending on what you think, I'll have a word with Margaret – Mrs Grant, you know.'

'Dismiss Effie – but –' Christine ran a distracted hand

270

through her hair. She had many things on her mind just then, the welfare of her brother being uppermost, and the disposition of the parlourmaid was the least of her problems.

She gazed at Lady Marjorie with anxious blue eyes. 'I'm sorry, I'm not quite with you, I'm afraid. Why on earth should we even contemplate getting rid of Effie? Things are bad enough here without that, and the shortage of staff . . .'

'I know, I know, believe me, dear child, I wouldn't have mentioned it if I hadn't had a very good reason for doing so.' She paused in her pacing and looked Christine squarely in the face, twisting her hands nervously together. 'I honestly think we would all sleep safer in our beds at night if Effie – was to leave Dunmarnock.'

'But why? What has she done that's so bad, for heaven's sake?'

The other woman dropped into a chair and gazed long and hard into the fire that was cheerily leaping in the grate. For many moments she didn't speak and seemed to be having some sort of inner struggle with herself, then she looked up and in an oddly flat voice said, 'I have reason to believe that the girl tried to poison me, or at any rate put something in my food that would ensure I was kept out of the way for a while. You see, my dear,' she went on earnestly, 'she didn't like having to take orders from me, I saw her looking at me once or twice with venom in her eyes. Evander warned me to go easy on her but I just laughed at him – and the next thing I was ill in bed with dreadful stomach pains and no one else in the house suffered any such thing even though we must all have eaten the same things.'

Christine had to suppress a desire to laugh. The whole thing was monstrous – preposterous – the product of an over-fertile imagination – or the ravings of an unbalanced mind. She stared at Lady Marjorie and saw a woman who was entirely rational and in full possession of every one of her senses.

'But — how — how could she?' she began in a hushed voice.

'Oh, quite easy, my dear, every home is full of poisons of one sort or another, bleaches, disinfectants, old medicines — and of course there's always the garden shed, weedkillers, bugkillers, lots of deadly stuff, just a few drops of one or the other in the tea or sprinkled on the toast and exit nuisance guest for a few days —' She leaned forward, her dark eyes very dark, her face flushed. 'And what is more, Christine, I knew I was for it again yesterday morning when she brought my breakfast — such an odd look on her face — and her eyes — I saw such an oppressive expression of evil in them. I almost fainted and would have done had not Evander come into the room.'

Christine took a deep breath, her heart queer within her at the very idea of the things being mentioned.

Sitting herself down, she and Lady Marjorie discussed the affair at great length and in the end the latter agreed to wait a few days before taking the matter further.

'But I warn you now, Christine,' she said as she got up from her chair, 'if the girl isn't out of here by the end of the week I will be. I don't think I could bear to be in the same house as her for very much longer than that — and she knows it.'

Chapter Nineteen

It seemed, thinking about it afterwards, that everything that had cast a black cloud over Dunmarnock and the people in it came to a head all at once. Andrew, who had for so long maintained a deep silence about his innermost thoughts and fears, suddenly broke down one day when Evelyn was visiting him.

With his head in his hands he poured out his heart to her. He told her all about Effie, her visits to his room, her threats to bring some dire happening on his family if he so much as breathed one wrong word to them about her.

'She wanted me to tell my parents that I wished to marry her,' he sobbed bitterly. 'She kept on and on about it till I thought I would go mad and I very nearly did. That's when I landed up in here, I could take no more.' He raised a tortured, tear-stained face. 'That's why I must never go back there – to her, to her – her – evil. I never wanted to tell anyone about what happened, it's so filthy, I feel ashamed and degraded beyond measure. But I couldn't go on as I'm doing, I couldn't keep it to myself any longer, the dreams, the nightmares were getting worse and I knew I *would* go mad if I didn't get it out of my system.'

He clung to her hand, shaking, his fair head bowed in shame. 'Say you understand, Evie, say you don't hate me, I couldn't tell my family – or – or Grace, I never want her to know, but you, I always could talk to you as a dear friend – and I trust you not to breathe a word of it to any of them.'

'Of course I understand, Andra, and I certainly dinna

hate you.' Evelyn stroked his hair, her voice very gentle, a great swelling of compassion rising in her breast for this poor, lonely boy with his thin, young face and his haunted eyes pleading with her to show him kindness. 'I willna tell your family, or Grace, you can rest assured o' that.'

But she did tell David. That night, when the baby was asleep and it was just the two of them sitting at the fire, she confided everything Andrew had said and when she was finished he gave a little whistle and shook his head.

'Whew, poor bugger, poor lonely, demented young bugger. I can just imagine that wicked bitch, manipulating his mind to her way o' thinking. She saw a man who was sick and defenceless against a strength like hers and she made a full pitch at him.'

'Oh, God, I know.' She leaned against his knees, staring into the fire. 'But what can we do to help him? He canna stay at The Grange all his life, hiding, feart to come out because a bad bitch o' a parlourmaid has her talons into him . . .'

She stopped dead, remembering suddenly her meeting with Effie's mother, the accusing and malicious words that had issued from the little woman's thin lips. She had often wondered about that chance encounter, had asked herself over and over if it could possibly be true that someone as starched and as haughty as Effie had once led the kind of life her mother said she had. But then she would think of the evening she had come back from seeing David in Govan and the encounter with Effie outside the Big House and all the words of filth that had issued from the girl's twisted lips. And now there was Andrew, verifying the sort of woman Effie was, the kind of things she was capable of doing.

'Raggy Annie,' she breathed, 'and Gavin Galbraith.'

David grinned and pulled her hair. 'Now *you're* taking leave o' your senses. What connection have that two with Andrew Baird?'

'They both come from the Gorbals – Effie came from there, at least her mother said so – they might possibly remember something . . .' Then she realised that David couldn't possibly know what she was talking about and she hastened to tell him of her meeting with Mrs Barr.

'So,' he said thoughtfully when she had finished explaining, 'that tells us a lot about our Effie, and you're right, Gavin and Annie might be able to help. It's worth a try. If we could get some facts from them we could confront Effie with them and make her leave Dunmarnock for once and for all. I'll ask Gavin tomorrow to stay on here for his tea and you can invite Annie. It should prove an interesting occasion, whatever the outcome.'

The next evening, when the dishes had been cleared away and the baby was fed, changed and laid back in his cradle, David wasted no time in getting down to business. His dark eyes were glowing, his face animated as he began by asking the visitors if they had ever heard of a Gorbals family known as Barr.

'Barr. Barr.' Raggy Annie wrinkled her brow as she applied a taper to the end of a skinny cigarette. 'Only one Barr I knew of,' she volunteered after a few thoughtful puffs. 'Scum! Even the worst families called them that. The faither spent most o' his drunken life in Barlinnie for sexual assaults on young girls.'

'And the mother was a meths drinker,' supplemented Gavin now that he had ascertained that he and Annie were thinking of the same people, 'who plied her wares –' here he grinned – 'in the sleazy alleys round about Glasgow Green.'

'What about their children?' quizzed Evelyn, wondering how long it would be before the visitors grew curious as to the reasons behind the questions.

'Oy ay, the weans,' nodded Raggy Annie, flicking ash all over the clean hearth. 'Five poor wee runts, I felt sorry for them even though they would have cursed their ain

275

grannie black and blue. The eldest two lost their faither in a cut-throat rammy in Crown Street, the next never kent who his faither was, the next two were Sammy Barr's, both lassies, sly as weasels like himself.'

'Three left home as soon as they could,' supplied Gavin, settling himself comfortably back in his chair, thoroughly enjoying these unsavoury reminiscences about his stamping ground. 'One o' the lassies got ripped in a shebeen in the Rutherglen Road . . .'

'And the other?' asked Evelyn breathlessly.

'She walked the streets from the age o' fourteen,' Raggy Annie said pityingly, 'her face painted like a Red Indian, rouge, lipstick, black-pencilled eyes, no matter the time o' day. I used to pass her by in the morning when I was going to my work in a dairy and there she'd be, tottering along on her peerie heels, coming home to her bed after a night on the tiles.'

Annie paused to roll herself another cigarette, rejecting David's offer of a Woodbine saying they were too mild, and in the interval Gavin, quite carried away by now, took up the tale.

'She never gave the likes o' me a second glance, I was too tame for a lassie like Effie Barr, she could stand up for herself wi' the toughest o' men and it was said she carried a cut-throat razor in her bag.'

'Effie, her name was Effie, then?' Evelyn's voice came out in a squeak.

'Ay, Effie.' Annie took up the cudgels once more, in her excitement throwing her hands about so that cigarette ash rained all over her person and on to that of Evelyn who was sitting beside her on the sofa. 'She earned herself a helluva reputation as a wild one wi' the men she picked up. It was said they couldna handle her – and them the roughest wee keelies in the Gorbals. All her money went to keep her mother in booze and paid her faither's fines but somehow she faded out the scene and nobody kent where she'd gone though rumour had it she went the same way as her old man and landed up in the jail.'

276

'Why all this interest in the Barrs?' Gavin looked from one to the other of the young Graingers, suspicion and puzzlement suddenly clouding his eyes. Evelyn looked at David and, receiving a slight nod from him, she took a deep breath and told the visitors about her meeting with Mrs Barr, about Andrew and his fear of Effie and his vow never to come back to his own home as long as she remained in it.

When she had finished speaking a deep silence pervaded the room. Outside, the autumn wind rustled the trees, an owl hooted from the woods, a patter of dry leaves crept along under the window, a flurry of them rasped eerily against the panes before slithering down to join the others that were whispering and scampering round the house.

Inside, little Alex breathed evenly in his cradle, Snuffle and Sniffle, the cats, stretched and purred, one from her perch on Gavin's knee, the other from his place on the rug, Raggy Annie puffed her cigarette, an odd little 'prump, prump' on Gavin's lips came like the rhythmic dirge on a kettle drum.

'Never!' said Raggy Annie at last, so stunned by the revelations she forgot to flick her cigarette, causing a long, curving oblong of ash to grow and grow on the end of it and keep everyone's eyes riveted on it as if it was the only thing of importance in the breathless hush of the room.

'Never!' she repeated with even more emphasis. 'Thon prim, poker-faced parlourmaid wi' her airs and graces and starches and her snooty nose in the air could never be the same cratur as the one I a saw wi' my own een walking the streets o' the Gorbals.'

'I thought I recognised her.' Gavin's voice came low, filled with incredulity but a slow dawning of belief breaking over its edges. 'That day I went to the Big House to thank the Bairds for everything they'd done for me. My chair banged her on the shin and the glance she gave me could have killed. It was the first time I really saw her face and she hurried away, a strange, worried look on her when I asked her if I'd met her before somewhere.'

'Effie Jordan!' Annie sat back and stared aghast at Evelyn's earnest face, 'you mean to sit there and tell me I've been in the same house as Effie Barr and never even kent it? But how could she be the same as that wee slut wi' her painted face and her wild reputation wi' men? Yon lassie was a floosie, God help her, Effie Jordan's arse is that frozen I doubt the ice wouldna melt if she sat herself down on top o' a volcano.'

'The Effie you knew was much younger, remember,' David pointed out patiently, 'and, as you said yourself, you never saw her without paint on her face. Effie Barr and Effie Jordan are one and the same all right, her mother's visit and the way she treated Andrew proved that. We just wanted you to verify the things her mother told Evie, we had to be sure because Effie must be made to leave Dunmarnock, it's the only way Andrew Baird will ever get well or want to come home to his own house.'

'Ay, indeed she must go.' Raggy Annie was still reeling from the shock of the evening's revelations. 'I never liked the lass myself and some o' the things she said and did fair gave me the creeps at times. Look at what she did to you, Evie, snooping and prying and looking for trouble, and the lies! Telling folk she was an orphan. And all o' us believing the lying bitch. Ach, my poor, poor Andrew Baird, she must have terrified the lad for he's never been a strong cratur at the best o' times. She deserves to be run out o' that decent, God-fearing house by the scruff o' her neck – and I'd like to be the one to do it.'

'I'll deal wi' her,' said Evelyn hastily. 'The Bairds must never ken any o' this, Andra made me swear no' to tell them. Effie canna be dismissed, she must be made to go of her own accord.'

Gavin thought of Christine and how much she had worried about her brother. 'And you trust Annie and me no' to breathe a word o' this to anyone?'

'Ay, we trust you,' returned Evelyn simply. Both visitors looked at one another and nodded, each of them knowing that never by word or deed would they ever do anything to hurt the Bairds of Dunmarnock.

'Evie, are you sure you want to go through wi' this?' David asked next morning as she was leaving the house. 'I don't like the idea o' you and that cold-eyed devil being alone together. Why don't you let me handle it? She won't come any o' her funny tricks wi' me.'

'No, Davie.' Evelyn's face was resolute. 'I've dealt wi' Effie before. In a strange sort o' way we understand one another and the sooner it's over with the better for everyone concerned.'

He took her hands and kissed her on the mouth, a warm kiss, filled with tenderness and affection. It had been so good with him since their return from Kenneray, the dark side of him seemed buried in the uncertainty and unhappiness of the past though, just occasionally, he was moody and quiet and would pace restlessly, like some wild creature only half-tamed and longing for a return to the freedom that had once been his.

But mostly he was content enough working with Gavin, his hands sure and firm as he fashioned pieces of furniture, loving the smell, the feel, the look of the wood, and she left the cottage, his kiss warm on her lips, pushing Alex in his pram, his rosy-cheeked face peeping out from his woollen bonnet, chubby fingers pointing at anything that took his fancy, not glowering at her nearly so much now but still more aloof with her than he was with anybody else.

A chilly autumn wind was blowing, severing the dry leaves from the trees, sending them scampering and dancing into the woods. A few minutes later she met Twiggy May in a leafy lane. The old woman was carrying her sack and smoking her clay pipe which was stuffed with a mixture of tobacco and leaves. They exchanged a few pleasantries then Twiggy May disconcerted the girl by saying in a low voice, 'Be careful how you go the day, lass, I can feel your anxiety, your eyes are full o' trouble.'

Evelyn stared at her, wondering wildly if she ought to confide in this wise woman but before she could say anything, the deep, low voice came again, 'I carry secrets that go away back before you were born, lass, and they'll go wi' me to the grave.'

Evelyn took a deep breath and half against her will she told the old woman everything and when she had finished speaking there was a short silence.

'Effie.' Twiggy May spoke the name unwillingly, fearfully. 'The first time I looked at her I glimpsed the de'il in her een. She's possessed, Evelyn, possessed wi' all that's wicked and sinful and you mind how you go wi' her. 'Tis a big responsibility you take on yourself, and you such a young and inexperienced lassie.'

'Someone has to tell her,' Evelyn said a little desperately. 'She must be made to leave Dunmarnock before she destroys everything and everyone in it.'

The black eyes were on her, mesmerising, oddly hypnotic. 'Ay, but will she let go, even if she does leave?'

Twiggy May spoke almost to herself then with a swift movement she rummaged in her ragged pocket and pressed something into the girl's hand. 'Take this, keep it on you, it will help to keep you safe and mind, some part o' me will be wi' you as long as you are in danger.'

She went on her way, bent and old, but it wasn't her bulky sack which stooped her shoulders, it was an invisible burden that sat on them like a heavy weight.

Evelyn stared at the object nestling in her palm. It was just a twist of rough hair, bound round a tiny wooden hoop, a homemade good luck charm, one that the old woman had endowed with magical qualities known only to herself.

Evelyn slipped it into the pocket of her skirt and went on her way with the wind whistling round her and the autumn leaves skirling and rustling round her feet.

Effie, her sallow face twisted and livid with fury, glared

at Evelyn as if she would like to kill her. 'I'll never leave Dunmarnock!' she blazed. 'It will take more than a tink's daughter to make me give up everything I've ever dreamed of since I left the stench o' the gutters behind me. I've worked and sweated, bowed and scraped, and now Andrew's mine, mine, do you hear me, Miss High and Mighty Kitchen Maid! He'll come back to me and he'll find me waiting for him. I'll never let him go, not now, not ever, never, never, never!'

'He willna come back, no' as long as you're here.' Evelyn felt strangely breathless and kept a tight hold of the little lucky charm lying in her pocket. She kept her mind on Twiggy May, and somehow, strangely, the strength and power of the old woman made her go on, even though all she wanted was to run out of Effie's room with its gloomy, oppressive atmosphere. 'Andra despises you, Effie, you robbed him o' his dignity and trod him to the ground at a time in his life when he was too weak to fight back. You dinna love him, you only love yourself and used him for your own ends. Well, it hasna worked, I ken who you are and what you are and if you dinna leave here o' your own free will I'll no' hesitate to tell everyone all about you.'

'You filthy little slut!' Effie raged, her narrowed eyes glinting with hatred. 'You dare to lecture me on the rights and wrongs when all the time you're nothing but a cheap little whore who lied and cheated and pretended to us all you were something you weren't. But you never took me in, no' for one minute . . .'

For fully five minutes she ranted and raved and trembled from head to foot, then, exhausted, she dropped onto the bed, her breasts heaving, flecks of foam gathering at the corners of her mouth.

'What does it matter if the whole place finds out about the Bairds and their precious son? Why should I care what happens to any o' them? They're nothing to me now, I'll have to leave, one way or another, so I might as well go out wi' a bloody great bang.'

Evelyn felt sick, desperately she strived to hold on to the last remnants of her courage as she panted, 'You'll go quietly and respectfully from this place, Effie, because if you don't there is no' a house in all the land would dream o' taking you. You've built yourself up from nothing, for that I have to admire you, but knowing you as I do you willna jeopardise your chances for the sake o' one, glorious, destructive fling. So, go in peace, Effie Barr, and if you do you'll take references with you that will ensure you find a good place for yourself wherever you go – just as long as it's as far away from Dunmarnock as you can get.'

'Get out o' here, you bitch!' Effie had ranted herself hoarse but the look in her half-mad eyes said it all. 'But mind this, you bastard tink, I'll make you suffer for this! Somehow, sometime, I'll make you and everyone else who had a hand in this, pay for what you've done to me.'

Evelyn went gladly, her knees shaking so much it was all they could do to carry her downstairs to the homely sanity of the kitchen and a piping hot cup of tea from the ever-brewing pot.

'How very odd, Effie leaving like that,' Lady Marjorie confided in Evelyn some days later. 'Just in time too, if she hadn't, I would, for I tell you this, Evelyn, I could hardly bear to be under the same roof as the girl, and that's an honest fact.'

Evelyn merely nodded, not trusting herself to speak, still so shaken by the events of the last few days she could hardly bear to mention the parlourmaid's name.

Lady Marjorie gazed at the girl's face searchingly. 'Evelyn, if I was to tell you that I have reason to believe that the girl tried to poison me, would you think I was just too mad for words?'

'No, Lady Marjorie, I wouldna,' replied Evelyn and quickly left the room before the conversation became too awkward.

282

PART FIVE

Winter 1918/19

Chapter Twenty

There followed a time of great joy for everyone. Andrew came home from The Grange, still too thin, but his shoulders were straight and there was a sparkle in his blue eyes that reflected his hunger for living again.

Within days he was down at the stables, helping Burton with the horses, talking to his father about going back to work, looking at Grace with a light in his eyes and a new expression of vitality on his handsome features.

His family were overjoyed, Grace so delighted she agreed to accompany him on several small jaunts, one of them to Glasgow to shop and have tea in Miss Cranston's Tearooms in Sauchiehall Street, thereafter to take a tram along to the Kelvingrove Park where the trees grew over the River Kelvin and spread mysterious bowers over the shady lanes where lovers could stroll and talk and forget the world for a while.

'Are you in love wi' him, Grace? Just a little bit?' Evelyn asked, hugging her knees and praying that the answer would be yes.

'Ay, maybe just a wee bit,' agreed Grace promptly. 'But never enough for what you have in mind, you sly whittrock. I told you before, I love Gordon, he's the only man who ever meant anything in my life that was worthwhile. But Andra needs me just now and I'll no' deny him a bit happiness after all he's been through. In time he'll meet someone o' his own sort but until then I'll be glad to keep him company for as long as he wants me.'

*　　*

So that was that, life settling back to a happy routine at the Big House, the young folk meeting and going out or gathering for meals and ceilidhs at Maggie's house or over there at Fern Cottage where the burn purled over the bridge and the little red chimney puffed its busy smoke.

Lady Marjorie and Evander Forbes left Dunmarnock at the beginning of November, in a whirl of fond farewells and many promises to return in the spring, but just then it was London and the bright lights in preference to the country with its winter dark and quiet orderly days.

Soon after they left, Douglas Grainger came to stay for a short holiday in Fern Cottage. David was delighted to see his father again. They talked for hours, played with the baby, walked to the local inn, visited Evelyn's family, had tea with Seal and Ferguson and an evening of ghost stories from Grannie Currie, and when Douglas left there was a spring in his step and a notion in his mind that his life had taken on a new meaning just as long as he could occasionally visit the young folk in their country cottage.

And through it all Evelyn looked and sounded happy and content and tried always to be busy, but times of solitude inevitably came and with them the small, inner niggle of unease she tried to ignore but couldn't and knew she wouldn't as long as Effie's face came to haunt her peace of mind, and Effie's voice inside her head warned her that she would pay for what she had done.

Evelyn had freed Andrew of his nightmares and in doing so had transferred them to herself. The long, black shadow of The Devil's Door loomed again in her dreams and wouldn't go away . . .

Dreams, creeping, following her wherever she went, in waking or in sleeping, the dream that often seemed to her to be her own life, a strange mixture of people and places, loves and hates, and men who came to haunt her who weren't David but who were part of her life just the same, weaving in and out, in and out; her father; Johnny; Alan

286

Keith. Oh, Alan! Marching into war with the braw skirl of the pipes dirling in his head, fighting, dying, wanting to die for Florrie for what was his life without that golden-haired sprite with her teasings and laughings and the red blood of her life staining lips that had smiled and cried before death came to steal it all away. And Jamie, once a gypsy so gay, black eyes snapping with youth and love and caring, now withered and old-looking though times the light came back to his eyes when he remembered and forgot and stirred his own blood with fiddle music that carried him back from his exile to his peesies and the cool wind blowing over the faraway hills . . .

Davie, her Davie! Warm, warm, wildly warm and passionate, brave and often frightening with the look in his eyes of a lion in its cage and her in there with him, seeing not the bars that bound him but beyond them to the sky and the sun spilling over a land that was free – free . . . Gillan, dear Gillie of the black eyes and the youth and passion that was hers and his and beckoned her back, back, but no further than that for what was beyond but the guns and the wilderness of war and waste . . . The great guns of the Western Front, booming, booming, far-off and away beyond the night hills where there was no beauty, only death and destruction and Gillie, watching and waiting for the silence that never came yet never wanting it in case it was that final silence that would carry him off forever from the lands and people that he loved . . .

'Gillie.' She awoke, bathed in sweat, the name she thought she had screamed a mere hush of a breath on her lips. Beside her, David stretched and murmured and wanted nothing more than deathless sleep, and no wonder at that for the November night was still black out there beyond the window. Night, night, with its keenings and whisperings and sombre breathings, unheard by those in the deep quiet of their slumberings.

But she was past the sleepings and the dreamings and she stared and watched and waited with fast beating heart, she knew not for what, but eventually could bear it no longer and padded soft from the room to go downstairs and hug herself over the smoking embers of the fire, choked with dross but the poker soon stirring it to life and warmth that bathed her body which was cold from the flight downstairs in nothing but her nightgown.

'Oh, Gillie, why do I dream so?' she whispered to the empty room and, as if for answer, her eyes were drawn to the calendar pinned to the wall beside the fireplace.

11 November 1918. It meant something, she didn't know what, not yet, but she knew she would and she fetched a blanket from the kist and cooried herself into the chair and the fire and stayed like that, not dozing or dreaming, but staring big-eyed beyond the window till dawn filtered ghost-grey into the room to touch her with its cold fingers.

And later that day the world knew what she had half-glimpsed and as the big guns of the Western Front fell silent, kirk bells pealed and echoed and people stampeded and danced in the streets and threw their hats in the air. They kissed and hugged each other and just about smothered the boys in blue who happened to have taken a trip from hospital into town.

Everyone at Dunmarnock went wild with delight, farmers stopped in the fields to dance with the bringers of the news, old Jasper Pringle threw a dead rabbit in the air in his excitement while Big John Currie, the tidings flung at him from a passer-by on a bike, forgot himself altogether and, with nobody to kiss but a nearby cow, he did just that, plunk on the tip of her big wet nose which she twitched and snorted, while gazing at him out of wondering, long-lashed eyes.

In the Big House itself, Seal and Ferguson, forgetting their sore feet, did a Highland Fling in the middle of the kitchen and for the rest of the day work came to a standstill while everybody celebrated and went out and about to watch everybody else celebrating.

Night brought the bonfires, great plumes of fire and smoke, and the villagers and estate workers came to sing and dance and to roast potatoes and sausages in the embers, though they weren't too full to eat the piles of pies and cake and sandwiches that came down from the Big House in hampers.

In amongst it all was Lady Elizabeth herself, and the Colonel, pecking at charred sausages and laughing when little Union Jacks were stuck in their hats and wondering who had had the foresight to have them ready for the Grand Victory.

After that came the Peace outings and the Armistice medals and after that came the Spanish 'flu, spawned in the filth of the trenches and said to be the worst epidemic since the Black Death way back in the dark days of the fourteenth century.

Out from the wastes of war it came to inflict men already inflicted by suffering from the long fight, before spreading to the civilian population. In the Grant household Gavin was the first to go down, ordered to his bed by the overworked, wheezy old doctor, after he collapsed in a delirium of fever.

Christine sat by his bed as he tossed and turned, burned and sweated, even while the bed shook with his shiverings. She bathed him and soothed him and stayed with him all through his ravings and swearings, only leaving his side to drag herself home to her own bed and the deep sleep of the bone weary.

Grace was the next to succumb to the deadly virus. One night she went to bed light-headed and burning, the next morning Maggie took one look at her fevered face, felt her racing pulse, and ordered her back to bed.

'But, Mam, I'm fine, really,' she croaked, 'and I ken fine what's wrong wi' me, it's only a wee chill I caught in Glasgow the other day when I was there wi' Andra. I canna let them down at the hospital —'

She struggled to her feet only to stagger back into her chair, white to the lips except for her fiery cheeks.

'Just a wee chill, eh?' Maggie said grimly. 'You're a nurse to everybody but yourself, my girl, and it's back to bed wi' you this minute.'

Grace went, too ill in the next few days to know that Andrew haunted her bedside, while in the room downstairs his sister never left Gavin's side, not even to go home as she had done in the beginning, but fitfully dozing in a chair by his bed as he laboured to draw breath into his choked lungs.

Two days later he was dead from pneumonia, never gaining consciousness, the last of his fevered ramblings centred on Christine, his love, his delight of her, tumbling from his lips to his last breath.

She held him in her arms as he fell still and silent at the end, the sigh of her name trembling and dying away as his curly dark head fell to the side and she knew he was gone from her.

She stood up and kissed the ugly-attractive face that had so charmed her with its open, honest smiles and teasings, then she walked away from him, out into the weak December sunlight and no one saw her again till the black cold of the next morning when she walked into Seal's kitchen and asked for a cup of hot, strong, thick tea laced with a good tot of brandy.

During this time Evelyn flitted from Fern Cottage to Dunmarnock, from there to Wood Cottage, in and out and back again, seeing to David and the baby, never stopping from morning to night, driving herself as hard as she could to take her mind off Grace's fevered face; Gavin's tortured delirium; Christine's still, lovely young face, its expression hardly changing when finally he died and was taken away to be buried in the family plot in the necropolis where his dry-eyed old aunt said a place had been reserved for him and 'me too when my time comes'.

'So few to weep for him,' Christine said later to Evelyn. 'A man like him deserved so much love in his life.'

'You gave it to him, all the love he ever wanted or needed. He was aye happy when he was wi' you.'

'It wasn't enough to make him change his mind about him and me.'

'I know, he was like me that way, too proud and afraid to leave his side o' the fence.'

Christine nodded. 'You and Gillan, I remember that night we all had dinner at your mother's house, how passionately he argued about the class system. You loved him then, I could see it in your eyes. I think you'll always wonder what it would have been like – with him.'

'Part o' me will aye love Gillie, I'll never forget him.'

'Nor I Gavin, he was so real, so whole, so honest – now – it is finished.'

'What will you do?'

'I don't know.' Christine sounded bleak, very alone. 'I'll marry, I suppose –' she smiled bitterly – 'into my own camp. Guthrie Wilson Kerr is a good sort – if I don't marry for love I'll marry for goodness and have lots of good little Guthries reading me bits of the Bible. Oh God! I'm glad I never told Gavin any of that, he would have teased circles round me.' Her voice broke. 'How I miss him. He pretended to be tough when all the time he was as soft as butter. Last summer I watched him rescuing a butterfly from a spider's web and then he grew red in the face and said he only did it because he didn't like spiders. He believed in God, I did too when I was with him. He made me see things I'd never noticed before, now I don't believe in anything much, it's all so pointless.'

That night Evelyn wrote in her diary:

Joy and sorrow, sorrow and joy. Is that what life is really all about? When Davie came back to me I thought I had everything, now I know none of us can ever have that when the people around us lose the things they love. Their happiness is ours, their sadness is ours too and everything is nothing in the great merry-go-round of life.

* *

But joy came again for her, in a letter from Gillan, addressed to Wood Cottage and read in the privacy of the room in which Grace lay, getting better now and peacefully asleep with the daylight glinting on her chestnut hair and on the sweet repose of her lovely face, so pale now that the hectic stain of fever had left it; but at least she had survived, strange to think of that, Grace with her frail strength and almost ethereal appearance, winning through an illness that had taken Gavin with his rough and ready strength and his ox-like physique.

For a long moment of thankfulness Evelyn gazed at her sister's dear face then carefully she unfolded her letter.

My dear princess,

At last it's over. I never thought I would hear silence again and oddly enough can't sleep at night without the rumble of guns in my lugs. Something very strange happened to me in the dark hours before Armistice, that is why I'm writing this letter, to find out if you maybe experienced a little of what I felt. Knowing all about those eerie powers of yours I won't be surprised if the answer is yes.

I dreamt of you, princess, and you were so real I felt I could reach out and touch you with my hands. I honestly imagined you and I were lying side by side, comforting one another, knowing something was about to happen but not knowing what. Then I awoke, cold and stiff, but the ground at my side was warm, as if somebody had recently lain there and had only just got up. Once I was awake, of course, you didn't come back to me but I felt you were there just the same, watching and waiting with me for the dawn to break, and later peace was declared and I knew why you had come to me, to give me comfort and hope when I felt just about at the end of my tether.

Do you believe that people can visit one another in dreams? Not just in thought waves but in a far more tangible sense? No, I'm not crazy though I might sound it. Write and tell me what you think. If it was the case, think how wonderful it would be. I could come and visit you as often as I like, even lie in bed with you, and not another soul in the world need know about it.

God Bless you, my darling.

Gillie.

Immediately she rushed away to find pen and paper and was so eager to pen her own experiences to him the first two pages were just a jumble and had to be torn up and cast aside. Forcing herself to write calmly she began:

Yes, oh, yes, Gillie, I dreamt a similar dream to yours during the early hours of 11 Nov. I got up and went down to sit at the fire and just waited and watched for the dawn to come, and you were with me, Gillie, all through my dream and later when I got up. I wanted so much for you to be safe and well. I wished and wished it and prayed as well and willed for you to survive the war, and now you have and that special place in my heart that I keep for you is singing like a little bird inside of me.

We have had a lot of sad times here. Andrew was ill but is better again. Grace and Gavin both took that awful Spanish 'flu. Grace is getting slowly better but Gavin died. The doctor said his lungs had been damaged by mustard gas and he wasn't strong enough to fight off a bad bout of pneumonia. None of us could believe it and Christine is devastated. She loved him more than any of us thought and has gone away to Craigdrummond to be alone for a while.

Your parents were here in the autumn and your mother certainly stirred the place up a bit. It was wonderful to see them both again. It brought Rothiedrum closer than ever and Mam has been quiet ever since they left.

Sweet dreams, my dear, dear Gillie. I'm very, very

293

happy with David and the baby but as long as you come to me sometimes in my dreams I'll feel you have never really left me.

Evie.

She didn't tell him about Effie or the terrible trauma of her departure. Lady Marjorie would no doubt see to it that he got the news all right and would embellish it with all the drama of which she was capable.

It took Grace more than two weeks even to begin to recover. She had been so ill the doctor had privately thought that she wouldn't pull through but he didn't need to say anything to Maggie and Jamie. Their hearts were heavy with worry for this gentle daughter who had seldom given them anything but joy in all the days of her sweet young life. Between that, and their grief over Gavin, it was a time of great sadness in their lives, but one morning Grace opened her eyes and gone from them was the bright glaze of fever, instead they were great black pools lying calm and quiet in the pale beauty of her flower-like face. The first thing she asked about was Gavin, her voice hesitant in her parched throat, as if she already knew the answer that Maggie didn't want to give but couldn't avoid.

'Poor Chris,' was all she said, sad and quiet and turning her head away to look at the grey-dark of the December day, the low-slung clouds of it torn and weeping by the black claws of winter branches.

Andrew came after that, as he had come every day for the past few weeks, and she looked at the fair head of him, tussled and untidy, as if he hadn't taken time to brush it properly, down-bent it was, his blue eyes raking her face, black-blue eyes she had thought that then, so intense and searching as they gazed into hers, the young face of him taut and hollowed, his mouth firm and clean and trembling with emotions he might never voice in case she might think him too daft for words.

He said nothing, just made a little sound like an indrawn sigh, then he gathered her in his arms as if she was the most precious thing on earth, and held her like that, her head under his chin, stroking her hair till Maggie came up to wash her and sent him downstairs to make a cup of tea.

He smiled and went, the young Dunmarnock, who had never been much good at making tea till Maggie had changed all that; gentleman or farmer, they took their turn in her house and were glad enough to do it and feel that it was something grand to lift the big black kettle from the swee and nuzzle its steaming spout into the vast brown breast of the earthenware pot that always held a spare cup for any visitor that chanced in.

It took Grace some time to get back on her feet but when she did she told Maggie that she had best get back to her neglected duties at Dunmarnock, saying that she would manage fine on her own.

And Grace did manage fine, happed in a crocheted wool blanket there by the kitchen fire with General on her knee, reading letters from Nellie and Murn and Mary, liking it fine when one or other of the estate workers popped in to make tea and stay for a blether.

And through it all was Andrew, reading aloud little snippets from the local paper, talking about horses and people and things he loved and also about things he didn't, such as the war and the men who had fought in it and who would come home and be forgotten except in the singing and the praying and the remembering the dead and to hell with the living, they should be lucky to be alive, what more did they want?

Later, when she was stronger, they walked together in the woods, pale-shadowed in the winter sun, dead and cold-seeming but under the black-brown leaves the white-green of snowdrop spikes stayed snug and safe from wind and frost. Together they found these small quiet signs of hopeful spring and together they wondered at life, its strengths and its weaknesses, and he looked at the girl with her bright, shining hair and the sweet smile of her coming swift to her lips, and he loved her as he had never loved anybody in his life before.

And she never knew when or how, in those quiet, dear days, it came to her slowly like some secret dream of the night, the realisation that she had never known, or maybe hadn't wanted to know, the soul of the man that was Andrew Baird. Now, listening to his deep, dark voice, seeing the gleam and the glint and the kindness of his eager eyes, she thought to herself that he was beautiful in his young, sweet caring for her, for the things about him, for men and people he didn't know but cared about because life hadn't been too good or fair to them.

'You're a good man, Andra Baird,' she said to him one day and he raised his head to look at her, quick and wondering, and a small quiet sadness came to his mouth when he answered, 'You don't know me, Grace, or you wouldn't say such a thing. I hope you never find out about the real me.'

'The real you is standing beside me now, all o' us have things to feel guilty about but what's past is past and better buried.'

'But never forgotten, Grace,' he said huskily.

'Ay, maybe,' she smiled, a different smile for Grace, one filled with mischief and teasing. 'We have Adam and Eve to thank for that – or blame, whichever mood we happen to be in.'

He smiled back and took her hand, swinging it a little as they walked on, and she found herself wanting more than the touch of his hand, more than his blue eyes adoring her from afar. He had never tried to kiss her or touch her since his return from hospital and that had been fine then, she hadn't wanted more than his friendship. But she knew him now, had glimpsed something wonderful beneath the searing blue eyes that had once frightened her with their intensity; now she knew his shyness and his goodness and realised also that the strong bright flame of his love for her, that had burned so unwaveringly all through the days and weeks of her illness, was more than just a physical thing,

296

and the beauty of it touched her own soul with its spiritual light.

Grace was well now, well and strong, and soon going back to her work at The Grange, but first she wanted Andrew to love her, she wanted to give him something precious and private of herself that he might remember in times to come when the days were no more for them, the days to tramp the winter woods together, or to sit quietly by the fire, each of them lost and waiting as the slow tick-tock of the clock whiled away the hours that were left to them to be like this, warm and comfortable together, yet not comfortable inside where flames burned brighter than those of the fire and were mirrored and wanting in their eyes and their hands when they touched and drew away, embarrassed and smiling at nothing.

'Andra,' she said one day, her hand twining into his, her body trembling a little, 'it's all right with me now, I said daft things when first we met but now I want — I want you to love me. Gordon is always with me, you ken that better than anybody, but I was so alone till I met you, alone and lonely, I need to have your love in my life — even if it's just for a wee whilie.'

He took her head in his hands and looked long and tenderly into the soft flush of her face, then he gathered her into his arms and his lips merged with hers, eager and burning, demanding and hard, and for a few moments he went wild with a passion that consumed them both.

Then he pushed her away from him, his breath harsh and dry in his throat. 'No, Grace!' he cried. 'I musn't defile you, I mustn't touch you — not yet, not until I myself have been purged and freed from guilt and sin! Please understand, oh, understand, my darling, dearest girl.'

A great sob escaped her, she put her head against his heart, felt its wild beating, was aware of his hardness, the fiery heat of his wanting searing into her breasts. He stiffened and with a groan rose up, her in his arms, her face so close to his she could see a pulse in his temple beating like an imprisoned bird.

There was a strange light in his eyes, shining, shining, a glimpse into a restless soul that would never know peace until the madness that was in him was stilled forever.

She knew then that he would never be normal as other men. Something had snapped in him the day Barrett died in his fire and young Andra Baird would dream and follow the ghosts of his mind till, by some miracle, he was freed of their hauntings, and was made whole again.

The hurt and the sadness of that knowledge curled into her heart till it ached and tightened her throat and with a sob she took him once more to her breast, not as a lover would do, warm and waiting, but as a mother might take and comfort a small child who has found the world too big and frightening a place.

Chapter Twenty-One

It was peaceful inside Fern Cottage. The baby was asleep in his cradle, having cried and laughed his way through his usual nightly routine, his father bathing him in the tub in front of the fire, his mother feeding him and happing him snug in his long, flannelette nightgown, his eyes growing heavy with the heat, lying in his bed to girn for a minute, gurgle for another, before settling himself to watch, fascinated, the shadows prancing on the ceiling till his long lashes touched his rosy cheeks and his even breathings told his parents he was at last asleep.

There was no bathroom in the cottage, only a tiny water closet, and now it was David's turn for the tub. Topping it up from the steaming kettle he undressed and got in to lather soap all over his body and his hair while Evelyn washed his back then rinsed his hair with fresh lukewarm water from a bucket on the hearth.

He stepped out, lean and gleaming, towelling himself vigorously till he was pink and glowing and his head was a crown of dark, damp curls which she kissed, but absently that night, her head frequently to the door, the window, as if she was listening, waiting for something or someone.

She jumped when he touched her shoulder to indicate to her that he had freshened the contents of the tub and while he wrapped himself in his nightshirt and retired behind his newspaper she undressed quickly and lowered herself into the water, adding to it a few drops of rosewater in an attempt to invigorate its flatness. But at least it was warm. She stared at the tidemark of soapy

299

scum slopping round the zinc sides but she wasn't really seeing it, she was keyed up, inexplicably so, and was glad of the peace, and the heat from the fire, washing over her, soothing her, gradually making her limbs and her seething mind relax a little.

Outside the wind moaned, keened round the house, emphasising the warmth of the little house.

Christmas was only a few days off. David had brought home a tiny tree. Together they had decorated it and now it stood in a corner by the window, breathing gently of Christmas, the spirit of it, its remembrances, its laughter, its sadnesses. She caught her breath a little. So much had happened since that last Christmas at Dunmarnock with the snow and the fairy-tale woodlands sparkling and shimmering with frost, and Darling pulling the sleigh, her long legs stepping smartly out, sleighbell jingles tinging in sharp air that turned noses into cherries and cheeks into roses.

The laughter, the singing, the picnics and the stolen kisses under the mistletoe, the strange, sweet glances that weren't tears but very nearly so – Gillie – far away now, no longer the touch of his hand, the warmth of his breath against her hair ... He had sent a little Christmas card, somewhat stiff and formal: *To Evelyn and David and baby Alexander. From Gillan Forbes.* That was all but it was enough to make David growl a bit and grudge it a place on the mantlepiece beside the other cards ...

So different this Christmas, no snow, just lashing rain and bitter winds laden with the promise of snow that never came – no Gavin, no Gillie, gone, gone, the rough but kindly voice of one stilled forever, the strong, vibrant one of the other heard only in dreams that shattered with the dawn.

Gillie, oh Gillie! Would she ever see him again! He who owned a part of her heart that would never be for any other ...

She came out of her reverie with a little start. The water was growing cold, it was cloudier than ever, and the soapy scum was adhering to the metal. She glanced up at David, his face was hollowed by firelight, his drying hair was curling a little over his ears, his dark eyes were seeing nothing at that moment but the words printed on the paper.

How she loved him. Not with the breathless, unquestioning love of a young girl, eager only for the sound of his voice, the touch of his mouth on hers. He had hurt her too much for that kind of love to have lasted. Somewhere along the way it had flickered and faded a little but she would always be his, no matter what he did to her and she would love him till the end of his life . . .

What had made her think that? Which of the voices inside her head had pushed itself forward in her mind? Then she remembered. Twiggy May reading the cups, herself laughing in slight derision till she realised that the old woman knew more of her life than she did herself . . . Something dark and terrible seized her. Fear, large, looming, rose up black and terrifying before her.

She shuddered. Warmth and security slipped away from her – this house, this darling little house which she hadn't expected to love after King's Croft but did now with all her heart . . .

She turned her head sharply to stare at the fire. Sweat broke on her brow. She shrank away from the flames as they seemed to leap out and consume her . . . 'Effie,' she whimpered the name, then louder, 'No, no, not that!'

The sharp crackle of David's paper was like a crash of thunder in the silence. 'What did you say? It sounded like –'

'No, no, it was nothing,' she said quickly.

'Dreaming again. Come on, get up out o' that, the water must be freezing.'

'What time is it?' she spoke breathlessly, as if she had been running.

'Almost eleven.'

'Oh dear God! They'll all be in bed –' She rose up, water dripping from her body.

'Ay, and high time we were in ours.' He took a warm towel from the guard and wrapped her in it, his fingers lingering on her breasts, his mouth going to her throat, everything about him quickening as his hands moved downwards over her naked thighs, a sigh breaking from him at the feel of her satin-textured skin under his touch.

'No, Davie!' She broke away from him. 'We must get dressed, we must!' Her voice was ragged with panic, with the towel around her she ran to the window to peer out into the night. It was black-dark — except for an orange glow shining far off beyond the trees.

'Oh no, it's too late, too late! Effie!' She spoke in a hush but the words made David run to her side and stare with her beyond the panes.

'What the hell!'

'It's Dunmarnock! We must get over there at once to warn them. The baby will be fine, he's sound asleep and willna wake for hours.'

Without another word they hurried into their clothes and with hardly a backward glance they fled off into the night and the terror that awaited them out there.

The glow lit the sky, the glow made by Dunmarnock burning. It was the east wing that was ablaze, that part of the house along whose corridors it was said the Grey Lady walked in a flood of weeping for the lover who had abandoned her to a life — and a death — of lonely tears.

But it wasn't the Grey Lady who walked there now, it was a human being of flesh and blood who flitted from one window to the next to stare with mad eyes at the knot of people gathered below, insane laughter bubbling into her throat to be released in a hellish death knell of sound that would have frozen the blood of anyone hearing it.

'I warned that bitch I'd make her pay for what she did to me!' The frightful laughter rang out again. 'Ay, and all those other ungrateful bastards who dared to make me leave Dunmarnock! It's mine, mine, and if I canna have it

302

as it stands I'll take it wi' me as a payment for all the suffering I've endured!'

A bitter wind was blowing, fanning the flames to an inferno that shattered the windows and blackened the stonework. Someone had been dispatched to fetch the police and fire brigade and while they waited the crowd stood silent, hardly able to believe that such a noble house was afire, the house of Dunmarnock that had stood on that spot for the last one hundred years and more.

Young Jock Pringle, coming home late from some nocturnal outing, had spotted the flames and had gone rushing inside to warn everyone and get them out safely. Now they stood about, some only half-dressed, Seal still in her nightgown with rag curlers in her hair, Raggy Annie with her stockings rolled to her ankles, smoking furiously, the nicotine-stained fingers that held the cigarette to her lips, trembling in a mixture of nerves and cold. But blankets were arriving from the farms and cottages round about, together with brandy and whisky and anything else that could be fetched in a hurry. Cook with a Capital was very glad to hide her state of undress to the world and magnanimously shared her blanket with Ferguson who was shivering and muttering nearby and far too upset to bother his head about what folk might think of him pressing his old bones against the nice plump padding of a half-dressed woman.

Colonel Richard Baird and his wife stood very close together, his arms supporting her, for she looked ready to faint at any minute and was glad to gulp down some of the brandy brought to her by old Jasper Pringle.

'My, my.' Grannie Currie shook her head, her kind old face saddened and shocked. 'I never thought I would see a sight like this, the house o' Dunmarnock has stood here for more than a century and never so much as a candle flame to scorch her stones. I worked there for years as did my own mother before me. The de'il is at work here the night, I can feel the shiver o' his evil in my very marrow.'

'Look, look up there.' Someone pointed upwards. 'Is that your de'il, Grannie? Or is it the ghost o' the Grey Lady having a bit o' a last fling before the walls o' the east wing bury her forever.'

'It *is* someone!' The cry went up. 'And it's no ghost that walks yonder! Someone is there! Someone is still in the building!'

In common with everyone else Evelyn strained her eyes upwards and what she saw there made the hairs stand on the back of her neck. A figure of a woman was moving along the corridors of an upper storey, flitting from window to window, pausing at each one to press a featureless face against the panes and stare down at the people below – without hurry – as if she was enjoying the drama of that night when the big house was burning about her.

'Effie,' Evelyn whispered the name in dread, 'it was Effie – after all.'

'You said that once before tonight.' David stared at her. 'But how can it be her? She left the place weeks ago.'

'She's – come back.'

Her voice was very low but it was enough to make David shiver as he turned his eyes upwards to stare with everybody else at the figure above, its outlines blurred and shimmering in the haze of heat.

Effie looked at the people below and her lips drew back from her teeth in a triumphant leer.

At last! At last! At last! Notoriety was and would be forever hers now. In days to come people would talk about this night, the night that the house of Dunmarnock burned, and they would talk about her, she who had given life to the flames till now there was no stopping them.

The torch that was Dunmarnock would light the sky for miles around the dark countryside and people would stare and point and run to this place to gape further and whisper in awe at what their eyes were telling them. She had thought at first to do it on the night of November the Fifth but no! Why share her hour of glory with some faceless creature of the past? She would have her hour, her glory, her fame — but it wasn't enough — there had to be more, something that would ensure that her name went down in the annals of remembrance for all time, so that foolish nobodies would pass this spot and gape with hungry eyes at the ruin of the big old house, and, in hushed voices, would tell one another the legend — *The Legend of Effie Barr*.

An insane giggle escaped her, she could see the epitaph there in front of her vision in huge letters of fire burning into the sky.

And even when the ruin of Dunmarnock had just become rubble, after that just a lonely acre of grassy waste, they would still come to goggle at the site and remember *The Legend of Effie Barr* . . .

But for that to happen there had to be more than just herself alone in the burning house . . . the smoke was curling along the corridors, tongues of flame were licking at the staircase, devouring the banisters . . . She choked and rushed to a window to throw it open and gulp in great breaths of air, before opening her mouth to scream, 'Andrew! Andrew Baird!'

Just that, over and over again, till the name echoed and rebounded and rang through the woodlands and over the countryside. Scream after scream of insane sound, going on, and on, and on . . .

'Crazy! The woman's crazy,' muttered the Colonel.

'Effie! It's Effie Jordan up there!' Jock Pringle yelled, his eyes big and staring in his white face.

'Andrew, where's Andrew?' Lady Elizabeth moved away from her husband's side, a feeling of panic seizing her as she realized that her son was nowhere to be seen.

Andrew had moved away from the knot of people, he

had to be alone, to get away from that hellish sound that echoed in his ears till he felt he would go mad with its persistent cacophony. He would go into the woods where it was nice and cool and there was no one to jostle him and deafen him with their loud yells . . .

It was cool under the canopy of trees, more than that – cold – so cold, seeping into his bones, making him shiver. But at least the voice that called his name was fainter, more bearable. He looked back, back at that giant torch that lit the sky with a hellish glare. He was an onlooker, detached, nothing, no one could reach him now. He strained his eyes into the pitch dark of the woods. A small shimmer from afar seemed to be coming nearer, growing brighter . . . and now there was the sound, the sound of marching feet, growing in volume, and he saw now that inside the halo of light marched the stooped figures of men, torn, bloodied, their empty eyes looking ahead but seeing nothing – nothing . . .

Sweat poured from him, his disbelieving eyes stared wildly as the figures slowly approached him, the light that enveloped them gradually dissipating till there was nothing left but shadows without substance yet so real he felt he could reach out and touch them as they marched past him, one by one, on, on, towards the fire. He turned round and followed them, the fire filled his vision once more, the voice calling his name grew in volume till the world reverberated with it.

'Barrett.' He breathed the name just once. 'Hold on,' he implored, 'I'm coming, I'm coming.'

'Andrew!' Lady Elizabeth caught and held onto her son as he stumbled towards the house like a man in some nameless trance, drawn like a magnet to the flames, 'Andrew, you mustn't go in there, oh, please, please, listen to me.'

But he shook her off and began to run, leaving his mother to stare after him for one heart-stopping moment before she shouted as she had never shouted before: 'Andrew!

Andrew! Come back! Come back!' Her voice rose to a crescendo that rent the air in a fearful, protesting sound that no one who heard it would ever forget.

'Christ Almighty!' Colonel Baird took in the scene in one glance and made to dash forward but he was restrained from doing so by a dozen pairs of hands.

'Andrew!' Lady Elizabeth screamed again but it was too late, her son had reached the door leading to the east wing and the next instant disappeared inside the inferno.

A deathly silence enshrouded everyone like a thick blanket. Time went past in heartbeats that seemed to stand still for long moments that stretched and spun away into eternity. All eyes were riveted on the east wing and the figure at the upstairs window, now here, now swallowed into shadows that still remained in dark pockets as yet untouched by fire.

'Look!' The crowd found its voice, seconds, minutes, aeons later, no one knew, no one counted. Effie appeared again, only an outline without substance, wavering like a mirage in the heat. Beside her appeared another figure, that of a man, grabbing at her, struggling with her, two shadows in a deadly embrace that seemed to go on and on and both fascinated and horrified the onlookers.

The firefighters arrived along with the police. More noise, more confusion . . . no one saw Lady Elizabeth glide away into the house for the last time. She knew there was no hope for her son but something had snapped in her mind during witness of his death-throes with a shadow who was just one of the many who had haunted him for so long – for that was all Effie was to him in his final hour – and his mother knew it.

The fire brigade had put up a heroic fight, helped in their efforts by every able-bodied man and woman forming fire chains, passing buckets of water till their arms ached and they could hardly see for the sweat of exhaustion filling their eyes. Now it was over, the creak and groan of sodden timbers became less and less, the fresh air of morning was diluting the acrid stench of smoke. The greater part of the east wing was just a blackened shell but the main part of the building was still intact and after a thorough examination by the police and fire brigade was deemed fit for habitation.

It hadn't taken long to find Lady Elizabeth, she had been killed instantly by a falling beam in the hallway; it took longer to find the charred remains of Effie and Andrew, locked together in an embrace of death – but one arm of the young man thrown outwards, as if in some desperate last struggle to free himself of the bondage of his own demented mind – or perhaps just a feeble last effort to rid himself of the cloying clutch of Effie's possessive arms.

'She got him after all,' Evelyn whispered when the news spread through the waiting throng. 'In the end she got him.'

Colonel Richard Baird, in a state of shock, was taken away to hospital, the heartsore servants gathered in the kitchen to drink tea and quietly discuss among themselves the horrific events of the night.

Wearily the estate workers and the villagers dragged themselves homewards. 'Who started the fire?' They asked one another.

'Oh, I forget her name now. She was a maid at the Big House, I heard somebody saying so.'

'Ay, she got sent packing a month or two back. The old cook told me.'

'There was something about her being insane and right enough, only a madwoman would do a thing like that.'

'It would be her way o' getting her revenge.'

'Bitch! Murdering bitch! Thanks to her, both Andrew Baird and Lady Elizabeth are dead.'

'Ay, the besom deserved to rot in the ashes but to think she took these good people wi' her, I could cry, that I could.'

'They were never like gentry. Nothing snobbish or uppity about them.'

'Oh, they were gentry all right, true blue through and through, folk like that can mix wi' anybody yet never lose their dignity.'

'It's the Colonel I feel sorry for, losing both his wife and his son. He'll never get over the pain o' it. Never.'

' 'Tis a good job the lassie is away the now, but what a thing to come home to. I aye liked Christine Baird and she was that good wi' my Jimmy when he came home wounded from the war.'

'It's herself will be needing help now, she worshipped that brother o' hers and the poor lass already wi' an aching heart. There was a wee rumour that she had formed a strong attachment to that Gavin Galbraith who died recently – you know, the one without any legs.'

'Ach well, she aye did have some strange ideas for a gentry lass, even as a bairn she played wi' the local children as if she was one o' them.'

'They were the best o' the good families o' Renfrewshire, we will never see their like again for they will no' be staying here after this, it's a sad day for us all, indeed it is.'

David and Evelyn arrived home to the discovery that another tragedy might have occurred had it not been for the tub full of water which David, in his haste, had omitted to empty. Hot cinders had spilled into it from the unguarded fire to die harmlessly in the cloudy grey water except for one or two which had burned holes in the hearthrug.

'My God,' breathed a white-faced David. 'We might have lost Alex – everything we have in the house.'

Evelyn remembered her premonitions of the evening before and she shuddered to think what might have happened if it hadn't been bath night. As it was, the little house was serene and safe and she herself, despite the tragedies of the night, felt oddly at peace with herself. It was as if Effie had been cleansed from her soul leaving her free – oh so wonderfully, beautifully free! But everything had its price and both Andrew and Lady Elizabeth had paid dearly for the freedom that was now hers.

Even while her spirit floated out from its dark bondage her heart was heavy and sore for the loss of two people who had become very dear to her in the short time she had been at Dunmarnock.

Grace had been very quiet since the fire, her great dark eyes stared burning and dry into some far distance only she could see.

'I'm so sorry, Grace,' Evelyn said awkwardly, at a loss how to deal with her beloved sister's serene grief, 'I ken how much he loved you and I couldna help noticing you were growing fond o' him also.'

'Ay, poor Andra,' said Grace quietly. 'He died in his fire after all – gun-pit or mansion, what's the difference?'

'If it hadna been for Effie . . .' Evelyn began but Grace shook her head.

'No, Evie, it was what he wanted, you understand, what he aye wanted. He himself kent it all along – to go back and hide himself in the shadows o' war, to die wi' Barrett and the others in the fires o' hell. He was never happy, no one, nothing could have made him so. He's free now, Evie, can you understand what I mean?'

'Ay, Grace, I understand, he was a prisoner o' his own mind, but what a terrible way to go. He was such a fine young man, if it hadna been for the war he would have lived a happy, good life.'

'Ay, if it hadna been for the war, Evie, so many good men would be alive today, it goes on, doesn't it? Long after the guns fall silent.'

Chapter Twenty-Two

Some four weeks later Colonel Richard Baird rode into the woods. It was a fine morning, cold and crisp and clear, the Threep gurgled between its banks, the bright plumage of cock pheasants flashed in the undergrowth. It was the sort of day in which the hunt revelled, firm ground, bracing air. In his imagination he heard the baying of hounds, the blast of the horn, the tally-hos echoing, in his mind's eye he saw the flash of a red coat, the gleam of the horses' flanks – and off in the distance, occasionally glimpsed, the burnished flick of Reynold's brush . . . 'Poor bloody fox!'

The thought came unbidden. Self-reproach and self-loathing flooded his being. 'Poor bloody hunted beast. To run and hide and cower and finally die. It's for nothing, all for nothing, Andrew was right to hate it!'

He guided his horse to the edge of the moor. The winter-brown of the heather was like a vast thick mattress, great plains of it stretching away to meet the blue of the January sky.

He filled his lungs with the sharp air. Wine! Heady, fragrant, a raw edge to it on the way down. For a long time he breathed and stared, drinking his fill of life, knowing with a deep, calm pain how good it was to breathe and look and appreciate the everlasting beauty of earth and sky. Exhilarating. That was the word. Days like these had always exhilarated him with their promise and sweetness.

Major snickered softly, rather uneasily. The Colonel leaned over to pat and rub the strong, warm neck. 'Good

311

lad, Major, easy now, easy.'

He dismounted and walked a short way. A burn meandered at his feet, the purling music of it soothed into his head; a snipe rose up from the gorse in front of him, its zigzag flight carrying it off swiftly. He lifted his face. The wind blew over it, filling his nostrils with a myriad of moorland scents.

'Beth.' He spoke the name once. A shot rang out, the echo of it reverberating over the empty, windblown plains. Major's head jerked up, a red grouse rose up from the heath; '*goback, goback, goback*,' it cried in alarm. Then the echoes died away, morning settled peacefully back over the land, time drifted on, without hurry.

It was old Jasper Pringle who found the Colonel on that lonely, windswept spot at the edge of the moorland. He had died instantly, from a single shot to the temple, fired from the army revolver that he had carried all through his distinguished military career.

Jasper didn't weep or wail or do any of the things he wanted to do at sight of this beloved man lying in the heather in his last sleep. How could any man disgrace himself by crying when the Colonel himself was smiling — as if he had glimpsed a little bit of heaven before his own hand had carried him off to that eternal peace, somewhere away, away from the sadnesses and the tragedies of life.

'Goodbye Beardie Bum Baird.'

Evelyn stood on the brow of the hill watching the funeral procession, a great line of black-coated men stretching way back and disappearing under the trees. Gillan's father was amongst the mourners, so too was the Marquess of Inverbrora, representing his son who was still with the 'Auld Forty-Twa' in the Middle East and who would never have made it back to Scotland in time for the funeral. But he had written to Christine, a letter full of kindess and love and suddenly she could hardly wait to see again his strongly-moulded young face that was so filled with strength and character.

His parents had been pillars of support. They had taken her and cradled her in a cocoon of quiet understanding and after the funeral she was going back to stay with them at Inverbrora for as long as she wanted.

Time was what was needed, time to heal the raw wounds of grief and loss and for that to happen she had to get right away from Dunmarnock and all its memories.

It was strange, so strange and sad to see all those people gathered at Dunmarnock to say goodbye to Colonel Sir Richard Baird, KCB, who had preferred to be called by his military rank or simply just Beardie Bum Baird to the very privileged few to whom he had divulged his innermost secrets . . .

Evelyn's breath caught, a picture flashed into her mind, she and he sitting together on a fallen tree, laughing, laughing, in perfect joy of the daftness and delight of that hilarious little rhyme of his. She smiled at the remembrance and wanted to keep on smiling but sadness enveloped her instead and, turning on her heel, she walked back down the hill, the sun behind her, a drift of shadows and mist lying in the hollows below.

Gillan had written to Christine from Italy where he was still serving with the 2nd Gordons. He was grieved beyond belief by all the tragedies to hit Dunmarnock but he spoke to Christine in a positive way and when she finally folded his letter a small glimmer of hope glowed in her breast for the future. 'Gillan sends his love to you,' she told Evelyn before leaving for Inverbrora. 'He also said something rather strange and I quote: "Tell her not to forget the marriage of hearts and never to betray it by disappearing where my dreams can't reach her." Do you know what that means?'

'Ay, indeed I do,' murmured Evelyn and turned away to hide her tears. No promises had been made, therefore none could be broken, yet even so she knew the knowledge of that would be small comfort in the days ahead when she and her family must leave Dunmarnock and she would break her ties with Gillan for all time for, as things stood between them, he could never be part of her future nor she of his. He had to find a love and a life of his own, it was selfish of her to hang on to him when she had nothing to give him but a friendship that had grown too possessive for both of them.

Everyone had left or was leaving Dunmarnock, all except the tenant farmers who would remain till the future of the estate had been decided. Peggy and Violet went to another big house in the area, Raggy Annie went to work at The Grange because Grace had spoken up for her and had told 'Cuddles' the Matron that she could turn her hand to anything.

Seal and Ferguson were among the last to go. They were going to spend the remainder of their days in Islay whence Ferguson had sprung. The cottage of his birth was still standing, waiting for himself and his bride to make their home there, his bride being none other than Seal McWhirter who had 'aye been fond o' the old rogue'.

'We shared the same kitchen for donkey's years,' she explained with a gleam in her eye that fairly made poor old Ferguson wriggle in his slippers, 'so what more natural than we while away the last o' our years together. At least he has the advantage o' knowing I'm a good cook and will never go wi' an empty belly.'

The tears came at the moment of departure, the old couple gazing round the kitchen, *their* kitchen, for the last time, saying their silent farewells, remembering the happy years they had spent at Dunmarnock, then they went quickly away, two white hankies waving in the air before the trap disappeared among the trees and they were lost to sight.

Christine had told the Grants and the Graingers that they could stay on at the estate for as long as they wanted but they knew they too had to leave.

David had gone both job-hunting and house-hunting and one day he came home to tell Evelyn that he had secured a position as a ship's carpenter in Fairfields of Govan and that he had also found a house.

'It's a room and kitchen, in Govan, above my father's house, the rent is quite high so I'll have to start work right away.'

'My parents, they'll have to come too,' Evelyn said quickly. 'There's nowhere else for them to go.'

'Ay, them too,' agreed David but curtly, not relishing one bit the idea of himself and Maggie under the same roof.

Maggie didn't relish the idea either but was sensible enough to know there was nothing she could do about it for the moment.

'I never want Gillie to ken where we are,' Evelyn told her mother quietly, 'so dinna you go telling any o' the Forbes family — and tell Mary no' to say anything either.'

Maggie looked keenly at her daughter's face. It was blank, holding back its secrets. 'And why are you so anxious that Gillie should never ken your whereabouts?'

'Because there is no place for him in my life anymore, I canna share myself wi' two men and be faithful to them both and Davie will aye come first wi' me even though you canna thole me saying it. Forbye, I'm going to an area where Gillie's like has no place. No big houses in Govan, Mam, just tenement buildings and dusty streets and working men wi' dirty faces and the smell o' beer on their breath.'

'Gillan could aye mix wi' anybody,' said Maggie stubbornly. 'He wouldna turn up his nose at honest-to-goodness hard-working men wi' a bit dirt on their faces.'

'No, Mam, but they would turn up their noses at him and that's an end o' the matter. Lady Marjorie, Evander, Gillie, old Oggie, they dinna belong in our lives any more and we dinna belong in theirs.'

'No,' Maggie spoke rather wistfully. She would never

see her father again, of that she was now sure, nor would she ever sit at the fire drinking tea with her cousin whom she had once resented but who now held a very firm place in her affections.

Lady Marjorie had already written to express her horror and grief about the fire and the tragedies it had incurred. She had also waxed eloquent about Effie and how right she had been to distrust the girl. 'I sensed her madness from the start,' she penned flamboyantly, 'and just a great pity my dear Elizabeth was possessed with such a sweet and trusting nature or she would never have employed the girl to begin with.'

Now, as if on cue, another letter arrived from Lady Marjorie. 'You must all come back to stay at Rothiedrum till you have decided what you plan to do. The house is empty now that the military have all but left and it's far too big for just me and Evander. You know you will receive a most affectionate welcome and I'm sure all your old friends and neighbours would love to see you home again.'

Maggie smiled when she read the letter, knowing full well the soul-searching her cousin must have undergone before taking the decision to invite the Grants to stay at Rothiedrum House and all the inherent threats to her own peace of mind a situation like that would create.

'Can you imagine it?' she said to Jamie. 'You and me and the girls all there together at Rothiedrum House? What would Marjorie have us do, I wonder? We certainly couldna bide there just twiddling our thumbs, could we? She forgets we're no' the idle rich wi' naught to do in life but enjoy ourselves.'

Jamie knew fine what was on her mind. She would never be a servant to the Forbes family, her inborn pride would never allow it and, if *he* thought that, not knowing that his wife was blood kin to that same family, then Maggie's opinions on the subject were very decided indeed.

He nodded, not trusting himself to speak. Just for a few moments he had smelled and tasted the lands of Rothiedrum, he had seen the spangled rays of sunshine slanting into little woodlands that dotted the wide, patchwork plains. He saw too the rich, loamy soil of a newly-turned furrow; the flash of a Clyde's hoof; the birl and lift of the peesies in flight, calling, calling, in that strange, plaintive voice that could never be mistaken. He heard again the broad speak of neighbours and friends; the howl of the wind keening over the parks, fierce, rebellious, but part of it all, part of the whole spectrum that had once made his days and his nights a bitter-sweet allegiance to the land.

He looked lonely and alone in those moments. Gone were the days of his strength and youth, spent, all spent on that land for which he still grieved and longed for even if it meant pouring the last of his life into it, at least he would die in the country he knew, among the people he loved.

'Jamie, my man,' Maggie said softly, 'it can never be, it's over, that kind o' life, you have to see that.'

'Ay, I see, lass,' he nodded, dashing his hand quickly over his eyes. To her he put out his other hand, and she came to him, half-shy of all that now, but they needed one another very badly at that time and had to know there were still things in life worth living for.

Nellie also wrote, to the effect that they must all come to Kenneray till they had decided on their future. 'We'll squeeze you all in somehow,' she penned vigorously, 'and there's a but and ben close by, the original crofthouse, which could easily be restored back to a habitable condition.'

'Ach, God bless our lass,' Jamie said huskily. 'She's aye so eager to help and no trouble too much where her family are concerned.'

'Ay, she has a big heart,' agreed Maggie, 'but we have to be practical. Nellie may be a good lass but she was never the easiest o' people to live with and several women sharing a kitchen would try even the patience o' Job. Besides, what would you do? Go back to the kind o' work that nearly broke you once before. And me? No house to run or peaceful corner to call my own or any sort o' dignity in my life at all. No, it canna be. We left a croft o' our own in Rothiedrum and can never go back to that way o' life – much as it hurts me to say it.'

Jamie nodded and went outside to smoke his pipe. The stubby bowl nestled warmly in his palm, comforting him a little as he took a deep breath and braced himself for more changes in his life. He was too old now for this sort of thing, not so much in years, he was still just sixty-four after all, but he felt older, as if he had lived a long, long time in this world with its uncertainties and its sorrows and its habit of taking away from a man the only things that were worth living for.

He filled his lungs with the damp, musky smell of the earth and tasted the salt tang of his own tears and he hated himself for his frailties and his being no longer able to steer the course of his own life.

The day before they left Dunmarnock for the last time, Evelyn walked in the woods with her father. It had snowed in the night, only a light covering but enough to make her thoughts return to her first winter here. For a few moments she smelled and tasted and touched those lovely, lost yesterdays before they faded away and she was alone in the woods with her father, the frost-rimed leaves crackling under their feet, their breath condensing in the sharp air.

For a long time they wandered in silence, appreciating the other's needs for reflection and quiet. They had always been able to do this comfortably, father and daughter, at home with one another, attuned to what each was feeling and thinking.

'I miss them, Father,' she said at last. 'They were such good people. I grew to love them, Andra, Lady Elizabeth, the Colonel losing things, calling on Beth to find them. What a waste it all is, Father.'

'Oh, princess.' He took her hand and held it tightly.

'I myself canna see the sense in any o' it and find it hard to believe it ever happened. I feel that one or the other o' them will pop up at any moment and talk to us. Life is such a crazy affair. I never thought I would be happy anywhere else but Rothiedrum but I felt at home here, I felt *right* somehow — and now it's over — we're going away again, moving further and further away from the countryside where the natural order o' things somehow manages to keep you on the right road yourself. I dinna think I'll ever see Rothiedrum again. The grass and the moss will grow over King's Croft and smother it and no one will ken that the Grants once lived and worked there. If I could have died in my own bed it would have been for the best. You're young, lassie, your road will take many turnings and might one day take you back to the land o' your birth but I've had my life, there will be no place for me where we're going. I was born to the country, I need it in my soul . . .'

His voice broke, she took him to her breast and held him there. There was nothing she could say to him for the words he spoke might have come from her own heart. He was thin and little and old in her embrace. To think she had once thought him big and strong and immortal. But that had been a child thinking these things. She was grown now, she had watched the flowerings and the witherings and the dyings of people whose place in her heart was very often an ache.

She stood there, her father to her breast, his heart against hers and that of another yet to be born. Three hearts, beating, beating. Twiggy May had been right, there would be many children . . . Her gaze travelled slowly round the woodlands, the trees, strong, tall, reaching to the sky for light and air; others, stunted and frail but closer to the leafy earth which in spring and summer garlanded their feet with wildflowers. How like the pattern of human lives, she thought, the strong and the ambitious pushing their way to the top and just when they had reached those dizzy heights very often toppling down and breaking in the process; the more lowly, seeing life at their feet, never very strong or straight but getting life in perspective down there close to the earth.

She closed her eyes. Love touched her, coming to her on the breath of the breeze and she knew that Gillan was thinking of her at that moment and that somehow he was there beside her in the winter woods where they had walked and smiled, touched and looked, each of them knowing how precious were moments so fleeting, yet somehow everlasting.

She led her father to the edge of the woods – and there was the fallen log upon which she and the Colonel had sat so companionably together that day she had known Davie was alive . . .

'Beardie Bum, up the lum . . .'

The rhyme echoed in her head, then died away, and the woods slept once more, holding their secrets, keeping them safe from curious ears that listened and hoped but never heard.

'It will be all right, Father,' she assured. 'From Rothiedrum we took memories of people and places we will never forget. Dunmarnock has given us another store to hold in our hearts wherever we go and Govan will be the same, life is how you make it yourself and no one ever hated the Grants o' Rothiedrum.'

She turned her head to look back into the shadowed woods – and gave a little gasp, for there, on the log, sat a nebulous figure, one hand raised up in greeting – or farewell – she didn't know, but she lifted up her own hand and then the figure was gone and it was only herself and her father walking on the path together, an uncertain future before them but a host of friends waiting to welcome them on the road that was tomorrow.

Treatment of Cerebral Palsy and Motor Delay